Reminders *of* Greece

OTHER TITLES BY FRANCESCA CATLOW

Little Blue Door Series:

The Little Blue Door

Behind The Olive Trees

Chasing Greek Dreams

Found in Corfu

Other Fiction:

The Last Christmas Promise

Another Greek Summer

Greek Secret

Under a Greek Sky

Reminders *of* Greece

Francesca Catlow

LAKE UNION PUBLISHING

Published by Lake Union Publishing, Seattle

www.apub.com

EU Product Safety Contact:
Amazon Media EU S.à r.l.
38, avenue John F. Kennedy, L-1855 Luxembourg
amazonpublishing-gpsr@amazon.com

ISBN-13: 9781662526305
eISBN: 9781662526312

Cover design by Emma Rogers
Cover image: © Feel good studio © ajborges / Shutterstock

Printed in the United States of America

Firstly, and most importantly, I need to thank my mum. I remember sitting on the work surface in her old kitchen (the way I had since I was tall enough to do so) as she told me about an idea she had for one of my books. Her idea was to set a book in Kos with a mother who had worked there in the nineties, bringing her daughter to visit as an adult. That was back in 2023! I knew I'd write it one day. I'm so grateful for all our bookish conversations and the fun we have bouncing around ideas. Thanks for being the best mum. Love you millions.

This book is dedicated to
Sam (Samantha) Winters-Peabody
(1968–2025).
Sam, I wish I could thank you for your support and enduring kindness. I had visions of us having conversations that never came to be. I'm sorry for that. We always think there's time. I hate being wrong. All I can do now is dedicate this book to your memory in gratitude for the time you invested in people. Not just me, but so many.

Chapter 1

Sara 1998

It's not the first time a man has come within an inch of vomiting on my shoes, but it is the first time I've had second-hand carrot splatter from a complete stranger.

'Sorry, babe, he's had a few too many, haven't you, Kev?' A topless man slaps the hunched-over *Kev* between the shoulder blades.

I bite my tongue and gift them a wordless smile as I skirt the ever-expanding vomit puddle.

I should've known it was all going a bit too well.

Stepping off the aeroplane into the warm embrace of the late evening, getting a taxi with no hassle whatsoever, sucking in the enchanting buzz of island life through the window, all under the watchful eyes of olive trees and mountain peaks . . . it left me feeling strangely smug for the first time in a long time.

I'm free.

For the first time ever, I'm completely independent. Away from my parents' expectations of perfection, away from mediocre boys playing at being men, away from England and straight into a job with accommodation and the chance of a future that belongs to me and no one else.

When the taxi dropped me at the harbour, the first thing I noticed was the salt weighing heavy in the air, followed closely by the delightful smell of Greek cuisine dancing alongside it. My stomach had groaned in anticipation.

It's amazing what a difference three minutes makes.

The acrid smell of sweat and alcohol kicks me in the back of the throat, and back to reality, as I pass all the local watering holes.

I live here now. I work here now. This is it for the foreseeable future.

That's the problem with being sober when everyone else is having the *best party of their lives* – you still have your normal senses when everyone else's have been deadened.

For the first time since coming up with this hare-brained escape from the constraints of my life in England, nerves bounce around my abdomen. Up until now I've been living in the dream of it, the idea, and not thinking much about the reality. I might have accidently been romanticising life just a touch.

If someone had told me five days ago that I'd be alone in Greece, I'd have laughed in their face. I thought I was doing well enough. Things were plodding along as ever. This is until Lawrence – the last person I was clinging on to, with the desperate grip of a hook in a fish's mouth – dumped me for someone else.

The strangest part was, I didn't even cry. I felt more angry than sad. It was only after stomping around the garden for an hour that I realised, I wasn't even that angry about the fact the pompous idiot cheated on me. It was about the time I wasted on him and conforming to a life I'm really not sure I want.

My parents probably still think I'm staying at his place right now.

They were staying with some friends when it all kicked off. They might be back by now. They probably haven't even noticed I took a suitcase and left. Our family home is big enough for me to go about my day unnoticed if it's needed, even when they are in.

Coming here is all my mother's fault anyway.

Disappearing to Kos for work all started after I finished pacing the garden. I slumped down in her chair in the parlour, only to catch sight of an advert in her latest copy of *The Lady* magazine. She'd left it open on the coffee table and there it was, calling to me to apply for a job that would *whisk me away to far-off lands*.

I made a desperate and hopeful call, and was passed around several people before landing a five-hour interview in London the very next day. It included working through tasks in groups and finished with a one-to-one interview where I laid my credentials on thicker than Nutella.

It worked, because it ended with me getting offered a job.

Mrs Willis, the nice lady doing the one-to-one interview, informed me I'd get a telephone call confirming the offer and where my week of training would take place. Only *then* would I find out where I'd be posted in my new job as a travel rep.

I spent the next twenty minutes begging for anything that left within forty-eight hours. I told her I'd do anything, pay for any flight, leave then and there if I had to. I went into detail, again, about my extensive travels, independently organising my own excursions, my ability to strike up conversation with people from all walks of life and, of course, my first-rate education.

Twenty-seven hours from then to now and I'm walking along the buzzing streets of Kardamena in Kos. I've never been here before, but I've heard about its big reputation for friendly days and wild nights.

Apparently, a tour rep recently left her post here because she was too homesick. I guess it must happen, that people miss their homes and families enough to twist up their insides. It's just very hard for me to imagine.

I'm the opposite. I get sick just thinking about home. Surely that's what homesick *should* mean? When one is sick of being at home. Coming out in a rash at the thought of being there and vomiting like that *gentleman* back there each time you're near to it.

When I was at boarding school, I could hear girls crying into their pillows sometimes, missing their mothers. All while I glared into the darkness of the room, wishing I had a mother worth missing.

My suitcase rattles along the concrete beside me, followed by the eyes of drunk men. Even with the pumping bass spewing out of various bars, I can still hear the odd catcall. I'd be offended if I couldn't. If for no other reason than I'm one of the only people still able to walk in a straight line at 1 a.m.

I run my hand through my long blonde hair and pull my shoulders back to really give them something to look at. I made sure to dress to impress for the flight, in a fitted ice-blue T-shirt and a skort.

It's been a long day, possibly the longest of my life, and even though I could melt into an exhausted puddle with the heat, I know better than that. I know how to carry myself. I know how to gain attention. It's what my mother has spent my whole life making sure I was trained for. To be *something* or *someone*, or alternatively – and possibly preferably – to marry someone who is *someone*. It doesn't matter how far I try to push away my parents and all they stand for, it's hard to let go of everything.

Usually, I hate it. But at times like this, when I feel completely lost and alone, it helps to know that no one could possibly believe I'm anything other than cool and confident. When I need to, I can mask all the emotions God has given me. I'm able to box them up and put them away with all the other random things my mind kicks up.

I glance at the hand-drawn picture that was faxed over to London by someone called Tammy. It marks out directions from the harbour to where I'll be living over the coming months.

Even though I don't start my new job until tomorrow, I've made a point to dress the part, albeit my own version of it.

The interviewer told me I had to provide my own Marks & Spencer's court shoes and a few packets of tan-coloured tights; the rest would be provided on arrival. Normally, my outfit would be sent to me in the post, but there was no time. The lovely Mrs Willis took my measurements and faxed them to Kos, along with a stack of papers all about me.

After telling her I already had some M&S court shoes, I had hoped to get to the shops to buy some, but it turned out there wasn't time. So, they were added to the list of things I swiped from my parents before leaving. I took two pairs of my mother's shoes, and three unopened packets of tights from her drawer. The pair I travelled in are navy and almost as tall as skyscrapers. They're dreadfully uncomfortable and made worse because they're half a size too big for me. But these were the trendier of the two pairs, with the slimmer heel and a pointier toe. The others are perfectly sensible with a square toe, a sturdy thick heel and a faux silver buckle on the front.

'Are you OK, doll?' A slim Liverpudlian woman, with legs to die for and dark, alluring skin, steps out of a crowd near a bar, away from the swell of music and in my direction.

'Perfectly fine, thank you very much.'

'No one told me we was getting sent a toff.' She flicks her cigarette towards the ground and stubs it out with her platform trainer.

It's all I can do not to roll my eyes, but the exhaustion of the past two days is catching up with me, so words wriggle their way out of my mouth where normally I'd keep it shut. 'I'm not a *toff*.'

'You should never lie about who you are. It don't matter to me, you being a toff. But if you're a tosser then it might. Are you a tosser?'

The facade created by my mother cracks and laughter bulges and spills out. 'No, I don't think so.'

'Come on then, Sara, I'll show you where you're staying.'

I take a step back as she takes one forward and miss bumping into a group of cheering women by an inch.

I narrow my eyes on this woman. Her fine bone structure, her caramel-brown skin and her belly-button piercing. I'm usually quite good with remembering people from my extensive travels, but I don't recognise her at all.

'How do you know my name?'

'I'm Tammy, and that's my drawing you're holding. You've taken a wrong turning, so you must be a lucky one to bump into me here. If you'd carried on, you'd've ended up in the bloody mountains.'

'I guess I must be lucky then.' I watch as the group of women, all about my age, stumble past us together.

One pours with tears as the others prop her up and stumble along the road with her, all talking at once.

'Is it always like this?' I nod in their wake.

'Look, doll, if you're not up for a party, I think you're in the wrong place and I suggest you turn on those pretty lil heels of yours and go back the way ya came.'

'I was only enquiring. I'm just here to work, nothing more.'

Tammy raises a razor-thin brow before popping another cigarette in her mouth.

'This is tame,' she continues. 'Nothing like Malia or one of those big clubbing resorts. Everyone here likes to have a little fun, that's all.'

My head bounces in a sort of agreement as I scan the orange glow of burning the midnight oil that floods the winding streets of the fishing village.

The strange mechanical chime of a mobile phone rises up above the music coming from the bars. It takes me a full moment to realise the sound is emanating from my handbag. I've never heard the thing ring before.

I push the button to answer the call and press the phone to one ear and a finger in the other.

'Hello?'

'Hello? Sara? This is your number?'

'Hi, Mother. Yes, it is.'

Here it comes, the big fallout. Her spreading her wings of trauma and anger at me doing what I want without even asking her permission. Who cares that I'm a grown woman now?

'What's all that noise? Where exactly are you?'

'Greece.'

'The musical or the country?'

'The country.'

'Oh. I had wondered why you had left a scrawled number for me to call. I suppose now I have my answer. Am I to presume this is another of your rebellious acts or cries for help? Because your father and I will not rise to it or continue to tolerate it. We won't be paying for flights or anything obscene.'

Them? Tolerate *me*? My jaw clamps shut and it's all I can do not to drag the phone from my ear and end the call. I have never asked her to pay for a flight or to get me out of a sticky situation where money is concerned. I'd rather chew off my left arm than ask her for help. She really does have the cheek of the devil.

'I'm here to work,' I state calmly, holding everything in as always.

'To work?' The scoffing comes out clearer down the line than anything else. 'All the expensive education your father has paid for and you're working in *Greece*? As what, exactly? A waitress? Let me guess, you're there to drink cheap vodka and make an even greater mockery of this family?' My mother exhales so hard I can almost feel her Merlot breath on my cheek down the phone line. The worst part is, she seems more irritated by the idea of *cheap* vodka than anything else.

'No, Mother, I'm here to work, that's all.'

And perhaps escape in cheap vodka when it's required.

'W . . . was tha . . . ? I can't hear . . .'

'Mother? You're breaking up.'

There's a few more stutters as I step back a couple of paces in case a signal will return, before the line goes dead.

I look at the small square screen of my pristine phone and press the little plastic button six or seven times to end the already dead call, before stuffing it back in my handbag. I stare down at the bag for a moment. My mother calls it *ugly* and a *dirty hippie bag* just because it's purple cloth and has small circular mirrors on it.

I wonder what it would feel like to call her a bitch right to her face.

'Don't worry, chick, we're all here to escape something.' Tammy appears by my side in a cloud of smoke.

This woman who is all but a stranger to me, a seemingly sober one, slips her arm around my shoulders and guides me further down the road. 'You'll be all right here, mark my words.'

'Oi, Tammy, you caught yourself another stray, have ya?' calls a low and confident Irish voice from somewhere behind us.

I glance about and find a tall man with curly black hair walking in our direction, his hands in the pockets of his fitted shorts.

'Sara, this is Declan. Declan, Sara. She's the fresh meat we've been waiting for. Declan usually works in Kos Town.'

I raise an eyebrow at her insinuation of me being fresh meat, and outstretch my hand to greet the tall dark Declan.

'Nice to meet you, Declan.'

His grip is firm and warm as he looks me over in one grazing glance of eyes as blue as my outfit.

'Are you sure you can handle a party, Posh Spice?'

I slip my hand from his. 'Yes. I'm perfectly capable.'

All I can do is hope I'm right. I got this job because I've travelled the world and I can talk my way out of anything when I must, but this isn't like anywhere I've been before. I'm used to being swaddled to the point of strangulation.

'Come on, chick.' Tammy indicates with the tip of her glowing cigarette. 'It's this way.'

I follow on behind the two of them as they discuss me like I'm not here.

It doesn't matter. At least I only have to answer to myself now.

Chapter 2

Mia 2025

Mum snatches a breath and looks up at the trees encasing us. Their thick branches, wrapped in delicate fairy lights, reflect in her soft lavender-grey eyes.

Something isn't right, which should be pretty much impossible. How can there be something wrong less than two hours after landing on a moonlit Greek island and only ten minutes after arriving in the warm embrace of a resort that has a buzz like electricity.

She blows out a trembling breath.

'Everything OK, Mum?' I reach for her hand across the table, and she takes it in hers. Gentle and warm.

'Yeah, I'm fine, Sweetpea. It's just strange to be back after all these years. So much has changed. It used to be all loud and parties. Now it's . . . different.' Her face lifts into a reassuring smile. 'I'm so happy to be back here with you, though. I can't wait for our holiday to get started.'

'We're here! It *has* started.'

Nerves tickle my stomach. Is she picking up on my energy? She usually knows every thought in my head. How could she not already know I've decided to give up my steady singing job and run off abroad for an adventure? No. She'd have said by now if she'd guessed. I have to be calm about it. It's not like she won't be happy for me, she's the most amazing and supportive mum in the world. I just don't want to upset her.

Mum's eyes lose focus as she looks down the concrete street lined with shops.

This particular road has a low-key atmosphere, like we've stumbled into a comparatively peaceful street behind the vibrant ones closer to the sea.

It's a perfect place to sit and people-watch, as we're on a raised patio area outside a delightful stone building. A white chapel with a bell tower sits to one side of us, while opposite there's a sweet shop, a travel agent for local trips and a T-shirt shop with comic – and by the looks, rude – slogans waiting to be open again tomorrow. There's something perfectly Greek about having the chapel and the T-shirt shop in such close proximity. A realness that I've always adored about the culture throughout Greece.

This place must've been rammed with people back when Mum worked here, because it's pretty busy now.

She's told me all about her time working in this village, Kardamena, as well as her time in Malia, Crete, before I was born.

'I know the holiday has technically started,' Mum begins, 'but you know what I mean. When I wake up tomorrow morning after a few hours dreaming, I'll be ready to start relaxing. That's when it *really* starts.' Mum's shoulders lift to graze the ends of her long straight bobbed hair as she leans her forearms on the table.

'I do know what you mean, but we have to have our milkshakes first. It's tradition. And really that's when the holiday starts.'

Since I was eleven months old, we've been on holiday abroad together every single year. It's not an exaggeration to say my mum is my best friend in the world. Even when we're driving each other nuts, there's no one else I'd rather rant to about a bad movie, share my new favourite music discovery or explore a new country with than her.

Back when these adventures started, the only way Mum could get me to drink milk was by loading it with sugar and chocolate. My first holiday was to a place called Lloret de Mar in Spain. Everywhere we went, I asked for a chocolate milkshake. I'm not sure how well I asked at under a year, but apparently I made it pretty clear it was that or nothing.

The year after that, Mum took me to Rome. I can't believe she took a tantrum-prone two-year-old to the Colosseum, but she did. I think the only way to stay sane was to ply me with more milkshakes. She would spend the whole year saving every penny we had to take me on a week-long adventure.

Year after year, the association of hot holidays and milkshakes solidified, and now it *has* to be the very first drink we have when we arrive anywhere, or the holiday is cursed.

She came up with the cursed bit.

We're both superstitious, but Mum always takes it too far. One time we had champagne on arrival, as we were in the Champagne region of France, and we ended up having the worst time. It rained constantly and I got a phone call from our friend looking after our cat, Dragon, to tell us he had gone missing. It was dreadful.

'I'm sorry,' the waiter says before he's quite made it to our table, 'we are out of the chocolate milkshake.' He places a ceramic bowl filled with nuts in front of us. 'We have strawberry?'

Mum's eyes bulge at me, but I keep my cool.

'Strawberry will be just fine, thank you.'

The young man nods with a head full of short curls and a brief smile before swiftly making his way back to the bar.

'Mia, you said it's *fine*.' Mum abruptly drums the table in front of me with her fists before squeaking my name. 'Mia!'

I hold my hands up. I'm not sure if it's an act of submission like I'm under arrest, or to get her to stop. Maybe a little of both.

'It's still a milkshake. At least it's not like when we landed in the back of beyond of Cuba and we were left drinking God-knows-what and pretending it was milkshakes to try to keep the tradition alive.'

'They were *Batido de Trigo*. It's like a milkshake and they were pretty tasty,' Mum reminds me.

'The trip was still a disaster.' I shudder at the thought.

It wasn't as bad as our time in northern France, but it was only a few steps away. It included Mum breaking her toe, thinking she could dance the salsa. It was such a shame because the music, and passion for it, was truly incredible.

'Let's just focus on the good things, shall we? Like this lovely little street.' I wave one hand to the side of us and the golden glow that lights up the night.

Mum's eyes narrow as she studies everything in the direction of my waving, before twisting in her chair to look the other way.

'I know it's late, but I barely recognise anything. The church I remember, but I swear that's it.'

'How long's it been since you were working here?'

Mum's head tilts as she looks at me and her mouth slowly curves upwards just a little on one side.

'It must've been about . . .' – she shakes her head, still gazing at me – '. . . a year or so before you were born. It was the late nineties and a world away from this. Working here was my second to last job before having you. It was also my favourite.'

'What made you decide now was the time to come back? This trip was all very last minute, even for you.'

I've been afraid to ask this simple question for fear she wants to sit me down and ask whether I'm happy at work or what's going on. Maybe this holiday is her way of getting me away from it all to tell me she knows all the thoughts in my head.

I remember, when I was ten, wanting to quit guitar and learn piano instead. She sat me down and asked me if I was happy in my lessons before I'd even managed to formulate my own thoughts on the subject. She always paid that much attention to my every need, and I never want to let her down or leave her behind, because she would never leave me behind, not in a million years.

Mum presses her lips together and continues to shake her head gently. 'I saw this deal at work and thought it must be fate. Anyway, I've never heard you complain about a free holiday before.'

Maybe I'm wrong. Maybe this is just a peaceful holiday and the perfect opportunity for me to have quality time with Mum to tell her about the restructure of my goals and ambitions.

'Well.' I laugh a little, finally able to relax. 'I knew it must've been cheap when you said you were paying for it.'

'Oi, cheeky.' She tries to look cross, but the laughter catches in her eyes alongside the fairy lights.

Two baby-pink milkshakes in heavy glass mugs with thick swirling cream on top are placed down in front of us.

'*Yamas!*' I announce as I pick up my drink and hold it between us.

Mum swiftly picks up her glass, ready to clink it with mine.

This is it, the perfect time to both congratulate her for the thousandth time on her new adventure, and to tell her my plans to have my own adventure. I want to travel and work as a singer abroad. I need to tell her I'm fed up with rainy Essex. I've decided to spend my summers chasing sunsets instead of wasting my Saturday nights on everyone else's happily-ever-afters as a wedding singer.

It'll be a shock. Out of the two of us, I'm the *sensible one*.

It'll be fine, though. She's embarking on her own dream now. It's the perfect time to spread my wings.

She's supported every dream I've ever had, and I know she'll understand. I'll miss her like mad, but I have to do this. And it's not like it'll be *this* summer. This summer's almost over, but as of April next year, I could be anywhere. Greece, Turkey, Italy, Portugal, Mexico, Egypt . . . who knows.

'I would like to say how proud I am of you, not only for raising such a wonderful daughter as me,' – I playfully flutter my eyelashes – 'but because you're doing it. You're following your dreams all on your own. Eighteen more sleeps and *Travel the World with Louisa* will become *Travel the World with Sara*.' An involuntary squeal emits from my throat. 'Cheers! *Yamas!*'

Our glasses clink together, and we both sip through our straws.

I snatch a breath, ready to continue, but the look on Mum's face grinds me to a painful halt.

Her smile hasn't quite reached her eyes, and her jaw looks tense under her wafer-thin smile.

Every time I've mentioned her taking over the travel agent's up until right now, she has squealed and danced about, her voice hitting new highs as she's chimed, *I can't believe it, I can't believe it!* She was almost giving me a run for my money on vocal range.

'What's up?' I place my drink a little hard on the table, unintentionally making it rattle.

'Nothing, why?'

She does that thing, like I'm the mum and she's the adolescent. Her eyes don't meet mine and she begins to twitch a little under my gaze, fidgeting in her chair.

'Because this is the first time the takeover has been mentioned and you haven't burst my eardrums making noises only dogs can hear.'

'Don't exaggerate,' she tuts. Her nose begins to wrinkle like she's inhaled something she doesn't like the smell of. That can't be the case at all – the air is heavy with the scent of cooking and the salt from the sea. It's divine.

'I'm not exaggerating. I've booked an appointment with a hearing specialist and everything. I think you've caused me permanent damage.'

Mum rolls her eyes and quietly laughs into her drink as she takes another sip.

'That sounded like something I might say. You're only in your twenties and you're already turning into your mother. Poor thing.'

'Better than turning into *your* mother,' I grimace.

'I was going to say *I'm fine*. But now I feel rather ill at the idea of turning into my mother. And anyway, if I turn into her, that means you will eventually turn into her too, you do realise?'

I shudder at the thought, shaking it as far away from me as I can. 'Let's bring it back to the real point, please. What's wrong?'

'Seriously. I'm fine. How could I not be? We're on Kos island! Who doesn't love escaping to a Greek island?'

'Good question.' I narrow my eyes again, knowing she'll see what I'm saying behind them.

She pulls in a deep breath and hisses it out through her teeth as she slides her glass back on to the table. 'This tastes a little more like a smoothie, don't you think? Like a strawberry smoothie with crunched-up ice? Do you remember those smoothies we had in Portsmouth that time? From that place? What was it called? Doesn't matter. It's funny, they were more like milkshakes and this is more like a smoothie—'

'Please stop.'

Mum purses her lips. 'Bringing you up as my equal has its disadvantages sometimes, you know.'

My shoulders scrunch up around my ears before falling heavily back into their natural position.

She says this to me at least once a week.

I also know this is the time to keep my mouth shut. It took me a long time to discover that one. That keeping quiet makes other people talk, particularly my mum. She can't bear to leave a gaping silence in a situation like this one.

'I really don't want to do this now.' She continues, 'Can we talk properly in the morning? I want to enjoy this milkshake, cool off, unpack my case and sleep. I really don't want to be up all night explaining myself.'

Automatically, my right eyebrow arches at her and she quickly reflects the look right back at me.

'Do what? So there is a reason you're not getting all excited about the purchase? Is there something wrong with the loan? Or has Louisa backed out?'

'No, no, nothing like that.' She wafts her hands in front of her face. 'I mean it, Mia, let's talk tomorrow. Please.' Mum picks up her drink again and gulps it back like it's a big milky shot.

I don't follow suit.

Mum is rubbish at holding anything in. I could keep a secret, take it to the grave, come back as a ghost and still never tell another soul. Mum, on the other hand, ends up red in the face and looking like she might have a heart attack if she doesn't release the pressure of a secret. As a kid, I was always impressed when I didn't know what I was getting for my birthday each year.

I lean back on my wicker chair and scan the other people around us, sipping cocktails and enjoying the ambient music.

My heart begins to pound, each beat begging me to push her to spill.

I don't. It's always better to let her come to me. Let her wind herself up and she'll explode. Sometimes more so if she thinks I'm not interested.

When Mum doesn't immediately pop with information like she normally does, I have to respond, and hope it isn't the wrong decision. After all the travelling and the warmth of the late evening, I'm already feeling sleepy and can't be bothered to play her games.

'Fine.' I breathe out the word like it's much heavier than it is. As though it's a lot of effort to let it out. 'But if you don't tell me where your enthusiasm has gone in the morning, you'll wish that two-year-old me was back, because those sulky tantrums will seem like nothing.'

Mum tugs her cheesecloth shirt over her boobs to cover the top underneath and clicks her tongue.

'You have no idea what it is to be a self-made woman in her twenties with a two-year-old in tow. There's nothing you could do now that would be more embarrassing, stressful or soul-destroying than anything I've been through at some point in my career as a single mum. I've seen it all, done it all, put up with it all . . . If you sulk now, I don't have to discipline you, I can walk away and have a nap. Your threats are useless here.'

There's no argument that I can come up with, so I repeat my previous weighted, 'Fine,' and go back to sipping the milkshake that's left in my glass until the straw makes that cringy bubbly slurp noise.

A feeling lingers and a question sits on my shoulder with its arms firmly folded, scowling at my mum: *What on earth does she have to say that she doesn't want to tell me now?*

'Come on.' I put down twenty euros and leave whatever's left as a tip. 'Let's get back to the apartment and unpack. The sooner we're asleep, the sooner we can begin this holiday.'

Sliding out of our seats, we step down into the street. Everywhere is aglow with a golden amber haze from the few shops still open and the tavernas and bars crammed with people. When it's like this, I like to see if I can pick out all the different music playing and decipher what it is.

Most tavernas have their own chilled soundtrack playing and seats outside as we walk towards the square near the harbour and the navy sea beyond. There's definitely a bustle here I haven't seen in a while. It's not like a busy city, it's a large fishing village at heart, but there's a vibrant energy swelling in the streets, which is particularly true close to the harbour.

It would be interesting to see it in the winter. I bet it's perfectly quiet without all the tourists filling the seats. I think Mum said people do live here all year round, it's not a ghost town made solely for the purpose of tourism.

I link arms with my mum. We drift along past buildings with stone walls, arched entrances and tables sheltering from the moonlight under wide parasols.

It's a warm night and I feel sticky and dirty from travelling, but I have this feeling she needs me as her fingers gently clasp my bicep.

I really thought I'd be able to tell her I'm thinking of spending next summer away from her, and she'll have to visit me at whatever destination I end up in each year. I guess it'll have to wait until I find out what she's hiding from me.

Somewhere, I can hear a guitar. It's out of place with everything else I can hear. From the laughter to the bass thumping out of one taverna and karaoke in another . . . everything else is upbeat. But not the guitar – the guitar sounds sad, filled with minor chords.

The raw beauty of the notes is like a noose on my heart. I drop my eyeline to concentrate on it and pull it in. Whoever's playing has a strong and swift fingerstyle of playing the strings. It's not a piece I know, but I want to. I *really* want to.

As we near the sea, the sound grows. I scan the square and catch sight of the musician filling my body with his music.

His head is bowed so I can't see his face, he's too engrossed in whatever he's playing. He has strong, broad shoulders and his hands move over his instrument like it's part of him. He's to one side, sitting alone on a bench.

A few people stop to listen. He doesn't seem to notice. He's in his own bubble, enraptured by his own music. I don't blame him. I don't think I've heard anyone play like this live in a very long time. Maybe ever.

That's how I used to feel when I composed, consumed by the sounds and the beat. I just don't have the confidence to perform it. It's easier to sing and dance to someone else's beat than to share my own soul with the world.

'He's talented,' Mum whispers in my ear.

Even though we're linked together, I've been sucked in to the man with the guitar and have sort of forgotten she's here by my side.

'Very,' I agree.

I wish I could see his face. He looks maybe twenties or thirties, but that's guessing from his physique.

'Come on, it's this way.' Mum leads me away from the soft, wistful melody.

We leave it there to play out towards the dark shimmering sea. The notes play directly into my heart and reflect my sadness both at not getting to tell Mum about my new dream of working abroad and worrying she might be self-sabotaging.

Chapter 3

Mia 2025

'Wakey-wakey, eggs and bakey!' Mum opens the doors out on to the balcony, followed by the wooden shutters, pouring golden threads of light all over my face.

'You remember that I'm vegetarian, right? Bacon won't get me out of bed.' I tug the sheet over my face. 'Why are you in my room?'

I get flashbacks of teenage hangovers and Mum finding it amusing to wake me up before midday.

It's no use. The thin white cotton is no match for the brilliance of the Greek sun. I can feel its warmth making its way through the glass already, cutting through the crisp air-conditioned atmosphere.

'After four years of you looking longingly at my bacon sarnies, how can I forget? It's amazing you've got any saliva left in your mouth.' Mum chuckles to herself for a moment before continuing. 'How about the promise of coffee and something covered in sugar instead?'

'I'm up.'

Like a zombie rising from the dead, I sit bolt upright at the thought of coffee and sugar, my two weaknesses.

Mum's weaknesses too.

It's one of the millions of likenesses we share, including our lavender eyes, noses that would fit well on a mouse and boobs we both like to moan weigh us down. Not to forget our obsession with travel. That's the biggest one.

I like the similarities I share with my mum. My eye colour in particular. Although our eyes aren't shaped the same at all. Mine don't look like hers or my grandparents' either. My hooded eyelids, my hair and colouring have always made me wonder about my father – because for all our similarities, there are some big differences between Mum and me too.

I've got thick brown curly hair and can tan in the winter sun. Nothing like Mum, who has dark-blonde hair, although she adds subtle highlights to frame her face.

I tried to have highlights when I was seventeen and I looked too much like a badger with a perm to ever bother trying again.

I slide my hand towards the bedside table and tug on my phone to release it from the charging wire.

'You know,' Mum says as she pads out of my room, 'you shouldn't leave your phone on charge overnight. It's bad for the battery.'

Ignoring her, I glance at the screen to check for messages.

'Oh my God, Mum.' My voice falls down low in my throat, like a whingeing teen. 'It's seriously mean to wake someone up at seven a.m. when they only went to bed four hours ago. Why so early?'

'Because . . .' She hesitates in the door, pulling her neon floral blouse round her chest. 'Because I want to make the most of our time here.' She doesn't look back at me. Instead, I'm left with the sun in my eyes, wondering how long she's been up and dressed.

'It's a holiday. I know we like to explore and make the most of it, but come on, we like to rest too.'

My body turns to jelly, and I flop back down on to the firm mattress. The impact of my head hitting the pillow wakes me up enough to remember why I was struggling to sleep in the first place.

Questions race like sprinters through my mind again.

My blurry eyes open to sharp focus as Mum's travel slippers slap off in the distance.

No *real* holidaying is allowed unless all cases have been unpacked. Then, and only then, are we actually one hundred per cent on holiday. That's one of our other rules.

Last night's unpacking was done at super speed so I could get some sleep and be refreshed to give her a stern talking-to this morning and force her to confess anything and everything until I have every possible detail as to why she's backtracking on her lifelong dream.

All that actually happened was fifteen minutes of unpacking, then while Mum was lightly snoring in the other room, I tossed and turned, wrapping myself up like a mummy in the cotton bedsheet.

'Mum?' I wait all of three seconds before calling again. 'Mum? Mum? Sara!'

As I scoot off the bed, the mummifying sheet almost hitches a ride before I manage to kick it off.

My bare feet echo across the tiles of the open-plan living room. I scan the kitchen-diner. She'd be easy to spot in this place, with her neons. Every wall is bright white – the minimalist decor leaves space for the view from the balcony doors to take centre stage.

There she is, out on the balcony to keep an eye on the people walking about below. Which I guess is why she couldn't hear me calling her name.

I slide open the door with a whoosh. It's like opening a door to another realm that's a little bit like an oven. The heat touches every inch of my skin before I can even blink.

'As you've woken me up, it's time you told me what I had to wait all night to find out. I might be the patient one out of the two of us, but even I have limits.'

Mum's as still as the *Winged Victory of Samothrace* statue in the Louvre. She's not headless and doesn't have wings, but her head is certainly somewhere else as she stares at the blue dome of the church opposite.

'You look like a statue.' I fold my arms over my chest and watch her as she watches the world below.

'I feel like one.'

'Really?'

'Just ignore me.' She shakes her head and turns back to face me. 'It better be a good one. Like one of those Greek ones in Paris that they nicked.'

'I was actually thinking of that *Winged Victory* one,' I enthuse.

'Perfect.' Mum's face lifts and it's like she's shifted back into herself at our strange joint thinking.

'I love when we do that. Can you guess what I'm thinking now?' Mum leans back in her chair as she waits.

'That you're going to tell me why you've decided to self-sabotage?'

Mum makes a noise like an angry buzzer. 'Wrong! Get dressed and I'll tell you over breakfast. That's what I was thinking.'

She presses her hands into the arms of her chair to stand, then moves past me with the fluidity of a ghost. Something isn't right and I hear my heart ripping away from the ligaments that usually hold it firmly in place. Maybe she does know about my desire to travel alone, and she isn't taking it well and wants to have a serious talk. That, or it has to be some sort of self-sabotage if it isn't Louisa pulling out of the sale or anything like that.

If it's because she doesn't want me travelling alone, I understand, but I can't let my life ruin hers. I don't want her to give up on her dream to fit in with mine. Knowing her, she'd stop everything to travel alongside me or something.

I know I was an accident and she wouldn't want the same thing to happen to me, I get that. That doesn't make me feel unloved, I just know she would want things to be different for me. I'm sure she'd be worried history would repeat itself if I went off on my own. Maybe she's going to suggest delaying her dream to support me in mine and come travelling with me? Or ask me to stay for another year to help with the business, not that she needs me at all for that.

I'm utterly confused, possibly even more so than last night with the million strange reasons that flooded my head as to why she'd have lost her enthusiasm for owning the business she's been desperate to acquire for years.

I march back towards my room, calling out, 'Swimwear?' as I pull the door shut behind me.

'If you like,' Mum calls back. 'Beach after breakfast?'

'Perfect.'

I grab the first bikini that comes to hand and a beach dress, before dashing to the bathroom.

I move around the tiles in a dream, wondering what the hell is going on and whether this is all my fault. Each thought leads to questions, and I have to tell myself to stop before I make myself dizzy.

With a shaking hand, I press down on the new tube of toothpaste and a large glob shoots over my brush. I don't care. I begin frantically brushing it all in, until my gums burn with the minty overload.

'Done,' I announce as I step out in record time.

'Me too. I've been ready for ages. Let's go.'

I follow on behind, out into the morning heat. It's like I'm a little girl again, following Mum and waiting to find out what would happen next. Each holiday was like walking out on to a new planet, a new realm, and my mum always master orchestrator. She would have the books with all the answers and lists of places to explore.

It's funny how different we've always been to other families. Or at least, to my friends' families when I was growing up. Every family is unique, with their very own version of right and wrong. I always thought that ours was the best. It was better to be just the two of us, it meant that I never had to share my mum with anyone. If I needed her, she was there. She still is.

Mum often let me help with the decision-making. I got to pick my own clothes and have my own identity from a really young age. It helped me to develop a secure sense of self and gave me the scope to discover who I wanted to become. Having that space to grow gave me a strong voice and, apparently, a practical mind.

I didn't feel like I was the child when I was one. I felt like we were partners in crime. Us against the world.

There have been times I asked about my dad, and Mum said I cried once when I was very little and asked why I didn't have one, because some boy at nursery was mean to me about not having one. But I think that was because I thought it was weird that he did have one.

Mum doesn't know who my father is. She told me as soon as I was old enough to understand that she had forgotten him as soon as she'd snuck out of his room. I don't even have a first name for him. She's never even hinted at a race or country of origin, only saying she can't be entirely sure.

It happened when she was working in Crete. That was back in the late nineties when she was working just outside of Malia, a big nightclub hotspot. Or it was a clubbing hotspot then, anyway. I guess it still is.

He was a tourist. A holidaymaker. A twenty-something. That's all I have of him.

Other than what I see in the mirror when I look at myself and wonder about him.

We did go there once, to Malia, a few years ago. While we were there visiting, I had this strange notion that we would bump into my father and that I would get to see the man who had a hand in my making. Not that it bothers me not to know him. Equally, it would be a lie to say I'm completely disinterested. But I've accepted that he is, and always will be, a complete mystery.

I take a deep lungful of sea air and the sweet scent of lavender and citrus as we pass a gift shop filled with rows of handmade soaps decorated with flowers in all different colours.

It might be a tourist resort, but this place has some very interesting quirks that stand out even after only a minute of walking, like half a bicycle sticking out of a wall with flowers tumbling out of its basket.

I wish I could appreciate it all in the moment, the way I usually can, from the quiet winding streets lined with buildings adorned with ocean-blue shutters to the bustling shops that spill out on to the road. Normally, it would be easy to get lost for an hour or two spending money on stunning trinkets and soaps. Not today. My heart is in my throat as my flip-flops slap along the concrete.

'Blimey, so much has changed. Right up until now, my time in Kardamena felt like it was about five years ago but . . .' – Mum's eyes skirt the lines of boutique shops and their handmade jewellery – 'it makes me realise just how long it's really been.'

She stops outside a taverna with a sign announcing coffee and a list of breakfasts. 'This looks good, it's got coffee and cakes, what more do we need?'

'Looks good.' I'm pleased she's found somewhere straight away. I want to know exactly what's happening, and whether it's all my fault she's being odd. 'Mum, can you tell me what's going on before we order? You've really freaked me out.'

Mum manoeuvres a chair that's been left at an angle between tables covered in lemony-yellow paper cloths.

'It's nothing, it's just . . .' She lowers herself cautiously into the chair and slowly leans back. 'I've decided to delay the purchase. That's all.'

I feel my muscles crumple into confusion. Mum's shoulders round over her hands as she clasps them together and leans on the table. She dips her chin and looks like a child anticipating a telling-off.

All the words trap in my throat at once, leaving a series of glottal stops and puffing air passing my lips.

This is the worst-case scenario. She must've been reading my mind about leaving and this is all my fault.

Eventually, I manage, 'You're kidding?'

'Nope.'

'This doesn't make sense. Louisa said it had to go through quickly or she'd sell it on to one of those bigger travel agents who want her position in town.'

'I know. I've spoken to her, and she understands my concerns.'

My palms feel sticky and the heat is making me a little dizzy. Or maybe it's just knowing what I have to ask next.

'Is this somehow my fault?'

'What?' Mum sits tall again and she tilts her head to one side. 'How would this be your fault? I've asked for a little thinking extension, that's all. I need a little more time to think. Why would it be to do with you?' Her pupils become lasers, boring into me.

'I don't know. I just can't think why you would need time to think. I mean, you? Think? Of all people, I couldn't see that being the reason. You needing time? It doesn't make sense.'

'Neither does you saying it could be your fault, and yet here we are, that's what you said. Why would you say that?'

'Let's not change the subject.' I shake my head and hope to shake off the limelight.

I rub my hands over my face, only to realise I forgot to put sun lotion on. This whole situation has left me feeling so on edge, I haven't even managed to achieve simple tasks. If I'm not careful, she'll turn that limelight she's casting on me into an interrogation torch and then I'll be doomed.

I need to get this back on track.

'Mum, you've always gone head first into everything. Do you remember when you wanted to start a business bringing antiques back from France for some extra cash? You'd barely said the idea out loud and you'd booked a trip to buy things. You don't know the first thing about antiques. You thought it would be this amazing side hustle to pay for my singing lessons and it was a massive waste of time. But this . . . this is what you've always wanted. You always said getting that job working for Louisa was a dream come true. How is it *now* you want time to think?' I round the words *time to think* with exaggerated finger quotations. 'And if that's all it is, why make me wait all night just to say that? It's not even a reason.'

'Because I knew you would be like this. Thinking you're the mum, but you're not. I'm not your responsibility, Mia. I'm a grown woman, and if I need a nice relaxing holiday with my daughter to think about what's going to happen next in my life, then that's what I need. I want to be a little careful. I'm getting older—'

'You're not even fifty, you're basically a child.'

'No, I'm not. See, there it is again, you thinking I'm a kid.' She rolls those wide lavender eyes of hers back in her head in a way she thinks I won't notice, but she doesn't close them quick enough so I still see the action. 'Anyway, I keep thinking, more and more people buy holidays online, and, yes, there are a lot of older people who like to come in and book face to face, but . . . I just think I'd like to take a couple of weeks to consider my options and Louisa said that would be OK. I knew you were going to make a big deal out of it, so I didn't really want to talk about it last night. That's all. End of story.'

'I'm not making a big deal out of it. I'm in shock, that's all.'

'No, you're lecturing me the way you love to do, like I'm the kid.'

'That's because you like to act like it.'

'Thanks. I whisked you off on a last-minute holiday, that's pretty childish, right? How about we do something else, without giving it too much thought?'

'I don't know.' I sit back in my chair. 'When you put it like that, it sounds too choreographed.'

She exhales hard. 'Blimey, I can't win today, can I? If I think about things, it's out of character, if I do things last minute I'm childish.'

'I just thought this was a big fun holiday to celebrate your dreams before you knuckle down into your new role as owner. Now you're saying you're not even sure if you *want* to buy the place. Like, what? It might close. Or the next people who buy the place might change it and get rid of you. What happens then? You won't have a job or anything.'

'I'll still have you.' She flutters her eyelashes.

The weight of my reliable role sits on my chest, suffocating me, and my mum's words make the pain so much harder to take.

I briefly squeeze my eyes shut, as though I'll be able to see better or hear differently when I open them.

'That's true,' I whisper. 'You'll always have me.'

Chapter 4

Mia 2025

'I really wish I'd waited until after a caffeine shot for this conversation. Where's the server?' It's still pretty early and I already feel exhausted and uncomfortable in the bikini under my dress.

I want to get some breakfast inside me and get to the beach as soon as humanly possible.

I look around and catch the eye of a woman deep in conversation. Her shiny black hair is pulled tight on her head. She talks more with her hands than her mouth, although even that is running quicker than a train. She's chatting away to a woman, maybe my age. I get the impression they're mother and daughter by their heart-shaped faces. They briefly kiss cheeks and the younger woman leaves, jogging down the street.

'Sorry, sorry.' The woman flaps her hands as she comes over to us. 'My daughter is leaving for two weeks and who knew how much drama this causes. *Kalimera*, ladies. What can I get you?' The woman's hands drop to her hips, and she looks from me to Mum for the first time.

She physically jumps back and the whooshing sound of air dragging into her lungs at great speed makes me jump as well.

'Sara?' She gawps at my mum like she's looking at an alien. 'It can't be you? It has to be, you haven't changed. What is it? Twenty years? And you haven't gained a single line on your face, and not one grey hair. Although you have shorter hair, it used to be so long.'

Mum pushes her chair back to stand, embracing the woman who talks with her hands.

'More than twenty! It's been too long, my friend.' Mum lets out a shaky breath as she pulls out of their embrace, leaving the woman touching the ends of Mum's blonde hair, then her face.

They stand for a moment, hands clasped together. The nameless woman's fingers are laden with heavy-looking gold rings. Unlike Mum, who always wears one ring on her left middle finger.

Only she's not. It's not there.

The gold band, with a pale rectangular aquamarine stone in the centre, is gone.

I want to point it out, tell her that maybe she's lost it, but she's already lost in this moment with what I can only assume is an old friend. So much so that she seems to have forgotten I'm even sitting here, waiting for caffeine and sugar.

'I always thought you would come back again, I thought maybe it would be sooner,' – the friend laughs to herself – 'but better late than never? Yes? After you left—'

'Mia. I haven't introduced my daughter, Mia. I'm so sorry, this is my daughter, Mia. Mia, this is Alexandra.'

There's something about Mum's voice that's riddled with nerves, like I'm dragging her up to sing karaoke and she's stone-cold sober. She's talking too fast and at a much higher pitch than usual.

I stand to shake Alexandra's hand but instead she pulls me in for a hug and rubs my back. I'm hit with the aroma of luxury floral soaps mixed with freshly ground coffee beans.

Alexandra then holds me at arm's length, inspecting me. I'm suddenly aware of the speed at which I got ready this morning and wish I'd made a touch more effort to be presentable.

'I wish I had noticed you both sooner, you could've met my daughter. How long are you here for?'

'Ten days,' Mum and I chime at the same time.

'Then we must catch up. There is so much to say. Now tell me, are you like your mother? Are you waiting for a big Greek coffee with many, many sugars?'

'Oh my God, I would love that so much. Yes please.'

'I will make you both a special breakfast.'

'Thanks, Alexandra.' Mum pushes her hair off her face and tucks it behind her ears.

As Alexandra disappears out of earshot, I lean in towards my mum.

'Firstly, where's your ring?' I stab my index finger towards her hand. 'And secondly, I want to know everything about you and Alexandra.'

'I took it off, it was feeling a little tight in the heat.' She rubs at the empty space where that ring has always been, then wiggles her fingers at me.

'Seriously? We've been backpacking in Chile, volunteering in Malaysia, driving through the outback . . . but here, now, this is where it's *too hot*.'

'Maybe I'm fatter now than I was back then.'

'In your fingers?'

'Maybe,' she shrugs.

A growl escapes my stomach, like a cat that doesn't like the presence of something coming in too close.

'Alexandra has worked here since back when I was here. Not here though.' Mum taps her fingernails on the tablecloth. 'Another place in Kardamena. A place that probably doesn't exist anymore. I'm not sure if there's even one place that's got the same name as it did back then. Even the sea is different. I mean the beach. There used to be these big rocks by the sea . . . it's all gone. Anyway, I'm going to pop to the loo.' Mum slides her chair back and disappears in the same direction as Alexandra.

An older couple sit down at a table close to ours. He looks like something from a seventies' rock band, with long hair, and they laugh and chat together peacefully, like they're newly-weds. It's nice to think they might be. That maybe Mum could find someone to spend her days with still.

Mum's got lots of great friendship groups, we both have, but we share a disastrous inability to date. When I was growing up, Mum never mentioned dating anyone.

When I got into my teenage years, I made it my mission to find my mum *The One*. Believing her to be the best mum and overall human on the planet, it seemed only right to find a great bloke to look after her.

Sadly, I never managed to fulfil my goal to sprinkle magic on her love life. There was one girl at school who had a reasonably cute dad that I was sure was single, so I befriended her and kept inviting them over to our house. It was only after a few months, when Mum announced how great it was to have a gay man in her life to gossip with, that I realised I had got everything wrong. Although, she and Malcolm are still very good friends to this day.

At least sitting here, with the breeze fluttering my hair and cooling my skin from the prickle of the sun, I know deep down her life is not my responsibility. I can only be here with open arms to commiserate when she comes back from another disaster, the way she does for me. Or hopefully celebrate if she finds someone nice.

My rumbling stomach contracts at the thought of not being there for her with open arms if I disappear to travel.

There was Scott last year. He gave me hope that she might be happy and have someone else to have adventures with that wasn't me. I thought there was a chance she'd found someone for good, but it was only six months before she called it off. She hasn't dated anyone since. It's lucky Mum is so independent and happy to chat to just about anyone when left to her own devices.

I glance through the door, expecting her back at any moment.

In a shadow at the back of the taverna, Mum and Alexandra lean in close to each other, almost touching but not quite.

Alexandra begins to nod before gripping my mum's arm and pressing her hand to her mouth in what could be surprise.

Mum flicks her hair off her face and I know she's about to turn with it. Without thinking, I look the other way so she won't know I have been spying on her.

Not that I was spying.

I was looking.

It's not as though they were somewhere private and I was creeping about listening at doors.

I'll ask her when she gets back to the table. It's easy to look suspect from a distance, whispering. Mum was probably just catching her up on the past twenty-six years and how I was in no way planned.

Mum pulls her chair out opposite me and slides back on to it, exhaling with a smile.

'All OK with Alexandra?'

'Oh, yeah, she says it's all well on its way. It won't be long until you've got more sugar and caffeine in your circulation than blood.'

'Just the way we like it,' I smile.

I wait for more information, but it doesn't come. I have no way of knowing what they were actually talking about, but I'm sure that wasn't the extent of their conversation. Even in the poorly lit corner, I could see a puckering of Alexandra's face that looked something like concern or sympathy. A face that wouldn't match telling someone their order is coming along nicely.

I wonder how much Alexandra really knows about my mum and her upbringing.

I think people imagine my mum came from a much poorer background than she does. More like I did, I guess, as I wasn't blessed with the privilege Mum had as a girl.

My grandparents are actually really well off. They live near Epping Forest in something resembling a manor house, with two ageing stone lions beside the gates. They even have their own library.

Mum always says they had her as a box-ticking exercise. All their friends were having kids, so they had to have one too. They didn't really consider how much work might be involved in looking after a child.

The only thing she gained from being their daughter, she says, was her love for travel.

She's an explorer, we both are. That's why she ran away to work in Greece.

I look up to watch Mum with a smile on my face, knowing how hard she's worked to give me everything I do have. There's no way I was a box-ticking exercise. In fact, I'm sure I was one she never wanted to tick off, but she's a better parent than my grandparents ever were to her.

Mum squints as she looks into the distance, down towards the sea.

I hope she's happy. She deserves to be happy.

After all she's done for me, her happiness is always at the top of my list.

Maybe I should rethink travelling, at least for a year, just while she decides what's next in her life.

Chapter 5

Mia 2025

'Come on, come on!' Mum tugs my hand as we march along the street.

Our feet slap the pavement in time as she guides me through the narrow roads. The air is filled with the scent of cooking meats and freshy caught fish from a taverna somewhere in the distance. I want her to slow down and let me take my time to look in windows or around each shop we pass, but she won't. She's like a kid that's had too much candy and all the ultra-processed sweeteners and colour additives are making her crazy, while all I want to do is look at salt-and-pepper shakers hand-carved out of olive wood or some of the beautiful pottery I'll never be able to fit in my case but would if I could.

This isn't unusual for her, though. She'd do anything to cram everything life has to offer into every second of every day. To see everything, to talk to everyone . . . Although so far Alexandra is the only person who has recognised her and actively said so, which is one more than when we were in Crete to see my place of conception.

Ever since this morning, and her insane announcement about having to *think* about taking over the travel agent's, she's been her larger-than-life self again.

It's probably my fault.

I said she was being out of character with all this *thinking* and that was totally the wrong thing to say. We've spent most of the day on the beach or swimming in the sea, but she point-blank refused to let me read my book, claiming we had to *seize the moment* and *feel the sea salt on our skin, talk about life and people-watch*.

At least now we're dressed and back on dry land. I thought we would have a relaxing evening with a glass of wine and a feta salad. Now I've decided I probably won't go travelling next year, not unless I'm sure Mum is settled and happy, I thought I might be able to relax a little.

While I feel shattered, as though the sea air has battered the energy from me, she looks invigorated, like it's put new wind in her sails and now she could keep running about all night too.

She's already treated me to a pair of circular handmade earrings in gold and beige as well as an emerald sarong that I didn't even hint I wanted. She just said it would look great and purchased it. I tried to point out she needs to save money for her new business venture, but she hasn't listened at all.

The sun is starting to set at our backs and the moon is stealing its limelight over the sea, and I'm already stifling a yawn.

'Did I tell you I've been having the craziest dreams lately? Every night for about two weeks?' begins Mum as she holds up T-shirts in front of me then refolds them before putting them neatly back on top of their piles.

'Nope. Are they crazier than those ones about Nina Simone rising up from the grave and telling you that you have a better singing voice than me?'

'Way crazier than that. That's a firm fave, not a weird one at all. In these dreams, every night everything is a new colour.'

I lift an eyebrow. Partly in response to the *I love Kos* T-shirt she's pressed to me and partly because I have no idea what she's on about.

'You know,' she says, 'like one night everything's pink, the next it's green. Our skin, the sea, the sky. All of it. What do you think it means?'

'Don't drink milkshakes before bed?'

'I was wondering about auras and what they mean. But it's always a different colour, so it can't mean that. Maybe I'm meant to paint the house. What do you think?'

'Where are you in the dream?'

'That's the best part, it's like that music video from around the time you were a baby, "*Blue (Da Ba Dee)*". You know the one? I'm almost invisible because I match all the rooms. My face, my hands, my clothes . . . I'm not sure where I am.'

She tries to sing the song but doesn't make any of the right sounds in the right places. Luckily, I recognise it well enough.

'Maybe it's about hiding? Like camouflage?' I offer.

Mum falters and the T-shirt in her hand sags. 'What do you mean?'

'Well, if everything's the same colour, it's pretty easy to hide there. Right? Maybe it means you're hiding in plain sight?'

She begins to pace, still clutching the white T-shirt with the evil eye shaped like a heart on the front.

'Maybe. Or maybe we're overthinking it. Maybe I just need to paint the house?'

'Maybe,' I shrug, before subtly stretching out my arms from all the swimming this afternoon.

'My back's starting to ache with all this running around. I'm not sure how much more shopping I can do. Shall we head out for dinner now?' Mum's face has settled into a deep frown.

'Oh, thank God. I could've gone for dinner an hour ago, I'm starved.'

'You should've said.' Her spare hand slaps down by her side.

'I did. But you kept saying *one more shop*.'

Mum begins to walk towards the entrance, still clutching the T-shirt.

'Mum, aren't you forgetting something?'

She turns to face me and cocks her head like my words are a complete mystery to her.

My eyes slide down to her hand and back up. It takes a full moment for her to look at what she's holding. She gasps in complete surprise, as though she's never seen the T-shirt before, then splits the air with a high-pitched squeak.

She holds it out to me. 'Do you want it?'

I shake my head vigorously, making my curls brush over my shoulders.

'I really, really don't. Thanks though.'

I take the soft cotton T-shirt out of her hand and put it back where she got it from before thanking the person at the till and exiting into the sharp heat in the street.

'What would you do without me?' I shoot her my most angelic smile.

She pauses and reaches out to push a curl off my face.

She hasn't done that since I was a little girl. I'd all but forgotten the action. It's only in the doing of it that the memory of a feeling floods back to me and the sweet perfume on her pulse races me back to childhood.

'I couldn't be without you, my sweet child.'

As quickly as the action arrived, her hand vanishes, and a bright smile lifts her fine features. 'Come on then, let's not waste these sexy outfits on shopping. Let's find a taverna.'

The moment might have passed, but the sensation of pain lingers bitterly on my palate. She's just said it herself, she can't be without me.

I take two fast steps to get in line with Mum, and she slows her pace for me.

'I still think you should seek proper advice for your back, not just Louisa's friend Sue with the crystals, but an actual doctor.' When she doesn't say anything, I push harder. 'You seem off, what's wrong?'

'I'm not made of milk, I don't go *off*. I'm more like a vintage Champagne, I'm worth more every day.'

'You know what I mean. Has your back been bothering you a lot?'

'On and off. You know how it is. I need to start doing Pilates or something, that's all. How about this? I promise I'll see a proper doctor about my back when we're home, as long as you don't treat me like a dairy product.'

'Deal.'

Mum links her arm into mine and we meander back down towards the sea as it switches from bright turquoise to its dull midnight shades.

It doesn't take long to select a taverna – they all look and smell divine. Some are too full to pick though, and I think we might have to book in advance for some places.

We order whitebait and big bowls of salad filled with olives and thick slabs of feta. Everything flows like it always has. The wine, the food, the laughter.

We chat about all the things we want to do on this trip, like heading over to Nisyros tomorrow and the three-island boat trip.

The waiter comes over to retrieve our crockery, which looks as though a stray cat might've jumped up and licked it clean – that, or they forgot to put food on the plates in the first place.

‘Can I order some chocolate ice cream, please?’ I beam before he scoops up our scrunched-up napkins. ‘Anything else for you, Mum?’ I tilt my head, knowing she can never resist a lemon sorbet.

‘No, that’s everything for me, thanks.’

The waiter nods and disappears with our plates and bowls.

‘I think I’m going to go back to the apartment. My back still feels tight. It’s my own fault for overdoing it. I still think I’m your age.’ Her lips twist into a half-smile. ‘Sadly, my body disagrees with me. You enjoy your drink and your ice cream, and I’ll tell this rubbish back to sort itself out before tomorrow so we can catch that boat to Nisyros.’

‘How can I enjoy life without you?’ I meant to say enjoy *the night, my drink, my ice cream*, but my voice came out like a squeaky mouse’s and the word *life* slipped out instead. My concerns over her living without me have likely caught up with me.

‘One day you’ll have to, my girl.’ Mum stands and plants a kiss on the top of my head. ‘Finish your drink, fall in love with someone not on an app, and don’t get brain freeze from your ice cream.’ A wide grin spreads across her lips before a laugh spills over into the warm night air.

‘Well, there’s no way I’d find luck on an app, that’s for sure. They should put all the apps together and turn them into one app that’s called *Leftovers*.’ I roll my eyes and join in with her laughter.

‘I have to keep some hope I *might* find love again,’ Mum muses.

‘When did you find love in the first place?’

It isn’t meant to sound harsh or mean, but that’s one hundred per cent the note I strike. In doing so, the metaphorical string breaks and whips Mum in the face.

I begin to flail and backtrack, starting five different sentences with *I mean* or *I didn’t mean to* and *Were you in love with Scott?*

‘It’s OK, it’s OK. It wasn’t Scott, but you’re wrong. I have been in love. I love you, and that one’s for ever. Enjoy your evening,

Sweetpea. You can explore and tell me which cocktails are worth trying tomorrow night.'

It's not the first time Mum's turned in early on a trip. We're both independent and like to chat with *all and sundry*, as Mum would say. Sometimes I've gone to bed and she's stayed out late, chatting to people.

I watch as she moves away, rubbing her lower back, circling the sacrum with her fingers. Maybe she can get a massage on the beach tomorrow instead of getting on a boat; we'll have to find out whether that's possible here. I wasn't paying enough attention today, or Mum wasn't letting me.

I want her to be fighting fit because I've got my heart set on going over to see the volcanic craters on Nisyros. There's a ferry every day and tours up to the volcano itself. Mum said it was something she did years ago but would love to do again at some point.

I've always had a morbid fascination with volcanoes. Maybe because when I was little Mum took me to see Vesuvius and all the plaster-cast bodies of Pompeii, caught like flies in amber. Trapped forever in their own natural disaster. I suppose the sticky amber rolling towards insects must be like the miniature version of the rolling waves of hot lava from a volcano.

Chocolate ice cream piled high enough for three is placed down in front of me in a glass tumbler, along with a silver sundae spoon.

'*Efcharistó*.' I smile at the waiter.

'*Parakaló*.' He nods in return.

Drips of chocolate begin to roll down the sides of the glass, tumbling like tears. There's no way I'll be able to eat it fast enough alone.

A pang of sadness resonates in my chest. I'm not usually bothered if Mum heads off before me, but today it feels like I've been hyped up only to be abandoned.

I shovel in a few big mouthfuls of ice cream with instant regret as I'm hit with the stab of brain freeze. The one thing Mum told me not to do.

It's time to give up.

I put money in a shot glass holding a bill and gather up my phone and my handbag.

I begin to meander towards the sea. Sweat gathers on the exposed area of my lower back and beads form over my lip. It might be past ten, but the power of the sun can still be felt in the sultry nights. A quick paddle in the sea to refreshen me up, then I might as well head back too. I'm not in the mood to chat to strangers in bars tonight, even if Mum did say I should try to find love *not on an app*. Which wouldn't happen anyway. What are the chances of finding someone a million miles from home, and then, how annoying would it be to live so far away. Long distance is worse than not having a relationship at all.

All roads lead to the expanse in front of the harbour, like rivers running towards an estuary, opening out into the mouth of the central square. It's possibly the busiest area, with cocktail bars on every corner and the overwhelming ring of laughter and joy in the air from people on low-slung wicker chairs, sipping through thin black straws.

The mellow vibe of the winding streets spills out to here, where a large heart made of red wire sits at its centre, filled with plastic bottle tops to be recycled for charity.

Something glitters on the floor just ahead of me. It looks like the hook of an earring sticking out of a crack in the tarmac. As I reach it, I bend forward to retrieve it. It's not an earring at all, it's a two-euro coin that was balancing on its side.

I slip it into the pocket of my flowing skirt and wish Mum was here so I could do my usual, *Find a penny, pick it up, the rest of the day you'll have good luck. Give a penny to a friend, and your luck will never end* bit. Only for her to point out it isn't even a penny.

A little way in the distance, the street lights reflect in the inky-black sea and the flashing dot of a plane looks like a shooting star having a dream of its own as it edges past.

The fragrance of fresh cut flowers and the gentle sound of a guitar float along on the sea breeze.

It has to be him. The man from last night.

The guitar at least, perhaps not the sweet floral scent.

He's there on the bench to the far right of the heart. His eyes are on his fingers and his back to the white wall in the quietest part of the square. A family of four are gathered not far from him, absorbing each elegant note from every pick of his fingers on the strings.

The family move away to watch a man on stilts at the other end of the square, who's already gaining quite an audience. Kardamena really does have a little bit of everything.

Keeping my distance, I stare at the man playing guitar under the stars. He doesn't seem to notice the family leave, or me arrive. He only has eyes for his music, and I can't blame him.

My critical ear wants to pin it down, but I'm quite sure it's an original piece. Today's music is a little more upbeat than yesterday's, but there's still that sultry summertime feel, like it's inspired by an impossible heatwave that's burning into his soul. Or maybe my soul.

Goosebumps ripple over my arms as I watch him. I rarely feel such an instant connection to music I don't know; my analytical mind likes to pull it apart into its raw form, seeing the mathematics in sheet music and the value of each note dancing across it. But this man's passion and love for his instrument fills me up instead.

I slip my hand into the pocket of my skirt and feel the smooth edges of the two-euro coin I found on the floor a moment ago.

As the music comes to an end, he still doesn't look up at me. I pull the coin out and gently wave my hand.

'Where do I put the money?'

He looks up at me with the widest ebony eyes I've ever seen. He's somewhere around my age, perhaps . . . twenties or thirties at a guess, anyway. There's a dark and brooding look to him that fits a little too nicely with the way he plays guitar. The look in his eye, almost unblinking on me, is enough to chase away the goosebumps and bring back the heatwave over my chest.

His face shifts and he looks bewildered for a moment, making me question whether he speaks English. It was silly of me to assume. My Greek isn't good enough to say more than simple pleasantries. If he speaks Italian or French, we might be able to get by. I had to learn a few languages for operas I was in, and even did a joint honours degree in music and Italian at university.

As I try to conjure different words in my mind, his face slips into the curve of a smile.

'What money?' He pouts and relaxes back into the bench.

I wave the coin in my hand for effect. 'This money. For the beautiful music.'

Suddenly, a two-euro coin feels a little insulting for the skilled music he's been filling the air with, and because my intrusion has now stopped it.

'I am practising. My sister is sick of hearing the same songs. She kicks me out to rehearse. You can have my noise for free. In fact, if you find her, maybe she will pay you to stop her having to hear it.'

'Oh.' I wrap my fingers back around the coin.

Heat rises along my spine and lands on my cheeks.

'Well, you're very good,' I continue. 'I can't imagine ever being bored of hearing you play.'

His teeth sink into his full bottom lip as he lifts one eyebrow. It's enough to make my head feel like it's spinning.

'I better go.' I turn and swiftly walk back towards our apartment, because a face *that* handsome and hands *that* talented can only bring trouble.

Chapter 6

Sara 1998

'Come on, doll, let's get some peace and quiet before we have to get on the next sweaty coach.' Tammy nods her head in the direction of the sea, and I follow on next to her.

The sun must be rising higher in the sky somewhere behind the clouds. The tarmac smells of warm rain and there's a sense of walking through a damp cloud as more people begin to emerge on the winding streets to look in shops and find their first pint of the day.

A moped swings out to go round us, the person on the back holding an umbrella over the rider's head. It's not the first time I've seen such crazy driving this week.

I don't really know what I was expecting from all this when I arrived.

I'm not naive enough to believe all holidays are the same. Not all *people* are the same. I didn't want to look down my nose at everyone the way my parents do – but the times I've had away with my parents are so far removed from this, it's been a complete eye-opener. I've been clubbing, and partying, even sneaked out to a rave or two, but not every single day. Everyone who comes here seems to be living life like they're on death row, and as soon as they get back to England, their lives cease to exist. It's almost as though I've slipped into an alternate reality without consequence, one where alcohol, particularly beer, is the sweet elixir of life itself.

It's been a week since I started my job as a travel rep in Kardamena, and so far the rain has also had an interesting effect on people. It's almost like it's been laced with something that triggers more anger than that of a testosterone-ridden honey badger. I've seen more fights, more men pissing up walls and more vomit washed down drains than ever before.

The more time people have had to spend indoors, the more time spent exchanging an empty beer glass for a full one, with undesirable consequences.

The people I work with are nice and the local bar and taverna owners are great, and even with the red-hot anger some holidaymakers feel at the touch of a warm summer rain, I'd still rather be here than back in England being told I'm not good enough by my parents.

Here, shadowing Tammy, I get nothing but praise. And even though a lot of the men want to fight about a puddle they then fall in, so many people spend their days laughing and their nights dancing that it's strangely intoxicating . . . until a fight breaks out, that is.

I'd heard about this sort of set-up, of course, where people arrive by the coach-load and party until they drop, usually into bed with another holidaymaker.

The people here have been working hard all year for their one week's holiday. All my mother does is read her copy of *The Lady*, smoke cigarettes to stay thin and scream blue murder if anyone tries to come in the house with shoes on.

My mother always has a strict itinerary on holiday, which I do my best to ignore. My parents usually have a personal concierge in our hotel – a travel rep like me, I suppose – who organises everything they want to do. Strictly in private, of course. There's no way my mother could book a package holiday and get on a coach with lots of people pushing for a seat. That wouldn't impress the people at my father's golf club at all. We always have a private transfer. Most people do at the places we stay.

My mother would never be seen dead at one of our group welcome meetings.

So far, the meetings are actually my favourite part. We have to walk around the hotels slipping notes under doors in the dead of night, informing people their presence is required in the morning. When they arrive, they're always impressed at the cocktails being placed down in front of them. We want to make their holiday great, and usually so do they. It doesn't matter that the cocktail is watered down to within an inch of its life, people are determined to enjoy themselves.

This week I've mostly been studying the smiles and sales tactics of Tammy and my other roommate, Tina. They use their brightly painted lips to sell various excursions around Kos, as well as organised bar crawls. Although the sign-ups to bar crawls far outweigh anything else we offer.

So far, more people have asked about when it will stop raining than booked to go to the volcanic island of Nisyros by boat or take a tour to 'bubble beach', where the water bubbles delightfully.

Tina goes along on some of the more interesting trips, while I've been designated clipboard holder at the airport to make sure I collect everyone and get them safely on a bus to their accommodation.

With the harbour in our sights and the sea beginning to glitter with a hint of reflected sun from a break in the clouds, Tammy makes a left to face the mountains, which look like a watercolour backdrop to the village. Thinning silvery clouds have been painted above them today.

She stops at a place called Blue Note and heads for a table for two.

'So what's next?' I place my clipboard down and look eagerly at Tammy for my next instructions.

'Lunch. Next on the agenda is lunch. But you gotta be ready, because the sun is back this afternoon, and everyone who has missed it this last week will stay out to get every last ray. That means they'll be burning. That also means we're gonna be chocka with people complaining of heat stroke and wanting to know where the doctor is. I know, I know,' – she holds her hands up like I'm about to say something, but I haven't even opened my mouth – 'they were given all that crappy information, but they're on holiday, who cares when you're on holiday? You mighta noticed, everyone thinks they're Superman. They got their holiday-brain in.'

'How do you know the sun is coming out today?'

'Declan told me. Don't ask me how he knows, but that fella *always* knows and he's never wrong.'

It hasn't rained yet today and, to be fair to her, the clouds over the mountains look as though they might be thinning out from silver to white, with pale-blue lines filtering through.

The mountains and the sea have to be my favourite part of being here. With the sea in front of me, rugged mountains split the earth in the distance to the left. Their dark, looming presence isn't menacing, though – it's rather beautiful. There was nothing like that where I'm from in England. It's one of the reasons I love to travel – other than meeting all sorts of people, I like to see all the shapes planet Earth can make.

'So.' Tammy leans her cheek on her fist and squints at me. 'You got here one week ago. Ready to leave yet, *Toff*?'

'No. And please stop calling me that.'

'I pegged you for being like that last girl they sent here, running back to mam's at the first sign of a fella waving his prick about for a piss.'

'No amount of urinating in the street would send me running back to my mother.'

'No.' She sits up straight, but still looks at me like she's reading a tricky textbook. 'You're different, you. First toff I've been mates with. They must've taken the stick out your arse at birth.'

'Thanks . . . ?'

A smile spreads across her mouth, displaying her shining white teeth. 'Yeah. I think you'll be all right staying here. Better company than tight-arse Tina, that's for sure.' Tammy glances over her shoulder before leaning in towards me to whisper, 'And I notice Declan's been coming around more since you been here.'

'Really?'

'Oh yeah, we only used to see him every other month, for a knees-up. We've seen him three times in the past week. Can't be a coincidence now, can it?'

'Maybe,' I shrug.

He's good-looking, and has the wicked charm of most Irishmen I've met. It's true that I don't always notice the subtleties of someone liking me in that way. Not that it matters. I'm here for an adventure – if he is part of that, then it's fine, but it's not all that important.

'And guess what?'

I tuck my chair closer to the table and lean in towards her as she pushes a dark strand of chemically straightened hair from her face.

'Next week, you're doing all the welcome meets so I get a lie-in. No more following me about like puppy love. Twice as many people arrive next week and that's when the real fun begins.'

'I thought you were going to tell me a secret about Declan.'

'God no, I'm not a matchmaker. I've said all I've noticed. Just warning you that this' – her finger waves around the paper tablecloth – 'this is quiet right now.'

Twice as many people.

No wonder they wanted another person here to help out. There will be more meetings, more problems to solve, more people to herd along on bar crawls and more boozy boat trips.

'Do you think I could do one of the non-alcoholic excursions soon?'

This week I've been involved in three bar crawls and nothing that meant going further than Kos Town.

'Guess so, but you'll have to fight it out with Tina. She likes to have a nap on the coach. I think she's got her eyes on a fella over on Nisyros too.'

I squint out to sea. I've watched the boats disappearing into the haze over the water and out towards the mysterious volcanic island. I'll ask Tina tonight if I can shadow her and escape with her on the next adventure.

That's what I'm really here for, after all, to escape. I'd do just about anything for an adventure right now.

I don't like to tell her that I pawned one of my great-grandmother's necklaces to pay for the flight out here. I took it right out of my mother's third-best jewellery box. She's told me I'll inherit the lot one day, so it seemed pointless to wait when I know she'll never even notice it's gone.

Chapter 7

MIA 2025

'It's OK, we can go tomorrow.' I shake my head in defiance.

'No.' Mum's tone is enough for me to know she means it. That she won't let go. That she'll make my day miserable unless I do as I'm told.

She has never been a shout and *do-as-you're-told* kind of mum; she's been a *I'll-sulk-you-into-regretting-being-born* kind of mum though. As a youngster, I always thought I had complete free will to make my own choices, but what Mum was really doing was teaching me to learn to live with whatever decision I made, and to think it through first, because if I made the wrong one, I'd sure know about it.

She's adamant I need to enjoy myself and not watch her read and sleep on the beach.

'I promise, I will come with you later in the week or something, but I'm knackered after yesterday. I'm not up to walking around Stefanos Crater in this heat. You do that bit today, and I'll come with you later to look at all the shops and buy volcanic rocks we can exfoliate our feet with. I've been over there a million times before, remember? You go and enjoy yourself and tell me what it's like and whether it's changed.'

'How will I know whether it's changed?'

'Good point.' She waves her finger at me like it's all very serious. 'And more reason for me to join you later in the holiday. It needs at least two trips to get a real taste of it. Trust me. You'll only scratch the surface today. And anyway, I've arranged to meet with Alexandra for lunch.'

'You kept that quiet.'

'No, I didn't, I just told you now. I bumped into her when I was walking back last night and we arranged it. Now, go and have some fun, will you?'

'All right, bossy. I'll see you this evening, OK?'

Mum blows me a kiss then returns to her book, putting her feet up on the chair opposite her on the balcony.

I walk with pace out of the apartment. The ferry leaves soon and I'll be late if I don't get a wriggle on. I don't want to miss it, because if I do, Mum will accuse me of doing so on purpose.

At first, I take long strides between people, sheltering my eyes from the blinding sun so I don't knock into anyone as I go. My sunglasses case has slipped to the bottom of my backpack and I don't want to stop to fish it out.

I spot a familiar face with a halo of curls smiling at me, marching in the opposite direction.

'*Kalimera*, Mia!' Alexandra beams. 'Have fun at Nisyros!'

'*Kalimera*, have a good lunch.'

We exchange another smile as we pass by each other.

My feet begin to skip underneath me to catch up precious seconds, my focus completely on getting there quickly. For all I know, the ferry fills up this time of year, and I might not even get a space.

My feet jar as I trip over a thought. How did Alexandra know where I was going, and why did Mum make plans last night to see her when she said she hoped she would feel well enough to come with me?

If she wanted to catch up with Alexandra without me there, she could've just said. Clearly, Mum had something to say to her the other night that she didn't want me to hear. I bet she was just using her back or being tired as an excuse to ditch me.

A new heat flushes my cheeks, and not just from the rays of the sun and the pace of my feet. I'll have to wait until tonight to quiz her on it. There's no point turning back now just to have an argument and watch Mum sulk about it. She might as well have her lunch and then I can find out what all the secrecy has been for when I'm back.

As I reach the ferry, it looks like it might be almost ready to go, with everyone already on it. I step towards the metal bridge resting on shore. On the lower deck there's motorbikes and an old moped strapped to the inner wall of the large vessel, next to a topless man counting tickets.

'Excuse me, I think I need to pay you.' I tap him on the shoulder lightly. Heat radiates out from his olive skin.

As he turns, the boat engine vibrates to life and I bump my fistful of notes right into his naked chest.

I look up and my heart drops down to my flip-flops.

'I told you, I'm not asking for your money.' The guitarist with the pitch-black eyes looks down at me with a laugh on his lips.

An older gentleman with a face like leather appears from somewhere inside the boat and tells me the fare I'll need to pay. Gulping back some strange lump that's formed in my very dry throat, I do my best to give the correct person the required money for the return journey to Nisyros without embarrassing myself further.

The boat lurches into the swell of the sea and I bend my knees to stay on my feet without brushing myself along the guitarist's smooth skin again.

He shoots me a lingering smile then makes his way to the stairs leading up to more seating. It's a hot day, and the sheltered area on this deck, with its worn leather seats, is already filled with people and bags. Mostly families with younger children, who need the shade and to be well away from the danger of falling off the upper deck.

Without even looking at him, I can feel the heat of the guitarist's eyes prickling my skin as he pauses to glance back at me before heading to the upper deck.

'The volcano? Also the volcano?' the leathery old gentleman asks.

'Erm, yes, please.'

He gives me the correct change and two tickets, one for a bus upon arrival in Nisyros and one for the return boat trip. The man turns away from me and follows the guitarist up the stairs. I don't have anywhere to sit down here, so I guess I'll be following behind the guitarist too.

Trying to keep my footing, I head for the metal steps to the left of the boat and grip the cool banister. As soon as I step into the sun, the banister becomes fiercely hot, even at this time in the morning. I keep hold, because I'd rather a cooked hand than to fall down.

As I reach the top, I scan the open central deck of the boat. Every possible seat is already filled with people in shorts, hats and sunglasses, many snapping photos of each other or the sea. Some, I'd say, live around here and others, like me, are looking for an authentic experience rather than an organised day trip.

I turn to the run of solo seats along the left side of the boat. There's one last white plastic seat that's empty, right at the front of the row. It would normally be perfect, but today the man in the seat behind it will probably think I'm stalking him.

Without making a meal of it, I swiftly walk past all the other people hanging their heads over the safety bar to look down into the waves and take the free seat at the front.

'You ran away,' he whispers close to my ear.

'No, I didn't.' I twist in my seat and scowl at him. 'I didn't run away.'

'No?'

'No.'

His chin rises and falls with a slow nod of faux agreement.

'What is the name of the girl who is always trying to give me money?'

'I'm not *always* trying to give you money. Twice, I've only tried to give you money twice.'

'The only times we have seen each other is twice.'

'That's not strictly true, I saw you the night before, too.'

'My playing wasn't good enough that night to offer me money?'

'No, I—' I stop before I begin defending myself. I don't have to answer to anyone but myself.

'So,' I begin, 'I guess I'll be in front of you for the next hour. My name is Mia.'

'Leonidas.' He scoops up the receipts I thought were boat tickets and thrusts them in his wallet before adjusting to slot it into the back pocket of his shorts. 'It's nice that you can't run this time.'

My eye bulge and my jaw drops slack.

'Not *can't*. That's not what I mean.' As Leonidas stumbles over his words and his cheeks bruise to a lovely shade of purple under his tan, I can't help but laugh.

'It's OK. I understand.'

'Thank you.' He clasps his hands together like giving thanks to a possible god.

His silent prayer, and the tilt of his chin to the heavens, gives me enough time to really look at him in daylight. The slight bump in his nose, the defined line of his jaw, his neatly cut hair with a ruffle of curls on top. He's not conventionally handsome, he's stunning. Like a puzzle that fits perfectly together, but the picture printed on it is something unexpected.

He has that musician's air about him. Confident in his half-naked state. And so he should be, with broad shoulders and arms that look like they could carry me about, let alone a guitar. He's rugged and perfectly imperfect.

My pulse racing for a guitarist or drummer or singer is something I do my best to avoid. The first band I was in fell to bits because the drummer broke my heart. But that was ten years ago, and I'm not sixteen anymore. I learnt not to fall for sexy musicians ever, ever again. It never works out.

That doesn't mean I can't indulge in flirting with the gorgeous man behind me.

'Have you been to Nisyros before, Mia?'

'Nope. I was hoping to hire a quadbike or something and have a look at Stefanos Crater. But I've just purchased a bus ticket . . . I think. I guess that was obvious, right?'

'Maybe a little. But if you want the authentic experience, I could show you up there? My godfather gives private tours, and sometimes I like to help him. I know a thing or two about it all.'

'I wouldn't want to take you away from your plans for the day.'

'My plans start this afternoon. We have a big family dinner. Before that, I was going to play guitar on the beach until my fingers cry blood. I can give my fingers a rest if you like?'

This wouldn't be the first time I've let a perfect stranger be a tour guide for me. I can't count the number of times Mum and

I have got chatting to people and jumped in at the deep end. In all the years of travelling and backpacking, the open and trusting nature I've inherited from my mum has only got me in trouble twice. Both times I had an itch about the situation and both times I was right to keep my guard higher than normal.

If anyone gives me a big itch feeling, I politely make excuses and find a new place to be and a new crowd to hang out with.

'Maybe you can entertain me for the morning? I have spent two days now entertaining you and you still have not paid me.' He raises one eyebrow and bites his lip like he's trying really hard to hold back a grin that's waiting to split his face in two.

Nothing about Leonidas gives me the scary itch, so what do I have to lose by saying yes?

'OK, sounds good.'

And there it is, the beaming grin framed with dimples to offset his unrefined beauty perfectly.

Damn.

I'd be better off keeping my eyes on the undulations of the sparkling sea at our left, instead of that sparkling smile, but it's going to be a tricky one.

'What are you thinking?'

My eyes flick back to him. He looks genuinely interested to know.

'The sound of the waves and the boat. It's loud, but . . . it's strangely peaceful.'

The engine makes a fast beat like a rapid heart and the waves sound like a thousand silver cabasas playing all at once.

'No. It's not peaceful. It is more like a war cry from the sea. The boat is splitting the water into two like a knife and the sea, she roars back with an angry belly.' Leonidas balls one fist and looks out into the waves.

'I love that,' I splutter, completely taken aback by his deeply thought-out description. 'Have you been thinking about that for a while?'

'No. It's just the words that found me when I hear it. If you couldn't see, would it still be so peaceful?' He closes his eyes.

It's something I love to do in nature. To close my eyes and listen. It's almost impossible to stop the smile that's tugging at the corner of my mouth.

Chapter 8

Sara 1998

'Tina? What are you still doing here? You need to get up, you have about six minutes to get ready and get to the boat, otherwise you're going to be in serious trouble. You've already missed the pick-up coach.' I study the mass of blonde hair protruding from under a thin white sheet.

A low groan emanates from somewhere inside.

'I can't go. I'm not well,' Tina whines.

I want to call her out, but I bite back the thought. It's been a month, but I am still very much the new kid.

'That's crap. You were up all last night drinking your weight in vodka shots. You can't now pretend you're *ill*.' Tammy joins in, gluing her hands to her hips next to me and looking down at the same lumpy bedding that has Tina in it.

Tina yanks the sheet from her face, displaying make-up smears and a fine smattering of glitter all over her cheeks.

'That's not it. I'm not well. I started to feel sick last night, I didn't really even drink that much.' She shuffles herself up the bed to a sitting position, the bed creaking and moaning under the movement. 'Sara.' Tina clasps her hands together as though she's about to pray to me. 'Pretty please could you take the group today? You're so good with all the welcome meetings and talking to everyone you meet. And the guy who runs the tour does everything, all you have to do is count heads at the start and the end. Please? Pretty please with sugar and cherries? I'll make it up to you, I'll take the next two groups back to the airport for you and all your early welcome meetings for a week?'

Tammy folds her arms across her chest and rolls her eyes towards her tightly gelled ponytail.

Tina knows very well not to ask Tammy to do it, because there's no way she'll say yes. If I don't agree, then there's no one to meet the people doing today's tour of Nisyros, and it'll be on all of us if things go wrong or someone goes missing.

I know deep down she'll probably only do one welcome meeting for me, and that's it, but the idea of going to Nisyros would be worth it for me anyway. I asked her weeks ago if I could shadow her on one of the tours, and she let me go on one of the drinking cruises, but I haven't had the time to follow anyone about for more training since then. It's been a case of get on with what's in front of us.

I take a deep breath and sigh out my answer to try to make her feel guilty. 'Fine. I'll do it.'

Tina claps her hands at a ferocious speed before slumping back on to the bed, tucking her sheet under her chin and closing her eyes, an angelic smile resting on her face that clearly doesn't belong there.

I exhale hard again and leave the room, followed by Tammy.

'I can't believe you're doing her a favour *again*, doll. The more you help her, the more she's just gonna use you.'

'I know, but I'd rather the people had someone there to take their tickets and make sure they all get on the right boat than leaving them with no one. It's not like I was going to do much else today.' I lean in closer to Tammy's ear. 'Don't tell her, but she's doing me a favour, I've wanted to do the Nisyros trip since I arrived.'

Tammy's face lifts in a sly smile. She knows as well as I do that it's best we keep that information to ourselves, otherwise Tina will never return the favour.

I scrape together everything I need into my backpack. Lip gloss, a few extra pens and my brand-new Nokia 5110 that I got before coming to Kos with some money I took from my father's hidden jar of cash.

Not that he'll ever notice the money's gone. It was the minimum parting gift a father should give his little girl before she disappears into the night.

It's pointless to bring the phone, really. It's like carrying a small brick round with me that no one will ever call. My parents do have the number, but my mother only called it once to ask where I was and why I left a note with a random number on it. When I said I left for Greece, she didn't call back, and that was weeks ago.

Lastly, I pick up Tina's list of names and the clipboard she's left on the kitchen table. Usually, Tina has to get on the coach that collects people from all the hotels and then lead them down to the boat. Today, she's so late she's missed the coach and now I'll have to make a run for it. We'll just have to hope everyone who was meant to get on the coach is on it.

Nerves jumble with excitement on my empty stomach as I jog down to the harbour. Usually when we start taking people on trips, we've done it once with someone else before. Not today. Today, Tina has thrown me in at the deep end. I can handle it.

Last week, she blamed her period and said that was why she couldn't get on the coach to the airport for the transfers, but she was fine to go out drinking later while I was still on the stuffy coach organising the drop-offs.

As I'm the new girl, I just want to fit in. Unlike Tina, Tammy has kindly taken me under her wing. There's something about her melodic Liverpudlian accent that's soothing and helps to keep situations calm. Even a crazy situation, like last week when someone tripped over and broke their wrist. We were all there and dealing with it, but Tammy took over and was so calm, it was like she was ringing for a taxi, not an ambulance.

I duck and dive between people as I make my way through the winding streets of Kardamena and down towards the port.

There's already a group of people milling about and waiting when I get there. The coaches must've already dropped people off, or they've made their own way down here from their hotels in the village. The boat's captain is looking out across, waiting for me. Well, not me, Tina. Or at the very least someone with my bright yellow blouse and the correct logo on the front.

The creases in his brow relax when he sees me and he waves frantically. I jog towards the crowd, holding up Tina's clipboard to get myself seen.

'Hi everyone, my name is Sara. If you're here for the tour to Nisyros then please come here to check you're on my list, and we can get you settled on the boat for a beautiful crossing to a very exciting island. I've got all your tickets here, so please come and collect them from me now.'

People push towards me to get their group ticked off first and find the perfect place on the boat. The seat with the view out across the clear crystal blue. I don't blame them – one of the perks of being a tour rep is getting to live next to the glittering sea.

It's not a holiday anymore, though. It's my life.

It takes fifteen minutes to get everyone on the boat, making us five minutes late heading out.

I'm amazed I've managed to catch up that much time, with the stream of families with kids not *that* much younger than me wearing something from the Bang on The Door brand, usually the Rabbits or Groovy Chick bag or T-shirts. That, or fourteen-year-olds in Spice World or '100% Babe' crop tops. Most teenagers are here with their parents or their families for free holidays and box-ticking.

I was them once, not that long ago.

Standing out on the top deck, not too far from the captain, who's behind the shield of the water-scarred screen, the sea breeze whips my ponytail from side to side like a metronome.

The view across to Nisyros glitters. I could happily stay on the water all day, gliding along. The island's not visible yet, but it's out there.

The sun has been blazing all week – I can barely remember what a cloud looks like now. Part of me is dreading trudging round a volcano in this heat. I can only imagine it's going to be like walking into a furnace on a sunny day, but the freedom of trying something new far outweighs any reservations.

Before becoming a travel rep, I never really *had* to work. I have worked, but there was no big need for it.

As long as I showed up and smiled at the right events and kept out of the way the rest of the time, life was pretty easy. My parents were paying for food and shelter, so life has been worry free.

They wanted me to trot off and go to uni like a good little girl and get a first-class degree so they could call all their friends and brag that I got a first because I'm *oh so clever*. After I finished my first year, I couldn't see myself there. Every second felt like it wasn't my life. It wasn't me . . . so I left. But living back at home for even a matter of months has been too much.

I've had a good education already, anyway, why bother doing more? I've had a private education my whole life, with some of the best teachers. Not to mention being thrown in the deep end at an all-girls boarding school – which really should've been called Boring

School. That was when my parents were worried I might be more interested in male attention than school. Which of course I was.

It was all mapped out for me. Every detail. All my parents wanted me to do was look pretty, get the good grades, smile at all the right people, marry the right man.

They wanted me as an accessory . . . I've been quite the disappointment.

The best part of my life so far has been seeing the world and travelling. That is the biggest gift my parents have ever given me. Bigger than the ponies. Bigger than the cars. Bigger than all the other box-ticking exercises they've attempted over the years. Better than spending money on me rather than spending time with me.

I don't want to be a handbag anymore. I want to be *me*.

It's funny when people talk about freedom, it means different things to different people. Freedom to buy whatever they want, have whatever they want, freedom to walk down the street without abuse, freedom to date who they want, sleep with who they want, dress how they want . . . I'm here for *my* freedom.

I just don't know what that is yet. All I know is I need to be away from my parents to find out.

Staring out across the glassy turquoise sea, I know I've made the right choice to find it here.

Nisyros is soon upon us. The volcanic earth rises up out of the sea in almost perfect lines. The undulating land is layered, like it's made of paper and someone concertinaed it in neat rows then opened it out again. I wonder whether it's layers from volcanic eruptions or man-made. Here and there, it looks like small walls have been constructed to hold it all in place. To the right of the stepped earth, the whitewashed town of Mandraki sprawls along the coastline, waiting to be discovered. At least, that's what the printed handout says that I've given to everyone taking the tour today.

That will have to wait for now though. As soon as we're off the boat, the first stop will be the volcanic craters.

The captain swiftly and easily manoeuvres the boat into the port of Mandraki.

As soon as the boat is secure, he throws down the gangway and I have to almost elbow people out of the way to get to the front ready to guide them towards the correct coach. If I don't, they will be meandering around not knowing which bus to get on, all because they didn't let me go first. That's something Tammy warned me about.

I grab the captain's hairy arm as he steps away from another tourist thanking him.

'Nikos, do you know where . . . ?' I look down at my clipboard, scanning and hoping I can find the tour guide's name, but I can't see it. '. . . the tour guide is?'

'*Nai*,' he nods, 'the coach. He will be waiting.'

'Thank you so much, Nikos. *Efcharistó poli*.'

'Good luck.' He taps my shoulder with a sweaty palm and laughs loudly as he turns back to the boat to help more passengers off one by one.

I hold my clipboard above my head and walk slowly backwards to let the crowd of people follow me. Luckily, there's only about thirty. Surely that can't be too hard to manage.

I scan the coaches, looking for a pink board in the window with the correct number.

I spot it, T7.

'This way, everyone. Please follow me.'

'Excuse me. Excuse me, please,' a tall woman with a posh English accent says loudly next to my ear, 'my daughter needs a restroom.'

The woman is wearing tailored chino shorts and a neat white blouse. She's holding the hand of a girl who looks to be about ten years old, dressed in the cliché Groovy Chick T-shirt. It's neon green, with the cartoon girl walking down the street. In the weeks I've been here, it must be the fiftieth time I've seen this printed on a bag, T-shirt or notebook.

'OK, sure, give me one moment and I will do my best to find it for you. Please wait here.'

I jog over to the coach and trot up the steps inside. There's no one sitting in the driver's seat, but there is a man sitting behind it with a Panama hat over his face. His arms are folded and his right ankle rests on the opposite knee. He doesn't move and for all I know he could be sleeping.

'Hi, excuse me, do you know where there's a toilet?'

His fingers link together and he extends his arms out in front of him, curving his back in a stretch before pushing his hat back off his face and looking up at me.

Burnt-umber eyes peer up at me from under the rim of his hat. He scrutinises me from top to toe. It's hard to make out any more of him with the blinding sun pouring in from the window behind him. He's a silhouette and his face is in the shadow of his hat.

'You're not Tina.'

'Correct.'

'But you wear a costume like Tina. Is she playing sick today?'

My eyes begin to adjust and I can make out his mouth curling up in a brief smile.

'Something like that.'

'And you are the new Tammy? Normally, she replaces Tina when she cannot be bothered.'

'I guess so.'

It's news to me that Tammy would ever do anything for Tina.

'Excuse me,' an abrupt voice sounds from behind me. 'My daughter really *does* need the toilet quite desperately.'

'Let me show you.' The man brushes past me as I hover on the stairs of the coach.

He steps off and points them in the right direction, also telling everyone else lingering ready to get on where it is and that we leave in five minutes, but that there is a toilet at our destination in the centre of the mountains.

The man steps back up towards me, removing his hat entirely, and greets me with a broad smile. He has straight teeth and golden skin. 'Dimitri.'

I've never been so taken aback by a face before.

I've seen many handsome men over the years but there's something about this man, this face . . . his sharp cheekbones and his eyes that don't seem to blink . . . something under my ribs feels both tense and liquid all at once.

Dimitri's hand engulfs mine. I'm hoping he can't read my thoughts as I try my best to keep my knees locked in place.

'Sara.'

Chapter 9

Mia 2025

'You're doing it wrong.' Leonidas hops off the boat in front of me.

Discarding his guitar, he turns back and reaches out his hand to escort me safely off the boat.

My fingers melt into the safety of his grasp.

'What am I doing wrong? Getting off the boat? Is there a wrong way to walk over a slab of metal?'

I hop down next to him.

'No, getting off is easy. It's what comes next that is not.'

I hover while he picks his guitar back up, staring at his profile, wondering whether he understands how that sounds to an English ear. Or, at least, to *my* ear that's always attuned to a double entendre. I suck in my cheeks for a moment as I contemplate telling him that, *yeah, that's pretty much an accurate description of half of my relationships with men.*

We begin to walk across the concrete port of Mandraki together, simultaneously tugging our bags higher on our backs. He has to juggle with his guitar on his left shoulder, but he has more than enough muscle to make balancing it all look easy.

'You see all these buses?' he continues.

He nods to the people streaming off boats like sheep, only to be herded on to one of the perfectly aligned coaches instead.

'They will all go to Stefanos Crater now. It will be filled with more people than this island has cats.'

'I take it there's a lot of cats?'

'*Nai*,' he nods, 'more than I would count. If you like, we could go for a walk, have some lunch and I will take you to the volcano when it is quieter?'

'It sounds a lot like a *hot date*.' I grin up at him and playfully raise my eyebrows.

'It does? To me, it's sharing my home with a kind woman for the morning.'

'First off, I was *trying* to be funny, because volcanoes are hot, and second . . . What makes you think I'm kind?'

'You're always trying to give *poor me* some money. And you like my guitar, so I think you must have very good taste.'

We meander, necks twisted to maintain a moment of eye contact.

There's so much to learn from someone's eyes. Mum taught me that. She said that people who don't want to hold eye contact are often hiding something.

Leonidas's eyes are so dark they're almost black, yet somehow they radiate and reflect light. Maybe it's the slight squint with the sun high in the sky, but to me, it's like he wants to share in jokes with me. Like he's holding in a laugh.

'OK, that would be lovely. Let's go for a walk,' I agree.

'Good, wait here for one moment.'

Leonidas puts up a finger for me to stop in my tracks, then dashes into a taverna on the seafront. The white building seems to be empty. Wooden chairs are neatly placed around tables, even spilling out from the open sides of the building where they've placed red and blue parasols for shade. It's still early, and it seems

Leonidas is right – everyone's getting straight on to buses headed for the craters.

He comes back with no guitar and two bottles of water.

'Now we are ready,' he says as he waves them in my direction.

The seafront is lined with a handful of tavernas ready for the lunch rush, but there's only a few people on foot, like us. Mostly people who were on our boat. There's a delightful sea breeze catching my curls. Without it, the heat would be sticky and uncomfortable. I'm as grateful for that as for the water Leonidas got us.

'So where are we actually going?'

'Up to the monastery, then further to the ancient fortified walls. It is very beautiful, and very old.'

We wander along with the sea a constant presence on our right, gently brushing itself against the rocks. Shops selling pumice stones and black lava face-wash skirt the road to the left, before we move into meandering streets. They weave their way up to higher ground. People's homes protrude snuggly at either side of the cool grey paving slabs.

Leonidas fills the gaps between the walls with tales of a long-gone past as I snap photographs of cats lazing in doorways. Everywhere is immaculately clean. Each white building is crisp, as though it was freshly painted for the season.

I don't know whether it's the town of Mandraki or the whole of Nisyros, but it's both exceptionally Greek to look at and unique to anything else I've seen. Although there are swathes of whitewashed buildings and neat blue doors, there are many houses made from the large volcanic stones.

Outside some of the houses, front steps have been decorated with small black and white pebbles, set like mosaic tiles. There are many beautiful and intricate patterns, from geometric shapes to some styled into flowers set in the ground.

'This is beautiful.' My fingers brush along the steps to someone's door where clean white pebbles encase dark ones in the shape of a four-petalled flower.

'If you like that, you will love the town squares. This way.'

I pause to take a photo of potted plants and some buildings so close together that the balconies above almost kiss.

'When I was a boy, I would run through the streets here with my bigger sister chasing me. Usually, I had taken her bouzouki because I wanted to play so mutz. She is five years older than me.' Leonidas does that typically Greek thing I love to hear, pronouncing the English 'ch' as 'tz'. Every time I travel, I enjoy hearing how any English can be twisted around different tongues and how every alphabet creates something different.

It reminds me how much our upbringing influences our view of the world, and how important it is to venture out and see everything from a new, different perspective.

How can we really know our place in the world, if we haven't even seen it with our own two eyes? Mum used to say, and sometimes still does.

'Do you have any other siblings?' I'm always interested in the relationships between siblings and families. Having only my mum, everything else feels so alien to me.

'Also two younger sisters. My oldest is Foteini, after my grandmother. Then me, then it is Antigone and Ismene. They are twins. Normally twins are seen as lucky, but my mother named them after a Greek tragedy because she says they ruined her little body. I don't like this so much because the brother dies in the story.' Leonidas twists his lips into a grimace before breaking it back into a smile.

'This is it,' – he points towards an opening from the narrow street – 'one of my favourites. It is not the biggest though. You might like others more.'

Leonidas turns to me, his intense eyes focused on me, waiting for my reaction to his favourite place in his hometown.

In the small square, there's a large circle of black stones with a helix pattern of white pebbles running through it. Inside the outer ring, three dolphins in black pebbles swim around a trident.

'When I was very small,' Leonidas begins in a low voice, so close to my face I can feel the warmth of him, making my skin tingle, 'a dolphin saved me, and my godfather tells me this circle was to show how they are always here to help us, sent from Poseidon himself.'

I bob down and touch the smooth lumps that form one of the dolphins. Each pebble has been worn until it's soft and smooth from people walking across them for years.

'That's really funny actually, because I *saved* a dolphin.'

Leonidas is quick to crouch next to me. 'Is this a joke?'

'Nope.' I shake my head, making my curls whip from side to side.

'Then how?'

'I was diving with my mum, and a few other people. I think I was about fifteen, maybe. Yeah, fifteen, because I was in high school but it was before GCSEs. Anyway, we were swimming about under the water and this dolphin seemed to appear from nowhere, and it was coming up to me and showing me its arm. I mean, fin. Not arm.' I roll my eyes and stand. 'It had a hook and line caught there—' I point at my armpit, hoping it isn't too sweaty. 'It seemed to want my help specifically. So the guide and I, we untangled her together. It was one of the most amazing things that's ever happened to me, to be singled out like that and be trusted to help. Mum was super jealous but said the dolphin probably knew I was a kind and calm person.'

I think back to the change in the dolphin's body language once we had disentangled it. It was so long ago, but I can see it clearly in my mind's eye. How it was gently nudging me with its nose and how it seemed to smile once we'd freed it.

'So what about you? How did a dolphin save you?'

With wide eyes, Leonidas shakes his head at me, his right hand lingering over his full lips.

'It is the exact opposite.'

'What? You were the one caught in fishing wire?' I snort a laugh but his expression doesn't change.

'It was a net. My legs, they were caught. The dolphin swam me to the surface, back to my boat. At first no one believed me, but it is real.'

A silence falls like no other I've ever experienced as we dive deep into each other's eyes.

My throat feels dry and my pulse quickens to a new, dizzying height as words disappear and all that's left is a very real energy circling us.

'I don't normally tell that part,' Leonidas mumbles. 'It sounds pathetic, to fall in the sea like this, and it was. I think I was about fifteen also, but usually I tell it like I was younger.'

'When you tell the girls you normally pick up and show around Mandraki?'

'Maybe. None like you. You are different. Very different.'

He begins to walk away down another alley. I lick the salty sweat from my top lip. There's more to this man than meets the eye, that's for sure.

I wonder what his top lip tastes of.

Chapter 10

Mia 2025

After meandering around Paleokastro castle with its huge heavy stones, it's creeping towards midday and time to find a taverna before they're all flooded with people back from the volcanic crater.

We take our time walking down the dusty path that leads back into town. The roasting air around us is filled with our conversation and spotting local wildlife, from birds to lizards. Leonidas has been impressed by my basic knowledge of birds, and didn't even laugh when I told him it was because I love the music they make. As a child, I used to nag my mum to find out which bird sung which songs, so she got me a subscription to the RSPB magazine so I could learn more about them.

A young boy skips past us and down towards the end of the street, where the whitewashed houses pinch closer together. He has floppy dark hair that flaps as he skips.

'Milo,' a woman's voice calls not far from my shoulder. She says the rest of her sentence in French.

A man and a woman overtake our slow pace to reach him. They pause and the man looks up at us.

'Excuse me.' His English is surprisingly perfect. 'Could you take a photo of us? Please?'

'Sure.' Leonidas and I both step forward to take the man's phone, then laugh before inviting the other one to step forward and take it.

Eventually, I'm the one who takes the phone and snaps off a round of photos of the attractive young family, all in matching denim shorts.

'I like the matchy-matchy,' I say as I pass it back.

They all look down and the woman laughs. 'It was not intentional.' She has a subtle French accent in her English, unlike the man, who might actually be from England.

'Thanks for doing that,' the man beams as he looks back at his lovely little family. 'Do you want me to take one of you two?'

'Yes,' the woman adds. 'You're a very beautiful couple, you should have photos too.'

Leonidas and I start talking over each other to explain that we're not a couple, that we've only just met, that that's very funny, very sweet in fact, but no, no, not a couple.

At the end of our awkward laughter and verbal diarrhoea at this idea, the boy, Milo, tilts his head, a frown wrinkling up his forehead.

'I think maybe you should be. My mère is much happier with Ralph.'

'OK, thank you, Milo,' the woman says. 'Thank you again for the photos. Have a good day.'

They usher the boy away and we stand still for a moment, and if Leonidas is thinking what I'm thinking, it's to give them space to escape this moment without us trailing two steps behind them.

Not that it bothers me too much – it was a compliment, after all, and said without malice.

We look at each other before exhaling one final laugh and taking a step forward.

'So, you live here? On Nisyros?' I begin, pretending five seconds ago didn't actually happen.

'I used to. Most of my family still does. I now live with my sister and her husband in Kardamena. There isn't much work for a musician here.'

The empty streets speak for themselves. While we've been walking, we've seen Milo and his family plus nine cats. Although anyone who lives here is probably working or hiding from the midday sun, which would be the sensible thing we should be doing right now.

Despite melting in the heat away from the sea breeze, I've enjoyed every moment of this morning, walking through the town of Mandraki guided by Leonidas and his knowledge of his home.

'And what about you, Mia? You have spent all morning hearing my voice, learning about my home. Tell me about your hometown and the things you love, other than listening to the birds. What job do you do . . . Or you don't have a job? You are born so rich you can give all your two euros to men on the street like me?'

'No, no. I was certainly not born into money.'

The image of the council house we lived in when I was small pops into my head. Mum did her best to make it look beautiful, but she had to paint some walls every month to cover the mould, and she worked hard and never spent a penny on herself so we could have enough money to travel once a year.

Looking at where Leonidas was brought up, it's a world apart. This is like a dream filled with clean air, more vitamin D than my body would even know what to do with and swimming in the clear sea daily.

'I'm a wedding singer. I'm classically trained so I often do the wedding service and the reception party too. What about you? Is it all guitar or do you have another job?'

'You're a singer?' Leonidas's feet scuff the ground and he steps ahead to walk backwards to face me. 'This is why you like the singing birds.'

'Yeah.'

'I think you are a very good one.'

I am, but it's strange to believe someone is good at something when you've never experienced it in real life.

'I would like to hear you sometime.'

'Sometime,' I shrug, intentionally flicking my eyelids down and back up.

Whenever he faces me head on, the urge to flirt with him rises up in my chest. That little family had something right – he, at least, is very beautiful.

Not pretty. Not cute. Beautiful. Beautiful with character. Painfully beautiful, like glancing at the sun and having it imprint on my retinas. Equally not a cliché like a flower or a sunset, more like the beauty found in a tree that's been struck by lightning.

If he was put through a filter, AI might straighten out his nose, or soften the intensity of his eyes, but that's why AI can never create something truly stunning with depth and heart . . . because beauty comes from the art of unique difference. Something this man in front of me has in bucketloads. Something that could never be artificially crafted. Just like the magic of his fingers on a guitar, or the string of words from his mouth.

I hate how my body is responding to him, but how can it not? Not only is he interesting and gorgeous, he's a talented musician. He makes me want to screw up the imaginary paper in my mind that says Never Fall For Another Musician and set it on fire with the heat in my chest.

I could sing for him now. I rarely hesitate when given the opportunity to do what I love, but it's like a cotton thread is pulling on the nerves in my abdomen at the idea of singing for him, or better yet, singing with him playing by my side.

'I hope sometime soon?' He sounds urgent, like he doesn't want to leave the idea alone.

'Maybe.' I do my best to keep things light and playful, opposite to the grinding tension in my chest. 'I guess you'd have to feed me first. I don't feel like singing on an empty stomach.'

'Then I shall fill you up,' he declares.

There goes my mind again, wondering if he could possibly mean that in something a little more sideways than just eating lunch.

He turns to walk forward again after his slow backwards detour.

I press my lips tightly shut and shake my head, trying to retrieve my mind from somewhere in the gutter.

'Is it weird to live in a place where people take pictures of your front door all day?' I pause to take another photo of an attractive blue door with potted plants outside that cascade with flowers.

'Why? Does no one take photos of your doors?' Leonidas folds his arms over his bare chest and it's almost enough for my mind to fall back into the gutter, but what I enjoy the most is his humour.

I guess when your life is this beautiful, it's easy to forget how lucky you are.

Chapter 11

SARA 1998

The air-con in the coach is close to useless and, as it's completely full of people, I'm shoulder to shoulder with Dimitri. I can only hope he can't feel the heat emanating from me every time I look at him.

I'm not sure it's air conditioning at all. It might just be blowers. It's more like how I imagine it might feel to be in a fan oven.

Before the coach lurched away from the port, Dimitri took the microphone and began to share facts about the island with us all. I don't know how he does it, but he makes everything sound so sensual, so meaningful. Between his soft accent and his low dulcet tones, it's not just the heat from the sun making every other woman on this bus melt.

So far, I haven't been able to retain one single fact he's uttered. Every word has slipped over me like olive oil.

I think maybe he said something about the age of the island or the volcano or about how the volcanic rocks are used, I can't be sure.

'We will be arriving very shortly. You can leave your belongings on the coach. Remember, please, to take some water as it will be very, very hot.' Dimitri clicks off the mic and puts it back on its clip on the wall of the coach. 'You have the water, yes?' Dimitri furrows his brow at me.

Sweat pours like rain under my blouse as panic swims along my veins. 'No, Tina never mentioned bringing water. Did I leave it on the boat? Oh my God, did I leave it on the boat?'

Dimitri's elbow finds my ribs and gently nuzzles them. 'I am kidding. They bring their own.'

I exhale a laugh of relief, but my body's left tingling with the small shot of adrenaline he's given me.

'Sara, how long have you been on Kos?'

'Almost a month.'

'And have you been to Greece before?'

'Loads of times with my parents, but never to Kos. We've spent time in Athens, Santorini, Crete, but never Kos.'

'Do you like it?'

'Yeah, I really do. Usually, I prefer staying in quieter places that feel a bit more . . . authentically Greek. But I needed the work, so Kardamena was perfect. It's not that I don't like drinking and dancing, it's just a bit more . . . alcohol than I'm used to. But the island is beautiful, and the people are great. What about you? You live here, right?' I point to the floor of the bus. 'On Nisyros?'

'For all my life.' He leans closer to me, untroubled about leaving me without any personal space. 'Do you think it is not authentic? Kardamena is not *real* enough for you?'

'No, it is.' I'm filled with regret at my wording. I wasn't trying to offend him. 'I guess I like to go off the beaten track, you know? To places where tourists don't normally go. My parents tend to take me to certain types of places and usually I run off and try to do my own thing.'

'Then I think you will like it here on my island.'

I could point out we're on a coach stuffed with day trippers and I'll be stuck to them all day in case they need anything. And twice a week this same trip happens, and tourists are beating down this track, not steering away from it to find something new.

The coach pulls into a car park with a handful of other coaches.

Standing up, Dimitri tugs the microphone back off the wall and turns to face his adoring audience.

'We have arrived. As I have already told you, I am Dimitri, your guide, and you have the lovely Sara also at your service. I have the red umbrella so if you are lost, look for the red umbrella. Let's see a real, living, breathing volcano, shall we?'

Dimitri hops off the coach, swiftly followed by a river of holidaymakers.

I stay where I am, counting heads to make sure I know the exact number we need to come home with. That's about my entire contribution to this trip, as I have no idea what is going to happen next. On the itinerary there's something about lunch and shopping in Mandraki after this.

I'm barely off the coach and Dimitri's already got his umbrella in the air and devoted fans hanging off his every word. I linger at the back, making sure everyone stays together as we move along and look down across towards Stefanos Crater.

Dimitri begins by talking about the cluster of earthquakes that have taken place over the last few years, and that it's been some time since the last major eruption, so we should be safe to walk round and down into the crater itself.

From up here, it's like looking down into a giant crème brûlée, only the burnt caramel here and there is actually mustard-coloured sulphur.

We begin the decent towards the largest crater, Stefanos.

As I've been to a few volcanoes before, I know that it smells like horrible eggy sulphur, and the stink lingers. There's an odd savoury smell to it, too. Like a sulphur stew with a sprinkling of dill.

Sadly, a lot of the holidaymakers did not know this was part of the trip. One teenage girl with '100% Babe' written across her crop top looks quite green already. She's gripping her nostrils so tightly she might do herself some damage.

'Make sure you keep sipping your water. You'll get used to the smell soon,' I reassure her.

Her mother doesn't look convinced.

Dimitri does a good job of layering facts and entertainment into his tour, asking his audience what they think the answers might be before giving them the facts. Like asking when they think the last eruption was, when they think the last big earthquake was, what they know about hot springs, among other things.

When we make it inside the volcano itself, everyone has free time to wander around and discover things for themselves. They're given a meeting time to be back at the coach.

Lingering just behind Dimitri's shoulder, I don't really know what my role is now. *Not really knowing* seems to have been my primary role all day.

'Are you looking forward to lunch?' Dimitri turns to face me, tilting his head like he almost forgot I was here.

'I guess. I haven't really thought about it.'

'Tina usually finds somewhere to smile sweetly at a man and get a free drink, maybe food. Is this what you'll be doing?'

'I guess it depends on who the man is.'

Dimitri takes off his hat and places it on my head. 'That never seems to bother Tina.'

'Well, I'm not Tina.'

I lift the hat off my head, inspect it and put it back on because it gave a nice relief to the heat hammering down on me.

'No. I don't think you are.'

'I was thinking something very similar earlier.'

He studies me for a moment, like I'm on display in a gallery. I can't imagine it would be a very high-end gallery, maybe a local village hall displaying art by the old ladies to get together on a Tuesday morning.

'Would you like to come to mine for lunch? There is time, if you want?'

'Yeah, I'd like that. What's with giving me your hat?' I look up towards my eyebrows before going cross-eyed and contorting my mouth.

It has the desired effect of making him chuckle.

'Excuse me, Dimitri, how did you say the volcanoes got their names? I've forgotten what you said.' A woman, maybe in her late twenties, clutches a small handbag to her chest as she flutters her eyelashes at Dimitri.

I touch his arm and lean in close. 'I'll see you back at the coach. Don't worry, I'll look after the hat.'

He briefly looks down at my hand resting on his bicep, then meets my eyes with a glancing smile across his lips.

'You will.'

I turn on my heel and begin marching my way out of Stefanos Crater.

It's only been a month since my break-up, but it could almost be a year ago. Lawrence was the only person keeping me back in England, back in Essex. When I realised what a cheating scumbag he was, I had no reason left to stay. Getting a job as far away as possible was the best option in the world.

I didn't message him to tell him I was leaving. I didn't even leave a note. I assume he turned up at my house one day and I wasn't there anymore.

My parents didn't like him anyway. I guess they had to be right about something eventually. I'm sure they had great satisfaction telling him that I had left for Greece and I wasn't coming back in the foreseeable future.

In some ways, I'm surprised they didn't like him. At least he's on track for a first-class degree in Spanish. Really, they'd prefer a doctor or a lawyer though, I suppose.

It would've been good to see the look on his face. Those cold-as-ice blue eyes, stunned.

I think Lawrence was the first guy I went out with that I *really* fancied, and that blinded me. The pursuit was totally on my part. I don't want to do that again.

There's something about Dimitri, a beauty that shines from within him that has me a little bit terrified I'll make a mistake here and fall for someone I shouldn't. There's no way I want to fall for someone based on looks alone, ever again. To believe someone is something they're not because they've got a face.

I need to be careful. I didn't come here to get hurt again.

I did, however, come here to live a life of my own, and have fun . . . Going for lunch with one handsome guy isn't against the rules, because I get to make up my own rules now.

It's not on my agenda to be a complete sad act, and how much harm can a little fun *really* do?

Chapter 12

Sara 1998

'Can I keep my shoes on?'

'Yes,' Dimitri shrugs.

Thank goodness he didn't ask *why* or make me take them off in his home. I've been wearing the same Marks & Sparks court shoes with tights in the burning heat for the past month and they're starting to smell like they've been left in a prehistoric swamp then dipped in a blue cheese fondue for good measure.

I can't bear to think how they'll smell by the end of summer.

'Nice place.'

There are small alcoves with plates stuck on the walls inside them, and various religious icons dotted about. In the kitchen there's a circular table with a floral plastic tablecloth and four wooden chairs around it. Another image of the Madonna lurks in the corner.

It doesn't look much like a bachelor pad. Not one I've ever seen before. I'm more used to men feeding off their family businesses, with minimalist flats just outside of London and cleaners that come in every other day. Even Lawrence had the nicest uni house I've ever seen.

Dimitri starts making excuses like he's reading my mind and seeing my thoughts as a negative, but they're not. It's good to be different.

'It is my mother's place. But she is visiting an elderly aunt on Kos, she is very sick and my mother is looking after her.'

'Is a salad OK for you?' he continues as I hover behind him.

'Great. I mostly live on ouzo at the moment. Or that's how it feels, with all the bar crawls we have to go on.'

There's a moment of quiet as Dimitri sticks his head in the fridge. I'd quite like to join him, but I'll keep that to myself for now.

'I'm sorry to hear about your great-aunt. I hope she's better soon. It's nice that she has your mother there with her.'

'Thank you.' Dimitri pulls a jug from the fridge then turns to a low cupboard, taking out two short tumblers. The juice glugs as he pours, before handing me the ice-cold glass.

'You really have been spending too much time with Tina and Tammy if you live on ouzo.'

'It seems to be the norm. Most nights anyway.' I take a sip of the fresh tangy orange juice before placing it on the kitchen table and shuffling it to line up with the pattern on the plastic cloth. 'Have you ever invited Tina or Tammy to your house for lunch?'

'No, no. My mother would not approve of those girls.'

'But she would approve of me?'

'No, but she's not here today.'

Typical, another mother who wouldn't approve of me. Just like my own.

He pulls out a ceramic bowl from a cupboard and raises his eyebrow at me.

'I hope you're not expecting something . . . nefarious. And that's why she wouldn't approve of me?' I narrow my eyes on him.

Dimitri takes some tomatoes out of the fridge and begins juggling them, as a small crease forms between his brows.

'I do not know this word, *nefarious*.'

'Illicit.'

'No. Nor that one.'

I fold my arms over my chest and step back to rest my shoulder blades against the cool stone wall. 'Naughty.'

Dimitri stops juggling. 'This is a shame. I think maybe you would be good at being naughty.'

It's hard to keep the smile from my mouth. I do my very best to contain it, forcing my lips to control themselves.

'This is not why she would not approve. You're not a good Greek girl.'

I begin to laugh. 'And that's why my parents wouldn't approve of you. You're a good Greek boy, instead of some doctor with the right family name. God forbid I ever marry someone with a name they can't pronounce. It would be worth doing for them to disown me. What's your last name?'

'Georgallis.'

'Nah, that's too easy. I'll have to annoy them by marrying someone else.'

Dimitri chuckles to himself as he slices up the salad, cutting into a plump onion.

It's nice to have someone who understands what it is to be judged by their parents. If any of the people I went to school with felt that way, they hid it well. Even the ones with the hyper-competitive parents seemed to thrive on it. I've always felt out of place in that world.

'Do you find it hard? Having an overbearing mother judging your decisions?'

'Do you know what I think is best?' He stops cutting and turns to look at me instead, giving me his focus as he leans his weight into the counter. 'To live your own life. They are our parents, we have to respect them for giving us life. But . . . does my mother have to know everything about me? I think, no? And what about you,

Sara? Do you tell everything to these parents who do not approve of a good Greek boy?'

'Oh, God, no.' Automatically, my head begins to shake. 'I didn't even tell them I was coming here to work. The more I can keep my life separate from theirs, the better.'

Dimitri watches me in a way I'm not used to. Like he's actually listening, not waiting for the right time to tell me something *he* thinks is important about himself.

We're sharing in conversation. I'm used to being talked at, not talked to, by many of the men in my life. This is refreshing.

'Not that it matters if they approve or do not,' he continues, 'there is only time for food. No time for *naughty*. Not today. Even my mother can approve of eating next to an English woman.'

Something about the way his mouth moves, the way his lips pout over the word *naughty*, makes my chest crush and my body fizzle.

'Come, you can help me now. You cut these tomatoes and I will do the rest.'

He places a wooden chopping board on the kitchen table, along with a knife. I peel myself off the wall and take a seat to begin slicing open the round fat red tomatoes. It's hard to keep an eye on my fingertips and not on him.

This would not be the time to lose a finger.

I'm already pretty concerned that if I'm not careful, I'll lose my knickers, and if I'm really unlucky, my heart too.

Chapter 13

Mia 2025

'She looks a bit . . . scary. Like I'm afraid to touch her because I might do something to . . . upset it. I mean . . . *her*.' I'm glad my eyes are hidden behind my sunglasses so Leonidas can't see how much they must be bulging.

'No, no, she's fine, she's fine. She has never hurt anyone.' Leonidas firmly slaps the cracked leather seat of a very rusty red scooter he calls Bia.

He swings his leg over the scooter and shuffles forward on the seat. 'Come on, it's only a short ride.'

'I'm not getting on it while you're topless. No way.'

If I do get on the scooter with him in a state of undress, he will certainly feel my heart pounding in my chest.

'And what is wrong with me?'

'Nothing.' It's hard not to choke on the word, because at least to look at, *nothing* seems to be sharply accurate, in my own opinion. 'I just don't think we should push our sweaty bodies together just yet.'

'*Just yet?* His eyes meet mine and that light that seems to shine from within grows stronger than ever.

Oops, I shouldn't have let the dirt dropping from my mind into the gutter so many times today fall out of my mouth.

'That's not what I meant . . .'

His eyes drag over me for a moment. I can tell by the twitch on his lips he's doing everything he can not to laugh, to the point where he rubs his hand over his face to cover it. I wonder whether he meant to make things sound rude earlier, because he caught on to that one way too quickly.

He turns away for a second before passing me an open-face helmet that was hanging on the handlebars. There only seems to be one.

Leonidas swings his backpack off his shoulder and tugs open the zip to pull out a cotton short-sleeve shirt, the one he put on for lunch and then took off again as soon as we were out in the sun. I thought it was only the British crazy enough not to cover up in the afternoon, but apparently he is of the same mentality. I did like that he put it on to eat though. It had an old-fashioned gentleman vibe about it that hit just the right note.

He puts it back on but leaves all the buttons open, his flat stomach still on parade.

'Better?'

I place the helmet firmly on my curls and shrug playfully. 'I guess.'

This is going to ruin my hair, but I really don't want to be vain about it. I'd rather be living my life than tied up in concerns about the way that I look. I'll still be crossing my fingers that it does look OK, but it won't stop me doing what I want.

Swinging my leg over Bia, I can hardly imagine she'll start, let alone get us up to the mouth of a volcano, even if it isn't a big cliché funnel shape. Not from what I've seen online, anyway.

With one turn of the key she's ready and purring happily in a way I didn't expect.

I slip my arms around Leonidas's waist, knowing this is the safest way to travel, but also acutely aware that with his shirt unbuttoned, I get the pleasure of my fingers locking together over his abs.

He pulls away from the harbour, leaving the busy tavernas and bustling shops behind us.

Everything feels fast on an old scooter. We could be going fifteen miles per hour and it would seem fast. Glancing over Leonidas's shoulder, I'm quite sure the speedometer is broken, so there's no real way to tell our speed.

We buzz along winding roads, climbing the layers of the earth. First lush greenery skirts us, but it isn't long before we reach swathes of dry and rough terrain with scatterings of olive trees. The road is a beige line that curls around the volcano.

Excitement bumps along the road with me. I've seen volcanoes before, I've been up close and personal with one or two, but I've never been *inside* a crater before. This will be something completely new.

Wrapped up in our surroundings and the feel of the breeze rushing over my skin, I squeeze a little bit tighter to Leonidas. I close my eyes, glad he can't see the blush on my cheeks that I'm sure will be there.

I'd lost all awareness for a moment, which seems strange. I must be really comfortable with his energy already. A few years back, I dated someone for a while, and I felt hyper aware of our knees touching under the table, like I wasn't truly comfortable with him, so I broke it off.

I can feel the warmth of Leonidas there in my hands, but it feels comfortable, not awkward. My hands feel happy around his waist.

What's Mum going to make of this when I tell her? She told me to fall in love away from an app, but I'm still pretty sure she wouldn't really want me to have a holiday fling if it could end in tears or babies.

◆ ◆ ◆

We abandon Bia in the car park, close to the toilets and café.

What strikes me most as we walk closer and closer to Stefanos Crater is the smell. I knew it would be here, just as I knew that the heat would climb in the air. But it catches at the back of my throat and my nose like an eggy punch. It's been lingering in the air from a little way off, but the sulphur pong intensifies with every step. It fills our lungs and leaves its mustard stain on many of the rocks. I hope it doesn't do that to our insides.

Sweat gathers in every pore – with the sun high in the sky, no shelter and the threat of lava just under our feet, it's pretty intense. This is probably why most people come up here in the morning.

'How often do you come up here?' I rest my finger under my nose momentarily, waiting to get used to the smell.

'I guess more than most people. I sometimes come here to help my godfather. It is known that the volcano has erupted at least thirteen times. A few years ago there was an earthquake, a big one – it made it to 5.3 on the Richter scale. And you know about the hot springs near the sea?'

'Yeah, I'd be interested in seeing them.'

'And you know the volcano is 160,000 years old and is still the baby of all the volcanoes in Greece.' Leonidas becomes more animated and there's a distinct spring in his step. 'According to the ancient Greeks, the smoke and the sounds coming from Nisyros were the actions of grumbling giants moaning and moaning and moaning. There are many myths about wars of gods here, fighting between Titans, Poseidon, Polyvotis. If you ever meet my godfather, I'm sure he would tell you mutz, mutz more. If you're interested?'

'I'd actually love that.' As soon as the words pass my lips, I'm struck by the feeling that I've been invited to something concrete instead of something hypothetical. That maybe I will be lucky enough to have a chat with Leonidas's godfather about the history of the volcano and the island, instead of it being something said in passing. *Yes, I'd love to meet your godfather. Sure, we should definitely meet for coffee soon. I'll call you. I'll join the gym soon* . . . and the million other things we mean when we say them, but which don't ever happen. This feels like something I might actually make happen. Something I'd like to be real.

I stutter to find more words to soften my enthusiasm. 'I love learning about any history. The myths of Greece.' I frame my words with a hand action like I'm in a pre-Shakespearian play. 'I just love to travel. Everywhere I go I like to find something new. It's the same with my mum. We love to meet people, talk to people, go on adventures. That's what life is all about. For us, anyway.'

There's a pause in conversation as we edge down the last part of the track and have to watch our feet with every slippery, stony step.

My feet suddenly skid along before I catch my balance again. Leonidas grabs my elbow with one hand and his other finds my lower back.

'Are you all right?'

I do my best to laugh it off. I'm completely unhurt, I just feel a little silly.

'I'm fine, honestly. I just thought it would be funny to cause a minor rockslide.'

'Here, take my hand. If we fall, we can fall together.'

He slips his hands off my back and elbow and holds the right one out for me to take.

'Honestly, I'm fine.'

There's no response. Not a verbal one, anyway. Instead, he stays with his hand out, but his muscles relax a little, as if to say he'll just keep waiting until I agree.

I roll my eyes and take his hand. It's as sweaty as mine, but it's a comfort to hold on to him as we take the final steps down into the large crater.

There's a moment as we break our connection, an awkward exchange of smiles as I thank him.

We step across the crust of the crater. I wonder how thin it is before reaching the magma below.

Towards the cordoned-off centre of Stefanos Crater, I have a feeling we might find out. The ground moves in places, and the smell of eggs takes a stranglehold. Smoke and steam rise up in swirls. It's like standing next to a blazing fire on a hot summer day. But that's not the reason I think we might find out. There's a large woman in a very short dress bending over a Pringles pot, using a spoon to dig a hole in the ground to fill the pot.

'Stefanos, the biggest of the craters, he is five thousand years old and big. His diameter is a hundred metres. Do you want to look at the other craters? The smaller ones.'

'Of course. I want to see everything.'

'I don't know about everything, there is too much in this big universe for everything, but I can show you Mikros and Megalos.'

'I guess we'll have to start with that then. What is that woman doing?' I cock my head in her direction.

It seems Leonidas has been too busy looking at me to notice her. I'm not sure how. Her dress is so short, she's exposing her striped knickers in bending forward. And not a little, but a lot.

He turns in the direction of the woman, then calls out to her, 'Excuse me, what are you doing? You can't take that.'

She hurriedly pops the Pringles lid on and begins to walk away. Leonidas then calls out to her in Greek, taking a step towards her. She briefly looks over her shoulder before carrying on in dismissal of understanding. I then call out in Italian, but all she does is walk back out of the crater at a quicker and quicker pace.

'That was so weird. Does that happen a lot? People stealing dirt?'

'People would take the whole volcano if they could put it in their bags.'

Half of Leonidas's face slips into a smile, and I catch his profile as he looks at the ground ahead. It's enough to make my insides burn almost as much as my skin in the sun.

We don't let the strange encounter ruin our time, but we do end up going into a big discussion about human behaviours, ownership and sharing. We seem to have very similar ideas about leaving things as they are for future generations to enjoy and about not using up more than is needed.

As we wind our way back out of the crater, leaving it bubbling to itself, our conversation takes a turn as we both pile in on ranting about AI not only stealing creativity, but stealing water for cooling systems. And for what? We both agree it's dulling people's ability to feel free to create and compete as creators.

It's nice to find someone who doesn't look like they're going to fall asleep when I go into a passionate speech about the harmful and frightening realities of AI flooding social media to get people to argue with it, thinking it's a real person. Or how angry it makes me when people steal dirt and put it in a Pringles pot to take home.

The other craters are similar to the first, only smaller and with their own unique shapes from their past eruptions.

Checking my phone, I see a message from Mum that says *Having a weird mother builds character*, with a picture of a mum and daughter doing handstands with their knickers on display. Mum should have been forced to see Pringle-woman's knickers, like us.

Guilt nips at my heels as my teeth nip in my cheeks. She's been over there in Kardamena looking at memes while I've been exploring without her. I know she made this happen, so I shouldn't really feel guilty about it. After all, she pushed me to go off without her and made plans of her own behind my back.

I check the time as well as my messages. It would be a good time to head back to the ferry. I say as much to Leonidas, and we make our way back towards the car park and Bia.

'You know, when I was maybe twenty,' Leonidas begins, 'there was a musical performance in the crater of Stefanos, under the moonlight. It was so magical. I think my godfather knows more about why it happened. I was only there for the music.'

'Are you sure there'll be anything left for your godfather to even tell me?'

'Am I boring you?'

'Never.'

A contained smile is shared between us before he puffs out an almost silent laugh and walks on ahead.

However much I'm enjoying the personal tour from Leonidas, and our own fun friction, which I'm sure could outdo the movement of the tectonic plates, there's still part of me wishing Mum hadn't wanted to ditch me. She was meant to be the one giving me a personal tour.

We were meant to be here together, with her telling me tales of her last visit. It was meant to be our last holiday before the mania of owning a business settles on Mum's life . . . and before I up and leave for months on end.

I am very much enjoying Leonidas's company in a way that would never have played out if Mum had come along for the ride, but this was never the plan.

'Is everything OK? I know the smell is very strong here—'

A short laugh jumps right out of my mouth as I realise my brow is furrowed and my face is tight with tension.

'No, I just, I wasn't expecting any of this.' I wave my finger between us. 'This. Me and you. I expected to be alone today or with my mum. Suffering the gross eggy smell with her. But . . . that didn't happen.' I decide to leave out the part where Mum over-exaggerated a bad back to meet up with a friend instead of hanging out with me. 'Instead . . . I found you. So, I guess you got stuck with me, or I got stuck with you . . .'

'You're stuck with me now?'

I watch him as a pout rounds his lips. Maybe I've truly offended him. I don't know him well enough to gauge. It's not what I meant. It came out all wrong. In not wanting to open up too much, I pulled away too hard.

'No. Not at all. I'm grateful for you showing me around today. If I'm honest, I feel a bit pissed off my mum isn't here with me, or I did. I *did* feel pissed off. I don't anymore. Today turned out better than I could have hoped.'

Leonidas leans his back against the rocks, biting his lower lip. After about a second and a half, he launches himself in the air towards me, letting out a horrible guttural yelp followed by a string of Greek words I imagine I don't understand for a reason.

'What's wrong?'

He sucks air in through his teeth and the veins around his forehead pop.

'My arm. I leant against one of the rocks and—'

That's when I look behind him. Steam trickles out of a small hole in the rocks. He twists his arm, trying to look at his triceps, and there it is, a burning kiss from the volcano.

It's my turn to suck in air through my teeth as I look at the red patch of skin that might as well be steaming.

'It doesn't look great.'

I whip my bag off my back and yank the zip with satisfying speed. I dig my hands in, scrambling from one pocket to the next. I know that somewhere my neon-yellow mini first-aid kit is lurking. I take it everywhere with me. Mum got it for my eighteenth birthday and it gets refilled every now and then.

'We need to put something on it. You can't have it exposed in the sun, it'll only get worse.'

'I'm sure it is fine.'

'Maybe, but it won't be if you're not careful. Here, I've got some aloe vera gel.'

Pulling open the plastic box, there's a tube of gel waiting for all the scrapes and burns that adventures can bring. I pull it open and squeeze a pinch on to the fingertips of my right hand.

I lift my fingers at him. 'Do you want to do it, or shall I?'

'You.' He nods at me.

Carefully, I place one hand on his shoulder and begin dabbing the gel on to the wound with the other. His muscles go taut under my touch, making me grip him a little harder.

'You need to keep it out of the sun. I'm going to put a plaster on it as well, OK?'

'Do you have any pretty ones? Maybe with ponies on?' He begins to chuckle.

'No, no, just glitter and rainbows.'

He splutters a louder laugh and glances over his shoulder at me.

'Who has a first-aid kit always in their bag, huh?'

'Me.'

We exchange something that lingers when it shouldn't. I don't know what this energy is that keeps passing between us.

'Thank you.'

There's a flirtation, sure, but it's like there's something else that's been growing ever since we shared our stories about dolphins. With each new moment, something else is being laid down, like soil waiting for something to grow. It doesn't mean it will, but I'm certain something could . . . if it was given the right time and care.

I go back to my first-aid box, ripping open one of the plasters that really do have rainbows on, because Mum thinks everything is better with extra colours and is always a firm believer in celebrating Pride all year round.

I let out a sigh at my own handiwork.

'I thought you were joking about the rainbows.'

'I never joke about rainbows.' I carefully tap the plaster again. 'I don't know how well it's going to stay on your sweaty skin.'

'Thank you for the compliment, I know how you British people love sweat.'

'You're very welcome. Yeah, I don't think it's *just* us who have such a paranoia about our natural bodily functions. You lot from the Mediterranean never seem bothered by sweat. I like that.'

'When you grow up closer to the sun, you realise sweating is important. It's only not helpful when you're trying to keep on a rainbow Band-Aid.'

'Put your shirt back on and let's get back to Bia before we end up late for the boat. Mum will kill me if I miss it.'

'There's thirty minutes to drive fifteen, there's plenty of time.'

I look at my phone. 'No, there's twenty-five and we have to get back to Bia. Come on.'

Leonidas has barely stopped the scooter as I pull off my helmet and run to the edge of the harbour.

Not that it matters. I'm too late.

Based on how far off the boat is, about three minutes too late.

I shake the helmet in my hands like it's got Leonidas's head in it and it's all his fault I'm late.

But it's not his fault. It's mine.

I could've pushed to leave sooner, not let him show me around. Hurried up with the plaster instead of enjoying holding on to him.

'I'm so sorry, Mia, today there is no evening boat, only this one.' I hear Leonidas's voice behind my shoulder.

A loud whistle splits the air as tears sting in the back of my eyes.

The sound slashes through the air again but I ignore it as I pull my backpack off and reach for my phone from one of the pockets.

With a few angry hits of the screen, I begin the call to tell my mum. I'll have to find somewhere to stay, maybe she can meet me here tomorrow, or I'll see when the first boat will be heading back to Kos.

'Leonidas,' someone calls behind me, before a stream of Greek that I can't understand.

I keep my focus on the buzzing of the phone in my ear.

'Hey, Sweetpea, are you on the ferry? My back's feeling a bit better so I thought we could go for a nice meal and make some plans for tomorrow. If you're not too tired from your busy day?' Mum chuckles. 'Did you enjoy it?'

'Bit of a change of plan. I missed the ferry, so I'll be staying here tonight.'

'Oh. Oh, OK, not to worry. These things happen.' Disappointment saturates her voice. I know it all too well from those frivolous teenage moments where children like to disappoint parents.

It's like the time she gave me money to go to the cinema, and instead I spent it on whisky when I was only seventeen. It's the same tone then as now, like she can't tell me off because the same thing would probably have happened to her, but she's not exactly pleased about it either.

'I've got to find somewhere to stay, and, well, I met someone here.'

'You *met* someone?' Her voice switches completely into something bouncy and interested.

'Yeah, I mean . . .' I turn to look at Leonidas. He's chatting away to a handsome man with thick hair that's greying at the temples. They look nothing alike, so I doubt it's his dad, but the age gap would be about right, so it could be. 'He seems nice. He was showing me round.'

'Oh, OK, I get it now.'

'No. I genuinely missed the ferry . . .'

'Yes, it's fine. I understand. Out of interest, how old is this man?'

I lower my voice and take an extra step away, just in case Leonidas suddenly decides to listen in. 'I don't know, a grown-up, maybe late twenties or early thirties? I didn't ask for ID. Why?'

'No reason, just interested. You have some fun and I'll see you tomorrow. Love you and be safe, promise?'

'It's not like that, Mum.'

'Love you, bye.'

'Love you too.'

The call ends and I turn to face Leonidas, suddenly feeling like a lost lamb now all the other sheep have left the island.

'Mia, this is my godfather, the one I have told you about. He was my father's best friend. This is Dimitri.'

'Nice to meet you.' I hold out my hand and he takes it, but he doesn't let go.

Chapter 14

Mia 2025

'Mia? That is a good name. It's from the Greek for Maria.' Dimitri's accent is softer than Leonidas's. His voice is very smooth and low. I wonder whether he's also a singer.

'Well, actually, it's Mia Zoí. I think Zoí was going to be a middle name, but Mum filled out my birth certificate wrong or something.'

Dimitri raises one thick eyebrow. 'Mia Zoí? You know what this means in Greek? One life, or a lifetime.'

'Really? In all my travels, I actually didn't know that. But then I rarely tell people my full name.'

Dimitri tilts his head and his eyes search my face before his other hand lands on top of our still-clasped hands. 'It's very nice to meet you, Mia Zoí. Are you coming along to the party?'

'I need to find somewhere to stay. I missed my boat.'

'Leonidas has told me. We will get you settled at Three Brothers, it's just over there.' Dimitri points behind us.

There, not far from the sea, is a hotel with a few tables outside.

'I will talk to them. Stay here.' Leonidas jogs towards the hotel and disappears through an archway in a slate-grey wall made of what I imagine is volcanic stone.

I let out a heavy breath. I can't believe I've let this happen.

'Are you here alone?' Dimitri enquires as we slowly begin to take steps along the harbour.

'Erm . . .' I think of my mum back in Kardamena by herself. 'Yeah, I guess I am now.'

I've been to boyfriends' homes before.

I've been to some of their family parties over the years too.

It's normal to be put on parade a little bit the first time round, when every great-aunt wants to get a look at the new girlfriend. But I've never walked into a room and had everyone stop talking before.

Not until now . . . and Leonidas isn't even my boyfriend.

I guess I've never been on show at a Greek family party before. People are everywhere, yet word of us walking in spreads across the room quicker than water out of a broken glass and everything falls into a strange hush.

'This is Mia Zoí,' Dimitri announces in a booming voice before Leonidas can even open his mouth. 'Leonidas made her miss her boat back to Kardamena, so now she is here for dinner with us, and we have found her a room at Three Brothers for tonight. I have already assured her there will be plenty of food here. Be kind, she is a very good friend to our Leonidas.'

He raises his eyebrows at Leonidas with a smile spreading over his face as he then goes into Greek. I assume repeating what he's just said for those who don't speak English, as somewhere in among it he says my name.

There's no time for me to react before Dimitri places his hand between my shoulder blades and ushers me into the centre of the crowd.

'Leonidas, you must introduce Mia Zoí to everyone,' Dimitri continues, but it's too late, it's as though someone hit play and put the volume on high.

People are already holding my face and pressing kisses against my cheeks, some welcoming me in Greek, others in English.

'This is Leonidas's mother, Kalista, and his sister Antigone,' I hear Dimitri say over the crowd, but I'm not even sure who he's talking about – the ones kissing me, or someone else? 'Where is Ismene?' he demands. 'There she is, hiding with her book as always. Leonidas, did you come across with Foteini?'

'No, no, she came across yesterday.'

I turn around to face him, squinting before stepping away from the next person in line to hold my face. I lean towards him, knowing half the room is paying attention to every single thing I'm doing, but equally not caring.

'I thought you said you were bothering her last night and that's why you left the house to play guitar?'

Leonidas shrugs. 'I didn't want to say I was bothering the dogs.' A smile lifts his cheekbones, and I can't help but reciprocate.

A short and round woman who I've already kissed, with elegant flowing clothes that swish as she walks, steps towards me.

'It is so nice to welcome you into our home, Mia Zoí. I am Kalista. I think this is the first time Leonidas has brought one of his . . .' – she pauses, squinting at her son – '*friends* home before.' Kalista smiles broadly, showing slightly crossed teeth, as she takes me from Dimitri like I'm a bunch of flowers being handed around for everyone to sniff. 'Come, come, you can carry on with the rest of the family later, let's find you a nice drink.'

Kalista takes me back down the stairs and away from the throb of people.

Leonidas doesn't even attempt to follow us. He's caught in the kissing machine, answering questions. I can only assume at least ninety per cent are about me.

Everyone upstairs carries on chatting again as we clop away and out of earshot, passing various family photos and icons on the walls. I'm half expecting her to lead me right back out the front door and on to the street, but she doesn't.

The house is compact, or maybe it's just bursting with people. It's hard to tell. It's equally full of decorative plates on the pale-pink walls as we move into the dining room.

There's a sideboard filled with food. The smell of rich tomato sauce and oregano cooking somewhere in the belly of the house fills the rooms. One more room and we're there, in the heat of the kitchen.

'Tell me, what would you like? We have the white wine retsina, ouzo, fresh orange and many others. You like it, you have it. You're at home here.'

Kalista turns and begins to pull glasses down from a cabinet, moving swiftly around the kitchen, her floral skirt twirling around her ankles as she goes.

'That's very kind of you. I'll have whatever you're having, thank you. I'm so sorry to inconvenience you like this. I really didn't mean to miss my ferry.'

'No, no. We know what Leonidas is like with time. He moves at his own speed, like snails. It would not be the first time he has missed that boat. I am amazing he has made it here for his godfather's birthday.'

I don't correct her English, it's a million times better than my Greek will ever be, and as long as someone can be understood, then they're speaking a language perfectly as far as I'm concerned.

'Mia Zoí, I am Antigone, this is Foteini.' I whip around to find Leonidas's younger sister in front of me with one hand delicately placed on her hip and Foteini, his older sister, looking me up and down without flinching.

Antigone is tall and slim, with fine features and thick straight hair cut at a perfectly angular line around her face. Foteini, on the other hand, is short like her mother, with curved hips and a round face behind her wild hair. They're both well dressed like their mother. Unlike me, who looks perfectly dressed for hiking in shorts that were clean on this morning, but now . . . not so much.

'It's really nice to meet you. I'm sorry I'm so underdressed, I had no idea . . .' I turn back to Kalista, thinking about what she just said. 'I had no idea it was Dimitri's birthday today, now I feel even worse. I didn't know I was crashing a birthday party without a gift.'

'Don't be worry, don't be worry. *Yamas!*' She hands me a freshly made concoction and raises her own glass towards me in cheers.

We clink before both beginning to sip, leaving an opening for Antigone to talk.

'*Mitéra*, it is *don't worry*, not *don't be worry*.' Antigone rolls her eyes towards her sister. 'It is all right, Mia Zoí. Nothing would give Dimitri greater joy than finding a nice girl for Leonidas. Isn't that right, *Mitéra*?' Antigone raises her eyebrows like she's goading her mother, or *mitéra*.

'Oh yes, he would. It would be good for all of us, yes. Very good. But I prefer he is finding a nice Greek girl. Are you Greek? A Christian at least?'

I begin to stumble over words, coughing over the sweet drink she's given me.

'It's not like that, *Mitéra*, leave her alone. I'm sorry for this.' Leonidas whispers the last part so close to my ear I can feel his hot breath in my curls.

He waltzes around me and then round the kitchen, pours a shot, necks it then heads back towards the dining room. 'Feel free to take as much food as you like,' he smiles.

If in some strange world we were to become a *thing*, a *real* relationship, I'd be terrified to tell Kalista that I have no idea what I am, other than half English at least, and Mum brought me up with music and dancing in the kitchen as our religion.

'He's right,' I confirm to Kalista and Antigone, 'we really have only just met. Please, excuse me.' I follow Leonidas back towards the dining room.

Dimitri and a handful of others are there, filling plates with food. They smile at me and speak to Leonidas in Greek while looking between me and him.

I smile along, unfazed, knowing we have become the most interesting talking point even though there's nothing to say.

All the food is beautifully prepared and ready to be devoured. Piles of salad, stuffed vine leaves, bowls overflowing with olives and peppers, moussaka with a rich tomato sauce, and loads of things I'd need to try to see whether I could identify them or whether they're a brand-new experience for my tongue. It's nice to see loads of fish and vegetarian stuff too. There's plenty for me to sample. My stomach ripples in response to all the delights, begging me to fill a plate.

'I won't be offended if you want to run.' Leonidas lowers his eyeline all the way down to the floor.

A wrinkle has formed between his eyebrows and he's biting his bottom lip, but not in the way he was earlier. Not in that delightful seductive manner. He's chewing it, more like he's the one about to run away.

'Do you want me to go?' I indicate towards the door with my glass.

'No.' Slowly, his lips rise into a shy smile.

'Then I'm happy to stay. I told you, I like to meet new people, try new food and get the *real* experience wherever I travel to. I'm grateful that you're willing to feed me and look after me. And anyway . . . everyone seems very . . . friendly.'

'They are. I am grateful to have you here, you know.'

There it is. The energy again pulsing between us – that's how it feels, anyway. Maybe it's just in my head, but it's like my heart is trying to lurch right out of my chest and straight into his.

I'm being ridiculous. I barely know him.

'Mia Zoí, do you know why your mother came up with this beautiful name for you? She must be a very interesting woman.' Dimitri pauses at the other side of the dining table.

'I don't know. You'd have to ask her.'

'I would like that very much.'

'Well, you can if you like. She's over in Kardamena, waiting for me. You're welcome to come over and speak to her.'

Dimitri picks up a thick slice of red pepper and pops it in his mouth, chewing slowly before continuing, 'So that's who you've left behind. And what is your poor mother's name?' He slips another pepper into his mouth.

'Sara.'

Dimitri coughs with a closed mouth before hammering his own chest and spluttering over his food. Voices increase in volume as more people enter the house and others begin to walk down the stairs to welcome them or to get food in here.

'Are you OK?' I step towards Dimitri, with Leonidas close behind.

'Fine, I'm fine.' His voice is gruff as he continues to cough. He points towards the kitchen. 'Water,' he croaks and scurries away, weaving past people as he goes.

'Something I said?' I tilt my chin up towards Leonidas.

'No, no,' he chuckles. 'Why? Is this the effect you always have on people?'

'Yep, everywhere I go, people always leave the room choking on food.'

Leonidas's face breaks away from the furrows of concern and leaps into laughter.

'Then soon the house will be quiet, and I can keep you to myself,' he whispers.

A shiver rolls over my spine from his breath on my cheek, making goosebumps ripple over my skin.

Maybe I *should* leave, but I know I'm going to stay.

Chapter 15

Sara 1998

'He invited you in *for lunch*? He's never invited *me* for lunch. Tammy, has he ever invited you in for lunch?' Tina pads round the apartment in her miniskirt and bra. It's a cute skirt, with a three-inch slit up the leg. It doesn't suit the incredulous tone in her voice and the burning cherry red of her cheeks.

She paces her minuscule body back and forth. I can't help but wonder why he did ask me back and not her. She looks like Gwyneth Paltrow in *Great Expectations*. My ex, Lawrence, has a major crush on the actress and took me to the cinema to watch it for his birthday. It wasn't long before I realised the reason he picked that film was to see more of Paltrow's skin than I'd have liked.

'Why do you care, Tina? You've shagged more men since the season started than you've had hot dinners.' Tammy leans on the door frame to our balcony. She brings a menthol cigarette to her full lips and takes a deep drag.

'That's only because we mostly eat salad here.' Tina flicks strands of white-blonde hair off her shoulder. 'So . . .' She pouts her lips like she's also sucking on a cigarette. Or perhaps a lemon.

'What was he like? Great, I guess. That voice alone is enough to get me going.'

She marches towards the kitchen and picks up the open bag of crisps strewn on the counter, thrusting one in her mouth, crunching while she waits for my answer.

I cough, but it sounds as fake as it is. 'Actually, nothing happened. We ate a feta salad, then I went back to meet the people taking the tour to get them back on the boat. All above board. No pun intended.'

I miss out the part where he asked whether I'd be coming to take the tour again and him catching me off guard with a lingering kiss against the cold hard stone wall of his mother's kitchen.

The heat of his body has imprinted on mine, and had I not had exactly ten minutes to meet everyone to get on the boat, I'd have probably stayed to see where that kiss would go.

'Is that it? You *actually* had lunch? Maybe he thought you were uptight.' She reaches for another fistful of crisps.

'As if. We just got on well, that's all. Anyway, I don't care whether he thinks I'm uptight.'

'Well, he's never tried anything with me. I'm pretty sure he has a girlfriend or an arranged marriage or something.' Tina purses her lips for the hundredth time.

Tammy puffs out smoke and laughter. 'You're not all that, Tina. You might have blonde hair, perky little tits and legs up to your arse, but that's nothing special, and it's not anything new. Anyway, this is Greece, not India or Pakistan. Can't say I've heard anything about *arranged marriages* since I've been working here, doll.'

Tammy steps on to the balcony and stubs out her cigarette in the ashtray before shooting me a wide-eyed look as if to say *oh my God she's a sad act* about Tina.

'Whatever, Tam. You can be such a cow-bag,' Tina growls.

'Hard words coming from a twig in a bra.' Whenever Tammy gets irritated, she leans on her Liverpudlian accent a little harder, just like she is right now.

'OK, OK.' I hold my hands up between them. 'That's enough. We get enough moaning from people on holiday, let's not turn on each other. Tina, you promised to do welcome meetings for a week, remember? So no staying out all night and missing it, because I won't be doing them. I'm free tonight and I want to enjoy it. I don't want to waste it listening to you two get irritated with each other.'

Tammy strolls up to me. 'You can help me with karaoke if you don't want to be a Billy No-Mates? It's gonna be mega, I'm dressing as Scary Spice. Everyone loves when I dress as Scary Spice, and Alexandra said she would be Posh. She's gonna pull her hair into a tight pony for it and everything. Without straightening it to death like mine, I have no idea how she'll do it. Her curls are pretty wild.'

'I'm going as Baby,' Tina pipes in. 'Declan said he's there too, if you're interested?' She winks.

'I've got some Adidas poppers if you want to be Sporty?' Tammy adds.

I shake my head and my hands for emphasis. 'I would die in this heat if I wore those.'

'Nah, you just have 'em undone to the top. You got the legs for it.'

'Honestly, I'm good, thanks.' I scoop up my mirrored bag and pull it on to my shoulder.

'Have fun at karaoke. I'm going for a stroll, then an early night for me so I can be up for an early morning swim.'

'Don't be waking us up at the crack of dawn again,' Tammy tuts. 'We'll need our beauty sleep after tonight.'

I shout a goodbye as I close the door behind me.

Maybe I should've gone for a swim now. I could do with the refreshing salty sea on my skin. Anything to cool off the thoughts of Dimitri.

The golden-cinnamon rays of the setting sun beat down on my shoulders. My heart skips faster than my feet with the thoughts of that same heat from Dimitri's parting lips.

I snatch a breath and keep my eyes plastered open, because even blinking is enough to see that smouldering look in his eyes.

This is a time of evening where people are getting ready for their night out. It's the perfect hour for people-watching. Bars begin to flood with English tourists aged between eighteen and thirty, ready to drink their weight in booze.

Not all of Kos is like this, and there are definitely crazier places for it than here, but this particular resort thrives on the buzz of nightlife.

Tonight, I just want peace. A quick walk to calm my mind, then sleep, ready for an early morning. Anything to keep Dimitri out of my mind, and to give me space to figure out how to ask Tina if I can take the same tour of Nisyros in three days' time.

Chapter 16

Sara 1998

The sun hasn't yet peeped up from below the horizon. Behind me, Kardamena is still asleep after a heavy night.

Slipping off my flip-flops and my dress, I step on to the coarse sand down to the water's edge. The fresh smell of salt and seaweed fills my nostrils. I like to come down to this smaller beach on the outskirts of the town. It has a few more pebbles and some rocks, but it's a lot more likely to be peaceful.

I stretch my arms over my head and my mouth falls open for a gaping yawn. I ended up going for a long walk last night, and didn't sleep as well as I'd hoped. I couldn't stop my mind from scuttling right back to Dimitri, no matter how hard I tried.

In front of me, the water doesn't care about any of it. The sea has its own rhythm. The life within it has no idea what people do. The water will throb and sway at its own pace, regardless of me.

As I get closer to the water, I balance along shingle muddled into the sand. When I can't see into the shadows of the water, I bend at the knees, picking my way as the cool sea nips at my toes before biting at my ankles.

When I was a teenager, I went to Loch Humphrey in Scotland with my parents and their friends. I escaped as often as I could from their pretentious conversations and made friends with some local lads and lasses.

We decided to pack a picnic and a few bottles of whisky and hike up to the lake one evening. After a few drinks, someone suggested taking a swim. Even though it was a warm summer's evening, the water was freezing, and we had to wade through the squelchy peat. We laughed and swam to get warm. It was my first taste of cold-water swimming, and I quite enjoyed it. It makes getting up early on a Greek island for a swim feel rather cosy by comparison.

I like finding the cooler waters around the world, and it's worth waking up early for.

Morning twilight seems like the only time I can find real peace since becoming a travel rep. Someone always needs something. It could be information or a crazy toe-stubbing emergency, or advice about which bar sells the cheapest vodka shot. But when I'm in the sea, no one can find me. It's perfect.

When I was a kid, my parents used to pay for swimming lessons as part of the myriad of extracurricular activities they made me do. Swimming was one of my preferred sports. The worst by far was gymnastics, I had no natural ability for it.

In their own crazy way, they were giving me the best by ignoring my protests and passing me on to the top teachers Essex and London had to offer.

I used to think I would prefer to spend time with my parents, but when I really got to know them, I think leaving me to other people was doing me a favour.

I brace myself in a star shape and take a moment to float on the surface, letting the sea rise and fall around me as I bob aimlessly, weightlessly, perfectly calm.

Closing my eyes, it's like I'm a baby being rocked to sleep in her mother's arms. I wonder if my mother ever rocked me to sleep, or whether she would let me cry until I tired myself out. I think it's probably the latter.

As darkness begins to lift off the sea, the first rays of sun turn the navy-blue rippling fabric from a solid-looking duvet to something light. It's as though the sun is tickling the water with a warmth lighter than a feather.

The dawn tells me it's time to head back to shore.

Tina is meant to be doing my welcome meetings, but I can't guarantee she'll be up in time. I shouldn't be needed again until this evening if I can skip out on the welcome meetings.

Before my feet can even feel sand and shingle beneath them, I notice there's a shadowy figure sitting next to my bag on the shore. I tread water for a moment, not knowing whether to head back or to swim away further down and sprint back to the apartment.

I don't really want to go without my towel and my phone and everything else I've left on the beach.

From here, I can't tell who it is. Their head is bowed. I'm going to assume they're male, based on the broad shoulders.

I take a look around. The rest of the beach is empty and the street behind seems to be empty too. Even if I did scream, who would be awake to hear me? Most people are comatose in an alcohol-induced sleep. It makes people deaf in the dead hours of night.

I have no way of telling what the time is now. Maybe it's getting close to six? Maybe some people will be awake. People who like to get to their sun loungers before everyone else.

I don't have a choice. I need to get back to my bag.

I begin to swim towards the shoreline, waiting for my feet to find the shelf in the sand that leads back to dry land.

Different scenarios play out in my head.

I'm fast enough to try to run. That was another activity my parents forced me to do, road running and sprinting. I was never going to win any of those things, but I never came last either.

As I get closer to the beach, I can see the person's head still bowed in thought, or maybe I'm lucky and they've fallen asleep.

I step up the shelf into the shallows, doing my best to stay silent in the water, but the impossible splashing of my legs cutting inelegantly through the sea alerts them.

He lifts his head, and his dark eyes flick up towards me.

For a moment I'm taken aback and nearly fall back down the shelf.

'Dimitri?'

Chapter 17

Sara 1998

'Tammy said you were in the sea. I did not believe her. Luckily, she said to come this way or I might still be looking for you.' Dimitri's soothing tones carry on the sea breeze.

I push my dark-blonde hair out of my eyes. It looks almost muddy in this light, and saturated in salt water.

I've never felt less like a Bond girl getting out of the water than I do right now, stumbling towards him scraping at my hair in complete surprise.

'Yep. I like to start my beach parties early,' I grin.

His lips twist into a guarded smile. 'I was looking for you.'

'And now you found me. How did you know where I live?'

'I didn't. I knew where Tammy and Tina live. They were not happy with me waking them up.' A cheeky smirk crosses his face. 'I was wondering . . .' Dimitri watches me as I reach into the brightly coloured Body Shop bag I use for my swim stuff and pull out my towel, quickly wrapping it over my shoulders.

'Sara, I don't know what you've done. Maybe it's that you didn't throw yourself at me like Tina . . . No. I think it's those eyes of yours.'

'My eyes?'

Dimitri puts his hands underneath him and pushes himself off the sand to stand in front of me. He dusts his hands over his thighs then pulls himself tall to look down at me.

'You sound surprised? I can't be the first man to tell you they have never seen eyes like yours. I wish the sun would hurry up and lift into the sky so I could see them in the light again.' He takes a step closer. 'Not blue . . . something else. Like the rising mist on the sea on early mornings before a heatwave.' He speaks slowly, methodically.

He steps towards me again, leaving only inches between our bodies as I drip on to the sand.

His tongue passes over his bottom lip as he studies me.

'Sara, would you come back to Nisyros with me?'

'Now?'

'We can talk, I can show you Mandraki. I told you yesterday, I think you would like Nisyros. The *real* Nisyros, before any coach arrives. And anyway, there is no coach trip today.'

'Now?' I repeat like a skipping CD, as my heart skips along with it.

'Yes, why not?'

'Because there isn't a boat right now?' I shiver in the cool morning air as water tickles along my spine.

'Do not worry about that.' Dimitri picks up my bag. 'Are you coming?'

I glance from left to right. From tavernas to rocks, as though they might tell me what to do. But I already know what I want to do.

'Yes. I'd love to.'

Dimitri's lips slide into a smile as he begins walking up the beach.

I slide on my flip-flops and clatter along behind him.

From the moment Dimitri found me on the beach to now, clambering into a small wooden motorboat covered in chipped paint, my heart has been doing its best to try and jump right out of my mouth.

I had heard rumours about these types of holidays, and the things that reps get up to on a daily basis, before coming out here. But parties and sex and booze aren't what brought me here. I came here to escape, and so far I've managed to avoid joining in with any of the activities Tina is getting up to. I've managed to avoid most drunken advances completely. I might joke about living off ouzo, but I'm always a good few drinks behind everyone else.

There's something about Dimitri, though. Something that could make me want to change all that. There's something so appealing, so alluring. I'm not sure I could say no to him . . . I'm not sure I'd want to.

All of five minutes ago he was standing in our apartment waiting for me to shower quickly, then watching me pack random items of clothing into my mirrored bag while Tammy slept on and Tina moaned I should take my own welcome meeting because we woke her up after thirty minutes' sleep, giving her a headache.

She forgets that I've seen her party all night, barely sleep a minute and start all over again.

'Is this yours?' I study the motor at the back of the boat hovering in the water.

'It belongs to my family.'

Dimitri unties the rope and walks the boat along like it's a dog, taking it to a ladder that goes down into the shadows of the sea. He ties the boat there, takes his shoes off, throws them into the boat then climbs down the ladder before hopping into the boat from there with a bit of a wobble.

'Your turn,' he calls, reaching a hand back towards me where I stand on the edge of the grey concrete, looking down at him.

Without another thought, I pass my bag and my shoes down the ladder a little way and take Dimitri's hand into safety. Dimitri waits for me to sit before he goes back to the ladder and unties the rope again.

He pushes the boat further out to sea and then pulls the motor to start. Then we're off, back towards the electric energy of the volcano.

The sun scatters blinding glitter over the waves as the boat cuts along with ease, puncturing and breaking through the glitter and sending it in all directions.

Watching the sun rise over the dotted islands and the water, with Dimitri guiding the way, feels like coming back to the home of my soul. I like nothing more than to be one with nature. I pointlessly shade my eyes and squint, scanning the water hoping to see something break through the surface like a dolphin or a whale, as seabirds fly overhead. It's the most perfect morning I could've possibly imagined.

The air whipping around my neck is enough to make my body tremble and break out in goosebumps, but it doesn't deter the heat in my heart.

'You're cold,' Dimitri shouts over the engine.

'I'll be OK.'

My body almost jerks from the chill rattling down my spine. I've coiled my hair around my hand to stop it whipping across my face. It's still wet underneath from the shower, which isn't helping to warm me up, but watching the sun peeking up and shining on this corner of Earth again *is*.

The island isn't far now and it's as though we are being drawn in by its gravity, in the same way I feel I am by Dimitri. Those earthy eyes and the defined lines of his cheekbones and jaw make him stand out as attractive, but his energy, passion . . . and, quite honestly, showing up to whisk me off for the day make him as irresistible as ice cream in summer.

He came all the way over to Kardamena across inky water to find me, because he couldn't sleep until he saw me again. He's got my attention, that's for sure. He did already, but now I'm on high alert.

It's just past seven when we arrive in Nisyros, and although the morning is warm, I'm still chilled through from the crossing.

After tying it up, we abandon the boat entirely. Dimitri undoes his buttons and pulls off his shirt. Taking my bag on to his arm, he exchanges it for his shirt, which he wraps over my shoulders, covering the spaghetti straps of my dress.

His fingers outstretch towards me, his open palm waiting for me. I take it and we kick up sand and head off towards the street.

Barefoot, we practically jog along the narrow and winding roads with shoes in hand. There's no sign of life here yet. At this time of morning, it's probably still quiet over in Kardamena too.

We burst into Dimitri's family home. He keeps hold of my hand, pulling me into the house and switching on lights as we go.

We tumble towards the kitchen table, where he pulls out a chair for me, and I thank him as I take a seat in the same place I sat to have lunch only yesterday.

Dimitri is still displaying his golden tanned chest. A shiver rolls over my skin, but it's not from the cool morning anymore. It's an entirely different sensation as I wonder what it would feel like to run my fingers over his chest.

He tugs open a drawer and takes out a packet of matches, striking one and lighting a yellow tea light on the table before turning out all the other lights we've just put on.

'Why are we sitting in the dark with the shutters closed?'

'Because I don't want all the old ladies to tell my mother everything I get up to.'

My shoulders rise and fall without question. I can totally understand the feeling.

I hated my mother knowing anything I got up to. Mostly because she'd use it against me or to manipulate me in some way. The past few weeks have been blissful, knowing she can't do that anymore. I'm earning my own money and finding my own path, far away from her.

I wonder whether Dimitri finally feels free with his mother back on Kos.

'There's two issues I have with that.' They're not really issues but I want his attention.

Dimitri cocks an eyebrow at me over the glow of the candlelight.

'First, if they're *that* nosy, they probably saw us running along the street, and second, you have shutters . . . they can't see in.'

'Well, maybe I think the candle is romantic for breakfast.'

'Do I look like I would be so easily impressed by a little candle?'

I don't want to tell him that I sort of am. That I am actually *really* impressed he came all the way to get me and bothered to light a candle. All the men I've dated seem like boys and Dimitri seems like a man. He might still live at home with his mother, but he has a job, a life and a look in his eye like he has everything mapped out. It must be what inner confidence looks like.

'How does it make you feel to hide things from your mother?'

'Guilty sometimes, but it's not my fault. If she could think about what I want, not what she thinks I need and want, it would be easier.'

I nod along. 'I feel exactly the same about my parents. It's like I was born a circle and they've been trying to force me into the shape of a star. But I'll never be that. I can't be seen and not heard, I can't listen to someone drone on just because they have a good education or something. I don't want to look down on people because they're different to me.'

'So what do you want?'

I'm sure it isn't . . . it can't be . . . but this feels like the first time someone is looking me in the eye and asking me what I want, and they don't just mean for dinner.

'I don't know. For a long time it's been more about not being them than who I want to be. I guess I just want to be happy and see the world. Beyond that . . . I've got no idea.'

'It sounds like a good start to me. Should I blow out the candle?'

'No, I sort of like it.'

The flame flickers between us, like it has something to say but there's no way of sharing what it knows.

'Good. You may not be very impressed by the candle, but' – he turns a wooden chair round and sits on it so his arms rest on the back, still facing the table – 'I feel a need to impress you. I never feel this way with women. Around anyone. To be honest, I'm used to women trying to impress me.' He stares into the flickering flame with a new-found intensity before adding, 'That sounds very bad. Like I am thinking a lot of myself and what I'm trying to say . . . badly . . . is I am interested in you. When you talk, I don't think you're trying to' – he circles one wrist, as if doing so might pull out his words like fish on a line – 'tell me things I like to hear. You're saying things in your head without guard. I like that.'

Never one to take a compliment well, I puff out a breath laced with denial of what's true. I'm not trying to impress him, because I'm too busy taking him in.

Although, had he given me a critique of sorts I'd have fared a lot better. Perhaps because I'm used to hearing criticism, I can take it like a real champ.

In a fashion my mother would be proud of, I sidestep the compliment and home in on something else instead.

'You haven't tried to impress the other reps then? I know Tina was quite upset you asked me to lunch, and you saw how she was about today.'

'No, no.' He shakes his head with a new enthusiasm and leans away, like there's suddenly a foul smell emanating from the candle. 'Tina, she is *very* obvious. She might as well walk around naked and beg *please someone, someone notice me*. Maybe this works for many men. In fact . . . I think it does, for many men. Not me. I find her . . . Boring. It's too easy.'

'Yeah. She is kind of sad. Wait, you like me, what, because you think I'm challenging? There's more thrill to having to chase your prey?'

'No. That's not it. I've said why I like you. I don't know why else I like you.'

I draw my lips into my best sarcastic smile. 'You're such a charmer.'

'I don't mean it like this. You are beautiful. That is easy. And I feel this desire to impress you . . . it's not just the way you look, it's the words you say, the way you hold yourself, how you want to see more of the culture here . . . I want to show you something authentic.' Dimitri rubs his thumb and forefinger together as though authenticity is right here in the air. 'Kardamena and its people are authentic—'

'I didn't mean it like that – before, I mean. Everyone's been so lovely. People are welcoming, happy . . . it just feels more *party* than traditional Greek life. I still think everyone has been so welcoming and fun.'

'You did not let me finish. If you think it's *party* now, you should have seen it ten years ago. But the people *are* authentic, they *are* fun. Why else do you think everyone started coming to Kardamena? But I understand you want to see another side, the side we all see in the winter when it's only the people that live here. Maybe you would prefer the sleepy fishing village it becomes? I want to show you this side of my island. We don't have the same tourism here, it is mostly day trips, it is not so . . . changed.'

'I'd like to see it.'

'But first,' – Dimitri drums his hands on the table – 'breakfast.'

Chapter 18

Mia 2025

'Who else is there to meet? I feel like everyone's kissed my cheeks at least twice.' I turn to Leonidas. 'I haven't met your dad yet, have I? There's so many people upstairs it's a little bit dizzying.' I stretch my face into a grimace behind my glass before taking a sip.

'No, you won't be meeting my father. Not unless you want to take a trip to the cemetery.'

I squeeze my eyes tightly shut and drop my forehead into my hand.

'I'm so sorry,' I mutter.

'It's OK, you didn't know. He passed eight years ago. He and Dimitri were best friends. It was my father's dying wish for Dimitri to keep an eye on us all. He is divorced, no children of his own, he says that Baba said it to help him as much as us. That's what Dimitri tells us, anyway. He was with him when . . . I should stop talking.' Leonidas plasters an unnatural smile on his face. 'What about you, when will I meet *your* father?' He lets out a short laugh. 'You are meeting all my family at once. It is only fair I meet yours. Is he with your mother in Kardamena?'

I press my lips together, knowing that my answer is stranger than his.

'How about, you can meet him when *I* meet him. Sound good?'

He narrows his eyes on my lips, like I'm speaking a new language and he's trying to figure it out.

For some reason, I'm never able to part with the information sensibly the first time I tell people about my fatherless situation. It always comes out like I'm telling a joke with a really poor punchline.

'I've never actually met my dad. I don't know who he is. Not even a name.'

I do my best to grimace playfully again and laugh it off, but the awkwardness is palpable as Leonidas mutters what I can only imagine is swear words under his breath and shifts from one foot to the other like he wishes he could run.

'I'm sorry. I've asked the wrong question.'

'Not at all. It was me who asked the wrong question to start with. Look, it really doesn't bother me. It is what it is. My mum is enough of a handful that she counts as all my family members. You meet her, you've met everyone.'

Leonidas meets my gaze and settles there. A smile slowly creeps up his bronze face.

Slowly, he says, 'I would very much like that.' The words hang in the air between us like bubbles before he carries on. 'I'm going to get a drink. Do you need a drink?' He looks down at the glass in my hand, which is still pretty much full. 'No,' he answers his own question. 'I will come back.'

Leonidas edges backwards out of the room in the direction of Dimitri and half of his family.

For a brief moment, I'm alone in my thoughts. I step out of view of the kitchen door and unclasp my hands, shaking my fingers loose.

I take the steps up towards the living room. It's possibly the only place not filled with people, all stuffed in like vine leaves.

Ismene's in the corner, and there's a large group of middle-aged women talking with their hands, frowns digging deeply into their foreheads. I wonder whether they're talking politics, or something heartbreaking perhaps. Or maybe I'm reading too much into it, it's hard to say.

There's also a group of people outside on the sweeping balcony. There's a mixture of all ages, laughing and talking, some holding plates of food, others sipping wine.

Ismene's chin is dipped, as though she's hiding under her mass of frizzy hair. The biggest difference between the twins seems to be their hair.

'*Kalispera*,' I say in her direction.

In one swift movement, her eyes skim over me in the same way her older sister's did, as though she's assessed me and taken a mental Polaroid.

'You are Mia Zoí? This is an interesting name.'

'Most people just call me Mia. But yeah, Dimitri told me it means one lifetime or something.'

She slowly nods and isn't forthcoming to say much more, stuffing her nose back into her book. I take a seat next to the window, hoping I can take a minute to hide unnoticed.

Maybe I should drink my drink and run back to the hotel.

This was never meant to happen. Mum is all on her own and I'm in a house that has more people in it than there's room for. I like Leonidas, but I'm still pissed off with myself for missing the boat. I shouldn't be here at a party when Mum is all alone.

Unless this is some strange karma for Mum pushing me to come here, with no intention of joining me.

Maybe she's still with Alexandra now and she's not alone at all.

Or maybe she's found some other old friends to hang out with. I take my phone out of my pocket to message her.

‘Here.’ Leonidas appears by my side. ‘I thought you might like this.’

He sits down next to me and tries to hand me a plate filled with food, including pitta bread and some dips. I quickly put my phone away and almost snatch the plate from him. Hopefully, it comes off as helpful and not greedy. He is balancing his own plate and a drink, after all.

‘I remember you don’t eat meat, well, this is *pythia*. It is made of chickpea here on the island.’ Leonidas goes on to tell me about the other dishes he’s plated up for me and why he’s picked them, based on our conversations over lunch.

It’s nice to feel heard.

I’ve had so many disastrous dates lately, from being catfished to toxic-masculinity vibes.

We begin chatting and sharing food together while people eat and chat around us, often bringing us into their conversations where they can.

Even though the house has filled way past a fire safety capacity, thick stone walls do their best to keep the building cool. It’s not enough tonight, not with so many people moving from one place to the next, and with the sun leaving its mark on the land well after sunset. I feel sticky in the clothes I’ve been wearing all day and desperately want a shower to cool off.

I’ve enjoyed being here and getting to know Leonidas’s family, but it’s getting late, and I need to be up and ready to sort transport back to Kos in the morning.

‘Mia Zoí, Leonidas, have you seen Dimitri?’ Kalista looks from her son to me.

We both shake our heads and Leonidas adds, ‘Not since he was coughing up his food earlier. That was hours ago now. He must be downstairs talking, or outside.’

'No, no. I have been looking for many minutes and I cannot find him.' She continues on in Greek, her hands held high before finishing on her hips.

With that, everyone begins calling for Dimitri, tiptoeing to look over each other's shoulders for him.

It seems Dimitri has managed to disappear from his own birthday party completely unnoticed, but no one is sure for how long. One of his older sisters believes she saw him not that long ago, but she can't be sure.

Kalista goes around the house double-checking with everyone, and Leonidas calls his phone. It goes straight to voicemail.

'Maybe he went home. Do you want me to look, Mama?' Leonidas puts his hand on his mother's shoulder and she rests her hand on top of his.

'Would you?'

'Of course.'

I'm confident they were speaking English for my benefit, so I step a little closer to join the conversation. 'I think I should probably get back to my hotel now and leave you all to find Dimitri. I don't want to be in the way. It was really lovely to meet you. Thank you for your generosity.'

'You are welcome in our home any time. Leonidas, you must walk Mia Zoí back to her hotel after you check for Dimitri. You call me to tell me he is home.'

'Yes, Mama.' Leonidas kisses both of his mother's cheeks and I do the same before I follow him down the stairs and into the street.

'He does not live far from here. Only a couple of streets away.'

All the patterns on the ground look different at night. As we pass the dolphins, they don't seem as jolly as they did in the day. Sporadic street lights guide us, but at the end of each street, cats cast eerie shadows. Each shape is enough to make me feel glad I didn't walk back alone.

'Do you think he's OK?'

'Dimitri? It would not be the first time he left a party early.'

'What's his deal? Single? Maybe I could set him up with my mum.' I grin up at Leonidas.

'No, no. He is divorced with no children. He seems happier alone than when he was married to Ourania.'

'Oh, maybe not right for my mum then.'

'No, probably not.' We walk in perfect step along the empty streets of Mandraki.

'How does your mother feel about you not having a father?'

'How do you mean?' I can feel the hairs on my neck stand on end, prickling and ready for anything he might throw at me. I've had every question or comment possible over the years, and all the raised eyebrows too.

'You say you want to *set her up* . . . Maybe she is unhappy there was no father for you?'

'I don't think it was that she was *unhappy* that I didn't have a dad. Not that she ever let on. And as a kid, I didn't know any different. It's only as I've grown up that I've realised she might be ashamed that she doesn't know who my father is. That she can't give me more information about him. She shouldn't feel ashamed. Not at all. It was the late nineties, and she was working hard to escape my rubbish grandparents. She's not the first person to have a one-night stand and hardly remember it, and she won't be the last.' My words rattle off with increasing speed.

'She got unlucky. Most people don't get stuck with a baby at the end of casual sex. Not that she's ever made me feel that way. Like she was stuck with me, I mean. I've always felt really wanted by her, and she swears that as soon as she found out she was pregnant, she knew she wanted me. My mum's more than made up for not knowing my dad. She's been my mum, dad, grandparents, best friend. There's nothing she can't do. She inspires me every single day.'

'She sounds like a very interesting person. I look forward to meeting this Superwoman.'

He's right. She is Superwoman. The muscles in my face pull upwards in delight at his apt description.

'It must be hard for you both. You're not even close to your grandparents? Here, there is a big community. Everyone was looking out for us when we were children. Everyone was helping to bring us up.'

'My mum had a small network of other mums. Not that many though, when I was very little. There weren't quite as many single parents back then. I do know my grandparents. Sort of. I don't think Mum wanted me to be alone with them. They wanted to pay for me to go to a boarding school but Mum wouldn't have any of it. They aren't bothered about me, and I'm not bothered about them. I haven't even spoken to them in years.'

'Why not?'

'I don't really know. It's not that we had any big falling-out. They just don't bother with me. If I don't call them, they don't call me. So I don't and they don't. It's funny though, I bumped into one of my grandma's friends in a supermarket, one that I'd met at a dinner party once, and they knew so much about my life, but like, only the good stuff, but they listed it off like it was something amazing. From the travelling to my degree in music and Italian. They even knew about an upcoming event I was singing in. My grandparents would be the only ones to tell them all that. I've just never been able to work out if they are genuinely proud or would do anything for bragging rights.'

'It is important to be proud of people we love, no?'

'Yeah, but when you love people you want to spend time with them. They were more interested in spending money on me than time with me. They bought me an iPad once and Mum gave it to a charity shop. She didn't even open the box.'

It was over ten years ago now, maybe fifteen. I didn't even know what an iPad was because it was back when they first came out. If I'd really known what Mum was giving away, I'd have told her to at least sell it. But that was the thing, she didn't want either of us to rely on their handouts.

Leonidas stops outside a door. The mint-green shutters are closed so it's hard to tell whether anyone's home. Raising his fist, he firmly knocks three times.

We wait. I squint a little, as though that will help me hear whether someone is moving on the inside.

I don't hear anything.

Leonidas knocks again. As if in response, his phone pings from his pocket.

He pulls it out, the bluish light on the screen illuminating the street.

'It's Dimitri. He must be hiding inside. He says he is fine and to tell my mother he is sorry for leaving the party.' Leonidas closes the screen and rolls his eyes. 'Sometimes he wants to be out all night with us, sometimes he will hide at home. I don't think he is very happy to be fifty.'

Leonidas nods his head back towards the street.

'I guess we better get you to the hotel.' Leonidas looks as disappointed as I feel, knowing our time together has an expiry date that's rapidly coming towards us.

Chapter 19

Mia 2025

'When will you sing for me?' Leonidas nudges against me as we head towards the hotel.

'When will you play guitar for me?'

'You have heard me play.' Leonidas bumps his shoulder gently into mine. 'But I have not heard you sing.'

He stops on the corner where the path narrows and leans against the wall. He folds his arms and tilts his head, waiting under the dull glow from the next street along.

I lean my back on the building opposite, only a few feet from him. The stone wall feels cool on my back as I close my eyes.

Only one song comes to my mind. One I wrote years ago at university about the unrequited love for someone who, at the time, I desperately longed for. It's soulful, something like Joss Stone in the early 2000s singing 'Fell in Love With A Boy'. I was around five years old at the time, and I was obsessed with that song through most of my childhood. Her voice was a big reason I wanted to sing in the first place.

When I open my eyes, Leonidas's fingers are curled over his mouth and his cheekbones are so high they're almost digging into his eyes.

'You're beautiful. I mean—' His hand drops and he chuckles momentarily, biting his lip. 'Your voice, it's beautiful. Although . . . you are beautiful too.'

Our eyes lock together. My throat closes as sarcasm jams the path of all words. It's so hard to accept compliments with this intensity sitting behind them. He breaks the heavy silence before I can say something I shouldn't, in the way I know my mum would, the sarcastic way she always does if someone tries to compliment her.

I've had to fight the urge to say something flippant so I can evolve past my mum's almost allergic reaction to praise. I can take compliments now, but on the inside it still feels cringingly big-headed to come across like I'm in agreement.

'Thank you.'

'Did you write this one yourself?'

'Maybe.'

'I don't know it. Did you *really* already know this song, or did you make it now for us?'

Uncontrollable surprised laughter pops out of me with a slightly manic 'Pah' sound at the start. 'No, no. I wish.'

I debate telling him the truth, wondering whether it's better or worse. In the end, Mum always says, honesty is the best policy.

'I actually wrote it about one of my university teachers. I had a *really* big crush on him. I never told him or anything and I find it a bit . . .' – I contort my face into a grimace – '*icky* now.'

'Oh.' Leonidas rubs along the bridge of his slightly crooked nose. 'Well, it's a good song. You are very talented. You must sing while I play to you.' There's an urgency in his voice, like he would drop everything right now and have me sing along to his guitar.

I hold my index finger up at him. 'OK, but not tonight. You can send me some of your music if you like?'

I push off the wall and walk towards the sea and in the direction of the Three Brothers hotel.

Leonidas follows on behind a moment after.

'Fine. I will need your phone number.'

'You're welcome to it,' I call over my shoulder.

The tavernas along the seafront still have a few people sipping their last drinks, looking out towards Kos across the thick sea glittering with stars.

As soon as I get back in, I'll message Mum and find out how her day with Alexandra has been and whether she managed to enjoy her evening in the end . . . and maybe even pluck up the courage to ask why she ditched me in the first place.

We pause outside the stone arch leading into Three Brothers.

'Can I come up?'

'No. You need to get back to the party and tell your mum Dimitri is fine. Remember?'

'I can message her. Not even to sing one song?'

'Nope,' I shrug.

If he does come up, I'm pretty sure he'll want to do more than hear me sing. Unless, of course, that's a metaphor.

'Then to walk you to the door? To make sure you make it up the stairs safely. Remember, that is what my mother told me I must do.'

I exhale hard and give myself a moment to mull it over.

In normal circumstances, back in England, when a man so fervently wants to know exactly where I live by walking me to the door, alarm bells go off in my head. I think they're going to come back later and break in. Usually, I find an excuse for them not to follow me. Not when I've only met them that day. Mum taught me better than that.

The problem is, Leonidas has already seen the one-bed apartment. He carried my backpack up to the room for me and paid for it too, as an apology for making me late and spoiling my plans.

I tried to stop him but he spoke in Greek and they took his money, not mine.

Mum would tell me he sounds like a keeper, and that chivalry is a rare gift, and that we should all be kind. Men shouldn't be the only ones holding open doors, but it's nice when they do.

'Fine, as you promised your mum.'

We walk in silence up the stairs towards my door. Our feet scuffing the steps is the only music we make.

'This is me.' Instinctively, I open the door and switch on the light.

'I remember.'

We walk into the white box room, with the crisp linen sheets and the two simple pictures on the wall.

'Thank you for looking after me, feeding me—'

'Making you miss the boat in the first place . . .' Leonidas leans on the door frame, arms folded across his chest, displaying those toned forearms of a guitarist as he watches me throw the room key on a grey desk and kick off my shoes underneath it. 'It was not on purpose, but I'm glad you had to stay. Can I see you again? And not just for music?'

I step towards him and take all of him in.

He's leaning there with all the confidence in the world, so it would seem, but there's a vulnerability to him. Something about the slight curve in his shoulders and the gentle incline of his head, like he doesn't dare stand too tall in case I knock him down. At least this way he wouldn't have as far to fall.

'Yeah. I'd like that.'

I take another step and stand on tiptoe to kiss his cheek, momentarily clutching his bicep and lingering in the fresh scent of his cologne. Like he's just slipped back into the ocean and the salt has cleansed him.

My mouth lingers to the side of his, making my feet, still tiptoeing to reach him, feel like they might give way.

Leonidas twists his lips to meet mine with a brief and tender kiss.

We stay, almost suspended, millimetres from the other, our breath mingling in the warm air of the room, the door still wide open.

I can't resist but feel the soft pressure of his lips again and take his lower lip between mine.

We tangle together, fingers acting like roots trying to find a place to latch on and grow.

Voices come from the direction of the stairs, chatting away in French.

We pull away from each other like we've been caught.

'I should go.' Leonidas turns to leave before turning a full circle. 'I don't have your phone number.'

'Milo, stop,' the man's voice from earlier calls out before the same boy stops outside my room.

The man stops about an inch from the boy. 'Sorry,' he grimaces at us. 'Oh! Hi again. Sorry, we were racing and he went the wrong way. Have a good night.' The man places his hands on the boy's shoulders and guides him back to a woman calling to them in French.

'No worries,' I call back to them.

In a very clear voice that pierces the air even as they walk away, Milo says, 'If they are not a couple, why do they kiss like that?'

Leonidas turns back to me. 'I think something else of our interruption, not *no worries*, as you said.' Leonidas's low voice rumbles, completely ignoring Milo's comment.

'Here.' I take my phone and pass it to Leonidas. 'Put your number in there, and I'll call you.'

I watch his fingers as they press against my phone screen and daydream about them pressing against me and maybe changing my mind and asking him to stay with me. If only his mum and family weren't waiting for him, expecting his imminent return.

When he's done, I take the phone and hit call. His phone flares into life with my number across the screen.

'There, now you can always find me,' I smile.

'Good, because I would be very stupid to lose a woman like you.' His lips touch my cheek before he turns and leaves.

I quickly close the door and lean my back against it, letting myself catch my breath for a moment. I don't want to watch him walk away because I'd end up calling him back. Shutting the door was my best defence against the feeling of desire burning my skin.

Marching across the room, I take my phone out on to the balcony to take a moment to message my mum.

The sea is there, only a matter of metres away, I can hear it gently singing everyone else to sleep. Not me. My body is tingling and my mind is swirling at a rate I've never felt before.

I stare at my screen, swatting away a moth intrigued by the light.

I'd like to tell Mum the main points face to face. About Leonidas and the day as a whole. I want her to meet him and tell me whether this is all in my head or if he seems like the person I think he might be.

Not that I even know what I think he is. I'm getting way ahead of myself about a man who lives an undesirable number of miles away.

I shouldn't get attached.

We barely know each other. One day isn't enough to start picking out crockery patterns together.

This isn't me. I never normally feel like I'm falling for someone spontaneously. Usually, I like to get to know them over time, letting my feelings get deeper. This is like my body has positioned itself perfectly for a diving trick and I've cut through the waves without a splash and now I'm plunging into the unknown. Today has seemed like a month of quality time with someone interesting and who's interested in me.

Someone who's a really good kisser too.

I have to stop. If my mum's anything to go by, holiday flings can be a dangerous game. Too much alcohol, not enough protection . . .

Only this doesn't feel like that, but then I guess that's what lust would say.

For a million reasons, spending more time with Leonidas would be a bad idea, and not just because he lives far away and I don't want to be like my mum, but because I need to focus on my independence.

Three knocks strike my door, making my chest pound almost as loudly.

Leonidas. He must be feeling the same way as me.

I glide across the tiles at speed, not knowing what to say or do when I open the door, only knowing that I want to find out.

Chapter 20

Sara 1998

The car Dimitri has borrowed, his best friend Manolis's car, rattles along the road. It has a strong smell of synthetic pine and cigarettes, but overall it's very tidy on the inside. All except a few of his kids' toys abandoned on the back seat.

In the middle of nowhere, Dimitri pulls the car over and it comes to a standstill. At first, I wonder whether it's broken down, but as Dimitri grins and undoes his seatbelt, it's clear the stop is intentional.

'If you are still feeling cold, this will warm you up.'

I've warmed up a lot from our early-morning boat trip. There's nowhere to hide from the sun kissing my skin.

We both get out of the car and Dimitri takes my hand again. Although it feels natural and comfortable in his, my spine shivers at his confidence in touching me.

He leads me over volcanic boulders and stones that are strewn all over the ground. Some have been moved to form walls and shapes.

'The tourists, they don't know about this place. We never show them.'

With a view stretching into the far distance across the sea as the backdrop, an entrance to what can only be described as the broken-down remains of *something* sits pride of place among the grey and white rocks.

As Dimitri begins to help me pick my way through the stones in my sandals, he tells me a little about where we are.

'This is one of the island's natural saunas. It is a cave that is heated by the warmth of volcanic air.'

We manoeuvre our way down between walls of large solid stones and towards an entrance made of a white sheet.

'It's going to be hot in there.' Dimitri releases my hand and pulls his shirt over his head. He folds it neatly, placing it on a rock to one side before pulling at the zip to his shorts.

My heart races as I wonder how far this is going to go. I swallow hard as I admire his skin glowing in the gleaming rays of the sun.

I take off the shirt that I've borrowed and place it on top of the one he was wearing, leaving me in a strappy violet dress. I didn't know what we'd be doing but I knew I'd want to look nice, and this is one of the only dresses I have with me that I've been saving to wear for something special.

I kick off my clear jelly sandals and wait to see whether Dimitri will be wearing less than his navy briefs. He settles his shorts on top of the pile and peeks behind the curtain.

He turns back to assess me over his shoulder.

'You might be hot in that dress.'

I shrug and follow him as he ducks down into the cave, one step at a time.

He's right. It's like a burning hot afternoon. The curved walls form a short tunnel with long stone benches pressed against either side.

Within moments, sweat is rising and tickling my skin.

'You're right, I'm going to take this off.'

There's no way I want to sweat all over my dress before the day has even started. I hop back up the steps and out into the light, slipping off the dress and carefully laying it on the stones along with the rest of the clothes.

I look down at my pure white underwear, glad that three weeks in Greece has blessed me with a tan, even if the tan lines don't match the underwear.

I never feel particularly attractive in my bras – my boobs are too big and my back is too narrow for all the pretty little ones, unless I want to pay a big price tag for them. A plain white T-shirt bra and a simple white thong was the best option for today. Although I had thought Dimitri might see me in my knickers at some point, if things went well, I didn't know it would be before 9 a.m.

As I pull back the curtain, I do my best to subtly cover my stomach with my hands linked in front of me while avoiding looking at my feet too much. I don't want to come off as nervous, but I can't help but second-guess myself.

I catch sight of Dimitri, his eyes almost popping out of his head. I hold in a laugh and hope I'm not blushing. With the thin white sheet across the cave, there's some light, but it's quite dark so hopefully he won't catch the rose in my cheeks.

'Come, sit.' He taps the solid grey slab next to where he's sitting.

'I'll sit here, if that's all right?' I take a seat opposite him, so I can look him in the eye.

I fear putting myself next to him and in direct contact. It might be too much heat and I might evaporate entirely.

As my bottom and thighs touch the stone, I'm surprised it isn't cool as I imagined it would be in my subconscious. In this heat, it's ridiculous to think it would be cool, but stone almost always is when left in a dark cave.

'You know, on all my travels around the world, this is my first time in a natural sauna. I've been in hot springs before, but nothing like this.'

'The hot air is enriched from all the minerals in the rocks. You know, Hippocrates, the father of modern medicine, used to come to this island from Kos to heal. The volcano brings much positive energy to the people who come here.'

'Is that why you brought me here? To bring me positive energy? Am I particularly negative?'

Dimitri leans towards me, placing his forearms on his knees.

'No. I brought you here to get warm.'

I join him in leaning forward until our faces are only a few inches apart.

'I thought perhaps it was to get me in my knickers.'

'There is that, too.'

His fingers graze my knee and our eyes stay locked together. The memory of our lingering kiss after lunch yesterday makes my heart race. His soft lips caressing mine and the warmth of his body against me. It had caught me off guard, like a daydream or momentary lapse in reality.

With each moment I spend next to Dimitri, I want to know more about him and his life, and I also want to feel his lips against mine to check the last kiss really happened.

Dimitri's thumb and forefinger curve around my knee as we both relax forward until our lips come together, slowly at first. I can taste the sweet honey on his tongue from this morning's breakfast. I edge closer for more, until I'm almost completely off the hard stone bench.

His right hand slides further along my leg, bringing me to him.

I trace lines of my own, my fingers slipping along his shimmering skin.

He kisses down my jaw and licks my neck. A giggle catches in my chest, as nerves and insecurities weave through my ribs.

'Relax, Sara, you want this, no?'

'Yes,' I moan.

He stops kissing me and takes my face in his hands.

'You're so tense, I can feel it.'

'No, I just keep thinking I'm all sweaty and probably red in the face and not thin enough or . . . I keep overthinking.'

His eyes move as they look from one of mine to the other.

'Who has made you feel this way?'

'No one.' I rack my brains to past lovers, but I've never had any complaints. *I* might have a few, though. I guess I've never felt completely comfortable with anyone. I puzzle over his words.

'The world is too hard on its beautiful strong women, but this feels like more than just believing the rubbish in magazines. Who has made you feel that you cannot relax, that you are not good enough? When you are perfect the way you are.'

A lump forms in my throat. Deep down, I know exactly who's made me feel less than ideal. Who, my whole life, has made me feel like a second-rate handbag.

The number of times I've heard something like, *Did you hear, Josie is off to Oxford University and Camilla is dancing on Broadway. Their parents must be so proud . . . I can't imagine how that must feel.* Or *You're not going to wear that, are you? It's not very flattering . . . for someone with your figure.* It's no wonder the easiest thing in the world was to walk away from my parents without even telling them I was going.

Negative comments burrow deep under the skin and settle there like parasites, slowly eating away at your soul without you even realising.

Tears cloud my eyes and I bite my lip to stop it from trembling. How did he sense this in me, when I've been hiding it from myself?

'You don't have to tell me. Let me help you heal. Lie back.' Dimitri takes the weight of my head in his hands, and kneeling next to me, he lays me down safely on the stone. 'Close your eyes and empty your mind.'

I do as instructed, trying to push all the micro criticisms I've had my whole life out of my mind.

The times my mother said it was a shame I got my grandmother's build from my father's side, instead of her *dainty* frame. Or the times my father ignored my hard work if it wasn't for something he thought held value.

Dimitri's fingers smooth over my face, gently pressing against my eyebrows, probably the only dainty thing about me in my mother's opinion.

Dimitri's voice fills the cave, low and smooth like dark molasses permeating the sticky air. He's speaking in Greek so I have no idea what he's saying, but the low vibration and the heat in the cave feels like the comfort of a warm bath after a hard day.

His hands move down my neck, swooping carefully over my décolletage and down my arms, gently squeezing out tension all the way to my fingertips.

As Dimitri moves over my muscles, almost chanting at me, I begin to relax. I'm not forcing him to spend time with me, which is how I've so often felt around people. Like I should be chasing them. My parents always made spending time with me feel akin to washing dishes or vacuum- cleaning. I've always had to run to keep up with their attention.

I was a job they wanted to employ someone else to deal with.

Even with ex-boyfriends, it's felt normal to be the one to chase. This feels uncomfortably safe, like something I've never known.

Time folds and curves as Dimitri's hands move from one place to the next, then he slips seamlessly into English, and it's like I'm hearing his voice in a dream.

'Many people in my family are able to heal. We think it comes from living here, but we don't like to talk about it too much. Keep your eyes closed and I will pass you my energy.'

I have no idea what this means, but with my eyes closed I can feel the warmth of him near to my skin when he isn't even touching me, and the energy feels like a beacon skimming light over me.

I never, ever want this day to end.

Chapter 21

Sara 1998

'I love this view. It's like the sea is made of a million aquamarines.'

Dimitri turns to look at me, I can feel his eyes on me.

His head tilts and he narrows his eyes on my lips.

'I don't know this word.'

'It's a type of stone. My favourite, actually. I love aquamarines. Probably because I love the sea.'

Since the passing of energy in the sauna, we cooled off in the shade before quietly getting dressed. We've been sitting holding hands and looking out to sea ever since.

'You know,' I begin, 'my mother put me on the contraceptive pill when I was fifteen because I wouldn't want to *ruin my life* with babies. My life has been riddled with never being good enough. If that isn't a statement about how she truly feels about me, then I don't know what is.'

'I could feel the damage deep inside you, but you are very strong. You can heal. You don't need people like that telling you lies about yourself and the world.'

I rest my head on Dimitri's shoulder and he slides his arm around my waist. The sea breeze is enough for us to be just the right temperature in the sun, even when linked together.

'How do you deal with your mother?'

Dimitri sucks air through his teeth. 'It's different for me. I'm her only boy. The negative words are different. It's more, why can't you find a nice wife? When will you get me grandchildren? And wanting to know everything I do so she can make sure it is right. Her controlling is because she loves me too much.'

'Instead of not enough, like my parents.'

'They must be very foolish people.'

'At least you can understand the controlling part.'

'Yes, that I can understand.'

We fall back into a moment of silence. I'm glad he can't understand the pain of feeling unloved. I wouldn't wish it on anyone. I've always felt a lot of shame feeling this way, because there are so many children in the world who are treated so badly, and my parents have given me everything. The only thing they have withheld is a healthy balance of love, but it's not like their hobby was to put their cigarettes out on me. I was ignored, not tortured. I'm grateful for that.

I replay Dimitri's healing hands on my body and how different he made me feel in that moment.

'What were you saying in Greek when you were massaging me?'

The weight of his head leans on top of mine.

'That you are complete, that you are worthy, that you deserve happiness, things like this.'

'I like that.'

I twist my head to face him and our mouths meet, soft and slow. I don't feel worried anymore about what he thinks of me. I already know. I've known people from birth and not really known how they feel about me. Had boyfriends for months and never known what was in their heads.

'It is a beautiful island—'

'I was thinking something very similar.' A smile touches my lips.

'You always are,' Dimitri says on a deep exhale before shaking his head in amusement. 'I was going to say, *and there is so much more to see*. Come on.'

For the rest of the morning Dimitri takes me on a guided tour of the island, which in no way includes the volcano and its craters. Instead, we visit a bright white and blue church that looks like it should be on a postcard from Santorini, as well as the huge fortified walls from times when the island needed to protect itself from invasion.

Interwoven in showing me the peaceful corners of the island reserved for people living here, we talk about our childhoods. In some ways they couldn't be more different, and in other ways we can connect. We both want to find our own path, away from the expectations of our parents. We have similar outlooks on the world and life, even though we're from different corners of Earth. It doesn't matter. We both want to spread kindness.

Dimitri has two older sisters who are already married off and living on Kos. Unlike me, with no siblings and no cousins. I'm an only child born to two only children.

Dimitri has focused on his love of his island, and sharing that with people.

'It doesn't earn as much money as some jobs, and all my mother wants is for me to marry and start a family. She thinks I'm too old to be living at home with her, which means she wants me to have children of my own. It is now my one job to father some grandchildren for her and to pass on the family name. But I'm her baby boy, so even when she is mad, I am still her favourite child,' he says as we climb steps through Mandraki town.

'At least she loves you and wants little baby versions of you. I'm sad to say it, but I think I'd rather your mother than my parents.' I hesitate for a moment, thinking about my wording. 'Although, if I'm honest, I can't stand the thought of being around any overbearing parents, not just mine. The idea that your mother might not like me because I don't fit the shape she wants, the same as my parents, is too much to handle.'

Silence burns like a magnifying glass under the sun and I have to switch it.

'And what about your father?' I begin.

'He was older than my mother. Fifteen years older. She worked him to death. That, or he is just sleeping for a little peace in his old age. He was a quiet man, but a good one.'

'Were you close?'

'In Greece, all families are close even if you don't like them much. We love each other and we argue and make up. I think the problem with your parents is you don't all shout. Have you ever shouted?'

'A couple of times, but they rolled their eyes and cringed, saying I was being too loud and that I should go away. They didn't listen to the words.'

We stop at the top of the steps and pause to look across all the whitewashed houses below and the sea shimmering into midday.

'I'm glad you are here, and not just for me, but for you. Here you will find space to grow. Nisyros will heal you. But now, I think maybe it's time to grow your belly.'

My head whips round so quickly I catch Dimitri with the ends of my hair.

'Not like that!' He begins to laugh. 'Not with a baby, with food!'

◆ ◆ ◆

In a taverna close to the sea, Dimitri introduces me to local cuisine, including a garlic dip called *skordalia* that is made with almonds on Nisyros, as they grow so many of them. We also sample some interesting cheeses, including *mizithra*, a goat's cheese I've never tried before.

After lunch, we meander along the streets of Mandraki and wind up outside Dimitri's door.

'You want to have the authentic experience here?'

I nod enthusiastically.

'Then I have to take you to bed.'

I raise an eyebrow as his thumb grazes my cheek.

'It is too hot in the day to do anything but sleep. And I did not sleep too well last night, I was thinking about you, so I got up and was out on the boat early.'

I stifle a yawn behind my hand. This morning's swim feels like days ago already.

'Come on then, let's get some sleep.' I tap my hand on his arm, but my fingers linger on his silky bicep.

Dimitri leads me through his house, up the creaking wooden stairs and to a bedroom with an exposed stone wall and mismatching patterns everywhere. The bed is covered in pale-green diamond shapes and the rug has pink roses with swirls circled around.

'This is your room?'

It's hard not to sound mildly stunned.

'Yes.' He flops down on the bed and it hardly gives an inch.

'Nice rug.' It's impossible to stop my eyebrows from drawing together.

'My parents made it for my oldest sister when she was born.'

Dimitri kicks off his trainers and I slip off my sandals before lying down on the bed next to him.

I fit neatly into his arms with the ease and comfort of someone I've known for years, not twenty-four hours. That's one thing I guess I have found in life: it doesn't always conform to what we think as children. Things we want to believe aren't always true, like parents will unconditionally love their kids, that the best relationships are founded in long friendships. It's not the same for everyone.

I've found wonderful like-minded people all over the world. With some I've shared a brief camaraderie while travelling, and others have stood the test of time. All have equal value in my life, because at that moment in time, I needed those people. I wanted them around me. I enjoyed their energy and they made me who I am today.

I'm enjoying being around Dimitri. No matter what tomorrow brings, I'm happy in today.

My arms wrap around his neck and my leg slides over his. Without thought, without judgement, without even thinking, we begin to kiss.

Hours slip away as we take time with each other, taking every part of the other in delicate kisses and touches until I feel I know his body better than my own. Soft and firm all at once.

His only focus is me.

Nothing but what I want is on his mind. It shows in every caress, every movement, every word.

For the second time, I've sent a silent wish for today to never end, as our bodies move together without a thought for the world outside this room or what the future might hold.

Chapter 22

Mia 2025

'I'm sorry, but I was thinking and thinking, and I know I won't be able to sleep tonight without hearing you singing again. I think a *whole* song. Only chorus, one verse . . . it is not enough.' Leonidas's lips twitch as he tries to contain his cheeky smile.

Even through the crack in the door, it's obvious he was trying to find an excuse to come back.

'You realised that in the five minutes since you left?'

'Yes. Can I come in?' He leans a little closer to the three-inch gap I've left myself to look at him through. 'Please.'

'I'm not singing for you tonight.'

'But I filled your belly with food, didn't I? I did what you asked and there was not even a whole song . . .' His head flops on to the door frame.

I step back and open the door, leaving Leonidas almost falling in behind me.

'You did, but I'm very tired now. I was almost asleep.'

Leonidas squints at me and his body shifts as he pulls himself a little taller. His shoulders square and he tilts his head to look down at me.

'Really?'

No, not really, but I'm not going to tell him I was sitting on my balcony, thinking of him.

'Yes.' I turn and step away because I can't face my own lie head on.

'It is very strange. I saw a girl looking very much like you sitting on a balcony here. Maybe it was a different girl. Maybe I should look and ask for her to sing me to sleep . . .'

I squeeze and contort the muscles of my face as though it will remove the venomous cringing that's just bitten down in my chest.

Regaining my composure, I twist on my heels to face him.

'Fine, you caught me. I was sitting on the balcony, about to call my mum.'

'Good.' Leonidas flops down to sit on my bed. 'Then you will sing?'

'Nope. You could've called me, you know. Or sent me a text.'

'I can't hear you sing in a text.'

There's always something enjoyable about playing this little tennis game with a man. To be the one who has all the outward power, even though my insides feel like a warm caramel puddle every time I look at him or hear his fingers caress the strings of a guitar. Everything about him is too much, in the best possible way. And it's nice to have a man unable to keep himself away from me instead of overtly looking for no more than a single night of my time.

'Fine. If you feed me again tomorrow, I promise I'll sing for you.' I walk round the bed and put out my hand to help him up, but instead he takes a firm grip and shakes it to cement the deal, then doesn't let go.

'I know I have to leave,' he says as he stares at our entwined hands. 'I know I shouldn't come back. I should go home. But I really was thinking about your voice. If you are as talented as you are beautiful . . .' Leonidas's head gently flops forward and sways back and forth before he stands, still holding my hands but now looking down at me.

'You frighten me,' he whispers.

I want to tell him I feel exactly the same. My lips part like I might, but then the fear makes me freeze in thought.

I'm intimidated by how much I want him to be the person I think he is, and for this to be real, not something I'm building up in my head . . . but I also don't want it to be real, because then what would I do?

At least there's a small satisfaction in knowing he's terrified too.

His fingers glance up my arm, along my neck and into my hair.

He doesn't move to kiss me.

He lingers, confident in his unbreaking eye contact. Holding me there like I'm caught on a hook. In our little tennis game, we were at deuce, but in this moment it's *advantage Leonidas*.

The anticipation of another kiss from his surprisingly soft lips is almost enough for me to launch myself into him and topple him back on to the hotel bed, but I don't.

We stay still for the longest moment.

'I'll see you tomorrow, Mia.'

'Make sure you call first next time, Leonidas.'

His mouth carefully settles on my bottom lip with a soft kiss that doesn't last quite long enough, yet stays on my lips even when his have gone.

'*Kalinikta*, Mia. I will call you . . . if I can keep myself from you.'

He turns and leaves and I'm completely speechless.

He's not the good-on-paper guy, the one with the steady job, who lives within a ten-mile radius and remembers to shave every single day. But who ever wanted to spend the night with a piece of paper anyway? Let alone a lifetime.

I run to the balcony to retrieve my phone, desperate to get it before he sees me back out there. I tug the door open, and barely step a foot out before grabbing my phone and dashing back inside.

A ridiculous urge to call my mum and tell her everything ripples over me. Like I can't wait until tomorrow. The screen comes to life, and I tap it and hit call.

Before the droning sound of the call can even begin, I fill up with regret. I'm jumping the gun, surely? Even teenage me didn't run to tell my mum I had a crush before it had gone on for a whole week, and even then I knew she knew before I opened my mouth.

I pull the phone away and cancel the call.

I've been sucked into Leonidas's world of heart-wrenching music, glassy seas and doors made for postcards. I have to rein myself in.

Three short knocks hit down on the door all over again. Maybe this time I should pretend I didn't hear them at all, because one thing I know from my mum is that a single decision can change the course of a whole life, and I have no idea whether I'm ready to have my whole life mapped out for me or not.

Chapter 23

Sara 2025

'You know, for me, you have been sitting here for more than twenty-five years. I imagine you and your cloudy eyes . . . they cloud my vision.'

I don't flinch at his voice.

I should, but I don't.

It's not so much that I'm not surprised, because I am. How and why he is here, late at night on the beach in Kardamena, is frankly unfathomable, yet . . . it's like I was waiting for him. This was our usual meeting spot, after all.

My lack of surprise is also probably because I hear his voice so often floating around my head. Even after all our time apart I replay the words he said to me, and sometimes make up new ones.

In my mind, he's followed me from the day I left here.

At times he saturates my dreams and leaves me in a cold sweat of regret. But when I wake, I know my choice was the right one. The only one.

Sometimes, conjuring his voice has been the only thing that would comfort me into sleep, particularly when Mia was a baby. I'd imagine him moving his hands and his energy over my body and I'd believe I could get through anything. I would pretend everything had worked out differently, that I'd told him about Mia and he had come to live with me in England, and he was only in the next room, not here in Greece.

It didn't always work. Sometimes it would end with my tears slipping down Mia's cheeks as though she was in my arms mourning him too.

It was always the realisation that we were over that left me feeling like I was being torn apart. Every part of me had been picked away, from my eyelashes to my innards. There were some nights where everything hurt.

One thing hasn't changed over the years, and that's how his voice vibrates through me. In the past, when we were together, it felt so soothing. Now it cuts the flesh around my heart, making it drop to my toes.

'I know it's you, Sara. Your daughter told me you were here.'

I close my eyes, letting my head gently sway back and forth.

Damn.

Only I could have this sort of luck. I'm about as lucky as a shark caught for shark fin soup. Mia, being the useful part of me, cut away, and now I'm left to sink to the bottom of the sea, unable to swim.

Mia led him here.

If she knows and it wasn't me who told her, she may never forgive me.

When I checked with Mia the age of the man she was spending time with on Nisyros to make sure he wasn't her own flesh and blood, I was reassured by her answer. Now I discover she still somehow managed to find Dimitri in less than three hours.

'The whole of Nisyros, and she finds you?' I pick up a handful of sand and let it fall away through my fingers.

'She found my godson. Manolis's boy. Do you remember him?'

A brief memory of a boy hurtles through my mind in the same way I'd seen him tumbling along the streets all those years ago. He was probably two or three. I remember being sure he would topple over at any moment, but he didn't. He was always trying to keep up with his older sister or wanting me to pick him up.

'Leonidas. Of course I remember him. He was a cute kid.'

I want to tell him I remember it all, and that half of my heart froze when I left, and the other half only beats for Mia.

I can't bring myself to turn and look up at Dimitri, let alone express the pain of being here. I keep my focus on the blanket of sea stretching to Nisyros, to my daughter. I'm already regretting sending her over there alone. I didn't want to be the thing to stop her exploring, all because I really wasn't up to it. Emotionally or physically.

This isn't how it was meant to play out. This isn't how any of it was meant to go.

I don't know how I thought it would happen, but this isn't it.

I thought she might go across and fall in love with Nisyros before I told her it was in part hers and before cracking open a can of worms that would change everything. Or maybe I was just too chicken to go there with her yet.

This can't be real.

If I take my eyes off the direction of Nisyros, off her, and look at him, it will all be real.

It would mean admitting to him that she *is* his daughter, if he hasn't already worked it out with her . . . he must have, or why would he be here?

Perhaps she is *another* daughter and she has met a half-sister or three. I have no idea how many children he's had over the past couple of decades. Alexandra would've told me at lunch, but I didn't want to know. I couldn't bear to hear how he has spent his time happily without me.

The sand and shingle move behind me, rattling under his feet until in the corner of my eye I can see black trainers next to me.

I do my best to keep focused on the distant island where my daughter is trapped, and yet Dimitri is here.

Maybe Mia has already worked it all out and that's why he's here, but perhaps not. I know Mia, and she's not one to hide from me. She might occasionally run away from an argument to collect her thoughts, but she always turns up at the start of one and she hasn't called or messaged me to demand answers. He didn't bring her along.

'If you've met Mia, how come she's over there, and you're here with me?' I begin.

I also begin to doubt my sanity. Maybe he's a hallucination. Maybe this is all in my head. I've thought about him so much that my mind can now create something that seems tangible.

Dimitri twists and winds himself down on to the beach by my side. There's a slight lack of grace that comes with ageing. Mia might be right to say I'm not old. I don't feel old in my heart, but I definitely don't sit down or stand up as sprightly as I did in my early twenties, and it seems neither does Dimitri.

'I should have offered to bring her back on my boat, but . . . I left her with Leonidas, enjoying my birthday party.'

'It's your birthday?' Instinctively, my head whips round to face him, the ends of my hair slapping me on the chin.

I instantly wish I hadn't.

He nods but keeps a serious look on his face. Moonlight glimmers in his eyes and highlights his cheekbones with a silver shimmer. He looks completely unchanged to the man I met twenty-seven years ago.

A lump in my throat threatens to choke me, and my heart all but flatlines.

How can his face be enough to make me feel so alive while also feeling like death would be a sweet release? Taking away the pain of whatever this is. The twisted agony of him.

Twenty-seven years of trying to believe that what we were was only a fling. When, really, it was a destroyer of every future relationship I would ever have. How could any other man measure up to what we had here? We were in a perfect bubble and however hard I've tried to love different men over the years, they weren't him. They weren't Dimitri.

Maybe to him, I was the summer fling. But for me, he became a yardstick no one could ever measure up to.

'Happy birthday, Dimitri. How old are you today?'

'Fifty.'

'That doesn't seem possible.'

It also seems impossible that I didn't know it was his birthday. How in love could we have really been, not to know such a simple piece of information? I thought we talked about everything: the way the world worked, our cultural differences, our similarities, the shade of blue in the sky versus the sea. It seems silly now.

The waves continue to lap over our silence and the stars continue to light up the night sky. Nothing has changed. Everything has changed.

'Do you come here often?' His expression stays the same, as blank as paper in the shadow of the beach.

I tilt my head. 'You didn't really just say that?'

A smile tugs at one side of his mouth and it's enough to lift my face along with his.

My body always responded to him, like it or not.

'I thought you might say *as if*. You liked to say that back then.'

'A lot has changed since the nineties.'

'It has. A lot has changed here, you may have noticed, unless you come to Kos often? That was what I meant – do you come to

Kos often? Have you and Mia Zoí been coming here on holiday, and I have not seen you?'

Mia Zoí . . . she never uses her full name, and yet here he is, knowing it already. She can't have spent that much time with him. She never mentioned him on the phone. How on earth does he know so much already?

'No. This is the first time since the last time,' I confirm.

He furrows his brow and his nostrils gently flare.

'You know what I mean.' I exhale my words.

'I do. Because it is you.'

The sea breeze kicks up a notch and hair dances across my face. There was a time when it was his job to push it back into place, but we both know that's not the case now. I tuck it safely away behind my ear without the touch of his fingers on my skin.

'Mai Zoí,' he repeats, then clicks his tongue as he looks out to sea. 'It's a good name. You know Mia comes from the Greek, Maria?'

'I know.'

'You remember me speaking of my mother, her name was Maria.'

'I know.'

I want to say, *I know because meeting her saved me from pursuing you and a life I couldn't bear to live.* And that *I know because when I was alone looking up the meaning of Mia, I read Mia came from Maria*. And that *Mia in a small way got that name as a nod to your love for your mother*. But I keep all of that in my head.

'And Mia Zoí, it means lifetime, or one life . . .'

'Or, *you only live once*. I know. I know what I named her.'

The sound of the waves continues to fill the space between us with their shushing and dancing up along the sand and stones. The hum of life in Kardamena behind us buzzes. Not as loudly as it once did, though.

I don't remember our time in the past being filled with silence. Perhaps time has filled those gaps for me. It stole the silence from my memory.

There have been many moments I've wished time would steal the whole damn thing. Times I wished our past would diminish and fade, but all it seemed to do was grow like a festering wound that never healed. Maybe it was me keeping it open, constantly picking at the scab each time one formed by wondering what he was doing or seeing his expressions there on our daughter's face.

My feelings have festered. They've eaten away at me, and now I'm paying the price.

Dimitri exhales hard before readjusting himself on the shingle and sand.

'I was telling the truth, for me you have been here, sitting, waiting. One or two times I come over to Kos and I see a woman with your hair or your shape and I think, there she is, but no. Never. Not that you have the same hair now. It was much longer back then.'

'It was. I've had a few different haircuts since then. My shape has changed a bit since then too.'

'No.'

'Everyone looks better in the dark.'

The low rumble of Dimitri chuckling rolls over the waves. It lifts me for a moment, only to trip me right over again.

'Anyway, I'm here now.'

'I'm still not sure. I think maybe I fell and hit my head.'

'I was thinking something very similar.'

'You always are.' I can hear the smirk in his voice.

My heart doesn't know whether to stop dead at the fact he remembers the things we used to say together, or whether to beat harder, like that will draw his heart closer to mine.

Dimitri rubs his chin and looks out across the sea. I turn and do the same.

'She's a beautiful girl.'

'Talented too.'

'Whose is she, Sara?'

'She's very much her own.'

I should just tell him now, put him out of his misery, but even when he has initiated the perfect moment, the perfect setting, it's like the words are blades and if I say them out loud they'll cut me in a way I will never recover from, and as they slice through the air, we'll both be hurt by it.

'Sara.' His voice is low and soft round the edges, but there's a core of steel to it, subtle enough that it could easily go unnoticed in the dark. But I caught it there on the breeze.

I lick my lips and catch the taste of sea salt, which flings me back to those nights where salt was the only thing that could be found between us as we took every opportunity to be together.

I close my eyes and recall the hundreds of times I've dreamt about telling him this, and in none of those dreams was it like this.

In my dreams it was when Mia was little, and we could be a family. Each time I woke up, knowing that it *had* to be me and her. That there was no choice.

Back then I was trapped and scared, and no matter what, I've had to live with that hard decision my whole life, and despite everything, if I was there again now, I would make the same decision all over again.

'Mia Zoí is yours.'

Chapter 24

Sara 2025

An overwhelming silence rings in my ears and a wafer-thin cloud covers the moon, throwing us into a darker place than we were before.

Dimitri doesn't move.

It's as though the knowledge of his new daughter has cast a spell on him and in the face of it, much like looking into the eyes of Medusa, he has turned to stone.

'How could you keep her from me?' The voice that crawls out from his lips sounds nothing like him.

It's broken.

Hollow.

It's enough to make guilt slap me in the face and leave a burning handprint.

'I didn't have a choice.'

My defence sounds so thin in the dark, but it's true. Maybe in hindsight it's not, but it was at the time. I felt that way deep in my bones.

Dimitri slowly turns to face me, like a predator stalking prey, eyes narrowed to the tip of an arrow.

'You didn't have a choice?' he scoffs. 'Sara, there were many choices. To take her from me and hide her from me was the worst of them all. What did I do for you to hate me this much?'

'I don't hate you. How could you say that?'

The cloud moves away from the moon and I can see the tears waiting in his eyes and the tension in his jaw and mouth.

'I can say this, because you took my child, made in our love, and did not even bother to tell me. You cut me out like I am an unwanted lump.'

Dimitri's fist connects with the sand as a tear reaches his lips.

'I didn't have a choice.' My tone is level, cool, as I repeat this, but my heart is racing. I feel like my soul is squirming inside my chest, trying to escape the shame that's burning me alive.

'Yes. You said that, but you *could* have told me. That was a choice.' Dimitri's voice rattles with anger, like his emotions are a hornet caught in a bottle and could easily explode out at any moment.

'I wanted to—'

'And how hard did you try?' he barks.

My words begin to rattle out like they're racing my heart to some unseen finish line. 'I came to find you, I was going to tell you, I spent more money than I had getting across here to find you and give you the speech that I practised so much I can still tell you exactly what I was going to say. *Dimitri, I have something to tell you. I'm pregnant, but I need you to understand, I'm not here to ask anything of you, I just wanted you to know the truth. If you want to be involved, you can be, but you don't have to be*. The whole journey here I said those words to myself, over and over.'

'Then why is this the first I know? Why is this the first time my ears hear this speech? Why do I have to be face to face with my own child and not know she is mine?'

His fingers pound on his chest and his anger fuels my own.

'Why don't you ask your mother?'

He recoils as a frown descends over his brow and his nose wrinkles. It's only now I realise just how similar Mia and Dimitri can be. However much I've believed my memories did him justice, it was like a photo of a shadow at best. Nothing like the man he is.

'I can't ask her, God rest her soul. She passed a few years ago.'

I lower my eyes to my knees and pull at my skirt.

'I'm sorry to hear that. If she were still here, she would be able to confirm I *did* come here to see you, but you weren't here. She told me you were off preparing to marry Ourania. There I was, pregnant, thinking we were the real thing after missing you for weeks, only to come back and be told you'd already moved on.'

'No, you must be mistaken. None of that is true, it was a long time after you left that I married Ourania and my mother had very little English, how could she tell you all that? You must have misunderstood her.'

I point at him in the white glow of moonlight, a self-righteous feeling filling my chest. 'And there it is. You would *always* side with her. I *didn't* misunderstand her – even in broken English, she made herself very well understood. She may or may not have lied to me, I couldn't know for sure. But it didn't matter either way, because it was right after speaking to her that it hit me. There were two possible truths. The first is she was telling the truth, and I didn't want my child raised by a man so fickle, or, she lied to me and I didn't want to run away from two controlling parents right into the arms of your mother, who was just as bad with you there backing her up. You used to say it yourself about her always trying to meddle in your life and know everything you're up to. I didn't want that for my child, to feel she had to bend to someone else's will and future instead of making her own.'

Dimitri falls silent and his eyeline drops to the sand.

Laughter echoes from the direction of the tavernas behind us as people make their way past us along the concrete road at the top of the slice of beach.

The resort might have changed a lot since I was last here, but people on holiday always like to have a few too many drinks and dance along in the dark.

'I am sorry my mother lied to you. For me, for you . . . and Mia Zoí. She could be very hard on Ourania once we were married. That is what Ourania would tell me . . . before she left.'

Dimitri's face falls and he covers it with his hands.

'Even with my mother telling this lie, even if you did not want to be with me or to live in Greece, you could have given me the truth. You have stolen all this time from me.'

My breathing intensifies and I shift my weight on the shingle and sand. My choices were my own, and he might be right, but it was all too overwhelming back then, too intense. In my heart, giving Mia a clean slate away from the judgemental eyes of her grandparents and the possibility of playing second fiddle to her father's *real* family, if his mother had been telling the truth, was worth being a single mother in the late nineties. It was worth the disgusted looks when I told people the lie of not knowing who her father was. I was putting her first in the only way I knew how.

'I was doing what I thought was best for my unborn child.'

Dimitri rips his tear-stained face from his palms. 'And keeping her from me was the best?'

'At the time, I thought it was, yes.'

Dimitri clambers to stand then begins to walk away from me, only to turn back and kick the sand up in my direction.

'Why now? Why are you here today? If I am so bad—'

'It wasn't about you. It wasn't about whether I thought *you* were bad or good, I wanted Mia to have a clean slate. I had to make a shit decision to be a mother when I never even wanted to be a mother. It was tough, really tough, and I can't go back and change it.'

'You didn't answer me, Sara. Why now?'

I knew this question would come, and just like all those years ago, I have prepared word for word what I have to say.

'There's something else you need to know.'

Chapter 25

Mia 2025

'Hey, Sweetpea.'

'Mum? How? What are you . . .' I poke my head out of the door to look past her in the doorway, expecting to see Leonidas not far behind, but he isn't there. '. . . What are you doing here?'

It's like I went to call her and manifested her instead. As though she knew I hung up and wasn't going to tell her everything, so she arrived ready to be all ears.

I carry on searching the concrete space outside of my door for some logic. I'm not sure what. Some sort of explanation in the space outside of my room? The captain of the ferry feeling guilty for leaving me here, so he brought her back hours later? Leonidas leading her to me as a bewildering surprise?

All that's there is a lizard, frozen on the wall like a decoration.

'I didn't mean to surprise you . . . well . . . I guess I did. Can I come in?' Mum looks past me at the empty bedroom.

'Yeah.' I step out of her way. 'Of course.'

Panic takes over from the shock of seeing Mum standing there instead of Leonidas. There's a strange air that follows her in, like she's brought a frost.

'How was your day?' Mum enquires as she looks over the lines of the room.

She looks smaller than usual, and her skin is flushed. It could be from a day on the beach, but I don't think so.

'What's going on? Has something happened? Are you OK?'

Mum runs her fingers through her hair before answering and even that feels like too long to wait.

'Mum?'

'I'm always OK, aren't I?'

'I don't know. Are you? Have I slipped on the tiles and I'm in some sort of coma? How did you get here? There were no more boats. I checked.'

'Someone else said something so very similar to that, not that long ago.' A distant smile drifts over Mum's face as she paces into the room. 'Anyway, that's true. There are no commercial boats at this time of night.'

I can hear my heart pounding in my ears, like the blood isn't in my veins anymore, and a greasy cold sweat coats my skin.

'What's happened?' I demand. 'I didn't tell you where I was staying.'

'Nope, yet here I am.' Mum's arms stretch open wide and she poses like she's in front of a famous monument and trying to show it off, before her arms flop down by her sides.

I turn away to close the door, then ditch my phone on the dressing table in a daze.

'I really thought you might be pleased to see me.' Mum crosses her arms like she's a teenager who's been told they have to be home at eleven, not midnight.

I whip back round to face her. 'I am! I just, I just can't believe this is real, I, I can't believe you're actually here. I *am* so happy you're here, but you're worrying me. Normally when we go our separate ways, you don't hunt me out.' I cut the space between us in two swift steps before wrapping my arms around her neck. 'I've got so much to tell you and I've felt so bad for missing the ferry, it's unreal.'

It's impossible to rid myself of the shaky feeling in my knees and my stomach. The adrenaline shot she's given me has left me exhausted and utterly confused. Even though she seems OK, this is way outside of her normal spectrum of odd behaviour. Something really isn't right, and I just wish she'd tell me honestly what's going on.

Mum squeezes my ribs a little too hard the way she always does, but normally she releases right after. This time she lingers a little longer, like she doesn't want to let me go. Not quite yet.

Maybe this is all to do with not wanting to let me go. Maybe even this was too much, if she has guessed I want to leave England for a little while. My mind races all over again.

Releasing our embrace, Mum sits down on the bed and smooths her hand over the thin cotton sheet, indicating for me to sit with her.

'I don't know how to do this.' Her voice is soft and measured and her eyes fall to her knees.

She watches her hand resting there.

Her face is obscured by her hair as it softly falls all around it like a curtain.

Even though I have no clue what she's about to say, I know her well enough to hear the edge of bad news in her voice. My stomach turns, my throat begins to close, and tears are already threatening to fall. I can barely breathe as each second feels like a minute of waiting.

'Do what?' My fingers coil around the dirty shorts I've been wearing all day and when she doesn't answer right away, I repeat it more aggressively. 'Do what?'

Mum's fingers strum over her knees. She's wearing her ring again. It matches the blue of her cheesecloth blouse.

Every nerve ending in my body tingles with an electric anxiety, like I'm about to be torn down by a headteacher but I can't remember what on earth I've done wrong.

The only time I remember seeing my mum like this was when she read me well enough to know I was hiding something big back when I was nineteen and my period was late. She knew to pull me to one side with a strange concern, not knowing how to word what she wanted to say to me.

Mum lifts my hands off my lap and holds them in hers, rubbing her thumbs along my knuckles.

'Mum, you're really scaring me.'

'I'm a little scared myself, Sweetpea.' She makes a silly muted scream noise, then tries to laugh.

'That doesn't help,' I whisper as my eyes blur with tears.

'No . . . it doesn't. No matter what, I love you. I'll always love you and I know that this isn't ideal, but.' Mum shrugs. 'I don't have a choice anymore now, do I? Not now.'

I grip her hand because my heart isn't sinking, it's falling, and I'm terrified it's going to crash into a million pieces on the floor.

Chapter 26

Mia 2025

'You met Dimitri tonight.'

'Yes . . . ?' I lean in, raising my eyebrows, urging her to spit out whatever this is before my heart stops beating completely.

'Over a thousand people on this tiny island and you meet him. Funny how life works.' She shakes her head, and for the first time since walking in, her lavender eyes meet mine properly. They're glittering in the electric light.

'Sweetpea,' – she cups my cheek – 'this isn't how it was supposed to play out. I was going to bring you here, suss things out . . . but . . . my emotions and my stupid back got in the way . . . I guess I got nervous, you know? Overthinking every detail. You know what I'm like, that crazy mixture of improvising and micromanaging—'

'Mum! Spit it out.'

'He's your father. Dimitri . . . he's your dad.'

A tickle of laughter erupts and splutters out of my lips in an awkward giggle as tears nip at my eyes.

For a moment, I was sure she was going to tell me something was really wrong. Like maybe she'd run him over with a car and we were going to have to hide from the law or bury his body. The first bubble that bursts inside me is that of relief that everyone's OK before my mind reverses back over her words again and again.

Dimitri is my dad?

'I thought you were going to say something had happened to him and you were to blame or that something was badly wrong with you or me . . .' Tears stream down my cheeks.

Mum looks down at our hands.

'Not today, no. Just that Dimitri is your dad.'

I take my hands back and hold them to my face before wiping flakes of mascara from under my eyes.

'How did you find out? I'm so confused. Was he in Crete all those years ago? I don't even know how you got here or how you know about Dimitri being here. I'm so confused, none of this makes any sense. How did you know I'd met him today? I have so many questions, Mum.' My hands drop down to my thighs as my voice squeaks out. 'What the hell is going on? What makes you think Dimitri is my dad? You said you met my dad in Crete.'

'I'm sorry, honey. I've always known it was Dimitri. It happened while I was working here.'

A burning sensation hits me right behind the eyes. It's so hot it's a blinding white that drills right into my head.

'You *what*? You've always known who my father is, and you've never told me? This whole time I've thought you were rubbish at keeping secrets.'

'I am, but this wasn't a secret. It was a lie.'

'How is that better?'

'It's not, but at least that was the truth.'

I bite back words I know I shouldn't say, running my teeth along my lips to hold them in.

'I can't believe you've actively lied to me my whole life.' I jump to my feet like I'm about to run. Instead, I stare down at her, my fists like solid bullets at my sides wishing they could strike out at something. 'And not about something small. About where I come from. About my own father.' My head begins to throb as it tries to run through every moment of my life where she could've told me the truth and decided not to. 'Does he know?'

'He does now. I think he had a feeling as soon as he laid eyes on you. It was Dimitri who came and got me and brought me here to tell you. He has a small fishing boat.'

It all makes sense now, the way he brought me into the house like he was showing off, the way he pushed to ask me about my mum and then disappeared when he knew she was in Kardamena.

'*He* made you tell me? What on earth, Mum. What. On. *Earth?*' My voice shifts as anger becomes uncontrollable.

'I know you're hurt—'

'Hurt?' I throw my head back in an outraged and incredulous laugh. 'Hurt. Hurt she says, like I've grazed my knee. *Hurt*. No, Mum, I'm not *hurt*.' My hands slice through each word before I step forward with my fingers poised ready to count off what I really am. 'I'm livid, broken, confused, humiliated . . . Why not tell me before? Why? Why not tell him?'

'It's a long story. I think we should get some rest, and I can explain it all in the morning.'

'Rest? You drop a sledgehammer on my heart and then tell me to go to bed like a good little girl? No, you will tell me *now*.' I point at the floor and stamp one foot.

Mum's lips twist and she grits her teeth. 'I know you're hurt—' she says again.

'I'm not *hurt*.'

'Fine, *livid*. But I'm not your child. Demanding and shouting is not how we treat each other, and it never has been.'

'Oh really?' I hold my shoulders square and dig my fingers into my hips to stop myself lashing out as I lean over her. 'Really? Because I thought we shared important facts and you haven't been saying you didn't want to bother telling me who my dad is, you told me he was an unknown tourist in Crete.' I almost spit the word Crete in her face.

As I continue, my voice climbs and climbs in volume and pitch. 'You're a liar and you have been a liar my whole life. I don't even know who you are.'

Tears burn behind my eyes, stinging the back of my nose as I sprint out of the room barefoot, jogging down the stairs like I'm being chased by a ghost.

I don't know where I'm going. All I know with certainty is, I can easily outrun my mother, even if I can't outrun her lies.

I doubt she would even try to follow me.

What's the point? We both know eventually I'll have to come back looking for answers.

Already I'm flooded with a million questions. Like, *Was it a one-time thing? Why didn't she tell him? Were they dating?*

My pace stays strong, my bare feet hitting the solid pavement with force as I keep the sea next to me, like my right-hand man, its comforting rhythm unstoppable – just like the pulse of emotions rising up, threatening to drown me.

As my quads begin to burn and tears cool my cheeks, I slow my pace, coming to a halt next to a low sea wall. I grip the jagged surface, sucking in sharp lungfuls of salty air.

I could've had a dad. My whole entire life, I could've had a dad, and I didn't.

She stole that from me.

The worst part is, Dimitri seemed nice. I didn't get to know him, but he seemed friendly and Leonidas spoke of him with so much affection, like he's a good guy.

I think back to his interest in my name and its meaning. I squeeze my eyes tightly shut to conjure his face, but it's not clear enough, my focus was all on Leonidas.

Someone else's fast-paced feet slap against the ground, gaining in volume. It's probably Mum, doing her best to chase after me.

I keep my eyes locked on the points and edges of the stones under my fingers.

The feet slow as they reach me. It has to be Mum.

'I don't want to talk to you,' I growl.

'I understand.' Dimitri's voice makes me physically recoil and my mind screeches to a halt as I turn around to be face to face with my father.

Chapter 27

Mia 2025

It's the second time tonight I've been surprised to see one of my parents, thinking they were someone else.

One of my parents, because for the first time in my life, I have two.

Dimitri and I are only a short sprint away from where we met in the afternoon, when I missed my ferry. I wonder what he thought when he saw my face. Did he suspect I was his right away?

'Mia Zoí—'

'Please don't say *I am your father*. I might throw up.'

His pupils look as wide and black as the dark side of the moon. He's probably saturated with the same shock I feel.

'I am, though.'

'No. You're a man who I met earlier today. I don't even know you and you don't know me.' I strike my own chest with my index finger.

'That is true.' He sits down on the wall only a few feet away from me. 'But you have the shape of my mother's eyes and her hair. You have your mother's mannerisms. Your hands are identical, and of course the colour of her eyes in yours is almost identical too.'

Automatically, I look from the backs of my hands to the palms, as though I'll find something new there that I've never noticed before.

'Almost identical?'

Most people say we have the same unusual eyes, they coo at them like they've never seen anything quite like them.

'Yours are a shade darker.'

He's right. He's spent all of five minutes with me, and not even standing directly next to Mum, and yet he knows my eyes are a shade darker.

'Did you know right away? That I was yours?'

'No, no. Not until you said your mother's name is Sara. Before that, I was wondering if you were a distant relation of Sara's. You're like the other side of her coin. You're not the same, but parts of her are imprinted on you.'

'And what about you? You *really* didn't know about me until today?'

I train my eyes on him to analyse his every word. Finding out Mum has been lying to me my whole life has left the bitter taste of mistrust.

'No. If I had, I would've given everything I had to meet you.'

My arms lock together in front of my chest like a shield as a lump in my throat threatens to choke me. I don't think he's lying. He looks genuinely cut up about it, the way I feel. He even got on a fishing boat at night to find my mum and force her to tell me the truth right away.

How could my mum do this to us?

My chest judders and I have no control over it. I do my best to stand tall and pretend I'm somehow immune to the confusion and pain coursing through me.

But I'm not.

Of course I'm not.

This was meant to be a fun little getaway and everything has been fractured and I have no idea what to do next. My whole life is a broken lie.

'Why wouldn't she tell you about me?' I try to steady my voice but it's hard.

'You will need to speak to her. It is not my place to put words in her mouth.'

'Do you forgive her? I don't think I can ever forgive her.'

Dimitri shakes his head, but he says, 'I don't want to, but I have to.'

'How? How can *I* forgive her?' My voice squeaks between gulping breaths.

My father takes a step towards me and reaches his hand to take mine before thinking twice and letting it fall.

I don't know what I'd have done if he had taken my hand in his. How I'd feel to have such intimacy with a stranger who has a family tag on him.

'You can forgive her because you love her and deep down, you know this wasn't to hurt you. She made a decision. Do I think it was the wrong one? Of course. But I can't change the past. She made it when she was very young. You didn't know her then. I did.'

'It sounds like you're making excuses for her.'

'Maybe I am.'

At least that confirms one of my many questions. They did know each other, it wasn't a fling.

'You said I'll forgive her because I love her. Why have you forgiven her so quickly? It can't just be because she made a decision when she was young. She's had plenty of time to contact you, even if she didn't tell me right away.'

Dimitri's lips fold in on themselves before coming back out with a quiet popping noise. 'I suppose . . . because I love her too.'

Chapter 28

SARA 1998

'I'm excited to meet your mother. Parents always like me. Not my own parents, but other people's always seem to.' My hand slips into Dimitri's as we meander across the smooth black stones of Hohlaki beach. 'Tell me everything I need to know to impress her.'

'Eat everything she gives you, and you remember never to touch the good towels.'

I think back to the first time using the restroom at Dimitri's and the sudden banging on the door to inform me not to use the *good* towels. They're more ornament than towel, apparently.

'Yes. I won't make that mistake again. If you ever meet my parents, please don't tell them that you have "good towels" because they'll start doing it too.'

Dimitri quietly chuckles.

'What if she gives me flowers?'

Dimitri looks down at me, his eyebrows resting heavy over his eyes.

'Should I eat them, too? You said to eat everything she gives me . . .'

His quiet chuckle pops open like champagne, filling the air with his melodic laughter.

'No, no. Just eat food. My mother might be a little hard on you. With me she is always asking *Ti tha káneis me aftí ti douleiá?* What will I do with my job. I'm no doctor and I don't own anything, so . . .' He shrugs. 'To her, I could be doing more. Then being with a girl who is not Greek . . .' He inhales through his teeth. 'Also, you must eat everything she gives you.' Dimitri's lips curl up as he suppresses further laughter. This time, at the fact he's actually said this to me at least ten times now.

'I'm sure when Mama finds out about you, she will plan a big feast. She will know about you already, from everyone I know calling her and telling her. But she hasn't said anything to me. We will find out soon. I was thinking, I might invite Manolis and his family. Little Leonidas is so taken with you, I thought this would be good for my mother to see.'

I bend down to pick up a small, shiny black pebble. One that fits perfectly in my palm. Studying the surface, hard yet delicately smooth, I wonder how long it's been sitting here waiting to be found. Like Dimitri was here, waiting for me to find him. I really hope his mother does like me. I know from the way he talks about her how important she is in his life. From what Dimitri has said, she might be a bit domineering, but the difference is, she loves him and my parents don't love me. Hopefully, she will see how happy we are, and she'll welcome me into the family.

Dimitri's finger curls under my chin and tilts it up until I meet his gaze.

'I don't think you will have to try too hard for her to see what I can see. I think she'll be pleased I've fallen in love with you.'

The stone slips out of my fingers and strikes against the others on the ground with a sharp crash.

I've imagined him telling me he loved me. Telling me that I was *the one*. I've nearly said it to him a few times over the past month, but I didn't want to be the first to take that step. I've always been the one to chase people, desperately seeking approval, and there's been something comfortable in the instability of not being one hundred per cent sure but feeling it all the same.

But, I guess, he didn't say he *loved me*. The classic, *I love you*. He said he is *in* love with me. A distinction as important as pauper to king. People say they love things all the time, I love Kos and Nisyros . . . but to be *in* love . . . That's something altogether different.

My jaw stays slack and my tongue becomes too big for my mouth, leaving me unable to speak. I'm sure it must have swelled enough to be putting pressure on my brain because it feels like it's lost all ability to think.

'I shouldn't have said it. It's too soon, I know, but it's impossible to hide what I know. And—'

'I'm in love with you too, Dimitri.'

Dimitri's hands glide over my lower back as I stand on tiptoe on the pebbles for our lips to meet. Every time is as good as the first time, only now I'm used to our sticky bodies at all times of day as summer creeps up to its full force, and enjoy the sensation of sticking to him, hoping we will stay this way forever.

'I have something for you.' Dimitri gently pulls away from me but keeps his left hand in contact with me while his right pulls out a small green box from his pocket. 'I hope you like it.'

He places the soft velvet box in my hand.

I click it open, and there, sparkling in the heat, is a simple gold band with a rectangular aquamarine in the centre.

'You remembered.' My voice comes out thin and breathy.

I told my mother once about my preference for aquamarines. The next birthday, she got me an emerald necklace and swore blind *that* was my favourite, as though she knew and I didn't. She then made a comment about how emeralds are worth more. As though that should be how someone decides whether they like something or not, by the price someone else put on it.

Dimitri's fingers move past mine to remove it from its box and slip it on my middle finger.

'Not for marriage yet.'

There's something about the way he says *yet*, like he's already jumping across the years of *us* and into a future filled with more of this.

He presses a gentle kiss to my finger, then one on my lips that lingers. His mouth moves slowly into mine. My body ignites from the inside out as I wrap myself around him.

I've never felt so lucky, so carefree, before. It makes me feel a little nervous. Everything's so perfect, something bad will have to happen eventually, but I never want anything to burst our bubble.

The alarm on my Baby-G jelly watch sounds from behind Dimitri's head, where my fingers are curling into his dark hair.

Our lips pull apart, but our bodies stay stuck together.

'I have to get back to the boat.'

'I will count the minutes until you are here.'

Our mouths meet again. I don't want to leave, not even for a minute, but I know I have to.

Reluctantly, I peel myself off him and we walk back towards Mandraki's port, hands still interlinked.

'When I left England, I didn't tell anyone I was going. My friends are spread out all over the world, and there's no one I see regularly enough for them to notice I was gone. I came to Kos because I saw an advert in a magazine. I thought I would do one season and decide what I was going to do with the rest of my life, but I assumed I'd travel far and wide before settling. It never occurred to me that I could meet someone I actually wanted to spend my time with.' I nearly say *spend a lifetime with* but am struck with vulnerability right before the words come out.

Dimitri wraps his arm over my shoulders. In response, my arm winds around his waist as we walk.

'I think it was fate,' he declares. 'The gods brought you to me for all my hard work spreading their myths.'

The pebbles begin to rattle, making my knees feel like jelly. The sea undulates unnaturally for a moment and Dimitri grips me tighter than before. The way he does late at night when we're together in his room.

I know this feeling and it's not Dimitri's romantic words.

It's an earthquake.

It rattles us from side to side and we automatically crouch down on the beach, gripping each other.

Nisyros and Kos have been having a lot of seismic activity for a few years, and this isn't my first earthquake, but it is the first one since being here, and the first time in my life I'm holding on to someone who makes me feel safe.

This might actually be the safest I've ever felt in my whole entire life, clinging to Dimitri's shirt while the earth below me lurches and churns.

It only lasts for a matter of seconds before everything's calm again.

There's nothing that could happen that would shake my core, not while I'm with him.

Chapter 29

Sara 1998

'While you've been swanning off over to Nisyros at every given opportunity, you missed a phone call. A really important one. Here.' Tina pulls a piece of paper off the dining table. I'm amazed she found it so easily with all the crap we leave lying about. 'They sent a fax too. You're off to Crete in three days.'

I snatch the paper out of her hand. My eyes dance over it, unable to read half the words because I'm suddenly very light-headed.

I tug a wooden chair out from the table, push the towel that's on it to one side and slide down into it.

'Pack your bags, babe, you're off to the next Greek island so you'll have to say goodbye to lover boy and hello to the next sexy Greek. It's OK though, I'll take good care of him for you.' Tina sways her hips as she leaves for her bedroom.

If I didn't need to read this paper so much, I'd ball it up and throw it at her.

There it is in black and white. Someone broke their leg and Crete is busier than Kos so they need me to go and work there instead. Before meeting Dimitri, I'd have been fine with trying out another place to see what's there, but now . . . Now I want to scream and quit my job and find one here instead. But I have no idea where. Every job is already filled this season.

I can't even speak to Dimitri right away. I'm not even meant to see him until tomorrow.

Tonight, he's welcoming his mother back from her time away nursing his great-aunt and I've got a bar crawl to host. All I want to do is swim across the water and get back to him now to find out how to fix this. Not that I could possibly swim that far, but with the anger that's pulsing through me I would give it a good go.

'This can't be right,' I call out in Tina's wake.

Tammy waltzes out of the bathroom with her hair wrapped up in a towel like a turban and another towel around her body that's so short I can almost see her bum cheeks.

'Hey, chick. Has Tina given you the bad news? I told her I should speak to ya, but you know how she is. We'll really miss you around here.'

'I can't go,' I mutter, more at the paper trembling in my hand than at her. 'I'll pay you to go instead of me. Everything I have.'

'Sorry, babe, this is my home now. I've been here for three years and I'm not going anywhere. Tina always wants more money for all her hairspray and lippy, you could see if she'll swap ya.'

'Tina,' I call across the apartment. 'Tina?'

'What?' She pokes her head around her door.

'I will pay you to go to Crete instead of me.'

'Why?'

'You know why.'

'Because of one man?'

'Stop toying with her, Tina, you know how loved-up she is. Stop being so jealous for five minutes.' Tammy tilts her head and her towel turban almost topples off.

'Oh yeah, I'm *desperate* for Dimitri to fall in love with me . . . *not*.' She sticks out her tongue and aims her fingers towards her mouth like she's gagging, but Tammy and I both know that given half a chance she would snatch him away for a night just to prove that she could.

But she can't.

We're strong.

I can't imagine Dimitri would pick anyone over me. Not anyone in the world.

'Will you help me out or not?'

'Sorry, babes, I'm in love with Kos. I'll throw you the best going-away party if you like, though?'

'No, that's all right. Thanks.'

'Suit yourself.' Tina's head vanishes back inside her room.

I stare at the paper in my hands. I'm required in Crete and I'll be picked up by taxi to head over there.

There has to be something I can do . . . I just don't know what it is yet. Dimitri might have an idea though. Or maybe he'll know someone who can give me a job.

This is unbelievable. For the first time in my life everything is going well, and now this.

Tammy's warm hand lands on my shoulder.

'It'll be OK, doll. It's only for a couple of months.'

A couple of months has never felt more like a life sentence than it does right now.

I look down at the ring Dimitri gave me. We're strong. Tammy's right, if he can't find a way for me to stay, at least it's only until the end of the season. After that, I can come back here for the winter and we'll work something out.

We can get through anything. I'm sure of it.

Chapter 30

Sara 1998

I stare out at the island of Nisyros as though I'm pulling it towards me with an invisible force.

As usual, Dimitri is already waiting for me. I can see his silhouette in the distance. He has an aura I can see, even from here on the boat. A physique that stands out. A presence.

Usually, he's sitting at one of the tavernas having a coffee, but today he's standing, patiently waiting for me to arrive.

The ring on my middle finger sits perfectly on my hand and it can't wait to be held by his again. To feel the comfort and reassurance of his skin, and his voice in my ear.

I wonder whether he told his mother about the ring. I'm glad I'll be able to wear it in Crete as a reminder of us every single day. I've got a few pictures of us on my camera too, but I need to get them developed before I'll know whether they're any good. I'm not sure there's anywhere here where I can take my SD card to get them downloaded and printed off in time. I'd like to have a photo of us to look at when I'm missing him.

Over the past few weeks of summer, I've become accustomed to casually reading a magazine on the journey across to Nisyros.

There's always someone who leaves one behind before travelling back to the UK or the USA and usually I'm there to snap it up when they do. It helps me to know what's in fashion and to read my horoscope.

Not today though. Not knowing what I need to tell him. I haven't been able to concentrate on reading and I've barely eaten since finding out I might have to leave.

To keep my job, I'll be spending the last few months of the season on a completely different island, all because I was the last one to arrive here. The one who knows this resort the least, so I might as well go off and know even less about Crete.

I tried to call someone, to figure something out, but it turns out they don't *need* as many reps here, but they need to maintain numbers in Crete this year, with Malia's ever-growing popularity.

It feels like a month before the boat is in the harbour.

I ready myself to be the first person off. I need to tell him what's going on before I meet Maria, his mother.

I hop off and straight into Dimitri's arms, kissing briefly so as not to smear lip gloss over his or my face before meeting Maria.

'I've got a box of cakes and a box of biscuits, just in case, but . . .' I'm about to tell him my big ugly news and ask for his advice when he takes a step back. I can tell something isn't right. Usually, he greets me with a toothy grin, or tells me he doesn't care about my lip gloss and kisses me deeply anyway.

Today, it's different. *He* is different.

'What's wrong?' I step forward to close the gap he's made.

He shakes his head. 'I am so sorry, my love. But there is a problem. A big problem.'

I cup his face in my hands, and he places his heavily over mine.

'Please, forgive me, forgive my mother . . .'

My heart drops. I can feel its pounding echoing through my bones.

Dimitri removes my hands from his face but holds on to them in his.

'She has invited a woman to stay with us. I think she hears about us from all the gossips in the village, and she wants to marry me off to a Greek girl. Her name is Ourania and my mother is trying to arrange a marriage with her and . . .' Dimitri takes a slow breath before tripping over his words. 'And she does not invite you to lunch today. I am sorry.'

I try to swallow but my throat has gone so dry it's like I'm trying to force out some of the pumice stones sold in the shops here.

Tina's words ring in my ears about Dimitri never trying anything with her because he was having an *arranged marriage*.

'What did you say?' I begin.

'Did you not hear? I said my mother has invited Ourania—'

'No, no. I mean to your mother, when she said I couldn't come to lunch. What did you say to her? What did you tell her?'

'I don't think I understand.'

My body grows tense and weary, the way it would when my mother went on a passive-aggressive rant. The ones where I would stay silent with her, zoning out. With Dimitri, my mouth runs at a new-found speed.

'She said, *that bitch is not welcome in my home*. So, you said, *but Mum, I'm in love with this girl, Sara, you have to meet her, there's no way I'll marry what's-her-face. If you don't meet Sara, I'll never speak to you again.*'

Dimitri's chin recoils and he releases my hand to put his on his hips.

'She didn't call you a bitch.'

'I don't care about that.' My fingers twitch and I pull my bag higher on my shoulder. 'That other stuff. Did you defend me? Did you defend us?'

'No.'

'So, what *did* you say?'

'Nothing. This is her house. *I* know how I feel about you, but I cannot bring you to her door and force her to meet you.'

'Why not?'

'Because . . .'

'Because what?'

'Because . . .'

'*Because? Because?*'

Dimitri lowers his brows, settling into a deep scowl.

'So why is it? Is it because you aren't man enough to tell your mother you can pick who you want to be with? Or because you're not *really* in love with me?'

'Don't be like this, Sara. A man looks after his mother and his family—'

'No. I've had enough of parents who dislike me just for existing and boyfriends who don't love me enough to stand up for me. I don't need that from you or your mother.' With a steely determination, I stare at his trainers.

How is this happening all over again? I thought here things were different. I was so wrong. I truly believed he would always be on my side, I thought he understood. He could see when I was tense and in pain, not feeling good enough, and now here he is, letting someone judge me and not even standing up in my defence.

It's easy to tell me I'm perfect behind closed doors, but now it's time to open them and he's already hiding behind his mother.

'What do you want me to do?' Dimitri looks like a loose stone ready to roll away.

My eyes flick up like a mechanical toy that's flared into life, but I keep my voice low. 'What do *you* want to do, Dimitri?'

'I want to kiss you, maybe take you to lunch . . . perhaps we could find a quiet place . . .' He takes a step towards me but it's my turn to take one back.

'But what about your mother?'

'What about her?'

'Would you marry me without her blessing?'

'She will come around. She just needs time.'

'You're a grown man.' I turn and pace for a moment, looking back towards the boat I've just stepped off, already refilling with people ready to return to Kardamena.

The morning sun beats down on the top of my head, making me dizzy, and my stomach turns over in acidy somersaults.

'I've got to go.' I point back towards the boat.

Dimitri catches my hand as I turn. 'Sara, stay.'

'Are you going to take me to your house to meet your mother? Are you going to defend me and tell her how you feel about me?'

'Please, let's not push for this today. She will see over time, we are meant to be together.'

'Because you love me?'

'Because I am *in* love with you.'

'But you won't take me to meet your mother.'

'Sara.' He rolls his eyes just like my father when I point anything out to him that's completely unfair.

'I've got to go.' I step towards him and press my lips to his one last time. Imprinting the feel of his mouth against mine and the smell of salt on his skin, knowing this is a forever goodbye, when I thought today would be the start of a very different forever.

I close my eyes and wish it was different, but I don't want to live in the shadow of anyone's mother. Not after everything I've done to escape my own parents. I won't let anyone dictate my life again, only me.

I'll get over him. I have to.

Dimitri presses his forehead to mine and his fingers dig into my arms. I think he knows as well as I do that this is over. If he didn't, he would've said something and told his mother how important I am.

'I know you need time. But we have time, and time is what my mother needs, yes? I will come and see you soon.'

'Goodbye, Dimitri.' I choke on the words.

Running back towards the boat, tears race down my cheeks, cool in the heat of the sun.

At least moving to Crete will mean I don't have to live with Dimitri on my doorstep. I won't have to try and avoid him. He'll be out of my life for good.

Chapter 31

Mia 2025

'You love Mum? *My* mum? You *love* her? How can you *love* her? You haven't seen her in . . . twenty-six? Twenty-seven years?' My breathing is shallow, like the thick sea air is too solid for my lungs to process it. 'And if she died today, and you never saw her again, would you stop loving her in twenty-six or twenty-seven years?'

Tears are out of control, rolling over my face, and my breathing is almost non-existent as I shake my head and tell him that even when I hate my mum, like right now, I still love her more than anyone else on the planet.

I'm not sure he can understand my shaking words as they contort on their way from my head to my mouth. They're too muffled as I choke on every thought.

He sucks his lips in for a moment, like he's trying to hold back. 'Mia Zoí, I can't stand for this. I must hold you, please.'

My shoulders rise and fall in a weak shrug as I do my best to hide behind my hands and curve my body into something smaller than it is.

Without another thought, he wraps me up in his arms and shushes me like I'm a baby in his strong embrace.

My forearms are high, like someone sheltering themselves from an attack. I was defending my face from view before it all crushed against his chest, making his shirt instantly damp with my tears.

This is the first time I've been held by my father.

The first time I've had him close enough that I can smell musk and sea salt ingrained in his clothes and on his skin.

For most children, this happens at such a young age they don't even recall it. Even the smell of their parents is so normal they probably don't even notice it.

Unlike this, right now. *This* will be scorched into my memory forever.

Meeting my father and being held by him in this way is so far from all the possible ways I've imagined over the years.

When I was a child, I thought he would walk through the door one day, and say something like, *hey, remember me?* to my mum. Or when we were in Crete, I thought Mum might recognise someone and it would all fall into place.

I've never once imagined she could have been lying to me about my dad. That she knew who he was and actively didn't share the information.

I mumble all my fears and questions into Dimitri's torso. None of them make sense to me so I doubt they'll make sense to him.

All the times I've had a broken heart, and he could've been there to hold me and make me feel better, and now it's Mum who's shattered everything and he's been left with the task of holding me together, and we don't even know each other. We've only said half a dozen words to each other.

'What do we do now?' His low voice vibrates through my bones.

I pull myself away from him and rest my bottom on the wall next to us to steady my shaking knees.

I try to calm my breathing and pull myself back together, but it feels impossible.

'If you love her so much, why aren't you together? Didn't she love you?' I sound like a child who's just found out her parents are getting a divorce. A child who's trying to simplify the complexities of human relationships.

Dimitri sits down next to me and looks back along the road we came from, back towards where I left Mum.

'I did look for her, but I didn't know where she was. I was told she would be in Crete, but when I arrived, they said she had quit her job and left. I didn't know where in England she was, or whether she had even gone to England. I was so angry at her for leaving me because she couldn't give my mother the time she needed to get to know her. My mother was old and stubborn. I've never felt so confused with the passion of hatred for someone. She took my soul with her, and she hid it from me. I married a woman to spite your mother, which was not a good idea. I do not recommend marrying for anything other than love.'

'That poor woman.' I can't help but question the sort of man who marries someone out of spite.

'Don't worry too much, she had an affair and lives in Kos with him and their two beautiful children. She is happy now. At the time I did not realise I was marrying her out of anger. I convinced myself we would be a good match.' Dimitri's head gently sways one way then the other. 'No. My mother convinced me we were a very good match.'

He turns and looks at me. My breathing has calmed a little, but my chest still jolts every now and then like it's trying to free itself from shackles.

'I cannot believe I have a daughter. I know you are hurting, but I want to know everything about you. All I know is your name and that Leonidas very much likes you. Which means there must be something very special about you. That boy is hard to impress. What is your job? What is your hobby? What are you passionate about?'

A smile touches my lips before I clear my throat. 'That's easy. I can answer all of those questions with one answer. Singing and music.'

'You are a singer?'

Even in the moonlight, Dimitri's eyes light up. He edges closer with an eagerness to know more.

This moment couldn't be more surreal. Thirty minutes ago, I didn't have a dad. I would never have a dad, and now . . . now there's a man in front of me with half my DNA and he wants to know everything about me. He's interested and engaged.

'I am. I sing at weddings mostly . . . but I'm thinking of branching out.'

'I hope you will sing for me one day. That would be the highlight of my life.'

'Even if you think I'm terrible?'

'Yes. To have a daughter to sing to me, even if she was terrible, would still be better than anything else that has ever happened to me. Not that you are terrible. Why would people want someone terrible singing at their wedding? It is the most special day, so they would pick the most special singer.' Dimitri sucks in a measured breath before pointedly exhaling it. 'But for tonight, I think you must talk with your mother. She will be worrying about you. Please, let me walk you to the hotel? I know she will be there waiting.'

My feet don't want to move. As though all the anger I feel has melted down into glue and stuck me to the spot.

I know he's right though.

The only way to move forward is to speak to Mum. She's the key to all of this deception, so she's the only one to unlock this mess.

Chapter 32

Mia 2025

I knock on my own hotel door.

I'd thought about what would happen when I got here as I'd trudged up the stairs. Would we stare at each other, wordlessly? Maybe she'll be angry at me for leaving and I'll be angry at her for not following me, and, of course, for lying to me.

The door flies open in an instant and my mum's puffy, pink, tear-stained face almost knocks me down.

She's always so strong. It takes a lot for her to look this broken up. She says she can hold everything in because she wasn't allowed to cry as a girl. It was frowned upon at best, punished as a nuisance at worst because my grandma didn't like the sound of it.

'Please forgive me,' she whispers, before crumbling away like a sandcastle being swallowed by the sea. She stumbles backwards until the backs of her legs find the bed to sit on. Tissues decorate the bedlinen like she's been carefully constructing a new blanket.

A big part of me feels sorry for her.

It's hard not to when you see someone you love so utterly distraught. But I feel worse for Dimitri and for myself. She chose this.

She ran away from him and didn't look back. This has been a long time coming and she's known that from day one.

It's too hard to look at her, seeing my pain all over her face.

'I've decided you're right. We should sleep and we can talk about it in the morning. I need a shower, it's been a long day.'

'I brought you some night clothes and a few outfits . . . just in case.' Mum marches towards the dresser and grabs one of her tote bags. 'Here.'

She walks over and places it in my hands. It's stupid, but right now I hate how thoughtful she is.

'Thanks.' The word is hard to squeeze out of my throat as a deep urge to cry stirs low in my gut.

I close the bathroom door carefully so as not to wake anyone in the hotel before allowing myself space to cry silently in the shower.

It's been a long time since I've shared a bed with my mother.

We've shared rooms loads of times on our travels, even the odd tent, but not a bed. Not one sheet between two.

I think the last time I slept in bed next to her, I was maybe fourteen. After chucking up at school due to a stomach bug, I didn't want to be left to vomit alone in my room. Plus, she had the en suite.

Tonight, or more accurately, this morning, sleeping has been a chore. Questions whizz and whirl around us in the dark.

With the shutters closed, even the stars have been left outside, without a hope of spreading their light towards us. Let alone the moon. The room has morphed into a black hole where light can't exist. It feels like all the light that once shone brightly in my soul has been sucked away, stolen, and I'm left praying it'll come back. Praying to a god Leonidas's mum believes in, but I don't.

I'm alone in the darkness of the unknown, while Mum has all the answers, able to snore softly next to me, completely unafraid of the black hole, because she hasn't fallen into it. She's on the outside looking in.

Not that she fell asleep quickly either. She did her fair share of wriggling before the audible breathing started. At least she's found sleep. I feel like I've been awake for a week.

I can't have been awake the whole time, it just feels like I have. But when I do manage to doze, I have dreams of us shouting at each other. They've been as clear and vivid as the reflection of the sun in the sea. But they can't be real.

Occasionally, I've checked the time on my phone and debated when morning really starts. Can I wake her up at 5 a.m.? Is that acceptable?

Probably not.

The light on my phone flares into life. Five minutes to five. One more hour and I'll make her give me answers.

I tug the sheet over my shoulder and twist to face away from her and towards the balcony.

I wonder whether Dimitri will tell Leonidas, or whether that's my job.

Maybe it is. Maybe Dimitri will take my lead on this, or maybe he's been running round the streets telling everyone. I hope not. I don't want congratulations from all and sundry on something I'm struggling to process.

It probably isn't my job to tell Leonidas. We hardly know each other. Unlike Dimitri, who has known him from birth.

He should've known *me* from birth.

My mouth flings open in another wild yawn when it wants to scream.

Everything aches. My calves, my quads, my back, my heart.

I close my eyes and let my mind recite the three questions I've boiled this down to.

Why didn't you tell him?

Why didn't you tell me?

Do you love him?

◆ ◆ ◆

'Wakey-wakey, eggs and bakey.' Mum's voice is comforting in my ear.

She's been saying this same phrase to me my whole life. Not every day of it, but so often it feels ingrained.

'One of these days you'll acknowledge my vegetarianism.' My eyes stay closed, but a smile tugs at my lips.

As my mind begins to drift back off to sleep, realisation hits me. The adrenaline makes me tingle and my eyes pop open.

'What time is it?'

Mum reaches for her phone on the bedside cabinet.

'About twenty to eight. You were snoozing happily, but I didn't know when you had the room till so I thought I should wake you up.'

Spending the whole night in a tired maze of questions left me to oversleep at the worst possible time.

'Let me get up. Kettle on, please. Is there a kettle?'

'I'll go and get us something to eat and drink, you get dressed.' Mum moves towards the door. 'I'll be back soon.'

◆ ◆ ◆

'Here. One strong, sweet black coffee and I've got some homemade *karydopita* . . . which is walnut cake.'

The mug she passes me has faded Greek words on it and a chip on the handle. Mum's is plain olive-green and has a chip on the rim.

I'm already washed and dressed and waiting on the bed for her when she gets back in. She's brought me tons of useful things across, including complete outfits. She can't have had long to put everything in, yet it all looks thought out, including my washbag, make-up and hairbrush and swimwear.

Damn her for always being delightfully thoughtful. She's so hard to dislike.

The faded mug doesn't look like anything I've been given in any tavernas before. 'Where on earth did you go to get this mis-matched lot?'

She walks towards the balcony and opens the door with a whoosh, letting the warm sea breeze roll in, pushing the air-con aside.

She pulls out a chair and places the clear food bag filled with cake on the table, alongside her mug.

I pull out the chair opposite and take a seat, patiently waiting for an answer to a question I thought would be my easiest of the day.

'Dimitri's place. Your dad's, I guess I mean. I knew he'd have slept as well as us. He had this cake from his party. That's what he said. Well, he actually said someone had left it in front of his door for him. It's his favourite.'

'Did he say anything about me?'

A smile lifts her face as she picks the bag back off the table and fumbles with the knot.

'Funny that, he asked the same thing about you.'

'You know he's still in love with you, right?'

Mum's fingers contract over the knot before stopping altogether.

I knew my words would garner a reaction. I just don't know what it will be yet.

It's only a brief moment of pause before Mum digs a fingernail into the bag and rips it open to retrieve a slice of cake wrapped in a piece of kitchen roll. She hands the first slice to me.

Keeping it in the kitchen roll, I place it back on the table. I can't bear the thought of food right now, not even for my usual glucose spike.

Mum takes her mug in both hands and pulls her feet up on to her chair, tucking one foot underneath her, and like bookends, I do the same.

'No. I didn't know that. Come on then. We both know you want answers, and now is your chance. You can ask anything, and I'll do my best to be honest.'

'Your *best* to be honest?' I lower one eyebrow in her direction.

'I won't lie, but a lot of what you'll be asking about happened a long time ago. Memory changes things. The best I have is my memories. True or false.'

'Fine.' I want to be annoyed by the answer but it's actually very reasonable and didn't contain any of her signature silliness, so I guess I should be grateful for that at least. 'Did you love him?'

'Yes.'

Her answer feels like a bullet nicking my heart, leaving a wound just big enough to slowly kill me off. How could she do this?

I try to control myself. I use my strong singer's core to control the sound of my voice in an attempt to stop it breaking. 'Do you still?'

Mum lowers her eyes towards her drink as though she might find the answer in there somewhere.

'How can I know that after all these years? I don't know. I don't know him. Not anymore.'

Like waves crashing against rocks until they break down to sand, part of me drops in the sea to be swept away. Until this day, I never thought Mum had *ever* been in love.

I do my best to push the grains of thoughts back together into a shape, like hands pressing the sand into a castle of questions.

'OK . . . well, I guess what I really need to know is, why didn't you tell him about me? Why deprive him of a daughter and me of a dad? If you'd told him and he didn't want to be involved, that I could understand. But we could've been a family, Mum. A proper family.'

'We *are* a proper family.' The sun rises up behind the one cloud in the sky and casts a shadow over my mum's face. 'How was I as a mother, Mia? Good? Bad?'

Her face is quite serious, almost aggressive. Defensive.

'You were a good mum. You *are* a good mum. You know . . . other than this . . .'

'And how were your grandparents? Were they always there for you? Did they stay up all night with you when you had earache?'

I shake my head.

'No. They didn't for me either, that's for sure. It would be Calpol and lock me in my room because hearing me cry was too distressing for *them*. Mum would complain I was upsetting *her* too much. You can't think about this situation from your point of view now, or even the point of view you think I *should* have, because you didn't know me back then. I had never been loved before Dimitri.

'My parents have never said they loved me. Not once. Within one month together, Dimitri was *in love* with me. He didn't tell me he loved me, he declared he was *in* love with me.' Mum's hands form fists in front of her chest and her whole body looks like a violin string ready to snap. 'I'd never had anyone tell me that before, nor since. That they were *in* love with me. I felt it too, like nothing I'd felt before. It was terrifying. Like being on a roller coaster in freefall without a safety harness, holding on and hoping it was true and I hadn't tricked myself, because who was I to know what love was? I had no experience. Wanting to believe it, but wondering how it could be possible . . . then finding out it wasn't. The next day, the *very* next day, he was telling me I'm not good enough for his mother and she *might* come round to liking me *one day*. I knew she wanted him to marry a Greek girl, but he didn't even try to defend me. Something inside snapped.'

Mum pauses, looking out across the misty sea before carrying on with a rapid spewing of thoughts and emotions.

'It's so easy now to say, *well, I was probably hormonal because I was pregnant*, but I didn't know I was pregnant. My mother put me on the Pill at fifteen when I'd only been having periods for a year. I didn't even have a steady boyfriend at the time. I didn't think it was possible to get pregnant . . .' Mum's hands fall limp on her lap and a heavy silence descends on our balcony.

I rack my mind to think of a way to respond that doesn't sound weak and childish, but Mum speaks first.

'Since Dimitri, the only person I have ever believed when they've told me they loved me is you.' Tears threaten in her eyes, but she keeps going.

'I didn't ever think I'd make a good parent, but as soon as I found out I was having you, I knew two things. I would do my best to tell you I loved you as much as possible, and I'd make you feel safe. I know I've hurt you by not telling you about Dimitri. I know I've hurt him too. I can't change that. But I did come back to tell him about you when I found out I was pregnant. I left my job in Crete to come here and find him, only to find out he was engaged to someone else. I'd been gone a month. One single month . . . and he'd already moved on to the woman his mother approved of. I didn't think having a dad who wasn't interested in you would make you feel safe or loved. I thought it would be better for both of us to pretend he didn't exist.'

'What the hell?' I roll my eyes and make sure to enunciate my words clearly for her. 'He married her to *spite* you.'

'Is that what he told you?' The corners of her mouth tilt ever so slightly downwards in the way they do when she thinks I'm lying, or at least withholding information. But I'm not.

'Yes.'

'No. Well, that's not what I was told at the time.'

Chapter 33

Sara 1998

Dimitri, I have something to tell you. I'm pregnant, but I need you to understand, I'm not here to ask anything of you, I just wanted you to know the truth. If you want to be involved, you can be, but you don't have to be. I've been repeating these words in my head for three days. They wait there anxiously, desperate to be released.

The boat glides over the sea like a very noisy skater on ice.

It's a calm morning, as though even the sea doesn't want to make today worse for me. Perhaps the sea knows as well as I do that when I get to Nisyros I'll be causing an earthquake of my own, one way or another.

My mild morning sickness is grateful for the easy trip too. It wasn't happy about my journey from Crete to Kos, that's for sure. I left more food in bags in bins than in my stomach.

When I arrived on Kos yesterday, I briefly considered asking Tina and Tammy for a free night back in my old bed, but instead I went with the less comfortable but entirely preferable option of Alexandra's broken couch.

If I'd stayed with the rep girls, they would ask a million questions I have no desire to answer. Even if I did answer, I wouldn't trust them with the truth. Tammy maybe, but Tina would swallow my news whole and spit it out in ugly pieces to anyone who would listen.

Alexandra didn't push me to answer any questions, but when she made me a special breakfast of stacked pancakes with chocolate spread and a milkshake, she did let me ask her about Dimitri. It was nice to see her again; she even told me she's dating Declan, the travel rep from Kos Town. He wasn't hanging about in Kardamena because he was interested in me, he was interested in her. I couldn't be more pleased for her.

She hasn't seen Dimitri in a few weeks – she's been too distracted with Declan – and so couldn't comment on his possible feelings towards me.

I was hoping to find out some piece of information, like he'd asked after me, but if he had, it wasn't her who was asked. Probably Tina told him I was gone before even stepping on the bus to take one of the tour groups.

As if I'd be lucky enough to find out something useful. I think my parents cursed me when I left, proving without them and their money I would fail.

I just hope they're wrong.

I hope I'm wrong about a lot of things, Dimitri being the most important. I hope he did care that I left, I hope he's missed me like I've missed him, and I hope he wants this baby the way I do.

As we near the port of Mandraki, I search the shoreline for Dimitri, wondering whether he'll be there, looking out to sea for my long-awaited return, like something from a movie.

I know he won't be.

It's not like I had any way of letting him know I was coming. I can't imagine Dimitri will ever bother to have a mobile phone. He lives in the same town as most of his friends so, as he has often said, what would be the point?

I try to conjure him in my mind's eye. Every time I do this, I see his face close to mine on his pillow, his fingers stretching to brush the long strands of blonde hair off my face.

He'll probably be sleeping on that same pillow right now, because he doesn't have work today.

I wonder whether our baby has a heart yet, and if it does, whether it's racing as fast as mine.

As the sun rises higher in the sky, light scatters over the white-washed buildings of the town. It's almost blinding, and it makes all the shadows harsher, colder.

My heart lifts at the familiarity of the lines on the horizon, and the recent memories of Dimitri holding my hand and telling me he was in love with me. It wasn't that long ago. Feelings can't change overnight. Mine haven't.

Nerves kick me in the ribs.

I was probably too harsh on him before. It's not like he said it was over, it was me who walked away.

Since realising I was pregnant, I've held on to the hope that he really *does* love me, and the baby will be enough for his mother to accept me, and that perhaps, once she's had the chance to meet me, things will be different.

I still think he should've stood up for me, but my feelings about it have cooled.

The biggest issue I have now is, I don't want a sense of loyalty or tradition to be the reason he stays with me. I've already prepared a speech explaining that I'm only here to inform him he is a father, but he doesn't have to be involved. I'll be keeping the baby no matter what, and that's on me. It's my decision. What he does is up to him.

The captain and one other man organise the boat into port, tying it up and putting out the ramp for us all to disembark.

I do my best to keep my eyes to myself, thanking the captain, who I recognise from a thousand crossings, as he takes my hand and helps me on to dry land.

He wishes me a good day, and I hope it is. More than any other day of my life, I really hope this one is a good one. One to look back on.

I clutch my purple cloth bag, tugging it up on my shoulder every few steps as my feet slap along the stone streets. I left my suitcase with Alexandra, just in case this doesn't go well. I didn't want to have to drag it from one place to the next. It has my whole life in it. Either I'm staying here, or I'm going back to England.

I pass all the bright-blue doors still snoozing in the shadows, where the sun can't quite reach yet, until I make it to his mint-green shutters and door.

I'm out of breath, but only because my heart won't settle down.

'*Hi, Dimitri, can we talk?* No.' For a second I pant like a dog. 'No, no. *I need to talk to you, can I come in?*' I rehearse my words out loud like lines from *King Lear* I had to learn at school. Each word has to be considered. It's the only way I'll get through this without falling apart.

Without further hesitation I rattle off four knocks on the door and take a step back, smoothing my hands over my violet dress. It's the one I wore on our first proper date. He always said it would be his forever favourite. My tummy isn't showing yet – if anything, I'm thinner than ever from not keeping all my food down.

When I close my eyes, I can still see his hands running over my hips.

The seconds of waiting at his door feel like an eternity as sunlight begins to creep along the street, reaching up one of my ankles.

The door swings open and I'm faced with a woman, I assume Maria, Dimitri's mother. She's quite beautiful, with Dimitri's deep-brown eyes and thick black eyelashes. Her eyes are shaped like his too, only etched with wrinkles. Maria's wearing all black. I remember Dimitri saying she hasn't worn colour since her husband died.

'*Kalimera*,' my voice croaks out. I hadn't prepared myself for her answering the door. Which is ridiculous, this is her home after all. 'Is Dimitri here?'

Her eyes narrow to slits as she looks me over.

I feel like I'm asking whether he's free to come out and play and she thinks I'm the naughty kid. The bad influence. Suddenly, I wish I'd worn something very different, but I don't own that many outfits.

'Are you the girl? Chasing *ton* Dimitri *mou*?' Her hands act as though they're joined to her mouth by a string, moving when her lips move and stopping when they stop. Maybe she thinks it might help her to be understood in English.

'I . . . no. No, I'm not here to *chase* Dimitri. I need to talk to him. Is he here?'

'No. No home.'

'When will he be back?'

'You come.' Maria points from me to the house then turns and marches in the direction of the kitchen.

I follow behind, watched by half a dozen icons on the way. I'm sure there weren't as many as this when I was last here. She probably added more to rid the house of my presence.

'Sit, sit.' She grips the back of a chair, grinding it along the floor. It's the same one Dimitri first sat me down on, then made me lunch. That could be a lifetime ago now.

She talks away to me in Greek as she places her *briki* on the hob and begins to heat coffee.

Maria hasn't asked whether I'd like a coffee, but as she has put out two decorative *demi-tasse* cups and saucers, I think I'm getting one.

'Will Dimitri be back soon?' I enquire.

'No, no, no.'

She pours out the freshly boiled mixture and carefully brings them to the table, putting one down in front of me and sitting to drink hers too.

Maybe this is a good thing. She's made me a drink, maybe she'll quiz me on my intentions with her son and, who knows, maybe my luck will turn and she'll actually like me and show me a kind and gentle side to her nature.

I wish I'd brought some cakes or biscuits as a gesture of goodwill. Or flowers. I've been so scatty lately, I didn't even think. My mother would be horrified at my lack of good manners.

'*Efcharistó.* Thank you.' I hold up the cup. 'It's very kind of you.'

'Yes, yes. Now we talk.' She rests her elbows on the table and wrings her hands. 'You need knowledge of Dimitri.'

'Yes, will he be home soon?'

'No, no. He is gone.' Her mouth turns down, making deep lines sprawl all over her face. I've seen the same expression now and then on Dimitri, but without the wrinkles. 'Explain me it. How this happens? You, him. I'm gone for no time and this . . .' She rolls her eyes.

'We're in love.' I hope this statement is still true. It's a bit presumptuous of me after my disappearing act. But even if I hadn't found out I was pregnant, I was going to come back. I made my mind up about that only a week after leaving Kos. My whole body ached for him, and I couldn't keep my mind on any simple task.

'No, we no want this.' She leans in towards me like she's sorry for me, but her thick accent sounds abrupt. 'He no want you. You too mutz late. He is married with Ourania, he goes now, to ask the parents for her to be married with him.'

'He's going to marry Ourania? He's going to marry Ourania?' I sound like a talking doll who's had its string pulled twice in a row.

'*Nai, nai*, yes! Ourania, very beautiful, very good Greek girl. Good Greek girl for my boy. Everyone happy,' she beams.

My stomach tenses to hold back the screaming words that burn in my guts, *I'm not happy!* – because I'm not. I can feel my chest begin to convulse, but I do my best to hide my pain with a simple smile. Everything turns hazy and grey, like a thick layer of grime has settled on what I thought we had.

That's it. That's my answer. We were a lie. Love is a lie and I'm an idiot.

In my mind I rip everything apart, pulling the icons off the walls and kicking over the table, tearing the wallpaper off with my fingernails, screaming until my lungs burn.

But outwardly, I keep perfectly still. If my parents had it in them to be proud of me, I think maybe they would be proud of my composure.

I build a dam in my imagination and do the damage behind my eyes. It's all in my head. It's always been all in my head.

I bring the coffee to my lips and drink it quickly, burning my tongue, numbing another one of my senses with fresh, raw pain.

'I'm happy for him. Thank you for the coffee. It was nice to meet you, Maria.'

I push my chair back to stand but she grabs my hand on the table.

'You are also beautiful girl. You will be good, I know.' She squeezes to reaffirm her words. 'You find a nice boy, I know. Dimitri says you are good girl too, but not for my boy.'

'Thank you.' My voice is suddenly shy, crushed down by the pressure building in my chest.

Maria crosses herself and says something in Greek as her eyes flick up to the ceiling. She pulls a cross from her chest and kisses it. She then continues to attempt to reassure me as she ushers me eagerly from her home.

With the door closed firmly behind me, I don't know what to do with myself for the rest of the day. The ferry back won't be until this afternoon. I'm stuck here with my heart torn from my chest as blood weeps instead of tears.

My feet carry the weight of me, but they struggle with the burden that's sitting on my shoulders. It's like the lava swelling under these stones in the streets has surfaced and now I'm burning with sadness and anger. Tears don't fall to put it out, the way I'd expect.

It all seems too unbelievable.

I will an earthquake of magnitudes I can't imagine to pull everything down on top of me so I won't have to feel anymore. That way, I wouldn't have to deal with all of this alone.

Not far from Dimitri's house is Manolis's door. He would confirm it all for me, whether Dimitri really has run off to be with someone else. We've spent afternoons together with his family on the beach. His son was quite taken with me. Manolis could tell me what happened while I was away, he'd tell me the truth of how one day Dimitri was in love with me and now he's marrying someone else.

I hover outside Manolis's gleaming blue door, dreaming of little Leonidas, and how every time I saw him, he wanted me to carry him about. He'd chat to me in Greek like I understood him, which I'm not sure I would've even if he was speaking in English.

My fist – the one wearing Dimitri's ring – hovers inches from the door. I could never bring myself to take the ring off. I wanted to hate him, but I couldn't.

What if Manolis confirms everything I've already heard? Only then is it real.

I strike the door hard and wait . . . and wait. I tap it again, and once more, because as the French say, never two without three.

Nothing.

'Shit, where the hell is everyone?' I mutter to the dead streets of Mandraki, only for a sleeping cat to open one eye in my direction.

I begin walking the streets towards the beach. I can sit at a taverna and wait. I'm not sure what for, a miracle perhaps?

As soon as I get to the waterfront taverna, the waitress recognises me. Her English is basic at best, although still better than my Greek.

'*Kalimera!* Coffee? Cakes?' She knows me all too well.

'Water, *parakaló* . . . and cake, please.'

She nods, turning on her heel towards the kitchen. She's back within a moment, holding a thick slice of walnut cake and a tall glass of water.

I thrust the cake in my mouth, taking a bite so big I can hardly chew, and crumbs fall like rain over everything. Even though there's no one else here yet, I cover my mouth with my hand to hide yet another mistake.

The events of this morning churn in my mind along with the cake in my mouth.

Even if I do decide to find Dimitri and tell him I'm pregnant, and his mother has in fact been lying to me, what are the chances he'll pick me and not her? And even if he did, by some miracle, tell me he loved me and wanted this child, there's no way I want Maria to be a big part of this baby's life if she's lied to me.

He wouldn't pick me. My own parents wouldn't pick me. They always knew I'd get everything wrong. They've always been right about me. I don't deserve love. That's why they put me on the Pill in the first place, to try to help me. To stop me making mistakes before I'd even started. Not that it helped.

Dimitri said to me a real man looks after his mother. Something like that. Which is true, I guess, but I've already left one set of controlling parents, I don't want to step right into another overbearing relationship. I might be a mess, but my baby won't be. I'll make sure they're loved and looked after.

It's only now that I can see it clearly. It doesn't matter whether someone is trying to control your life out of love or because they want to mould you into something more desirable or any other strange reason. It's still ugly. It still lacks the empathy of acceptance, and I may not really know what love feels like . . . I thought I did, but . . . I don't know. It doesn't matter. My child will know how it feels to be loved, because that's all I have to give them.

I might have been nervous coming here, but underneath it all, I was pretty confident that what we had was rare and special. It was to me. I'm such an idiot. I hate that my parents are right about me.

I swallow the lump of cake I've been chewing. It travels slowly down my gullet like a sinking stone. Almost in response, my diaphragm jolts like a hiccup. Only it's not a hiccup, it's the suppressed cry that's desperately clawing its way out. Like I've swallowed my love for Dimitri whole instead of the cake, and now it's desperately trying to escape. But just like me, it's trapped.

I'm trapped with a baby. Nothing can be what it was, because either he didn't really love me or his mother is as controlling as mine.

There's no happy ending for me here, not one I can see.

Sobs bubble up like warm water off the coast at bubble beach. Only these bubbles burn like boiling water, scolding me from the inside out.

How did I so easily let this happen? How could I have fallen for someone and ruined my life in a matter of months?

I push another chunk of cake into my mouth. It doesn't feel right, not since burning my mouth on Dimitri's mother's coffee. Or maybe it's not that. Maybe it's that nothing will ever feel right again.

I'm alone.

In six months, I'll be a mother. Something I never intended to be.

I guess at least I won't be alone anymore.

Chapter 34

Mia 2025

'Although I hated what Maria told me, ultimately I was grateful. She fixed the decision in my mind. She had stopped me from either humiliating myself right to Dimitri's face or worse, starting living here only to discover she was worse than my parents. Only here, there would be no place to hide from her. I didn't want that for you.' Mum vibrates in an aggressive shudder.

'How much have you spoken to Dimitri about what happened back then?' My skin itches with anger at my grandmother, because, if my father can be believed, that cow *was* lying to my mum. And no matter what Mum thinks, I know how strong she is, and if she and Dimitri wanted to make it work, they could've.

'We spoke a little . . . not much . . . we had other things to discuss.' Mum tilts her mug back to get the last dregs of coffee.

'I think you need to tell him everything you just told me. All of it.'

'What would be the point now? It's in the past. What matters now is the future. Your future. I know Dimitri wants to get to know you – do you want to get to know him? It might be nice to have a parent that isn't as scatty as me.'

'You're not scatty.'

Mum raises an eyebrow as she places down her mug.

'OK, maybe sometimes.'

'Well, Dimitri isn't. In fact, he has a rather beautiful calming effect on people. Or, at least, he used to. It's where you get it from.'

'He still does,' I confirm.

Mum's other eyebrow shoots up to meet the first.

'He chased me down last night. We talked, he was the one who said I should come back here and talk to you. Which I knew I'd have to eventually, as you are the holder of the lies and keeper of information. But without him talking to me last night, I don't know that I'd have come back quite so quickly. Maybe at all.'

'I need you to forgive me. Maybe not today or tomorrow, but please understand that this is the only time I made a big decision about your life without asking you first. It's been a weight on my soul from before you were even born, but I truly felt like there was no other way. I've never been that mum to tell you what you should or shouldn't do. I've been next to you while you discover this brilliant world of ours, but I've only ever been the guide. You know I've never pushed you in a direction. I've always left that up to you. Other than this . . . I guess if I'm honest, I was protecting myself as much as I was protecting you.'

'So what's changed? Why decide now is the time to drop this on me? Why not when I turned eighteen or twenty-one?'

'OK, when was it a good time? When you turned eighteen and you were stressing out about going off to uni, or when you turned twenty-one? Perhaps I could've announced it at your graduation? Nothing felt right. The more time went on, the more difficult it was. It's difficult to tell someone the truth the more you hold on to it. It's like holding on to a live wire and my hand locked in place and I couldn't let go. I was trapped in it.'

'That's all well and good, but you took me off to Crete to see where you met my dad. What was that all about? You must've been laughing so hard I'm amazed you managed to come up for air.'

'I was never laughing about this.' Mum's voice is as dark as a thunder cloud, and however much she's hurt me by all this, I know she's not lying now.

'What was that all about then? Letting me humiliate myself.'

'You pushed for that. You wanted to go.'

'You could've told the truth then?'

'I didn't want to hurt you. I didn't want to lose you.'

'But you're OK with losing me now?'

'No, I—'

Mum looks down at her hands then out across the sea and back towards Kos, before briefly shrugging. 'There have been a lot of changes lately. I guess it got me thinking about the past.'

Her words aren't enough. I don't think there's anything she could say that would ever be enough. Equally, I've never been in a situation like she was. I know she didn't do this to hurt me, but it's like she's hit me with her car, and even though she didn't do it on purpose that doesn't stop me needing a trip to hospital.

Sadly, no hospital can give me back the time I've lost or fix the pain in my chest.

'I cannot begin to explain the burning anger I feel that you've left it this long.'

Somewhere back in the apartment, a phone starts to buzz.

'Not mine.' Mum shakes her head. 'Must be yours. Mine's in my pocket.'

I jump to my feet to run towards the sound before scrambling on the bed to look for it, only to watch as Leonidas's name goes to unanswered.

'Damn,' I whisper as I pick up my phone.

I haven't told Mum about Leonidas yet. Not properly. I'm not even sure I want to now. She only knows he was the one to make me miss the boat.

'Was it Leonidas?' Mum calls from the balcony.

I roll my eyes. 'Maybe. Wait, I'm sure I didn't tell you his name.'

'You know, I knew him when he was a toddler. He was a cute kid back then.'

My mouth drops open. Not that Mum can see it. My back's to her, and I'm glad it is. In my mixed-up emotional state I'm weirdly irritated she knew him first, even if it was as a child, and not the man I know. Not that I *know* him.

The man I've met. Briefly. I don't *know* him. It turns out I barely know my mum.

I *should've* known Leonidas as a child. Another thing she has taken from me.

The phone begins to vibrate in my hand and Leonidas's name appears back on the screen.

I want to answer it, but I have no idea what to say. I don't want to lie.

'Just answer it. You know you want to,' Mum calls out.

I grit my teeth, but I do as she says and swipe to answer.

'Hey.' I begin to walk to the bathroom to hide from any possible further input Mum might decide to bestow on me.

'*Kalimera*, Mia. Did you sleep well?'

'Erm . . . No. Not really. Have you spoken to Dimitri?'

'No, why? Are you still worrying about him? I'm sure he is fine.'

'No, it's – well, I think we need to talk. Me and you. Soon. What are your plans for today?'

'I am free now?'

'Sounds perfect.'

'I will come up and get you—'

'No. It's OK. I'll meet you at the bottom of the stairs.'

'I will see you in ten minutes. *Antío*.'

'Bye.'

I hang up the phone and press it to my chest.

I need to process everything away from my mum, away from Dimitri.

Right now, my skin doesn't feel like my own, like it's been switched out for the shell of a waxwork, modelled on me, but it's not me. Everything's off.

I make my way back towards the balcony. Mum doesn't turn to face me. Her gaze remains fixed on an incoming ferry of people.

'I know,' she begins, 'you need to talk to someone that isn't me. If Leonidas is half as sweet as he was as a boy, then he's a good pick. Hopefully his English has improved since then though . . . or you've managed to learn Greek overnight.'

My arms lock over my chest. 'I hate when you do that.'

'Yep, I know you do. But sadly, I know you better than you know you, so I knew what was going to happen before you even answered his call.' She turns to look up at me with half a smile. 'Be safe and call me when you want me. Shall I see if we can have this room another night?'

'Yes. No. I don't know.'

'I'll try to book it. That way, at least we have options.'

I frown. 'Stop being the sensible one. It's unnatural.'

'I love you, Sweetpea. Please know that I did this to protect you, not to hurt you. I'm not saying I got it right. But I did what I could with the information I had.'

'I know. It doesn't make me feel any better right now, but maybe one day it will. Annoyingly, love you too.'

Mum stretches out a hand towards me, the one with the ring on. I cock my head, looking at the first signs of ageing on her hand before slipping mine into hers. I run my thumb over the aquamarine.

'He got you that, didn't he?'

I twist the circle of gold around my mum's finger. Her hand flinches slightly to resist the motion but she stays with it stretched towards me, never pulling away completely.

She licks her lips. 'Yeah.'

'You took it off in case you bumped into him, didn't you? So he didn't know you've been wearing it since forever.'

'Yep.'

I exhale hard, because there are times you realise that your parents are just people.

I worked this out back in primary school, because we were always late and she was always getting me to help with the washing and daily life. Other mums seemed too good to be true, turning up on time with their fair-haired daughters with perfect bunches. My wild curls were brushed into frizz, however hard Mum tried to make it look pretty. I knew she was human, and I loved her for it all the same. I always will, even when she does things I hate. I know she's always got her reasons.

'When did you put it back on?'

'Ironically, about an hour or two before he found me on the beach. Typical.' She rolls her eyes.

The corner of my mouth tenses with the desire to smile at her, but for now I'm not ready to gift her that.

'Bye, Mum.'

I walk back through the glass balcony door, grab my handbag and head towards Leonidas. I can't believe she was so *in love* with Dimitri all these years that she never took off the ring he gave her, yet still didn't tell me about him.

My hand locks on the door handle. She needs to know his truth, and not just her own.

I turn my head so she can hear me from out on the balcony.

'You should go and talk to Dimitri, about the past.'

'Maybe,' she breathes.

'For me.' I leave before she can answer, shutting the front door on anything else she has to say.

I've learnt over the years that putting a physical barrier between me and Mum is often a good way to win a discussion, particularly ones that may never resolve any other way.

I close my eyes and snatch a breath. I wonder how this discussion can possibly resolve. It's not like we can all start playing happy families now, can we?

Chapter 35

Mia 2025

I relay everything I know to Leonidas as we sit on a black pebble beach facing the sea. The stones are already hot to the touch from the morning sun.

The only good thing about this process of telling him everything I've found out since we last saw each other is watching his face morph from one expression to the next with each new layer of information. One minute his thick eyebrows are sky high and the next they're almost on his cheekbones with a frown.

When I'm done, he says, 'I knew your mother? I don't remember her. This is very strange.'

'Everything I've just said, and that's what you have to say,' I laugh. 'I'm half Greek and she's known this whole time and never even bothered to tell me that much of the story.'

I pick up a smooth black pebble and bounce it from one hand to the other before throwing it into the sea with a satisfying plop.

Through the clarity of the water, I can watch it sink downwards. It's the same way my heart feels knowing I've missed way over two decades of getting to know my father.

'Did you know my grandmother? Maria?' I move uncomfortably on the rocks, twisting to look at his gleaming eyes again.

'I did.'

'What was she like?'

'She was a force of nature. Very, very proud to be Greek, even more than my own mother. And her house was even cleaner than my *yiayia*'s, which is impossible. I remember her always cleaning her step and her windows twice as much as anyone. Maria had strong hands. I remember how she would pinch my cheek.' Leonidas sucks in air through his teeth and rubs his stubbled face at the memory. 'My *baba* would say her husband died for some peace.' Leonidas quietly snorts a laugh, then looks at me with a sudden expression of horror.

His entire face changes, his mouth drops and his eyes widen. 'I'm sure that is not true. It was a joke. She was a good woman. She loved her family very much. He died because he worked too hard with his farms.'

'It's OK. It's interesting.' I pick up another stone to feel the weight and heat of something other than the pressure in my chest. Every detail feels overwhelming in a way I never thought it would or could. She's a woman I never met and never will meet. What difference does it make that we are related?

It shouldn't make any difference, other than it does.

Maybe it's vanity, but something inside me wants as much information about the people that made me as I can possibly get.

I bounce the stone rhythmically in my hand. The consistent melodic thud sound against the shh of the sea soothes me a little.

'I really hope Mum goes to talk to Dimitri. I'm worried about how she'll react when she realises she was lied to by Maria.'

We fall into a silence and my hands still as the sea breeze rolls over my curls, moving them around my shoulders.

The peaceful shush of the waves fills the void while we slip into our own thoughts.

I wonder whether Mum will be there when I get back, or if she'll have done as I asked and gone to speak to Dimitri. It's so strange to think that they might both still like each other after all these years.

None of this is Mum's fault. Not really. I know her well enough to know that.

She came here to make a family with Dimitri, but my grandmother lied and stole the opportunity from her. That doesn't stop the stinging sensation every time I think about what could've been. Or the fact she could've told me when I became an adult. Uni or not, I'd have wanted to know.

'I'm sorry to unload all this on you.' I break back out of my bubble of thoughts. 'I'm going to assume this isn't what you expected me to tell you today.'

'No. It's not.' He laughs over the words. 'I thought *I* would be doing the talking.' Leonidas shifts his weight, making stones roll around him. 'I was going to ask if you would sing with me at Skala in Kardamena? It is right next to the sea. There is a gig in a couple of days . . .'

'That's short notice.'

'I thought you sing at weddings? You must know a thousand songs.'

A glowing energy shoots through me at the thought of how many songs I could sing without even a prompt from a band. 'More than that.'

'Well, I only want you to learn one.' He holds up his index finger and briefly bites his lower lip. His eyes fix on mine like they won't shift unless I say yes. 'Do you agree?' he urges.

It would be nice to have something else to think about other than the tangled web of family drama I've got caught up in. Singing and performing is my happy place, after all. Getting to know

Leonidas a little more and learning a quick song would be the perfect distraction.

I nod. 'OK. Sounds good.'

'Yes?' He holds out a hand for me to shake.

'Yes.'

Dropping the stone I've been clinging to, I take his hand. The electricity from last night, from before my life blew up, tingles through my fingers.

He draws my hand towards him, holds it to his chest and leans a little closer to my ear.

'Now all we have to do is write it.' A huge smile sneaks its way over his lips. 'The rest of the songs you can pick from the ones you know.'

'What?' I tug on his hand in mock irritation at his trick.

'It's OK, it's OK. We will write it together. I think it'll be good for you to get away from your parents. It will give them some time to work things out between them and—' He stops himself. He's still holding my hand to his chest, and as he looks down at the knot of our fingers, it's like we are both suddenly aware of it.

'And?'

The rhythm of his breathing shifts. I can sense when a beat changes around me, like his music has gone from something like a relaxed classical number to the salsa.

He keeps his eyes on our hands. 'And time for us to get to know each other.'

A tickle of lust and excitement rolls over my skin, but chasing right after it is a frisson of fear.

My mother was here once before, maybe sitting on these same stones, falling for the charm of a different Greek man. There's no way I want my story to end like hers. But I can't help myself, I want to see where Leonidas can take me.

Chapter 36

Sara 2025

'Have you told her yet?' Dimitri walks through the external door holding two coffees and more cake on a tray. He squints, turning his face as the sun catches him like a slap to the cheek.

He begins to organise everything neatly on the table on the sweeping balcony.

'That you're her father? Yes. You knew that? She told me you had a rather interesting conversation last night after you chased her down, and I've already seen you this morning . . . ? Perhaps you two had a chat about unicorns or dragons, or something else instantly forgettable?'

'That's not what I meant.' He clicks his tongue.

'I know what you meant, and I've already told you – I will, but I want her to get to know you for a few days first, to enjoy her time here. To maybe enjoy some time with me . . . if she can ever forgive me,' I mutter into today's second cup of very intense coffee. 'It's the way she's looking at me that hurts, you know? She's actually been quite good about it all. I don't know why I say *actually*, like it's a surprise. She's been good about everything, always. I don't know how she does it.'

'If I were to take a *wild guess*' – Dimitri puts on his best English accent for *wild guess* – 'it's because she has always had the support of her loving mother.'

Heat rises up to my cheeks. Normally I'd jump in with something sarcastic and silly, but I know how Dimitri always sees through all that, and how much he hated me mocking myself too much.

'I think it's probably that she inherited it from her father.'

He doesn't say anything in return. It must be such a strange time for him, and just like his daughter, he's taking it exceptionally well.

I press my coffee to my lips, because apparently this is my life now, sitting on balconies, drinking coffee and eating cake for half the day. If only life was as beautifully simple as it looks from the outside.

Dimitri's terrace-cum-balcony is rather charming. It's stuffed with potted plants filled with mint, thyme and chives with purple pom-pom flower heads.

It's nothing like it was when his mother was alive, although he does still live in the same home as all those years ago. There's only one icon per room now, or so he told me with a laugh.

How different things could've been with Mia dancing between plant pots instead of the ugly uneven concrete square we had next to our concrete shed in our first 'garden'. Our view was on to a broken fence that the council refused to fix. It was never safe for her to be out there alone.

Here, in Mandraki, I'd have felt safe for her to run along the streets with Leonidas as her guide as soon as she could toddle, with clean sea air filling her lungs instead of Tim next door smoking thirty a day not far from the broken fence.

Even inside our home was dreadful. Black mould edged the bottoms of the walls like we were growing a new type of skirting board. I used to cry at night, worrying about what it might do to her tiny lungs.

I did the best I could, saving our benefits and working as an Avon lady to make some money on the side while I figured things out. I'd push the pram around and knock on doors. Mia's cute face was normally enough to get at least the grannies to buy something they didn't really need.

It all could've been so different.

'Mia thinks we should talk over the past. Relive all the mistakes and make sure we are all very clear on the details.'

Dimitri folds his arms over his chest, waiting for more. His biceps still have their way of distracting me – although they're not quite as prominent as they were back then, he has kept well, like time has bypassed him.

'I was hoping it was your turn to talk? She seemed to think you had a different take on things.'

For a moment Dimitri is completely still, like he's been touched with a magic wand and turned to stone. Mia and I used to love playing that game when she was little.

'I said some things to Mia. Told her some of *my* truth. You know, I was thinking about when you came here to find me. It must have been when I was looking for you in Crete.'

'You came to Crete for me?'

'And you came here for me.'

My pulse quickens at the realisation that Mia was right, he did love me, he did look for me, but also that his mother was so hell-bent on keeping me out of his life, she was willing to tell a bare-faced lie about it. No wonder she kept crossing herself – she was probably asking for forgiveness from her Lord and Saviour.

'When I came back, I was very broken. My mother made me go to Kos to apologise to Ourania for my rudeness while she stayed with us. Her family treated me well and I was so angry at you for leaving. By the time I returned, I returned with her. All these years and I thought you left for nothing.'

'I did. Well, I was made to leave by work, in actual fact. Leaving wasn't my choice.'

'Yes, Tina was very happy to share the news that you were gone. At first I thought she was joking. She was never very funny.'

I've thought about it a lot, over the years. If my job hadn't moved me to Crete, I'd have stayed in Kos and maybe he would've made it right. But it wasn't meant to be.

Back then wasn't like today – Dimitri didn't have a mobile phone or social media. I couldn't pick up the phone and call him or tell him I was coming to visit before arriving. If he had a landline, I didn't have the number.

'I just can't believe your mother lied to me. Or to you.'

'You know, Sara, there are many reasons for mothers to hide things from their children when they think it is the right thing to do.' Dimitri purses his lips. 'My mother was wrong not to tell me you had come here, and worse to lie to you. But you were wrong to keep me from Mia. You seem to keep many things from her . . .' Dimitri shifts his weight, ready to pass on his thoughts on things I don't need opinions on. 'I think you should tell her—'

'I don't need you to tell me about my relationship with my daughter, thank you. I'm here for the sole purpose of you forming your own relationship with her, not for you to cast opinions on the one I have.'

'And I can help you with her. I can help you—'

'I don't need help. I don't need saving, Dimitri. I didn't need your help to bring up my daughter. You've met her, she's incredible. Kind, smart, talented. I was brought up being given everything I wanted but nothing I needed. Which made me independent. Resilient. I was twenty when I had her, and I did it all. All of it.'

'*Our* daughter,' he confirms quietly and calmly. 'She was never just yours. She is half me. I know I am a man, and some men have taken power from women's hands since Earth began. But not me. None of this was my fault. I did not pick my mother, and I didn't know what she did. I searched Crete for you and if I had more money, I would've come to England to search forever. But you never even told me where in England you are from. I had nowhere to start. I was so angry at you . . .' His soft voice trails off as he shakes his head.

I want to say something flippant or funny to fill the void. My stomach feels like it's been sliced in two and the contents should fill the void instead.

'I'm sorry.' I pinch the bridge of my nose in an attempt to hold back the tears threatening to fall.

'I don't like it. I will never like the decision you made.' Dimitri shakes his head gently and he chews on his lip for a moment. 'But I knew you then, and I understand why you did what you did.' Dimitri wraps his fingers around my arm. 'I am sorry my mother did this, I'm sorry I didn't get to Crete sooner, I'm sorry I didn't take you to my mother and tell her I was in love . . . I'm sorry.'

Dimitri's hand slips down my arm and slides into my palm. 'I'm here for you now, even if you don't need me.'

Our eyes meet and I swim in the luxury of being near him again. In the beauty of his dark, umber eyes. Every part of me wants to bring my lips to his, but I can't.

The pain of him goes beyond bone deep. It's cellular in a way I can't explain and haven't let myself believe until seeing him again.

I thought I'd be OK, but I'm not.

I slip my fingers free and gift myself the luxury of briefly cupping his cheek.

'Thank you.'

The pain is so urgent and overpowering, it strangles my ability to cry. I choke on it.

I can only pray that if a tear does escape, it'll evaporate in the sun before it can be noticed.

Not that anything has ever got past Dimitri. It's why I knew I'd have to tell him the truth before telling Mia.

Chapter 37

Sara 2025

Since becoming a mother, I've known so much about my daughter before she's worked it out, it's crazy. I could look at her situations and know how they would end. The boys she'd let break her heart, the parties she would get drunk at, the friends she'd spend time with because she felt sorry for them . . .

Right now, I know she's the other side of the door not wanting to come in because she doesn't know whether I'm back or not and she's planning what she wants to say to me.

I have no idea how my own mother could be so far away from this, from me. I guess she truly never cared. There was no instinct. No connection. No interest.

'Come in,' I call through the door in a silly, high-pitched voice, even though she hasn't knocked. I add in a stage whisper, 'People will think you're a psychopath hanging out there on your own.'

Mia growls and the sound of her hand striking the door echoes into the room.

'Maybe I'm not on my own.'

She is. I know she is. And not just because of her lonely shuffling feet, but because she's too particular. Mia enjoys planning ahead. Each decision she makes that she deems important is done with profound forethought. She'll probably come in and request I meet Leonidas, who I've already met, and maybe suggest we meet up with Dimitri at the same time.

Which is why I pre-warned Dimitri of the idea when I left his place after another slice of cake. I told him he needs to either get in some food or decide where he's taking us for dinner.

His gentle laughter at my demands filled me up and split me with cracks from the pressure.

Mia comes through the hotel room door at long last, doing her best to make it look like she's just arrived even though we both know that's not the case. Her eyes drag over me where I lie on the bed.

The chairs outside at Dimitri's were so uncomfortable, and I slept so badly last night, I thought I should lie down and get some rest.

'Did you manage to keep the room for one more night?'

'Yes.'

'Have you left the hotel at all since I went out?'

'No. Instead, I thought I would waste the last half of our holiday sitting in an air-conditioned box, moaning about the heat. That's very much my personality.' I throw her a delightful grin.

As usual she completely ignores me, knowing I'm being silly. I remember how, at three years old, she would call me Silly-Mummy as much or more than she called me Mummy.

'Did you go to see Dimitri?'

'Maybe. Or maybe I—'

'Mum, please can you take this seriously? I don't need a skit right now.'

'Fine, but you're asking me to be someone I'm not and I hope you can handle the boring ramifications of that.'

'When you forget yourself—'

'You want me to forget myself?'

'When you forget yourself,' she repeats with a principal-stern quality, 'you're actually a lot more normal than you think.' Mia flops down on to the bed next to me, making the springs creak. 'So, what did he say?'

There's a higher tone to her voice. A knowing tone. A tone she uses when she's trying to lead this horse to water and hoping I'll drink, all while thinking I might not know exactly what she's hoping for. Or perhaps she wants to come out and say something but would rather I said it instead.

'Yeah. Turns out one of your grandmothers cares so much about her kids she would lie to stop them marrying someone she deemed not good enough, and your other grandmother wouldn't bother lying for her kid even if it would get them out of trouble with the police at fifteen . . . Probably, of course – I have no evidence for that, other than that time I might have done something I shouldn't and ran all the way home and when the policewoman knocked Mum could've said I was in the whole time, but she didn't . . . Anyway, now you can breathe again because we've cleared up the past, and there is still absolutely no way to change it. Not unless you and Leonidas were discussing time-travel techniques while topping up that tan of yours?'

'Back up, do I know that police story?'

'Probably. I didn't go to prison, but I think if I had, your grandparents would've disowned me. Shame I didn't on that front. Honestly, it was nothing, I'd been drinking on a bench with some friends and dropped a bottle when I saw the cops . . . I got a telling-off, that's all. It was the nineties, babe.'

Mia exhales like I'm very hard work. I've always enjoyed winding her up in this way.

If I burnt the toast or told a crazy story about her toys waking up while she was asleep, it would all get the same Silly-Mummy coupled with a gentle head shake, occasionally an eye-roll and often the very same tired exhale. I really do miss that.

My hand glides along the cotton sheet and over to hers. I still remember how it was to hold her hand when she was small. How it would fit in the palm of mine, or when she would take her pudgy little fingers and press them into my cheeks and tell me she hoped she looked like me one day, only for me to explain she will always be better than me.

Emotions swell in my chest. Maybe Dimitri is right, maybe I shouldn't wait to tell her the real reason we're here. Maybe I should explain the whole picture now.

'Did he say anything else?'

'Like what?'

'I don't know, like how he felt about you?'

I narrow my eyes on her. 'He told me he followed me to Crete to find me, but I was off looking for him. Hardcore Shakespeare tragedy stuff.'

'The thing I can't get over, more than not telling me, is not telling him. Even if you didn't want to be together, he could've visited. No matter how I frame it, you were being selfish.'

Taking in Mia's words is like inhaling asbestos. It's probably how she feels too when I talk. It's like my lungs are getting riddled with untold damage at the hurt I've caused, and she has to live with the same damage too.

'Maybe I was. But I didn't see it that way. No. I guess that's not totally true. If he wasn't with that woman he married—'

'Ourania.'

'Yeah, Ourania . . . If he wasn't really with *her*, I wouldn't be able to keep myself from him and I'd be opening up the floodgates to a mother-in-law I couldn't handle. And if he *was* with Ourania . . . I couldn't watch that. Being on the outside watching him having a family would've killed me and I didn't want you to be left out. I know I'm not perfect, but we need to live with this now. It's that, or you never want to speak to me again? I'd understand, but please don't—'

'Mum, you've really hurt me, but I want to get past this. I want a relationship with both my parents. I'll never truly understand why you did it. It's not what I'd do in the same situation—'

'Please don't ever get into the same situation.'

'I won't, but if I did, I'd like to think I'd handle it better than you. I know half the reason for that is you, and not DNA, but upbringing. We're all a product of experience as well as DNA. My ability to handle all this is at least partly because you gave me so much stability and love.'

'You're a stronger person than me and that's not all upbringing. You're half him. But I'm more than happy to take credit for it.'

'It's true though,' Mia whispers to herself more than to me. 'I'm sorry your upbringing screwed you up so much at that age. I am proud of how far you've come.'

'I'm proud of me too. Look how awesome my daughter is. Clearly, I'm actually the best mum in the world. So how about this? We blame all my past mistakes, and possibly all my future ones, on Grandma and Grandpa? Sound fair?'

Mia's lips slide into a reluctant smile.

'Sounds fair to me.'

I might have loved Dimitri, maybe I still do. Probably. There's an indentation in my heart that he left, but what grew from that is the love I have for my girl, and it far surpasses any emotion I've had in my whole life. Parenting is hard and it really isn't for everyone, but I gave birth to my best friend. I'm the luckiest mum alive.

I put my arms out and hope she'll accept an embrace. She moves across the bed and slips into my arms and fits there perfectly, the way she has since she was small. I should've shared her, but I've also loved every moment I've had her to myself.

I do release her, the way every parent has to release their child and hope they can survive and find their own happiness and strength. We watch as everything we love travels off in the world, crossing our fingers they'll find kindness along the way.

'I was thinking. How about a meal with Leonidas and Dimitri tonight? It would be easier to have you and Leonidas there, you know, for some sort of moral support just in case we run out of things to say to each other. It might take the pressure off. It would be nice to do something before going back to Kardamena tomorrow?' Mia tilts her head in question.

'We're going back tomorrow, are we?'

'Yeah, I think so.'

'Maybe we could find a few hours just for us if we do? I don't want to take you away from your dad again, but I miss you.'

Shifting my weight, I swing my legs off the bed and head towards the bathroom.

'I'm sure we can find some time together,' Mia begins, 'but I did accidently agree to write a song and perform it with Leonidas at a place called Skala in a couple of days.'

'Sounds like fun,' I call back as I grope around in my make-up bag. I pop two paracetamol tablets, pick up the bottle of water I've left on the sink and knock them back.

'Mum, you still haven't answered about tonight.'

I turn back to the room and lean on the door frame.

'Dimitri and Leonidas will see us at eight, if that's OK? I told your dad to sort something out and meet us at the bottom of the stairs.'

Mia frowns and slaps a hand down on the bed.

'How do you do that? How did you know what I was going to ask?'

I shrug. 'I'm just perfect, I guess.'

If only I was.

Chapter 38

Sara 2025

'This is Leonidas,' Mia indicates with her palm.

I could tell it was him, he looks a lot like his dad, Manolis, from the slight bump on the bridge of his nose to the curve of his mouth. Manolis was cleaner cut, with neatly shaved hair, where Leonidas has that free-spirited guitarist persona oozing from him.

I grin up at him. 'It's good to see you again. But don't ask me to pick you up, OK? My back isn't what it once was.'

Mia laughs but the smile lingers on her lips and not in her eyes. I don't think it's because she's unhappy. She seems nervous.

I wish I could scoop her up and solve all her problems like I could twenty years ago. Things are so much deeper now. Nothing is as simple as a grazed knee.

Every single one of her fake smiles or nervous nibbles on the corner of her lip is like a match striking against me, and the anxiety I get at her anxiety is like lighter fluid.

She's swallowing more than normal.

She used to get like that before singing in shows at school. During one performance she drank so much water beforehand, saying her throat was too dry, that she had to run off stage halfway through to go to the toilet.

When Leonidas stops spluttering with laughter, looking from Dimitri to me, he asks with a distinct air of disbelief, 'You used to pick me up?'

'Oh yeah.' I begin to walk on, following behind Dimitri. 'Every time you saw me, you'd fly towards me and expect me to carry you around. Then you'd chat away to me in Greek, expecting me to understand you.'

'Wow.' Leonidas rubs his finger under his nose before pushing his hand through his hair and shaking his head. 'This is strange, I'm sorry, I don't remember you.'

'Why would you? What were you, two? Three? We knew each other for a month. I do have a photo of us together, though.'

Leonidas continues to shake his head in disbelief.

I suppose it is strange to fancy a girl and find out you've already met her mum a lifetime ago.

I let him process the information by falling into step with Dimitri, leaving Mia and Leonidas to have a moment walking alone together.

'Where are we off to, Dimitri? Things have changed here in the past twenty or so years. Although Kardamena much more so. I almost didn't recognise it. The heart is still there, that fun-loving soul, but now it's relaxed with age, like all of us, I guess. And you were right, that authentic soul was always there. Still is.'

'I think you brought out philosophy in me.'

'Oh no, that was always in your nature. That's why you do what you do, sharing your love for the energy and soul of Nisyros.'

Dimitri's knuckles briefly brush mine and it's like being sliced by a razor blade. I almost snatch my hand away from his electricity. It hurts too much.

'We are going to my home, I hope that's OK? I am cooking a traditional meze with Leonidas's help.'

'Sounds good.'

I glance over my shoulder and catch a genuine smile flickering across Mia's face. The light shining out of her is more than I've seen in a long time. I can't remember when she last actually *wanted* me to meet someone she likes. To be fair, her career has made it hard for her. Most people she meets are drunk at weddings, or catfish on the end of an app.

I lean my head a little closer to Dimitri's, but carefully so we don't touch. Just enough so I can lower my voice.

'Have you heard the latest news?'

'What news?' He mimics my lowered voice.

'These two are writing a song together and they're going to perform it at Skala the night before we go home.'

'Oh yes, Leonidas was almost blue in his face to share this news. I'm already worrying that I've only just found out I have a daughter, and I might have to speak to my own godson about . . . well, I don't even know. Something. Love, relationships?' Dimitri shoots me a wide-eyed look of terror at the thought of having to give someone the don't-mess-with-my-daughter talk. The one I gave so many times before it became second nature.

'Don't worry, I think they're more clued up than we were.'

Our eyes meet and I catch the golden sunset in his eyes.

If only it were the sunrise instead of the closing act.

'Mum,' Mia's voice carries on the sea breeze, 'if this cat doesn't belong to anyone, I think we should adopt it.' Her voice is barely a squeak.

A grey and white cat rubs around her ankles before moving on to the nearest taverna.

'Very cute, but sadly I don't think you can compete with what people drop on the floor when they're eating.'

'Shame,' she exhales.

My girl is so very beautiful, inside and out. A curl flutters over her face in the gentle breeze and her lavender eyes glimmer in a way that puts mine to shame.

I remember finding her curls a delightful nightmare when she was younger. It's nothing like my straight blonde mane, and I had no idea what to do with it. She was born with a thick mop, and I was bald until I was two. I can still remember how good she was about me trying to force a brush through it. She was so brave. She's always had to be brave.

We all carry on along the stone path. Dimitri and I used to walk hand in hand along these alleyways. Now it hurts just to be near him.

Dimitri swings open his unlocked door and the pungent smell of oregano and garlic whips around us. There's a strong sensation of coming home that floats along with it. That's how it was back then, with his mother away. We treated this place like it was our own, other than not touching her *good towels*, of course.

Since then, I've always seen anywhere Mia is as *home*, rather than one specific place. She is my home. Her smile is the house I do my best to maintain.

'This is such a beautiful home. Thank you so much for inviting us over.' Mia steps forward to keep up with Dimitri, following him round to the kitchen and the same table I sat at when I first came here years ago.

He falters, almost like he's stepped on his own shoelace, then he turns to face Mia with a sense of quiet importance.

'Thank you, that is very kind of you to say, Mia,' Dimitri begins, 'but please know, you will always be welcome in this house.'

A blush crosses Mia's cheeks and her mouth slopes into a shy smile. 'Thanks. Can I help with anything?'

'That is very kind. You can start by telling me what you would like to drink.'

'I'll have whatever you're having.' Her voice is bright and she rocks up and down on her tiptoes.

Leonidas chuckles at her response before his reply. 'Then let me make it.'

'I can't believe you haven't got a new kitchen table,' I cut in, and my fingers trace the smooth edge of the wood that used to occasionally hide under a plastic tablecloth.

'What's wrong with this one?' Dimitri's face crumples as he gestures towards it.

Mia's eyes land on the table then back on me. This must be really strange for her, after always wanting a glimpse into who her father might be. Now the past is right here in front of her.

'It looked old-fashioned back then,' I jibe.

'What is fashion anyway? The chairs hold my weight, the table holds my dinner.'

'Hopefully, a plate holds your dinner.' I tilt my head.

'I don't think you will ever change. I hope not.' A soft smile spreads across Dimitri's face.

There's a moment's silence before Leonidas's hands come together in a light clap. 'I shall make this drink. And Sara, for you?'

'I really *don't* want whatever it is they're having, thanks.' I nod towards Mia and Dimitri.

Mia looks between us all from the corner of her eye, her smile slipping a little.

'I'll have whatever juice there is, thanks, Leonidas.'

'Sara, will you take Mia upstairs, and we will bring the drinks and food soon.'

I nod at Dimitri before turning to Mia. 'This way, kiddo.'

'I'm not a kid,' she growls as we leave the room.

'You're *my* kid.'

'*Our* kid,' Dimitri's voice calls from the kitchen.

His words are enough to bring joy to my heart and hope back to my bones. A hope that hasn't been there in a long time.

I glance at Mià behind me, but she doesn't notice. She's taking in every detail of Dimitri's home. From the photos lining the walls to the wooden staircase and everything in between.

The double doors are already open, revealing the perfect suntrap for evening meals, the view over the muddle of flat white rooftops and out towards the sea. All the herbs are releasing their scents in response to the last warmth of the day, filling the air with fresh thyme and lavender.

'This place is kind of amazing,' Mia states as she touches lavender poking out of a pot, before giving in and dipping down to take a lungful of it.

'Yep.'

I take a seat to one side where there's a concrete bench against a white rendered external wall. It has a thick cushion on it, unlike some of the other chairs that are round the table. Sitting on one of those this morning was enough to give me backache and I really don't want to irritate it further.

Mia looks like something from an advert, her dark hair plaited to one side and a pale-lemon dress I brought with me for her to wear. It's the last of the clean clothes I came with, but I thought it would be important to have something a little special, just in case. She folds her arms, looking out across Mandraki, framed by the white walls of the buildings around her like a real-life Polaroid.

'What was that all about with Dimitri?' Mia doesn't turn to look at me, she keeps her head facing out across the sea of houses.

'What do you mean?'

'You had . . . a moment.'

'We've had many moments. How do you think you came to be?'

'Do you see more moments in your future?'

'No.'

She whips round like I've pulled on her hair. Her eyes narrow with complete precision on mine.

'But you two seem so—'

'*So* what?'

'So . . . something.'

'Very profound. Everything's *something*, just by existing. I had *something*, perhaps a *moment*, with a cat down the street but I wouldn't write home about it.'

Footsteps coming towards us halt the conversation. Thankfully.

Leonidas trots in first with a tray of drinks. He places it on the table, then picks off a tall glass of what I imagine is freshly squeezed orange juice and passes it to me.

'*Yamas*,' he smiles.

For Mia, he takes another tall glass that looks like it's all ice with a splash of water running through it. Knowing Dimitri, it's *koukouzina*. I've tried it before, but it really isn't my sort of drink.

Dimitri has a bigger tray, which he places on a separate table. That table wasn't out earlier when I was here, he's placed it there for the occasion and topped it with one of his mother's lace tablecloths that he told me once were saved for best. There are four small plates piled up with white napkins between, a bowl of fresh salad, some chickpea pies and delicious-looking dips. I know they'll be delicious because I've had them all made by Dimitri before.

I remember him asking me over for a meze and sitting on this very balcony, talking, touching and consuming each other as well as all the wonderful treats he'd prepared for us.

The sun set and we were still out here, enjoying the warm breeze and each other's warm breath. The stars came up and we were still here underneath them.

Dimitri looks across at me and for a moment I wonder whether he's having the same memories as I am. The memories of events that brought us here. The acts that fused us together in the form of Mia.

Leonidas passes Dimitri his drink and raises his own, which looks a lot more like mine, a tall glass of orange. I stand and we all move to the centre of the balcony.

'To family and being together. Mia, I am grateful for this chance to get to know you. Sara, thank you for looking after our daughter and raising her to be as strong as you.' Dimitri's eyes lock with mine.

We hold the moment for a second too long – it's enough to raise my heart to my mouth.

'*Yamas*,' I announce to break the tension, and we all come together to clink glasses.

As we bring our glasses to our mouths, I keep half an eye on Mia. I don't think she's stupid enough to think it could be water.

She takes a sip and her nose wrinkles.

'What do you think? It's *koukouzina*. I put in more ice for you, just in case,' Leonidas confirms.

Poor girl, we were all watching her drink it, waiting for a reaction.

'It's not what I expected. I was expecting ouzo and this isn't that. It smells a bit sour but . . . it's kind of like raki, but sweeter. What's it made of?'

Leonidas opens his mouth to answer but Dimitri is there to provide answers for his daughter. The excitement to do so is written all over him, from the widening of his eyes to using his hands to tell her about fermented grapes and figs, so much so he almost spills some of his own *koukouzina*.

I turn and head back to the comfort of the cushions.

As I sit, Leonidas places himself down next to me.

'It is so strange that you know me,' he begins.

'*Knew* you. I knew you as a very small child. I'm yet to discover the man you have become. But I always liked your father. And your mother, but Manolis spoke to me more as he was always more confident with his English than your mum, so we communicated more. How is your mother?'

'Good, thank you. I explained who you are. She was . . . shocked. Very shocked.'

'She knows Mia is Dimitri's daughter?'

'Yes, I hope it was all right I told her?' Leonidas shuffles on the cushion and grips his glass with both hands.

'It's not up to me anymore. It's up to them.' I nod towards the father and daughter getting to know each other, clutching at their drinks and sharing in their similar tastes.

I wish I'd done this twenty years ago, but everything is easy in hindsight.

Chapter 39

Mia 2025

This is the first time I've been alone with Dimitri since the night we found out the truth.

I follow him carefully down the uneven stairs, past all the religious paraphernalia and the photos of people I've never met and through to the kitchen. I've never felt more concerned about dropping a plate in my life. Usually when we've visited Greece, I've secretly been hoping for dropping plates so I could shout *opa!*

This doesn't feel like an *opa!* moment. It feels more like a nervous breakdown sort of moment.

'Are you very religious?' I ask as I put down the plates.

As soon as the words fall from my mouth, I hear them. There's a strange and accidently judgemental tone that doesn't belong and was entirely unintended. Of all the questions that had been running through my head, of all the things I could've said after offering to help carry down the dirty plates, why did it have to be that?

Dimitri turns to face me with a soft smile on his face. I can't help but study his features, trying to find my own somewhere in there, but I don't. Maybe there's something other than the dark hair, but nothing obvious to me.

'You are very much like your mother, aren't you?'

I don't know how to react to the question, but he doesn't give me a chance to before continuing.

'My mother and father, your grandparents, were always at the church, every Sunday, saying prayers, listening to the words of God. There was a time I would be there with them for hours of the day, listening. The words stopped making sense to me. I walk in sometimes, but not how I used to. It's because of the icons? That's why you asked me?'

Dimitri turns back towards the sink, a very light smile still adorning his lips. He puts in the plug and turns on the tap. The creaking of the pipes and water crashing against the plates forms the background music of our conversation.

'Yes, there's rather a lot.'

'Many less than there were. I feel I must keep some, to honour my parents. Having them looking over me is a reminder of them and their values. Your mother is right though, I should probably change a few things. It didn't seem worth it, living here alone.'

Dimitri twists the tap off now the sink is full, but he may as well have twisted a knife in my stomach. He's been here, alone, and I've been out there with my mum, plodding along thinking that by magic one day I would maybe find out something interesting about my father, convinced he wouldn't be interested anyway, he was a sperm donor at best. But that wasn't the case. It was never the case.

The slow drip of the tap hits my ears like needles.

'I'm so sorry.' The words sting the back of my throat.

'Why are you sorry?' Dimitri reaches out his hand like he might touch my arm but then retreats at the last second, the way he did before.

'Because you were here, alone, and I didn't know you were here.' I can hear my voice breaking in time with my heart.

I might forgive my mum on one level, because she was young and she'd been lied to and thought she was doing the right thing . . . but there'll always be a level lower, darker and more painful, that I'm constantly trying to rise above.

'I might have lived alone, but not always. And I have many friends too. My life isn't as sad as it sounds, please don't feel sorry for me. We are beginning *here*.' He points both index fingers to the tiled floor. 'Both of us, one step at a time. I hope one day you will see me as your *baba*, dad, something like this, but for now, having you here in my home is a dream. I can't believe how lucky I am to have you as a daughter.'

A flutter of embarrassment dances inside me, because it's tricky to take a compliment at the best of times, but this is a compliment I've only ever received from one other person in the world. It's been said to me so often that I'm almost deaf to it now from Mum, but from him it's something else. Something fresh and new and confusing.

I wonder whether it will soon be natural to hear from Dimitri, the perfect stranger in a kitchen I've never been in, on an island I only vaguely knew about.

Maybe this kitchen will become a familiar, comforting place. Maybe hearing his pride will be normal.

I hope so.

'I guess we should head back upstairs, otherwise they'll think we've done all the washing-up instead of just leaving it to soak,' I smile.

I'm feeling too vulnerable, like I'm on stage singing without knowing the words.

Dimitri nods and indicates for me to go ahead of him and back towards the icons and the narrow staircase.

I climb each step, beneath the eyes of the icons that have been here probably since before my mum arrived on the scene.

They've seen my mum pass them, now me. They represent my grandparents' choices, who they were. It's too much to comprehend.

I'm half Greek.

I know that now. It's a fact.

It runs through me, following back for generations. I wonder how many, how many generations have lived here on Nisyros. I'd like to sit down over a coffee and ask Dimitri a thousand questions on a day when it's just us.

I really want to come back here and discover who I am . . . who I could've been.

Not that I would change what I have with my mum, but there's always going to be a part of me saying *what if*, from the moment I found out until the day I die. What if my one life had been spent with two parents on a small Greek island instead of on a busy estate surrounded by strangers.

As I round the top step, I can hear my mum laughing at something Leonidas has said to her, followed by the words, 'It sounds like you're already getting to know my daughter rather well.'

They both look over to us and I raise an eyebrow, but I rise to the statement. I don't say a word about it.

'Leonidas, you said you had your guitar here? Can you play for us?' I ask.

He shrugs, like he wants to be cool about it, but there's something about the way his mouth twists to one side as he stands that says he is anything but nonchalant.

'I *can*, but . . . do you *want* me to?' He pushes up one of his shirtsleeves that's come loose from where he had folded it. He slides the fabric back over his olive skin before folding his arms.

I tilt my head towards my shoulder and take a moment to consider whether to release a bout of sarcasm, flatly say *no thank you*, or whether to be honest.

I decide on honesty. 'I do, yes please.'

'Then I will.'

As Leonidas passes me, his hand brushes mine and his little finger almost gets left behind trying to stay in contact with me.

There's so much here I want to explore, and although I don't want to leave Mum behind, she left Dimitri behind.

Every action has a consequence, and I'm starting to be swept down a path that was laid out before I was even born.

Chapter 40

Sara 2025

Music swells through the air as Leonidas fingerpicks his guitar alongside Mia's rich voice. Even simply humming out ideas is a treat for anyone who hears her.

She's too good to be wedding singing. I wish she had more confidence to break the mould. But security gives her peace, and I know how important peace can be.

Mia and Leonidas look relaxed and are working perfectly in tune with each other. Both nodding and smiling before scribbling things down in notebooks.

'Did we look at each other like that?' Dimitri indicates with his glass towards the two love birds before placing it on the table.

They must think they're doing really well to cover their intense desire, but they're failing miserably.

'According to Mia, we still do.' I sit forward, resting my forearms on my knees.

About an hour ago, Dimitri suggested we sit just inside the balcony doors in his living room, on the sofa. I think he was getting fed up with me fidgeting with discomfort outside.

'Really?' He leans forward too and fixes his attention on me instead of our daughter.

'She said we had *a moment*. She asked me if there would be more *moments*.'

'Don't all children want their parents to be happy and together?'

'I couldn't care less about mine. I can't imagine them separating would bother me particularly.'

'Now we have a daughter together, maybe I can meet them?'

'I like you too much to punish you like that.'

With Dimitri's left hand crossed over his right arm, his fingers relax not far from my own. In return, my fingers twitch at the notion of taking his hand in mine.

But I can't.

Tonight has been more than I could ever have hoped for already. Rich in laughter and hope for the future. I wanted Mia to open her heart to Dimitri and forgive me for not telling her about him sooner, and she has.

Mia is better than me at every turn. I don't know what I ever did to deserve her as a daughter. Even knowing her would be enough to improve the worst possible person. Not that I'm at all biased.

'Why did you call our daughter Mia Zoí?'

'Well, Mia was in part to honour your mother. I thought you would like that. You clearly loved her enough to put her before us, so I figured,' I shrug, 'she must be a mother worth naming our daughter after in a small way, even if she wasn't good to me.'

'She was a woman who would do anything she thought would help her family, even lie. It was good if she was on your side . . . If you had told her about the baby, you would have been married to me in less than a week, and she would have organised a big traditional wedding, like it or not. She thought she was doing the right thing, I know it.' There's a pause. Dimitri looks off into the distance as though he might be trying to conjure his mother before us.

He exhales through his nose and turns back to me. 'And the Zoí?'

I don't want to admit the next part, it makes me feel stupid even now, but I have nothing to lose anymore.

'Well, I remembered seeing something about a yacht named Mia Zoí and it meaning lifetime or one life and . . . I felt like I already had my lifetime, and it was here with you. She was the reason for it, for my one life. After being with you, I realised how I'd been quite miserable for my whole life up until then. I loved travelling because it was this constant wave of new people and not thinking about myself or the future, but with you . . . I could see a future that I liked the look of for the very first time.

'My lifetime is Mia Zoí . . . and once it was you. Not that it didn't terrify me, feeling that way.

'I recently saw this video about how people with parents who don't openly show love often don't feel loved unless they're chasing for it, because that's what their brain's been trained to believe. Love isn't love unless it's hard, you know? It had all been too easy with you. I didn't have to chase and it made me more sensitive, like I was waiting for the problem, the reality. Because how could our love be real if I wasn't chasing for it?

'When you picked your mother, and not me, it confirmed it. You weren't really in love with me . . . it was like the other shoe dropping, sort of? There was nothing to worry about, so I filled that void with fear at the first opportunity you gave me. When I was brave enough to come back, it's like that was it, that was the final confirmation. Love is pain, but I didn't want that anymore. I didn't want it for Mia . . . I don't know. I was a messed-up kid and I never wanted Mia to feel that way. She would be my lifetime because I was never going to have the rest of my lifetime with you.'

Mia begins to sing a few words in Greek out on the balcony before laughing at herself; Leonidas's eyes are aglow in the candlelight as he looks at her with complete admiration, urging her to continue.

'That is beautiful, but you break my heart with such sadness. What we had was my one life, too. Everything else is a shadow, and now you have returned, I've been allowed back in the sun at last.'

It seems as though we each trapped ourself in the other's prison, only I was lucky enough to have Mia with me. I could bask in all the little ways she's just like him. With a flair for history and geography, or her hair and the shape of her eyes, or the way she wrinkles her nose sometimes. There have been times it really felt like he was looking back at me.

I pull myself up tall, trying to stretch out from all the sitting.

Without a word, Dimitri moves too, placing his right palm exactly where it hurts on the lower part of my spine.

My head drops with such force my chin hits my chest.

I should tell him to stop, but feeling his energy, even through the cotton of my dress, is something I've spent at least ten out of twenty-four hours a day thinking about since I last saw him.

'Why are you doing that?' I curl my spine and tilt my head to look at him.

He curls forward too, bringing his face close to mine while keeping his hand on my back.

'Because you are in pain, I can see it in your eyes and the way you move. Please let me help you.'

'You can't help me. I told you: I don't need help. I don't need saving.'

Dimitri moves further into my space, an intimacy I haven't felt in years.

His face is no more than two inches from mine as he says, 'Let me take you back to the sauna. I can help with the pain.'

As my heart races, my head begins to spin, and before I can tell myself to say no, my mouth says, 'Fine.'

'We could go now?' He raises an eyebrow at me.

It's the same look he would give when he wanted to rip my clothes off in public but politely suggested we should go somewhere quiet.

'We can't now.'

'Why not?'

'That's why not.' I drag my eyes from his and focus instead on Mia and Leonidas. They're so absorbed in their own bubble we could probably disappear for a few hours and they might not even notice, but on the off-chance they do tear their eyes away from each other, I don't want to have vanished.

'I think they would like some time alone,' Dimitri chuckles.

'Maybe, but you should be getting to know her too.'

'We have plenty of time for that.'

I press my lips together and nod.

He's right. They do.

Emotions swirl like the start of a whirlpool, one that threatens to drown me.

'Sara, you know I still—'

'Please don't say it. I really can't do this.'

I push my hands down on to my knees and stand.

'Mia, we have to get the ferry tomorrow and it's getting late. Perhaps it's time to leave Dimitri and Leonidas. We'll stay in Kardamena tomorrow but be back the day after for a day trip.' I point at Leonidas. 'No making this one miss another ferry. I don't really want to pay for two hotels for a moment longer.'

Leonidas stands, placing his guitar to one side. 'Of course. I will happily pay for the hotel here—'

'That's not what I meant.' I walk over and kiss Leonidas's cheek. '*Kalinikta*, it was nice to see you again.' I look at my daughter, standing tall by his side, the candles casting a golden glow over her rosy cheeks. 'We'll give you two a moment to say goodnight.'

I turn away from them and catch the dad look of mild horror on Dimitri's face.

'Come on, you.' I nudge him towards the stairs and mumble, 'They don't need chaperones.'

When we reach the bottom of the stairs, Dimitri glances back up at them.

'They'll be fine.' I exhale the words with mild annoyance at his wide eyes.

'I was checking *we* will be fine.'

Dimitri's fingers slide into my hair and his mouth meets mine. I have no time to think, only react.

It's just like our first kiss, just after lunch the day we met. I hadn't expected it then either. The sharp sensation of the cold wall on my back. The meeting of his warm soft lips against mine and his strong hands on my body.

My body burns with the heat of the sun as our tongues collide in real time, not just in my memory.

In many ways, plodding through my forties, I thought my life would be the same as it was until I died. I'd get up and go to work, take calls from Mia and follow the delights of her life as it unfolded then make a meal for one at the end of the day, watch TV and go to sleep, ready to start again.

I'd given up on electricity.

Every man I've met on apps hasn't been worth the energy of swiping, let alone texting. I felt no satisfaction in dating them. I was content alone, but life was missing lightning. It was a delightful vanilla ice cream that Dimitri is determined to melt.

Dimitri ignites fire in my chest and makes me want to forget everything and curl into his arms, never to leave.

But I can't.

I gently push him away, my palms flat against his firm chest. It doesn't feel like he's aged at all. He's barely matured.

The timing is perfect as Mia arrives at the top of the stairs with Leonidas only two steps behind.

'Why are you two standing in the dark?' She laughs as she trots down the stairs.

I didn't even notice that we haven't put the lights on yet. There was enough light pouring down from the living room upstairs.

Mia reaches the bottom step and hits the switch, filling the hall with an unnatural orange glow, before she stands in front of Dimitri.

'It was really good to see you again, D—' Mia hesitates, like she might call him Dad. 'Dimitri.'

Dimitri places a hand on her cheek and his eyes reflect the light from the bulb with an instant glitter as though they are filling with stars, not dampening with the possibility of tears.

I think he knows as well as I do that she wasn't sure whether to say Dad. I'm glad he didn't push the point, however much his eyes gave away his desire for her to call him that.

We all chorus *Kalinikta* and goodnight as Mia and I step out into the street.

We're only a short way along the winding road, which isn't all that much wider than the two of us next to each other, when Mia begins to sink her teeth into questions.

'How did you know I wanted to come back the day after tomorrow? Are you sure it's OK for me to come back here to work on this song of ours?'

'Wait, I'm writing a song?'

'Not *ours*,' she tuts, 'mine and Leonidas's.'

'It's already sounding good.'

'Yeah, it is. But we might come up with something else. We're not sure . . .' Mia's pace slows. 'I really like him, Mum.'

'I can tell.'

Mia links her arm in mine and rests her head on my shoulder as we continue to meander back to the hotel. 'How did you know Dimitri was *the one*?'

'How can he be *the one* when we aren't even together?' I scoff.

'Because you're in love with him.'

It's hard to deny, but I don't want to admit it either.

All I can do is quietly tell her the only truth I know. 'No one knows what's around the corner. All you can do is follow your heart as far as it will take you. Life will decide the rest.'

Chapter 41

Sara 2025

'I was thinking, I'd like to get Dimitri something for his birthday. I know it's late, but better late than never. Any ideas what he might like?' Mia picks up a bookmark with Kardamena on it, only to put it down again.

'I'm so pleased that's your outlook on life. *Better late than never.* I guess that's why you didn't slap me for not telling you about him sooner?' I wiggle my eyebrows at her.

'I'd never slap anyone. Can you see me slapping anyone in the face?'

'Really? What about that misogynistic weirdo Andrew Tate? I think you could give him a slap and not think twice about it.'

'Yeah, maybe. I'd be worried he might like it though.' We both twist our faces in sheer repulsion at the idea of even touching him with a slap to the face. 'I guess the list of people I *could* slap is pretty long, actually. But don't worry, you're not on it. Even if perhaps you should be.' Mia tucks a curl behind her ear.

'Well, thank you for keeping me off the hit list.'

We move at a snail's pace to turn over every item in the shops in Kardamena. We've bought ourselves some fabulous handmade jewellery from a place called Pretty Greek. The jewellery is made in Corfu by MiNiMiS and has been crafted from recycled glass bottles. We fancied having some bright-blue Bombay Sapphire gin round our necks. It was right up Mia's street, with their tag line being 'The Art of Recycling'. The whole shop was bursting with items made in Greece. It was nice to take our minds off everything and feel like us again.

'So what sort of thing do you want to buy him?'

'Something he actually needs or wants.'

'A new kitchen table?'

'Too big.'

'Yeah, I don't fancy us taking that over on the ferry.'

An *ooo*ing sound almost purrs from my lips. 'What about a nice mug? Sounds dull, but it isn't. Remember those old mugs he let us use for coffee? He has a cupboard full of twenty-odd-year-old mugs. Probably his sisters got all the nice ones when their mum died.'

I think back to the pretty cups we had coffee in, the one and only time I met her. I think if Dimitri had those in his cupboard, that's what he would've given us to use. Unless, of course, he's still frightened to, even now.

'OK, good idea. Practical, useful, and he'll be reminded of me every morning. Perfect!'

I sing, 'You're welcome,' as we head towards the stacks of mugs.

Mia goes straight for the ones I would've picked. They're simple, white with a grass-green splash of colour diagonally across one side. A cup with matching saucer. They look elegant and yet masculine.

'I'm going to get them all,' she announces as she begins stacking up the last four that are there.

'Four? But he's only a one?'

'Yeah, but we'll be there all the time, and with Leonidas, so it makes sense . . .' She doesn't meet my eye. She keeps her focus on the handmade pottery between her fingers.

The lady behind the counter chats to Mia as she carefully wraps them all up in paper.

I do a little circuit of my own. Dimitri turned fifty so I'd like to get him my own gift, but I have no idea what would be the right thing, and I don't want to step on the thoughtfulness of Mia, even if I had secretly been looking for something.

I can't imagine what the right thing would be in our bewildering situation. It's probably best to steer clear and avoid making things worse. I step away from rows of beautifully hand-carved olive wood, only for a book to catch my eye.

The author is Dimitri Georgallis. It's a book about Nisyros, it must be him. How many other Dimitri Georgallises are there who are also experts on Nisyros?

I can't believe he wrote a book and never told me.

Not that he could've told me. Not until this week, anyway.

I pick up two copies, one for me, one for Mia. Gently, I flick through the pages. It's simply laid out, with photos interspersed with short blocks of writing. All in English. I could burst with pride at his achievement and can't wait to hand this to Mia.

'Mum, are you done?' she calls.

'One second.' I rush back to the till and pay without Mia seeing what I've picked up.

As soon as we are out of the shop, I pull it out of the bag. 'Look at this! Your father is an author. Did you know that?'

She takes it out of my hand and studies it, looking at the little blue door on the front cover with a cat sprawled in front of it, before flipping it over to study the blurb.

'No, he never said. This is so cool though.'

We both ramble along, flicking through our new books as we go. I can hear Dimitri's seductive voice as I consume his words about the fire in Nisyros's belly, and the healing powers of the soil.

'Oh my God,' I whisper at one particular image in the book.

'What is it?' Mia doesn't look up from her reading.

'Nothing, nothing. Can we go to Alexandra's place for a drink? I have an idea,' I say as I slip the book back in the bag to continue later.

'Sure. What's the idea?'

'I'm not telling you, just in case. But I'll hopefully be able to tell you in about fifteen minutes.'

There's a stifling heat today. Clouds have moved in and made the streets of Kardamena feel like they're making their own natural sauna. The heat from the sun isn't stinging my skin, but the moisture in the air is boiling it instead.

There are a few tables taken for afternoon drinks, but we squeeze into the same one we sat at before, only to stand up again right away to kiss Alexandra's cheeks.

'She knows,' I say with a smile.

Alexandra claps her hands together before throwing her arms open again, ready to pull Mia towards her and kiss both her cheeks again.

'You know about Dimitri now. He is a very good man.'

'You knew?' Mia says as she steps back from the kissing overload.

'Don't be mad, I told her because I didn't want her to tell you about Dimitri's and my relationship before I managed to say something . . . that worked out great, by the way. Alexandra, do you have a printer I could use, please?' I wiggle my eyebrows at her as I want to explode with joy at my idea.

'Yes, of course. Declan is in the kitchen. Through there? He will tell you how it works. I don't know,' she shrugs.

'Thank you.' I trot off towards the kitchen as quickly as possible to avoid any scolding from Mia that I told Alexandra so easily but didn't tell her.

I booked this trip primarily to tell Mia about her father, and in preparation I had a look at the old photos I have stashed away at home. I showed her once, when she was a baby. In that way, I *have* told her all about her father and showed her photos.

She gurgled in delight. I remember it vividly. It's not my fault she isn't one of those people who remember every second of their life in full Technicolor. If she was, then we wouldn't be here today.

As it is, I took photos of those photos on my phone to show her how we looked back then. It was only seeing a photo of Dimitri taking a tour in the nineties, with Tina hovering nearby, that I remembered them.

Declan is there with Kostas, a nice old boy who kindly helps me print out three images. I saw Declan again when I was here the other day. He still has that Irish charm about him, but his hair is grey now and he's holding more weight than he used to.

I look at the photos from a million years ago.

One of Dimitri on his own. One of us together on the beach, and one of us on his balcony, his arm outstretched to try and take a selfie before selfies were even a thing.

'They were good times back then.' Declan comes and glances over my shoulder.

'They really were. I love that you two ended up together. I'm so happy for you.'

'Thanks. I'm still hoping to see you do the same.' He lightly bumps my shoulder before turning back to a deep-fat fryer full of chips.

I almost skip back to the table with the photos in my hand.

Alexandra is busy with other customers, jotting down an order, and Mia is staring out at people in clusters looking in shops and finding places to stop and cool off.

She looks up at me as I pull out my chair. 'Alexandra was telling me how it was only the sea that could separate you and Dimitri when you were here. How she'd never seen two people more in love, but I'm not to tell her husband that.'

'Don't believe all the hype.'

'I do.'

'Please don't. Her husband's in there, if you want to tell him? They met at the same time as Dimitri and I.'

'I'm good, thanks. What were you printing?'

'These.'

I pass her the images. It's easy to tell who they are. We were both slimmer back then, but not so much as to be unrecognisable. We have that vitality of fresh-faced youth, but I don't think he's lost much of that.

'This is you two . . .' Her voice trails as she looks from one image to the next, her jaw slack and her eyes wide. 'Mum, this is you two. Here, well . . . over there.' Her head tilts in the direction of Nisyros.

'It is. We were younger than you are now by a few years.'

I tell her about when the photos were taken – as well as I can remember, anyway. At the time, I thought there would be plenty more photos to come. I never thought I would need to imprint the memories as they were all I'd have. I thought it was the beginning, not the whole story including The End.

'What's going on with you two, Mum? You're clearly still into each other—'

'Please, don't. It's not like that. We're here for you, that's all that matters.'

I dread to think how she'd react if I told her he kissed me. She'd start planning our wedding. I've never seen her like this before, not since she was trying to set me up with Malcolm. Bless her, she had no idea he wasn't interested in women like that. It took me ages to burst her bubble with that one.

'Are you sure this isn't why you put Louisa off, and delayed the purchase of the business? Putting everything on pause? Because after all these years, getting the dream business and everything lined up, maybe you realised *that* wasn't the dream, *this* was.' She taps a chipped nail on the table. 'Because a small part – or very large part – of you actually wants to move here on a whim and live happily ever after at last? Maybe at facing a forever future, you decided you had to see if he was still here?'

'No. It's nothing like that. I really am taking time to think about it. Yes, I've been thinking a lot about life and hopes and dreams and what's really important . . . that's in part how we ended up here. Anyway, I don't believe in happily ever after.'

'That's not what you've been telling me my whole life.'

'It's different for you, you can have whatever you want to have.'

'If I can, then so can you. I don't understand why you can't admit you like each other. I thought my generation was rubbish at being upfront about relationships but you two are so much worse.'

'Well, we win then, I guess.' I rest my elbows on the table and my chin on my fists. 'Look, I've been trying to understand it all since before you were born and I realised that I can't. That life happens outside of the control we think we have, so you're better off telling a joke and keeping a smile on your face than wondering about the past or even what happens next.'

'You can't always live life like there aren't consequences. Other people have feelings too.'

'Thanks, *Mum*.' I roll my eyes playfully. 'Who do you think taught you that? I know other people have feelings, and I don't want to rush into something and hurt anyone pointlessly.'

Mia's jaw locks. I've forced her to give up, but perhaps by using one phrase incorrectly, *I don't want to rush into something*. Now she'll have hope that because I said the word *something*, there must be *something*.

I slide the photo of Dimitri on his own a little closer to her. He's leaning next to his front door with a wonky smile. 'This one is for you to keep. I'm going to give the other two to Dimitri. I'll forward them to you, though. So you'll have a copy.'

'Thanks.' Her voice is only a notch above silence.

'I'm sorry if I've disappointed you.' I know I have. On so many fronts, I've let her down.

'You haven't. I just feel like you're lying to yourself, that's all.'

This would be the perfect time to tell her that I'm lying to her too, but I can't bring myself to do it. Not yet.

Chapter 42

SARA 2025

The reminders of the last time I was here, in this corner of Greece, are everywhere. No matter how much it's changed, its soul hasn't. The vivid blue of the sea and the way it glitters under the sun, the whitewashed buildings all layered in rows with their contrasting vibrant doors, the smiling faces of Greeks, the way the sea air feels thick in my lungs and the sun nourishes my heart. None of that has changed. I could almost believe it was still 1998.

It's seeing Dimitri in the distance with a fully grown Leonidas at his side that hits home how much time has moved on. If I squint, it could almost be him and Manolis, but I know it's not.

Everything has changed for us all.

In the past twenty-seven years, Leonidas has lost a father and Mia has gained one. Leonidas must be almost thirty now. Time runs on endless, unfathomable legs, silently and unseen, and I'd give anything to slow it down.

I shake my head. I wish I could turn back the clock, but I can't.

'What's wrong?' Mia says close to my ear, but loudly still, to be heard over the hum of the boat and people chatting.

'Nothing.'

Nothing I could possibly vocalise without collapsing in a heap on the floor at the swathes of missing time. The consolation I hold to my heart is that I got to see Mia grow up and hog it all to myself. The problem is it's like seeing a unicorn swimming in the sea under a pink sunset and having no one to turn to and say *did you see that?* and no one to now say, *do you remember when?*

◆ ◆ ◆

As always, I'm first off the boat, only this time it's with the exception of Mia, who I thrust in front of me at the last moment.

Leonidas and Dimitri help her down, arms stretched in anticipation. As soon as she's on dry land, they do the same for me. Leonidas takes my hand in his. The last time we held hands, his was so small, only the size of my palm. Now he has a firm grip, with rough fingers from playing his guitar.

We all greet with hugs and kisses as though it's been a lifetime all over again, not less than forty-eight hours.

'So,' Dimitri beams. 'Breakfast. We thought it would be nice to overlook the sea. Then we will meet later, yes?'

We take the short walk to a taverna I know well from many years ago. A young man takes our order, he's probably the son of the owner I remember. We take a seat at a table that's pressed against the sea wall so we can overlook the rocks below and the waves that gently foam as they knock against them.

We order milkshakes as Mia shares the story of our tradition of having them as our first drink on holiday, and the ramifications of not having them as our first drinks. The men laugh at her tales and our mishaps. They both hang on her every word as though her voice is that of an angel.

It's no less than she deserves, but I feel grateful to Dimitri for taking her in as his own so readily and easily. His anger towards me is probably much like the magma that pools underneath our feet – it's not likely to explode out again any time soon, but it's a powerful force that can't be changed, however much I wish it could be.

On a normal day among friends, either mine or Mia's or both, I usually like to throw in random bits into conversations, often silly things to open new ideas into the mix. But I keep my mouth closed as we munch our way through an assortment of sweet treats, all of which were chosen by Mia and me. I want her to find her feet without me getting in the way. I keep my mouth for devouring the yogurt with honey and almonds, pancakes and more.

'Oh, I nearly forgot.' Mia scoots her grey plastic chair back a little harder than necessary before picking up her bag and placing it on her lap. 'I got you a birthday gift. Happy belated birthday.' She pulls out a teal carrier bag from within her bag and passes it to Dimitri.

He hasn't even opened it yet, but he already looks delighted, with his cheekbones flying high and his pupils as wide as golf balls.

'You didn't have to do this, Mia Zoí. You being there at my birthday was the best gift I could have received. We only had a party for my birthday because I am so old now, you know we don't usually notice birthdays here.' He begins to peel away the paper methodically as he talks to Mia as though she's the only one here. 'When I was younger, my mother would never let me have a birthday party. We only celebrated name days and other celebrations for the church, never birthdays. Oh, Mia Zoí, this is very handsome.' Dimitri holds up the cup to display it for Leonidas and me.

'There's four matching for when we all come round for coffee. Mum thought maybe you didn't have any, then we saw these. Anyway, I hope you like them.'

I'm not used to seeing Mia like this, her posture curved and her eyes averted. I don't want her to feel nervous around Dimitri. The fact that she probably is falls heavy on my shoulders. I hope one day they can find a natural rhythm all of their own.

◆ ◆ ◆

As soon as all our forks have been discarded on our plates, and napkins have been scrunched up and placed on top of them, Dimitri sits tall like he's about to make an announcement. 'I have told Leonidas that you can use my house to rehearse. We will meet you here for the ferry, and we will both be coming back to Kardamena.'

'I was only staying here for a few days,' Leonidas interjects. 'I'm going back home to Foteini's to annoy her dogs with my guitar.'

'And I want to make sure I am ready for the big show tomorrow,' Dimitri grins. 'I called around and found a place to stay. I know you girls will want time together, but perhaps we can have dinner tonight?'

'I'd like that.' Mia pushes a wild curl behind her ear. 'But for now, I think we'd better get to work. Not only do we have to finish this song, but we need to come up with a full set, too.'

'That should be easy for you. Although I don't know about Leonidas, of course. If you have a strong repertoire too, you'll be fine. Based on what I heard yesterday, I think you'll be more than fine,' I shrug.

'It's finding songs we both know, making sure we know what key to play in . . . the usual stuff.' Mia shrugs back at me.

I know Mia well enough to be sure that she'll be ready for this gig in a matter of hours, but I agree to seeing them in the early evening for the late ferry that runs a few days in the week. It's important to give them space to find their own relationship.

They slide out of their chairs, and we wish them good luck. I watch as they leave the taverna, and like teenagers they wait until they're a little further away before their shoulders press and melt together like fondue.

I tilt my head towards Dimitri. 'If they're going to your house to rehearse, where are we going?'

'Don't you remember?'

'No.' I lean forward in my chair. 'I don't think you told me.'

'We are going to the sauna. You agreed.'

'I don't remember that.'

'Yes, you do.' Dimitri's tongue briefly touches his bottom lip and he leans towards me. 'Perhaps it was our kiss that made you forget everything else.'

His liquid voice covers me like honey, sticking to me and confusing everything.

'I hope you have your own car now. You can't borrow one from poor Manolis anymore.'

'I have a car now – well, it was his car. I bought it from the family when he passed. Come on, let's not waste a moment.' Dimitri looks at the bill, pulls out his wallet and places down a few notes to pay.

'Are you sure you don't want any money?'

'No, no. It is nice to have a beautiful woman to spend my money on.' His lips twist into a cheeky smile. 'Two beautiful women, in fact.'

I follow him out and back towards the port and the hotel where Mia and I stayed earlier in the week. There's a small white car there. Dimitri pulls out a key and the lights flash as it unlocks. I'm glad it's not the same car he borrowed all those years ago. I can't imagine it would be in very good shape now.

Dimitri opens the door for me, then jogs around the car to slide in next to me.

As we head off, I promise myself not to think about tomorrow, and the fact we only have two more days before facing the realities of England.

This is temporary. It has always been temporary.

People and places pass us by, the stone streets and a hundred shades of blue doors, cats trot along like the car is of no consequence and tourists barely look at us from taking selfies, until everything becomes sparse and we're out on the open road. We pass olive groves with their silvery leaves and the rough volcanic terrain of Nisyros.

I've missed this beauty and feeling the strength of the world under my feet, knowing an earthquake could shake my soul at any time. It couldn't hurt any more than this already does.

That sort of power ever present is quite unique. From the constant threat of shaking earth and lava to the vastness of the sea and the sky above . . . it makes me realise how small I am and how small my problems are compared to the infinite universe. I need that perspective right now.

The problem with life is there's always a pay-off, a balance, a piper that needs to be paid. Karma. Every action has an equal and opposite reaction and all that. Here, people live in a tranquil, stunning landscape with the sun shining like a jewel in a baby-blue sky and the constant rumbling threat of earthquakes and eruptions. Nothing is perfect.

'Do you remember the things I taught you?' Dimitri says over the rattling air-con.

'You taught me things?'

He chuckles and strums his finger on the steering wheel.

I don't want to admit that he taught me more in our short time together than anyone else I know. Apart from maybe Mia. But the life lessons have been very different.

'I would like to think so, yes,' he continues.

'We would all like to think so.'

'Nisyros and Kos are the home of modern medicine. Nisyros is very powerful.'

'I'm fine, I've told you that.'

'You did, you did. But we all need to heal from the past.'

I suppose he's right with that one – our scars run deeper than the white lines on the surface of our skin. They dig in with roots like pin-thin tendrils.

The problem is, I don't believe one day has the power to heal everything.

Chapter 43

Mia 2025

'Why here?' My eyes have been fixed on Leonidas's hands while he carefully tunes his guitar. It's been hard to keep my mind still and settled. All it wants to do is chase its tail, like a wild puppy.

Leonidas looks up at me, running his fingers through his thick dark hair before scratching his head.

'It's simple – because it's quiet, and Dimitri told me he was taking your mother somewhere and they would leave us to work all day.'

'Do you know where?' I stand up from the bench in Dimitri's sweeping balcony and walk into the sun.

'No, I didn't ask.'

I try to hide my disappointment as I look out across the muddle of houses and listen to the music of Nisyros. Closing my eyes against the sun, I can focus on the sounds around me. The birdsong, children laughing as their feet run along the stones, the indistinct chatter of life moving to its own beat.

'What are you doing?' Leonidas's voice startles me out of my bubble.

'Listening.'

'What are you listening to?'

'Life.'

He puts down his guitar and his feet scuff along the concrete towards me. I don't open my eyes. I listen and sense him coming to stand next to me.

'My sisters all think I'm very strange when I do this.'

I open one eye and tilt my head to see him standing next to me, rolling up the sleeves of his white cotton shirt with his eyes closed. He clears his throat a little before folding his arms over his chest, making his forearms look like the thick roots of olive trees.

'Are you mocking me?' I open both eyes and push my hair back over my shoulders.

'No. But I did think I was the only person to do this.'

'To close your eyes and listen?'

His eyes are still shut but I square up to him a little, sure he is mocking me.

'Not just to listen. Anyone can listen, but to hear. To hear what the world is telling me, the music that floats in the air and inspires everything. Sounds that people ignore because they're so embedded in everyday life, they're like the stitches holding your buttons on your shirt. People take them for granted, but they'd be upset if suddenly they all fell off.' Leonidas's words sound like my thoughts pouring from his mouth.

I tilt my head and imagine what he would look like if all his buttons fell off. Quite a few are already undone. Three beaded necklaces of varying lengths adorn what I can see of his tanned chest, like a well-deserved crown.

His eyes open and mine quickly flick up to meet his. I hope he didn't catch me staring.

'Were you staring at me?'

I shrug my shoulders and turn away from him.

'Yes. You were listening, I was looking.'

I take my place back on the bench and watch him some more.

He really is the perfect distraction from everything that's going on. I wonder whether that's how Mum felt about Dimitri. She had left England, arrived in Kos looking for some sort of escape from the life she was born to, and Dimitri was probably the perfect distraction for her too. Thinking about what happened to them is almost enough for me to leave and tell Leonidas our friendship shouldn't continue.

'What's wrong? You are frowning.'

I shake my head in an attempt to clear my thoughts. 'Was I?'

He nods as he begins to strum his guitar softly.

'Oh. My mind tripped and fell on the past.'

'You know, the past doesn't matter anymore. It's to educate you and help you to make better decisions.'

'You think so? It's all about making smart choices?'

'I know it.'

'Well, I was thinking I don't want this' – I indicate from him to me with my index finger – 'to end up the way Dimitri and my mum have.'

It hits me that my statement is a bit big for people who have only known each other for a couple of days and shared a few touches and a couple of kisses. However amazing those kisses might've been, it's probably not enough to compare us to them out loud.

'Do you think they regret being together? Regret making you?'

That wasn't the reaction I expected as Leonidas continues to let his fingers glide smoothly over his guitar strings, freely playing a soundtrack for our conversation like we're in a movie.

'No, I don't think they do. I hope they don't.'

'I don't think they regret it. They were living their lives. Isn't that what we should all do? Live for passion, art, music, food? What else matters . . . Mia Zoí?' His full lips twist into a smile as he says my name. 'I think I should write a song in Greek about your name.'

'That's up to you, but not for today.'

'Can I write about your shoulders in that dress?'

I run my finger over the seam of the cold-shoulder line.

'Or how my hands are always drawn to my guitar, but today they are drawn elsewhere?' He places the guitar down on the floor then turns to me, his dark eyes focused entirely on me.

'We need to write this song,' I breathe.

It's suddenly hotter than a moment ago, as though the shade has been filled with a glaring light.

'We do, you are right, but I think there is a lot of music we could make together. We need to be relaxed, *nai*? To make the sweetest sounds.' Leonidas moves closer to me, his face hovering near to mine as his rough fingers brush the hair from my shoulder.

I close my eyes and listen to the sound of his breath and the beating of my own heart in my head. His lips fall gently on my collarbone, and I tilt my head back in response.

'*Smart choices*. I like that. We should make a song about that?' I swallow hard, trying to force myself back from the edge of whatever this is, whatever this could be.

'Easily.' He begins to hum as his mouth moves up my neck. 'This is a *smart choice*.'

I laugh gently at the idea.

'We have to write this song.' Without thought, my fingers run along his forearm and tuck into his rolled-up sleeve.

'We are,' he insists as his other arm wraps around me. 'We are making our own music. You need to be open, Mia. Open to living this life, doing what you want, not for tomorrow, for now.' His fingers coil into my hair and his tongue traces a circle on my neck. 'Do you want this?'

My mouth feels dry as I try to swallow and pray for sense. 'Yes.'

'Then let's make music together today.'

Our mouths meet and I can feel myself relaxing. I hadn't even realised how tense I was feeling until my body released under the warmth of Leonidas pressing against me.

I close my eyes tightly shut and take in the micro sound of us. Leonidas is right, I need to start thinking about the life I want, and the things I want to do.

Chapter 44

Mia 2025

'This needs to stop,' I breathe as Leonidas's fingers slice under my bra strap like a knife that wants to cut it off.

I place my hand on his chest and while I seriously don't want to, I gently press on the soft, golden skin peeking out of his shirt. My fingers tangle into his necklaces, even though I'm doing my best to signal I really do mean we have to stop.

He moves back a few inches and I release the beads in my hand. His pupils are dilated and his teeth dig in his lower lip, as though he is having to bite back another kiss aimed at my mouth. He is quick to respect my wishes, though, and doesn't advance . . . however obvious it might be that he wants to.

'Not only do we need to sort out this set, but this is my dad's house.' I shuffle back on the bench and awkwardly circle my hands at the walls and the plants caging me in.

My *dad's* house. My *dad*.

'Dimitri,' I add, wishing to exchange the word *dad* for his actual name. 'This is Dimitri's house. It feels strange enough being here, but I don't think we should continue down . . . this path. Not right now.'

Leonidas's hot hand finds my knee. 'I want to tell you I can understand, but how can I? I only know losing a father, not finding one. I do know that Dimitri is a good man. My father trusted him, and so do I. Of all the men who could have been your father, you are lucky it is Dimitri.'

'Are you calling my mum a slut?' I lift an eyebrow in his direction.

'*Slut?* I don't know this word.'

'Someone who sleeps around.'

With that, Leonidas's head launches backwards and he grips his firm stomach as he booms with laughter.

It's hard to contain my own smirk of amusement.

Wiping his eyes, he says, 'No, no, I was not saying that. I am so sorry.'

'You don't sound sorry.'

It's impossible not to chortle along with his infectious laughter. It plays on the air like freestyle jazz.

'I am, I am.' He puts a balled fist to his mouth and clears his throat before calmly repeating himself. 'I am. What I was meaning is, before you knew it was Dimitri, it could be anyone. You thought your mother did not even know who your father was, so he could have been . . .' He squints and moves his head like he's searching the sweet warm air around us for words. 'A killer, or worse,' – he lowers his chin for dramatic effect – 'a politician.'

'How is that worse?'

'Come on, it's the same thing, *nai*?' He shoots me a cheeky look.

'Sometimes, I guess. Hopefully not in all cases.'

He shrugs and leans back against the wall with his chin lifted towards the dazzling blue sky.

A silence descends that's filled only by the high-pitched chatter of barn swallows and the hum of air-conditioning units.

'If you want to talk about Dimitri, your mum, anything, you can talk to me,' Leonidas informs me softly.

'Thanks. I think I've unloaded enough of this crap on you as it is, and honestly, I barely know how I feel about any of it. I thought that this holiday was going to have a completely different drama and now I'm more confused than ever. Can you play?' I look over at his discarded guitar.

'I've told you . . . I *can* . . .'

'Would you please play your guitar for me, Leonidas?' I make sure to give him my most sarcastic smile and strike each word with just enough staccato to emphasise it, but not so much as to sound bitchy.

'I would love to, but I would like to ask you one thing.' Leonidas stands to gather his guitar before pulling out a chair and dragging it to be opposite me. His focus shifts to the strings and his eyes lock on them with the same intensity as he looks at me, like there's nothing else going on around him.

'What's the one thing?'

'Tell me, what was the *drama* you thought you would find in Kos. Before you found out about Dimitri.'

'Oh . . .'

Leonidas's fingers move swiftly but carefully over the strings. The motion is both enchanting and intoxicating. For a moment, I regret asking him to stop the flow of his fingers over me.

I quash that thought and divert my attention to one of the chirpy swallows darting about.

My drama. I wish I could suck it all up and exhale it with my breath.

I think back over my plan to tell my mum that now she was settling into her new adventure with the business in the UK, I was going to begin my own. That I wanted to travel solo for a bit, sing in different parts of the world and do my own thing. Even now, the guilt of leaving her is like a dripping tap on the back of my neck sending a cold watery finger skimming over my spine.

'Well, my mum was meant to be buying this business, a travel agent's that she's always wanted to run. Which was great, her dream was coming true, she seemed really happy about it – it wasn't another hare-brained scheme of hers, it was a legitimate business opportunity.'

Leonidas takes his eyes off the strings but lets his fingers continue to create their own flowing song, only now I've stolen his focus again. Snatched it away from his first love and kept his dark eyes for myself.

'How is this drama?'

'It isn't. But, it meant she was happy. She had something that wasn't me that made her smile.'

A strange feeling rolls around in my stomach like a metal ball. I've never thought of it like that until it came out of my mouth. It *is* one of the very real reasons I'm afraid to head off alone, because I don't want her to be lonely. She's invested her whole adult life in me.

'My mum has always been there for me. No matter what, I've never needed to ask, I've always just assumed she would be there, and over the past year I've been really bored with singing at other people's weddings, only interacting with drunk people celebrating the love of others and . . . I don't know.' I shrug my shoulders and feel as deflated as a balloon as a vision of a hundred different drunk groomsmen, and one very stupid groom, propositioning me flashes before my eyes.

It's always the same thing. I'm on my break, they hover around or loudly think I'll be impressed by being asked whether I have a boyfriend. When I was starting out, I actually took a few of those numbers and went on a couple of dates. Some couldn't even remember giving me their number in the first place.

'You want to find who you are without your mother by your side. You need to know you can survive without her help, you want to have your own adventure but you don't want to hurt her feelings.'

'Kind of, yeah.'

'This I can understand. You know, Greek mothers are known for being soft on their sons. It's easy to understand when we look like this.' The corners of his mouth twitch as he barely suppresses a laugh. 'Some men, when their mothers are like this, they enjoy it. They take advantage of her love and let her do everything for them, then they look for a *good Greek girl* who will do the same.' When he says *good Greek girl*, he sort of sounds like a parody of himself. 'Not me. I move out, change island, make my own life. If I find a wife, I don't want her to be my mother.'

My fingers gravitate to my mouth as I try desperately to hold in words, but I can feel them clawing their way out.

'Haven't you moved in with your sister? And, also, to an island that's only a forty-five-minute boat ride away.'

He stops playing, tilts his head and pushes out his lips.

'And how far away do you live from your mum?'

I fold my arms over my chest and slouch down a little on the bench before muttering, 'About ten minutes away.'

'Exactly.' Leonidas places his guitar back down, turns towards the open doors and leans casually on the door frame. 'The thing you need to remember, Mia Zoí, is there in your name, yes? This is *your* lifetime. Your mother didn't have you to live in her shadow. She will be happy to see you happy, I think. They say they want this and that for us, but really, they smile when we smile. She doesn't want you to stay at home for pity.'

My jaw falls slack.

He's right. He's utterly right.

Like a hard slap to the face, he has hit me with a truth that can't be denied.

'You've had it too easy, too comfortable with your mama looking after you all the time. Now you have to find your own feet. It's hard, but when you come back to her, you'll both be with the biggest smiles. And you don't know, she might need to be free too. She has been your mother more than half her life. Maybe she needs to find who she is too.' He raises his face towards the sun and beams with a toothy grin.

This man has more soul than I could've imagined. I should've imagined it, by the way he plays his instrument, but I've learnt over the years not to use that as a gauge of maturity.

He's right. We both need space to find out who we are away from each other. Even when I went to university, I wasn't very far away.

Leonidas twists his weight from the door frame and moves towards the stairs down into the house.

'Where are you going?'

'To cool off. You have me mutz too hot. Are you coming?'

I stand up and reach for my bag that's been pushed under a table.

'Where's cooler than this?' I trot to catch up with him as he bounds down the stairs, jumping the last three.

'The ice-cream shop. You want some volcano flavour?'

'That doesn't sound cooler.'

'No, but it is, and it tastes good. A lot like you.' He turns and fixes his cool-guy smile on me.

'That won't help us write this song.'

'We can sit in the shade and write out the set. Come on.'

As we step out of Dimitri's house and into the blazing sun, I doubt we will find somewhere cooler to sit than here . . . but walking in step with Leonidas feels like I've been hiding in a shadow, and at last I'm gaining confidence to step into a light created by me.

I'm grateful that someone understands I need to spread my wings. He didn't make me feel bad for wanting to fly the nest, he showed me how it could be good for both of us.

After all, he's right – all my mum has ever said is she wants me to be happy, and leaving my old job behind and spending the summer away from England is something that would make me happy. It's something I have to do, now more than ever.

Chapter 45

Sara 2025

I can still remember exactly how to find the natural sauna, even though it's well hidden among the rocks. I can't imagine it's ever packed with tourists in this part of the island. Some of the other saunas might be. One is particularly easy to find, but not this one. Not at this time of day, at least. Although, I suppose with the rise of the internet, as soon as one person knows where something is, it can easily be shared with millions. The world has changed so much since I was last here, yet this seems like an unchanged corner of the world.

'God, it's nothing like it was. Bloody tourists change everything.' I stop to shake my head and look out across the neatly stacked volcanic stones and the sea in the distance.

Dimitri doesn't rise to my statement, or laugh, or anything much.

He just says, 'Nothing can stay the same. We all weather in the sun,' before continuing towards our destination. 'How is your back today?'

He takes my hand with the same confidence as when we were young, and we manoeuvre over the uneven ground together, edging towards the hidden entrance of the natural sauna.

'I took some paracetamol, but it's fine really. I just need to be a little careful. Sometimes my bum cheek feels numb or one of my legs goes dead. But I think being here in the sun helps. It was getting bad sitting at work all day.'

The only thing that has changed here is the sheet covering the entrance to the sauna. It's still a plain white sheet though, that's tucked under stones on top of the slightly sunken structure.

Dimitri begins to undo the buttons on his pale-blue and white striped linen shirt. We're reliving my favourite memory.

'I'm not getting down to my knickers again for this.'

'Fine, fine. We can be naked.' His eyebrows twitch up and a smile tickles his face.

I roll my eyes at him.

Of course, everything is different second time around. I'm both more confident and less confident all in one.

I'm not sure how that's possible, but it's true.

Since he last saw me naked, I've had a child, lived more than a quarter of a century and gained a couple of pounds. The positive is, I care less.

I now know there's way more to me than my physical form and that confidence at any age is sexier than any beauty of youth. Particularly as my confidence back then was lost in a hole somewhere.

None of that stops my stomach itching with nerves.

I hadn't forgotten that he wanted to bring me here. The idea grazed my heart and every now and then I'd sting with the thought of it yesterday while walking around with Mia.

I need to protect myself.

I need to protect him.

I don't think it's a good idea to throw ourselves together. Just like I was trying to explain to Mia, we can't suddenly believe we've slipped into another universe and the past is erased. Life doesn't work like that.

Dimitri folds his clothes and puts them on top of the rocks, leaving him in crisp white boxer shorts contrasting with his dark summer tan.

'Do you tan naked to look like that?'

'Maybe.' He folds his arms over his chest and a shy smile grazes his lips.

My skin burns at the image of him, and it isn't just the sun beating down on us. I didn't think it was possible, but he seems to have improved with age. Every part of him. That, or my memory hasn't been doing him justice.

'Don't stand and stare at me. I need to heal you . . . you need to take those clothes off.'

I shimmy my blouse down my shoulders and kick off my flip-flops, leaving me in chino shorts and a cami top. I fold the blouse and put it on top of his clothes.

'Done,' I announce happily, throwing my arms open in triumph.

Dimitri rolls his big dark eyes and pulls the curtain back for me to take the step down into the small tunnel-shaped room.

The heat hits me like stepping into a thunder cloud in a summer storm. My skin prickles and my shorts feel too thick and clingy in a way they didn't a moment ago.

'Bugger,' I mutter to myself.

Apparently, the image of Dimitri isn't the only thing my memory has diminished.

I turn around to the silhouette of Dimitri still holding the curtain outside, waiting for my realisation. I skulk back out to him. He's leaning on the wall of stones with his arms folded, chuckling.

He doesn't say a word. He doesn't need to.

I slip out of my clothes, leaving me in a matching black set with lace detailing. I can afford the nice underwear nowadays. My bra is almost akin to scaffolding, but it's worth it to see his face match the way it was all those years ago. I don't think anyone has ever looked at me quite the way he does. Like it hurts him not to have his hands on me.

I should shut this down. Walk away. I've done it before, and I already know I'll have to do it again soon enough.

Dimitri indicates for me to get back in the sauna. I hesitate in the doorway, taking a lungful of the dense air around me, filled with minerals from the earth and the memories of us.

The stones are warm under my toes and my skin itches with the heat. Shaded from the sun, the earth doesn't care. It's producing its own energy, doing its best to rival the sun with its own torturous furnace.

'Lie down.' Dimitri's creamy voice arrives close to my ear.

He's so close it could be his heat I'm feeling, not the burning lava not far from the surface.

I lay myself down in the same way as I did twenty-seven years ago. It's still a surprise when the stone bench isn't freezing cold in the darkness of the sauna.

The warmth of the stones soothes my bones more than a comfy bed.

I close my eyes, waiting to hear the softness of Dimitri's voice.

His fingers touch my face, pulsing a shot of adrenaline through my veins. I hadn't realised he was so close to me.

'I remember your beauty, but how is it possible that there is more now?' His thumb skims my bottom lip, making it tickle. I bite it away so he can't do it again.

I open one eye to find his face even nearer than I'd imagined.

'I thought you were going to heal me?'

'I am admiring you first. Sharing my soul with yours before I start.'

I hum a small noise of disbelief, making a smile lift his face.

'Fine, fine,' he grumbles playfully. 'Close your eyes and relax.'

He fills the room with Greek, sharing his energy through his hands, first with massage, then without even touching me.

Just as it did all those years ago, time slips away. The difference is, the future I'm thinking about now feels closed off. Back then, everything was wide open. My whole life was ahead of me. Now, more than ever before, I have no idea what the next few weeks will bring, let alone anything else. The past has taught me that everything can change in an instant.

Images of Mia as a little girl roll through my head. Her first steps, the first time she told me she loved me, the first book she read cover to cover all on her own, the first tree she climbed, the first song she sang to me . . . all of it. And how none of it was shared with Dimitri. She still has so many milestones I want to see.

At least I know Dimitri will be here to share in those now.

A pain I've been suppressing penetrates my chest like a meteor crashing through my ribcage. Tears as hot as the volcanic air run across my temples and into my hair.

My crying is silent, just as my pain has been. Silent and my own.

I can feel the heat of Dimitri's hands over my face, then the true touch of his fingers wiping my tears away as he stops speaking.

A distant sound pulls me out of the trance of him and my emotional pain.

Voices chattering and the crunch of footsteps over the loose stones, getting closer.

'Someone's coming,' I mutter, opening one eye.

He groans in recognition, his head flopping back. 'But we were here first, that is all that matters.'

'I don't think that would stop them coming in.'

'They won't come in. They will see the clothes and they will leave.'

'But they might not.'

‘*Yassou*’ is all I understand before something else is called towards us. It’s not English, nor is it Greek.

There’s plenty of space in here for a small group sitting on the stone slabs.

Dimitri sucks his teeth before standing up to respond. He takes two strides towards the entrance and hunches to walk up the steps without hitting his head, before poking his face out from behind the sheet.

I’m more aware than ever of our clothing situation, regretting leaving everything outside. The heat in the sauna is dizzying. I’m glad to be lying down.

Dimitri steps back inside.

He crouches down next to me and pushes the hair off my face where it’s sticking to my skin and tears. Leaning towards me, our mouths meet in a soft lingering kiss. It’s so natural I barely give it a thought until he gently pulls away.

‘They will come back later. They won’t disturb us again. I want to put my hands on your pain. Could you sit for me?’ He puts his hands out to help me up.

‘How do you want me?’

‘This is fine.’ He kneels on the hard floor between my legs and wraps his arms round me to place his hands on my lower back, right where the pain has been radiating from.

‘Now talk to me,’ he demands, but gently.

I look down into his eyes. The pupils have devoured his irises and created black pools of sorrow that I can’t bear to look into.

My head flops down on to his shoulder.

‘You don’t have to be strong for me, Sara. I want to be here with you. The past mistakes are for the past. I’m grateful you are here now.’

‘I don’t want to be scared, but I am.’ My voice cracks open with a ridge so deep I can feel it cut into my own heart.

I haven't told anyone about how afraid I am of what's to come. What's next on my journey. I've only told Dimitri the truth. I can barely admit it all to myself, but I know tomorrow I'll have to tell my baby girl too.

The words should've stayed inside, because tears pour out with them, and I can't hide from my fear anymore.

'I'll be with you. I will come back with you to England and I will stay with you.'

'You can't do that, your whole life is here.'

'I can. I can be there for you and for Mia. You can't stop me.' His voice breaks too and the wound in my heart that was left last time I was here rips wide open, because it never scarred up the way it should. There's always been a hole there eating away at me, and now I'm being pulled apart from the inside out.

'I need you to promise me that if things go wrong—'

'Please, please.' Dimitri shifts to press himself to me in a full embrace, pulling me softly into him. 'Don't say it. Everything is OK, I will help, I will be here to heal you too. You'll see. I promise.'

'You can't promise that. Don't ever make promises you don't know you can keep. Never to Mia. Please?'

Dimitri sniffs quietly into my hair. 'OK,' he agrees in a gravelly voice. 'But you must promise me something too.' He pulls away, his hands sliding up my body to wind his fingers into my hair and caress my face with his thumbs.

'Only if it's one I can keep.'

'That every day your eyes are open, you live. No one knows what is to come. No one knows how much time they have. Not one person knows this answer. I remember the day I lost Manolis . . .' Dimitri swallows hard, his eyes flicking away from mine.

Instinctively, my hands wrap behind his neck, as though this simple act will anchor him in the same way I need his hands on me as an anchor.

'There was nothing I could do. One minute we were laughing together, walking along the beach after a day of fishing, and then he says he feels dizzy, tired. We stopped on the rocks, looking out to sea. I was making jokes that he was getting too old, and then I looked at him. Really looked at him. His skin was pale grey and sweat dripped from his hair as he rubbed his jaw.' Dimitri closes his eyes, squeezing them shut like he can close the door, but I know all too well how these things are worse on the inside. How thoughts and feelings cut and scar in places no one can see. 'A minute later he was gone. I couldn't get help to him quick enough.'

The white sheet flutters in towards us, wafting in the breeze. It's as though Manolis's ghost has come to greet us. Maybe comfort us.

It doesn't work. We hold each other, knowing all too well that life is as fragile as a butterfly wing, and in a moment, even a simple one, everything can change and all too often we're asking how we could've done it differently and wishing we knew what could've been.

Chapter 46

Sara 2025

'I don't want to share you today,' Dimitri announces before we slide into the car next to each other. He keeps his eyes focused on the windscreen and the scorched landscape beyond.

'I was thinking something similar.'

'You always are.' He tries to shake a smile from his face, but it lingers along with mine.

We've been almost everywhere around Mandraki together in the past. From the charcoal- and rust-coloured walls of the ancient acropolis to the Venetian castle of Panagia with its panoramic views of the sea, and from museums to beaches.

I wonder which memory lane we might walk down next.

It's almost as hot in the car as it was in the sauna. Dimitri starts the engine and blasts the air-con on, making my blonde threads of hair flutter wildly around my ears. His hands rest firmly on the steering wheel but he makes no attempt to get the car to move anywhere.

Dimitri continues his stream of thought. 'I can't take you home, but I don't want to walk around where other people can talk to you and distract you. I want all your attention.'

'You remind me of Mia when she was two.'

Dimitri's head drops and his torso vibrates with laughter.

'You are right.' He twists his neck to look up at me from his curved position. 'I feel selfish in the same way children are. Is that so bad?'

'No. I feel the same.'

'I know where to go.' Dimitri sits up straight and taps his hands on the steering wheel with a new-found confidence.

Without telling me where we're going, he begins to drive, leaving another beautiful moment at the sauna etched into our past.

The road weaves through Mandraki, with the blinding blue of the sea on our left and the shelter of whitewashed artisan shops and seafront tavernas to our right. I turn the air-con down and open the window. I want to feel this place on my skin, like I can absorb it through each and every pore.

It isn't long until we're out of the town again and driving along a dusty road littered with olive trees, stones and spiky golden grasses that are probably as sharp as razor blades. The rugged beauty of Nisyros could never escape my heart. I've often wondered if I fell for this small island as much as I did for Dimitri.

'Tell me about Mia Zoí when she was small. Your comment about her at two has me wondering.'

'Well, at two, I was lucky if I managed to go to the loo on my own. She used to demand I carry her everywhere. She had this book that played nursery rhymes that she adored. She would carry that and I would carry her. My parents sent it for her second birthday. Things like that were out of my budget.'

'I wish I could've seen her, and been there to support you. I know you don't need saving—' He almost interrupts himself to qualify his point. 'But you know what I mean, yes?'

'I do.'

I let him have this one, because I know what a caring person he truly is.

As we curve round the volcano at the heart of the island, I share my heart with Dimitri, and all the memories I was thinking about when he was sharing his healing energy with me.

'Could you show me some photos when we are back in England?' Dimitri stops the car not far from a clean white monastery.

'I can. I also have some pictures of us for you in my bag, and . . . you never told me you wrote a book. I'd like you to sign my copy, by the way.'

'I cannot believe you bought a copy.'

'I got one for Mia too. She was up half the night reading it.'

'No.'

'Yep.'

Dimitri runs his fingers over the greying hair near his ears, the only obvious sign of him ageing since his twenties.

'It's strange to think of you in my house in Essex.'

'What's it like?'

I shrug as I think of the suburban life I've lived for so long.

It's not a big house, but it has two bedrooms and two bathrooms. It's probably a little bit smaller than Dimitri's. It's hard to say as the layout is so different. But I've got a square of grass out the back and I'm only a short walk away from a good pub and a pretty stream with a weeping willow. Plus, it's only a matter of minutes to the A12, so I can be halfway to anywhere in no time.

'It's a simple house, two bedrooms, a small garden. Nothing special.'

'Is it where Mia Zoí grew up?'

'No. That's a story for another day.' I open the car door and get out before he can ask more questions about the place we lived in back then. A shudder rolls along my spine at the thought of it.

Dimitri walks around the car to meet me.

'I'm glad it is a story for another day. It gives me days to look forward to.' His face lifts in a half-smile as his hand slips into mine. Still the perfect fit.

I smile back up at him, but I don't say anything in return. If I did, it would be flippant or silly, and I know sometimes that's not the best approach, however much I might want to burst into a skit. Lately, I've had less energy for it.

All that can be heard out here are the insects humming and our feet on the ground. A bird the size of my fist watches us from a string of outdoor light bulbs suspended over a courtyard, between a monastery wall and a tree. Sturdy-looking white benches are set in rows and there's no one about but us, yet everything is very well maintained.

'There is a big celebration here in July for St Panteleimon, as this is his monastery. There is a feast to honour him. The rest of the time it is often quiet. People who visit the island for a day don't have time to come this far south. They come for the volcano or the towns. I thought we might get peace here. Would you like to walk?'

'Yeah, sounds good.'

Even if I wasn't up for it, I'd say I was, because I made Dimitri a promise that I'd live, and I don't want to miss a moment exploring with him the way we used to.

'I forgot, stay here.' Dimitri runs back in the direction of the car, and I take a seat on one of the benches, still being observed by the sand-coloured bird. I've never been good with the names of birds, unlike Mia, who might actually be able to tell me what it is, but it's a pretty little thing.

Dimitri returns with a backpack over one shoulder.

'It is always good to be prepared.'

Dimitri takes my hand before I've even stood up, and we make our way down into an abandoned village. Many of the stone buildings don't look clean in the way they do at the other end of the island.

There's a beauty in the juxtaposition of the grey buildings, some without doors, looking out across the vibrant turquoise blues of the sea. Nature has reclaimed the village in part. People have moved on, but life always prevails in one way or another. With or without people.

For a little while we sit on the edge of the old harbour, Dimitri telling me all about this port village, Avlaki, and how it has stood still for decades now. It used to be full of life, but it's lain dormant for so long. Just like part of me, coming alive again now I'm here next to Dimitri.

When the sun becomes too much to bear on our heads, we settle back in the shade of a protruding rock. Dimitri pulls open his bag and takes out water, pitta – which he says we should heat up on the rocks, but I refuse to – a chickpea dip and more cake, all of which he has made from scratch.

Time whittles away in sharing details of the moments we've lost. We hold each other and listen to the waves, we kiss for even longer than we used to, until we both know there's no other choice but to head back for the ferry.

Dimitri moves first, collecting all our debris and putting it back in his bag. He stretches out a hand to help me up, but as I try to stand, my left leg doesn't work. I've had pain shooting through my leg now and then, plus the dull ache that's always there, but this . . . this is new.

'I can't stand.' I flop back down on the unforgiving ground. 'I think you're going to have to leave me here.' I laugh a little too loudly and I can feel the sting of tears behind my eyes.

'Let me help you.' Dimitri drops his bag and loops his arm under mine and round my back to take my weight, doing his best to get me standing.

It works, but my leg doesn't.

'Look at me, I'm a wreck. Sticking a fish to my hip would be more use than this bloody leg.'

I press my lips into a smile as hard as I can, but Dimitri doesn't even pretend to share in the laughter I'm faking.

Instead, he scoops me up in his arms.

'I will carry you.'

I press my head to his chest and listen to the rhythmical beat of a heart that I've missed so much. One like no other I've ever known. I close my eyes and inhale him, a smell that takes me back to our past and brings back even more love than I thought possible.

'I love you, Dimitri,' I whisper.

He plants a firm kiss into my hair.

'I have always been in love with you, Sara *mou*. I always will be.'

Chapter 47

Sara 2025

'Mum, where are you? They're getting ready to leave. Leonidas made them wait but—' Mia's voice is all squeaky, like she's had her mouth to a helium balloon.

'It's a long story, but we aren't going to make it. I'm so sorry. I think we'll come over on Dimitri's boat in the morning. Please, please forgive me.'

'I've been forgiving a lot lately.' She sounds as though she should add *young lady* to the end, which instantly tickles me.

She's been trying to mother me from her birth to now, I swear.

'You have, but I forgave you missing the ferry. We'll be over first thing. My back started to play up on a walk and it's slowed us down, that's all. I don't want to risk coming over this evening and making it worse. Dimitri thinks he can help. You have a nice evening with Leonidas, OK? Message me when you're safely at the hotel.'

'All right.' She does her best to sound deflated but there's an extra tone in there that tells me how pleased she is to get more alone time with Leonidas.

Her happiness is everything to me. It shines happiness on to me, the way the sun's brightness doesn't diminish joy, it enhances it.

'Love you, Mum.'

'Love you, Sweetpea. Forever.'

The call ends and my head rolls back on to the head rest of the car seat. I close my eyes as tight as I can, wishing I could shut out the pain.

Dimitri rubs his hand along my leg but all I can feel is pins and needles and a fresh dose of shooting pains in my back. He mumbles in Greek and I have no desire to know what he's saying. If he told me, it might hurt my soul more than my body does right now.

For a time, back when I had a tiny baby Mia strapped to me feeding all day and all night, I didn't want to live. I would have my eyes unnaturally wide open in the middle of the night trying not to sleep while she fed, and I kept thinking about how I didn't want to do any of it.

Not without Dimitri.

But there was no way to change it. I loved the bundle in my arms, and she was all I had left of him. But a part of me still wanted to waste away and die because nothing felt right.

Now I've been forced to find him, I realise all the time apart was for nothing and my stupid body thinks this is the time to be broken. It's like all the heartache and wishing my life away finally broke me, and now all I want to do is live.

I'm only young. Forties is nothing these days.

I want to start over again and I have no idea whether that's even an option for me.

'I'm never leaving you.' Dimitri's voice is so low, so dark, it's as though someone has told him they're about to take me off to hell and he's not having any of it.

I take the hand on my leg and put it in my own.

I can't speak. It hurts too much.

I keep my eyes closed and dream of what could've been if I'd made one different choice in life.

It's all so simple in hindsight.

◆ ◆ ◆

I'm aware of everything and nothing. Pain rises up and makes my head cloudy. I know Dimitri carried me into his house and laid me down in his bed. When Mia sent a message to say she was safely at the hotel, he read it to me and carefully replied for me, telling her we definitely won't be back until tomorrow. The whole time I've kept my eyes closed, wishing the pain would leave me alone.

I curl against him for what could be hours or could be days. His hands linger on my back as he quietly mumbles to me in Greek. It's almost like listening to a chant from a shaman. His energy resonates around the room, but I feel like I've already drifted away, in and out of sleep.

Eventually, the pain begins to subside enough for me to open my eyes. The golden glow of sunset ripples in through the curtains and catches like fire in Dimitri's eyes.

I've never seen such a hard look on his face. Like he's consumed by pure determination.

'I have paracetamol for you, but I don't know if this is enough.'

I carefully sit up with his help and he passes me two pills and a glass of water. I take both gladly, gulping back the whole glass.

'I can't live in this world without you anymore, Sara. I can't do it. Having you back now . . . it is like I'm awake again. I can't be without you.'

'No matter what happens to me, you have to live, for her.'

Our lips meet, softly at first, then more fervently. With the delicacy of a feather, Dimitri's fingers slip off my clothes. He travels around my body like it's lined with paths he remembers fondly, like he was here studying them yesterday, not over a quarter of a century ago.

He knows how to relax my body, how to make it rise and fall like the sea. There's only the here and now, with Dimitri's name on my lips.

He finds ways to awaken me and snatch my pain away, if only for the time we're alone in his room.

Chapter 48

Mia 2025

'We should probably sleep. We have a very important gig tomorrow.' Leonidas's calloused fingers trace circles around my belly button before sliding over my ribcage.

'Probably,' I breathe.

I pull on the cotton sheet and wriggle myself into Leonidas's arms, pressing my ear to his firm chest to listen to his unique rhythm.

It has to be past two in the morning, and I never want to sleep again, even though I'm exhausted. I've already decided I want to live here on Kos and explore exactly how far these feelings for Leonidas can really go.

I don't want to make the mistakes my mum made. I don't want to walk away without giving something or someone the attention they deserve. I don't want to look back and ask *What if*. . .

The pain on her face when she's around Dimitri runs deeper than anything I've seen – it's almost like she thinks she'll never see him again. I don't want to lose time with someone I want to be with just to be seen to be doing the right thing.

I really hope they've rekindled something and that's why they missed the boat. I'd do anything to see her happy.

'I don't understand how I can feel so deeply for a woman I barely know,' Leonidas sighs as I turn off the lamp next to the bed.

'That's the power of music.' I smile to myself in the dark then kiss his cheek.

I can feel his breath on mine. Our lips meet again, and I can already feel that the night isn't over.

◆ ◆ ◆

'Walk of shame?' I raise an eyebrow at my mum as she enters the apartment.

It's late afternoon and Mum's only just strolling in.

'Excuse me?'

'You're in the same outfit.'

'Not exactly. I've got some of Dimitri's pants on. They're pretty comfy. Wanna see?' Mum starts unbuttoning her chino shorts.

My face screws up and I take two steps back. 'I'm good, thanks. How's your back now?'

'Yeah, getting there.' Mum drops her handbag and a carrier bag on the kitchen counter and heads towards her bedroom.

'Where's Dimitri?' I cross my arms and march behind her.

'He's gone over to drop his bags at a friend's place. He'll be here in an hour or so.'

I'm glad I'll be able to see him before the gig, even if it is for a short period of time. All the small interactions lead to the bigger picture of getting to know him. I've already read his book cover to cover and I'm desperate to ask him questions about it.

'You know how you've always said you can make your hands really warm if you concentrate enough?' She begins to strip off and I get to see my dad's lovely black pants on my mum's bottom.

'Yeah.' I press my hands to my face and try not to laugh.

'Well, you actually get that from your dad. He has this healing power. I'm sure if you spend more time with him, he can teach you his crazy magic powers if you fancy.'

'So he can do it too? I haven't been imagining it?'

'Yep and nope.'

'Wow.'

'Wow, indeed. Now get out, I need a shower and to get ready for this gig of yours. Do you feel ready, or have you spent the last twenty-four hours staring deeply into each other's eyes?'

'We're ready for it . . .' I think back to last night and the smell of us on my sheets. 'But there might've been some staring in there too.'

'Five minutes, then I want to know everything.' Mum holds her finger up to pause the conversation and dashes off to the bathroom, clutching a bundle of items.

I take myself off to the balcony to finish my make-up. The perfect look for tonight's set is sexy and sultry. A smoky eye and a red lip. Classic.

I carefully lay out everything that I'll need to construct the look, the way I always do before any gig. Each brush placed neatly in a row and the various palettes piled in order of use.

I've only primed my face and my eyes and just finished my foundation when Mum appears in her dressing gown, a towel wrapped around her head and her make-up bag in hand. Her face is flushed red from the shower, and she looks rushed.

'It's OK, Mum, we don't have to leave here for an hour and a half.'

'Are you eating beforehand? We'll order food while you perform.' Mum ditches the entire contents of her make-up bag on to the other side of the table and picks out items with no thought whatsoever.

My eyes roll at her lack of method and total disrespect for order. She knows how I feel about her messy behaviours and doesn't care in the least.

'We had a big meal at lunch.'

'So, is he *the one*?'

She looks at me with one eye as the other hides in her eyelash curler.

I want to tell her my plan to come and live here to find out for sure, and how my heart already feels full when I'm near him, like this could be something incredible. We connect in art and conversation and physically. I'm yet to find a flaw, but then, it has only been a few days. Which is even more reason to take our time and find out.

'I don't think you can know that in less than a week. But I really like him. More than anyone else in the same space of time – probably ever.' My make-up brush hangs between my fingers in mid-air as I imagine what it would be like to be sure of *the one*.

'I'm really looking forward to seeing you both perform tonight. I can't believe we have to go home tomorrow.' She shakes her head.

I don't want to pursue this thought. I don't want to think too far beyond the gig itself because after that I'll tell her my plan and cross my fingers she's cool with it. I've even been thinking about asking Dimitri if I could live with him for a little while.

Mum throws make-up on her face like it's fingerpainting for children, but I know when she's done, she'll look well crafted. Even after all these years, I still have no idea how.

'Thank you for bringing me here, Mum. I know it must've been hard after all this time, but I'm so glad you decided to do it. No matter the reason, I'm really grateful.'

Mum's arms flop down on to the table. 'I'm just sorry I didn't do it sooner.'

'Better late than never.' I smile before turning back to my mirror and the smoky eye developing neatly on my lids.

'Thank you for being so understanding throughout all of this mess.' Mum's voice cracks.

'Don't cry, I haven't set my make-up and I don't have time to redo. Anyway, you were only doing what you thought was right with the knowledge you had. The lost time will always cut deep, but I don't want to ruin the future because of the past. Does my heart ache every time I think about the time I've lost? Yes. Would I go back and change my life . . . no. I've loved having you all to myself. I was the luckiest kid in school to have the young cool mum who let me have parties the way I wanted and didn't tell me off if I couldn't be bothered to do my homework. I've had the best life with you as my mum, so don't feel too bad.'

'I thought we weren't meant to make each other cry?' Mum splutters.

'Then concentrate on your make-up instead.'

'I don't know what I did to deserve you, Sweetpea.'

'Me neither.'

At this time in the late afternoon, the balcony is in shade, which is perfect for doing make-up. Natural light, but not squinting in the sun. It's easy to be distracted by people-watching though.

It's been a nice place to stay, with the view over the church on the corner and a karaoke bar not too far away. Different types of people are always coming and going.

Leonidas and I spent part of our evening out here watching people and laughing at some of the singing.

We talked more of me wanting to travel, and he suggested starting here. He'd like to travel too though – that and record an album.

He thinks we should record our song. We should. I wish I could record this whole strangely magical holiday in music form. I really don't want to leave.

A knot twists in my stomach. It's probably nerves. I can't tell whether it's nerves for the performance, or what's coming next.

Chapter 49

Mia 2025

Mum and Dad.

Every time I think *Mum and Dad*, it sounds beautiful and yet completely unnatural in my head. I still don't feel ready to say it out loud, or to call someone I don't properly know yet *Dad*.

When Mum and I arrive at Skala, Leonidas has already set up the mics and everything's in place.

I walk straight up to the man who was wrapped around me only earlier today. I gently kiss him on the lips. It's the first time we've kissed in sight of my mum or Dimitri. There's something that makes it feel more real. A true declaration of something serious. I guess it's my foreshadowing for her, so when I tell her I want to live here next summer, it won't be a big surprise. Knowing her, she already knows. Hopefully, it'll be an easy conversation.

'Is that all I get?' Leonidas purrs.

'Until after the show, yes. This lipstick doesn't transfer on to mics, but I haven't tested it with kissing before.'

'Then we must see what happens to it after the gig.'

'Sounds good.'

Our fingers weave together and we walk over to my parents' table for him to say a proper hello. Mum and . . . *Dad* . . . are taking their seats at a table at the centre of the horseshoe-shaped staging area. There's Thomas Grill & Meze to the right, which is also owned by Skala, I think that's what Leonidas told me. It's like one big restaurant, made of two smaller ones.

'It is good to see you again, Sara. Mia has been telling me about the problems with your back. I hope Dimitri has been helping you?'

'He has, thank you. Will your family be coming to watch the show tonight?'

'No, no. My sister is working and everyone else is still over on Nisyros.'

Mum nods. 'That's a shame. I'd have loved to have caught up with your mum while we're here.'

'Mama would like that, I know. Next time,' Leonidas beams.

Mum looks at Dimitri and nods. 'I'd really like that.'

'Right, it's half past, I guess we better get started.' My fingers contract at my sides like they're desperate to get the mic in them and my stomach feels like it's suspended above my head.

As Mum and Dimitri wish us a good show, we head towards the mics and guitar. No matter how many shows I do, there's always that shot of adrenaline that keeps me sharp.

There's a hum in the air, and it's not just the vibration of the speakers or the people chatting over their food, or the chant of cicadas outside. I think the nerves about leaving my mum are beginning to overflow. Once I say it out loud to her, it all becomes real.

I sit down on the stool that's waiting for me and adjust the height of the mic, my fingers firm on the cool metal as Leonidas slides his guitar in place before giving me the nod.

We're starting with eleven cover songs and ending with the one we wrote together.

'Ready?' Leonidas winks at me and it's enough to bring blood back to my brain, ready to engage it, instead of letting it all churn everything over.

I nod. He begins to introduce us, just as we agreed, then his fingers move over the strings, soft and firm to make the sound chime perfectly into his mic.

This is the first time performing for my dad. I've performed a million times for Mum. She says I came out singing. *Other babies had a high-pitched wailing sound full of snot, but you were always perfectly in tune. I think sometimes you were trying to harmonise with other babies.* Mum has assured me this is true on many occasions, with a wide, cheeky grin.

Nerves rattle around in my ribcage like it's made of tin, and I've suddenly got the urge to be a certified mouth-breather to calm myself. I haven't had nerves like this in a very long time.

Each week I sing a variation on the same set, only occasionally having to learn something new for a bride to walk down the aisle to, then most people want the same party band for the evening. It's easy. Simple. Almost entirely stress-free.

Leonidas and I play everything from Shola Ama's 'You Might Need Somebody' to 'Messy' by Lola Young, from Ed Sheeran to Elton John, as well as a Greek song by Giorgos Mazonakis, mostly sung by Leonidas with me joining in at the chorus and harmonising throughout. I've sung in Italian and French before, mostly while I was studying music, but it's been a while since I've had to stretch myself like this. I had to push Leonidas to sing, but he has an interesting voice with a lot of depth.

The songs flow and Mum and Dad watch in delight over their meal. Nerves fall away because Dimitri's face lights up with pride in the same way my mum's always has.

As we finish the last song of our cover set, my nervous flame is rekindled. I've always found sharing my creativity harder than singing other people's songs, however much I love writing them.

It's easier with Leonidas next to me. I pushed him to sing, he has pushed me to share this. He's dripping in talent, and this song is half him, so I know it has to be good.

I close my eyes and focus on the sound of Leonidas's fingers on the strings. Each note perfectly placed and waiting for me.

You trace dreams in my skin in the dark

And tattoo a map of your body on the back of my mind . . .

The song was inspired in part by my parents. About us. About finding someone and knowing they've left a mark, no matter where life goes. Something deep-set and raw.

I gain the confidence to open my eyes. Across the room, my mum's chin is trembling and tears push their way to the surface, golden droplets in the candlelight. She does her best to send me a smile but all it does is push another tear out, letting it free to follow on behind the last.

My mum's more likely to stand up and shout *that's my daughter* than bawl her eyes out at one of my gigs. In fact, she did just that at the end of a high-school show once. But cry? Like this? I've never seen it in public before. The lyrics must be harder for her to hear than I thought they would be.

Mum picks up a napkin, shaking it out and pressing it to the inner corners of her eyes. Dimitri slides his hand towards her and she takes it, gripping it so tightly I can see the whites of her knuckles from here.

I keep going, settling back into the chorus: *You got my heart with the heat of a devil's grip, I feel the burn of you there on my lips . . .*

Mum's shoulders begin to bounce as her chest gives way under the pressure of emotion. She stares down at her knees like she can't even watch anymore.

I have to close my eyes again, because I can't watch her either. I can't concentrate on the job I have to do if I'm also looking at my mum breaking down right in my eyeline.

The song ends and people applaud from their tables. Tonight was only a short gig, something I think Leonidas begged to get us, as usually it's only the weekly ABBA show, but the place is full and everyone seemed to like the music . . . other than my mum.

We chime *Thank you* and *Kalinikta* into our mics, but I can't get off my stool quick enough. I barely look back at Leonidas, instead swiftly gliding on my high heels towards my mum.

I don't make it before someone stops me to ask if we sing here often, then someone else to ask how long we've been performing together. It takes another five minutes of polite chat to various people before I make it to my mum.

'It can't have been that bad, can it?' I joke as soon as I'm in earshot.

'It was beautiful,' she sniffs, doing her best to control herself by smiling and standing to face us.

Dimitri stands too. 'It was beautiful, Mia Zoí, you are so talented. You both are. But I knew Leonidas was already, of course.'

'Thanks.' It's nice to know he enjoyed it.

'Thank you. Both of you.' Mum smiles at me then Leonidas, but her chin still wobbles. 'That performance was a true blessing. The song . . .' She closes her eyes and presses her lips together. 'It was beyond words. I mean, look what it's done to me. It'll be number one in no time.'

Mum rubs my upper arms, and a bigger, more natural smile lifts her features.

I know what I have to do now, before the subject changes or Mum starts listing the reasons I'm so perfect. I have to speak to her alone before something else comes along to derail me. After hearing that song and seeing what we can do, I know she'll be happy for me to make this change.

'Mum, I've . . . forgotten something, at the apartment. Would you come with me to get it? Please?'

‘I was thinking something very similar,’ she says, before turning to Dimitri. A soft smile lands on his lips and he nods. I don’t really understand what just happened. It’s weird seeing my mum defer to someone that isn’t me.

‘We’ll see you both in a minute. Why don’t you get some drinks in for when we get back?’ Mum nods like she’s made a big decision. ‘How about a nice sweet cocktail? Sound good?’

She looks at me and I nod. ‘Sounds perfect.’

I step towards Leonidas and kiss him on the cheek. ‘I’ll be back soon.’

Leonidas and I have spoken about next summer and he already knows that this is my plan, to speak to my mum.

‘Good luck,’ he whispers close to my ear.

As we leave, people continue to congratulate me on my performance and tell me how good I was. Luckily, I’ve gained the skill over many years of shows to thank people while maintaining momentum to get myself where I need to be.

I want to get this done. Mum has to hear this, and I’m hoping she’ll understand, and if I’m lucky, maybe she’ll want to come and stay in Greece too.

Chapter 50

Mia 2025

'Mum, I didn't really forget anything at the apartment, can we go for a walk? Maybe further along the beach?'

'I hope you're not going to berate me for crying, because tears are a natural expression of joy as well as stubbing your toe or breaking a fingernail, you know. You need to respect that.' Mum flicks her hair playfully in my direction.

I laugh as we move around other people walking the streets. It's so much busier here than on Nisyros in the evening. Kardamena is buzzing with life and everyone's smiling about something.

We walk next to the beach, lined with palm trees. When we get a little further from Skala and the port, we step on to the coarse sand. It's as though the moon over the sea has pulled us towards it, in the same way it creates the tides.

I'm only one step in before I sink in my heels and have to slip off the slingbacks I was wearing to perform, dropping them in the sand, trusting no one would steal them here.

We continue on, all the way to the lapping water's edge.

'Mum, I've been wanting to tell you something.' My mouth is completely dry. I wish I'd grabbed a drink after all that singing . . .

'And I think now is the perfect time, the only time, in fact, to tell you, because I wanted to say at the start of the trip, but then, well, you had a bit of a big secret of your own.'

'I did. It's funny, actually, I was going to say the exact same thing, about needing to have a chat with you.'

'Really?' I bounce on my toes in the sand at the idea she might be wanting the exact same thing as me, to come and see what it might be like to live the life of a Greek islander, here in Kardamena.

'Yep. You go first, though.' She smiles gently at me.

She looks like a silver statue in the moonlight, frozen, waiting for me to speak as I formulate my words.

'OK, well, here goes . . . I've quit my job – well, I've stopped taking on gigs for next year. Seeing you realising your dream of owning the travel agent's, it inspired me. It made me think about my life and what I wanted. I was considering trying to work in entertainment abroad, you know, join an ABBA tribute or something? But now, finding Leonidas and Dimitri . . . I've decided to come and live here next summer. Leonidas thinks we could get some more gigs, maybe some studio time, and, well, I'm half Greek so I should be eligible for a passport. You're not mad, are you?'

Even in the thin silver glow cast by the moon, I can see a tear rolling down Mum's cheek.

'Oh God, you're crying again. I thought you might be pleased. Don't worry,' I continue, 'you're not losing me to Dimitri, you'll be busy with the business, if you decide to go ahead with it, and it'll only be the summer.'

Mum smooths a strand of hair from my face. 'I'm not worried. I'm relieved.'

'Relieved?'

Relieved, thank God, everything is falling into place, I can feel it. The tingle of nerves in the pit of my stomach flips over into excitement. This is the moment she tells me she wants an adventure here too, I know it.

'Yeah. You've found something here in the same way I did. You'd be so happy here. I was an idiot to ever leave, to steal you away from this.'

'It wasn't your fault. Your job moved you and Maria tricked you.'

'I was a fool not to fight for it. To concede defeat and believe I wasn't good enough. I had no self-esteem back then. There's no way I thought Dimitri would pick me over some perfect Greek woman.' Mum exhales hard and her chin drops to her chest. 'I've been putting this off and putting it off and now I've run out of time. I never was an organised mum, was I? Do you remember how many times I'd be up until two a.m. making costumes I'd had weeks to make? Or buying you a sandwich on the way to school from the fuel station?'

'You always had so much more to do than the other mums.'

'Maybe. I doubt it . . .' Mum quietly sniffs before wiping her face with the back of her hand. 'Mia. My Mia. Mia *mou*, when we get home to England, I'm scheduled to have an operation. They found a lump on my spine. They don't think it's cancer, they said it's a benign vertebral tumour. But its position . . . it's not good. It's why I brought you here. I wanted you to meet your father before I . . .' Her voice fades to dust as my stomach turns all over again. 'Before the surgery . . . just in case.'

'What?' It's not that I haven't heard, or I didn't understand, but I can't think what else to say. Against the warm breeze of Kos, I'm frozen as goosebumps rise like mounds of snow, burying me in a painful chill. 'Surgery?'

'It's why I asked for an extension to decide about the travel agent's. Even if all goes well, I don't know when I'll be up and about, but . . . this surgery, it comes with a long list of risks.'

'Mum, I—'

'There's nothing you can do, or say. I just wanted a few more days where you didn't know and I didn't have to see that look in your eyes.'

'What look?'

'That look, the one you're doing right now.' She points at me and chokes out a laugh as tears stream down her face. 'You're doing the same face as when you see a homeless person and you don't have any change on you or you're running late and you can't buy them a coffee. It eats away at you, I know you. You're half me, half him, and I've watched you almost every day of your life. I've watched you grow and if I'm not around to see any more then at least it can be his turn.' Mum covers her face with her hands and I've never seen her shoulders look so narrow.

'Shut up, don't say that.' My voice doesn't sound like mine. It squeaks like a dog's toy.

My eyes overflow and I can almost hear the sound of a fracture splitting my heart at the thought of being without my mum, my best friend, the only person who I've ever been able to one hundred per cent rely on.

'Did you just tell me to shut up?' Mum's hands drop and she begins to laugh, a deep, slightly manic laughter, as she tries to speak through her tears. 'You cheeky cow, I tell you I've got to have life-threatening surgery, and what do you say? *Shut up?*' Her hand covers her mouth as she continues to laugh.

'I meant stop it, stop talking like that, like something bad might happen. You're going to be fine because you have to be. There's no other choice in this. That's it. The one and only choice.'

Mum presses her eyes under her lower lash line to catch more tears as the laughter gives way to her true emotions.

'It's not up to me. It's up to the surgeon and the anaesthetist and the nurses and the cleaners . . . everyone at the hospital doing their jobs well. I don't have any control over it. But I'll still do my very best. I'm sorry I've kept another thing from you. I promise this is it. Just like the only other secret I've kept, rightly or wrongly, it was half to protect you and half utterly selfish.'

It all makes sense now. Why this was the moment in time she thought it was right to tell me about my dad. If she hadn't found out about this, she would probably never have told me about him.

My emotions are like a coin being continually flipped, from the crushing hurt of lies to a fear so real, so tangible, it could actually be a solid lump inside my diaphragm.

My shallow breathing catches in my chest as I try to scrape together pointless words, but it's Mum who speaks first.

'Right now, Dimitri is asking Leonidas to host the rest of his tours this summer. He wants to come back with us to England and be there for both of us throughout the whole process . . . No matter what happens next.'

I grip Mum's hands like they're live preservers in the sea, because I can feel us both being cast adrift, like she's being pulled out further and I'm heading off to an abandoned island. I need her to come with me because I know I can't make it without her.

I can't imagine how she must feel. She's had all this to deal with alone.

'I wish you'd told me sooner. I could've gone with you to the hospital, I could've been there for you. If I'd known—'

'There would've been nothing you could do, but it would've spoilt your time getting to know your dad, and Leonidas! Who knew that would happen?' She sniffs gently and the thought lifts her face into a smile. 'I'm glad I didn't ruin that. Preserving your peace was all I had control over and even then, only for a few extra days. Anyway, when I went to the hospital I wasn't trying to hide it, I forgot to mention it because I really didn't think it was a big deal. I thought they'd say I needed physio or something . . .' Mum tries to shrug off the weight on her shoulders.

'I love you, Mum.'

'I love you too.'

Mum pulls me in like my arms are fishing line and holds me tighter than ever before.

It's fear that holds me together, gluing me into its sticky web of adrenaline. The sheer terror of living without my mum feels like an emotion that's impossible to break down or deal with. So I won't. I can't.

'I made a little promise to Dimitri.' Mum pulls away and holds my face in her tear-damp hands. 'I'm going to live every single day as much as I can, as long as the pain doesn't get to me too much—'

'That's a good promise to keep. You need to promise me no more lies and no more secrets. I still can't believe you've kept all this from me. You're a dreadful liar normally.'

She presses her lips together and exhales hard through her nose as her hands slide from my face to hold my hands instead.

'It's amazing what you can do when you believe you're protecting your child. It was also fun upsetting your grandparents by pretending it was a one-night stand with someone I didn't know, which, by the way, I've never technically done.'

She wiggles her eyebrows like this is a time to be playful again.

I close my eyes to shut out the hurt, because, ultimately, I could have told her my idea to leave England sooner. She was trying to protect me, and however much that grinds me up into dust, I understand the notion because I thought I was doing the same to her and she was supportive. Relieved that I could be happy here.

'You're going to have to take this seriously now, you know?' I demand.

'Maybe that's the real reason I didn't tell you sooner. I know what you're like for bossing me about.'

'Mum.'

'Mia.' She tilts her head at me, and I realise it's the exact tilt I'm doing at her.

'Mum, do you promise there are no more lies and secrets?'

'Only if you promise to have some fun and live like Dimitri made me promise? Oh, and presents don't count as secrets, right?' She smirks.

'I promise, and no, presents don't count. Now, do you promise not to cut me out anymore?'

'I was never cutting you out.'

I squeeze her hands a little harder, gently shaking them.

'I promise,' she agrees.

'I guess we'd better go and keep your promise to Dimitri then?'

'Good, but first I need to sort out your mascara because I knew I needed a strong waterproof, but you didn't.'

Mum hooks a finger under my chin, raises my face towards the light of the moon and carefully dusts away flakes of mascara from my cheeks.

'Perfect,' she whispers before leaning forward and planting a kiss in the middle of my forehead like she has done a thousand times before. 'I'm so proud of the woman you've become.'

My stomach squeezes and my knees buckle, but I've agreed to live too. Whatever that really means. Breathing is living, blood pumping is living, worrying is living, crying is living, there's only one act that isn't living and I don't want her to play any part in that, not yet. Not for a very long time . . . So living is exactly what we're going to do.

Chapter 51

Mia 2025

'It's time to say goodbye. Someone will be here any second to take you up. I'll see you again momentarily.' Dr Bouras smiles softly at us before turning and leaving the room.

'I like that you have a Greek doctor. As we invented medicine, it's only right.' Dimitri does his best to grin at Mum, then me.

I bend forward to kiss Mum on her cheek. My arms wrap awkwardly around her neck. She looks so fragile in her hospital gown, waiting for the last stage of the journey in her wheelchair.

'I love you and everything's going to be fine.' I squeeze her shoulders and kiss her soft cheek one last time.

I do my best to imprint the smell of her in my mind, as though I can call her back to me if I can conjure her perfectly in every detail. The floral notes of her perfume, the freckles she gained on her nose in Greece, the delicate highlights in her dark-blonde hair tucked behind her ears.

It takes everything I have to peel myself away from her.

The knowledge she needs to have this operation to get better is all that's holding me together. This isn't a choice.

Dimitri crouches next to the wheelchair and whispers something in her ear. She grips his arm like she doesn't want to let go, and it's enough to almost tip me over the edge into tears. I hold it together for her. I'll keep it all trapped in my lungs until she's out of sight.

He kisses her head, but she pulls him in and kisses his mouth. Instinctively, I avert my eyes.

This is the first time I've seen them kiss like this.

We've spent four days together and I haven't seen them even hold hands. I don't know why they've felt they should hide what is obvious to anyone who steps into a room with them.

Their love has carried through the decades and I hate that they've both been trying to deny it. I think she's been trying to hold him at arm's length to protect him, just in case the worst happens. But it's too late, he loves her and pushing him away can't stop that.

'Sara Barkley?' A tall man in scrubs walks in with a breezy smile and a heavy accent that I can't place.

Mum raises her arm at the elbow. 'That's me.'

'I'm Andrzej, I'll be taking you up. Have you said goodbye?'

She nods again, her lips pulling into a thin smile, one I've never seen cross her face before.

Andrzej walks around me and wheels Mum towards the door. She tries to twist and wave like she's being taken out for a spa treatment and she's really happy about it.

I wave back, holding my breath to stop my chest from heaving.

As soon as she's out of sight, Dimitri's big hand lands on my shoulder and the air falls out of my lungs as though a bullet has pierced right through them, collapsing them.

My hands press to my face, but it's impossible to hide it now. My shoulders shake and the sound of my quiet sobbing fills the hollow white room.

Dimitri takes me in his arms without a word.

Moments pass as I flood his shirt with tears for the second time in less than two weeks. Last time I was pissed off at Mum and overwhelmed at finding out I had a dad, now I'm more terrified than ever in my whole entire life, and I'd forgive anything in the world just to know she will be coming back to me safely. She's too young for this. She's not even fifty.

'Come on.' Dimitri's soothing voice breaks the sound of my snuffling. 'We should go to the café to wait. I'll buy you anything you want.'

I take a step away from his embrace, and in an instant Dimitri is passing me a fresh tissue. I gladly take it and carefully wipe my cheeks. My skin has been saturated with salty tears so often lately that under my eyes and the tops of my cheeks have started to sting every time I cry. I can't even use my normal face wipes to remove make-up without the feeling of burning on my skin.

Dimitri has a tissue too, to absorb the tears from around his own eyes. He's just got her back, and someone is wheeling her away to a completely unknown fate. It's hard for both of us.

'Coffee and cake?' I try to sound bright about it, but it doesn't sound natural.

'Sounds good.'

We make our way through the corridors of the hospital, most of which are made up like an art gallery to cheer up people like us who are wandering the halls. Some of the paintings are for sale, to raise funds for an ever-struggling NHS.

Nurses and doctors bustle along, shuffling papers and checking watches.

They're the opposite of us.

We move like starved, brainless zombies. Even if everyone in the hospital was dressed the same, it would be easy to guess why most individuals are here based on their walk and the slump of their shoulders.

I send a message to Leonidas to let him know they've taken her away. He asked me to let him know at every stage what was happening.

The café is stuffed with people like us. People who have been told to sit and wait. To pause their lives because there's something out of their control happening and they have to freeze for it. Some look sombre, but others laugh in the face of pain, making jokes that I'm sure even they don't really find funny.

Dimitri and I stand so close together in the queue, our shoulders touch. I'm so glad Mum decided to tell me about him, and that I'm not alone in this. That I'm not standing buying coffee alone, to drink it alone. I guess misery really does love company, because I don't know where I'd be without him right now.

My phone rings from my back pocket and I know it'll be Leonidas before I even get it out of my jeans.

'You find a seat and I'll get this,' Dimitri says in a tone that's not to be argued with.

'Thanks.'

Taking my phone out, I swipe to answer.

'Hey.'

'*Kalimera*, Mia *mou*. How are you feeling? It's a very stupid question but . . . it's all I have.'

'It's not. I'm glad Dimitri is here. He's been great.'

'He is a great man.'

I squeeze between two round tables to get to a free one behind them. We arrived at the hospital early this morning, but after the appointments to check Mum was Mum and get her ready for surgery, time ticked away and now it's way past nine and people are ready to fuel themselves with coffee and easy-to-grab food. It was almost empty a few hours ago.

I pull out one of the black plastic bistro chairs and flop down into it, harder than I should have.

Leonidas has been amazing with everything. He lost his father and lives with that every day. I've asked him about it, about how he manages, and he openly shared his pain with me, all while reassuring me. He's so strong, and our nightly phone calls have meant so much to me over the past few days.

I miss Leonidas and wish he was here to hold me, because however amazing Dimitri is, he's a father I don't know yet and I have no idea how to be around him at times. It's not a normal situation. Leonidas was my choice. Yes, the attraction came first, and the music, but with every moment together our bond has grown. It's been easy. Poor Dimitri has been thrown in at the deep end of parenting an adult.

I wish I could close my eyes and slip back to Kardamena or Mandraki and for the four of us to be laughing over drinks and food. If I had a time machine, I'd play one of the days before I knew the truth, and before this was real, over and over again.

Life can't be replayed, and holidays are special because they're perfectly short and sweet. But that isn't how life as a whole should be. It should be long and winding. It's an album full of songs that burst with different emotions. It follows from one song to the next like it's on shuffle mode. Mum has only lived half her life, her album can't be coming to an end yet – there's so much more music to play, I know it. It can't end yet.

'I wish I was there with you,' Leonidas's voice coos on the line.

'I wish you were too. It's nice to hear your voice though.'

I close my eyes and wish with my whole heart that this time next year we'll all be together talking about this moment and how scary it was and how lucky we all are. Fear scratches at my chest, making more thoughts bleed out, like what if finding someone I might actually want to spend the rest of my life with is in exchange for my mum getting taken away from me? I know it's completely illogical and egotistical, to believe such things hinge on me . . . but what if they do? What if I can't have the full pack of happiness?

Mum didn't. She picked me. She didn't get both. She never had Dimitri there on one side and me on the other.

I feel like I'm in a corset and someone has just yanked on the strings.

I close my eyes and listen to the world around me – shuffling feet, layered talking, the beep of scanned items at tills – then to Leonidas on the line.

'I've been up all the night thinking about you. I have a private tour soon. I really don't want to go. I want to be here for you.'

'But you have to.' I open my stinging eyes and search the anonymous faces of the hospital until I find the one I'm beginning to learn. 'I've got to go too, Dimitri is on his way over with coffee. I'll call you when she's out, OK?'

'*Siderenia*, be strong. I'll be thinking of you all.'

'Bye.' I hang up the phone with a heart made of pumice . . . not because it's light, but because it's full of holes.

I stand to help Dimitri with his overloaded tray. He tries to squeeze between people sitting at other tables but there's a strong chance he'll drop something if I don't come to rescue him.

I take hold of the other side of the tray as he tiptoes between chairs. We place it down on the table together. There're four slices of cake, two large milky coffees, a pile of sugar sachets and two large cookies.

'How many people were you buying for?'

'Only us.' Dimitri looks almost confused. 'I know you are like your mother. You two could drink a river of sweet coffee and eat a mountain of sugar every day, so I think today . . . maybe it needs to be a real mountain of sugar. Take what you like.'

'Thanks for this. It's really kind.'

'I'm happy to be here to help you. This isn't the perfect situation but . . . I'm grateful your mother came to find me and trusted me with you.'

The stressed-out, confused, anxious soul pulsating in my chest wants to be offended by the idea I've been passed from Mum's hands and entrusted into someone else's care like a baby . . . but I know what he means. I know they both mean well.

I take a plate with chocolate fudge cake on it. Even when everything feels rubbish, I've always been able to eat. Sometimes I've wished I could be the sort of person who didn't eat when they're stressed out, but there's nothing that's ever been able to stop me, or Mum.

We begin to eat our way through the piles of sugar in a comfortable silence.

Dimitri doesn't try to cheer me up or make me laugh. He's here for me, and that's enough.

◆ ◆ ◆

I was fine.

As fine as anyone can be when they have absolutely no power to change something and have to wait on the skills of someone else to save the person most precious to them.

One hour passed fuelling ourselves with sugar and two coffees.

For the second hour we read magazines Dimitri purchased at the shop. He got me one about home decor, because he wants Mum and me to come and help sort his place out when she's up to it.

I read the same article about colour palettes three times and still don't know what it said. It'll be a fun one for Mum when she's up to it though. She loves a decorating project, although I'm not sure what Dimitri will make of her taste in his house, with her bold use of colour and unique lamp collection. I don't think there will be space for his icons of the Virgin Mary anymore.

Dimitri then got me lunch, too. I ate half a tuna sandwich and two packets of salt-and-vinegar crisps, with even more caffeine on the side.

I paced the gift shop, afraid to buy Mum anything in case that jinxed her.

I went to the toilet more times than I needed to.

I looked around the one clothing shop, purchased three bags of chocolates for later and messaged Leonidas just to tell him I didn't know anything, knowing he couldn't reply because of the tour he was doing.

I replied to messages from some of the members of the wedding band I usually work with.

I replied to some of Mum's friends who were asking for updates.

But time kept passing . . .

It's right now that time has started running backwards. That's how it feels.

We've slipped into five hours since we left her and even the most patient of people, like Dimitri, can't stand this sort of waiting period.

Maybe if you're told in advance it'll be over five hours, it's bearable. But we were told two to three hours.

Two to three.

Not five hours six minutes and thirty-three seconds.

Thirty-four seconds.

Thirty-five seconds.

I open my phone and go back to the photos of our last night in Kos and the pictures of us all doing karaoke together. Mum said we had to. It turns out I get my singing voice from Dimitri more than Mum. It was a strange night full of laughter and stories, because no matter how much our hearts wanted to run and hide with fear, we carried on.

I turn my phone screen off and look up at Dimitri. He's trying to stay light but even he can't fight off the lines of worry digging into his forehead.

'What is your favourite memory of your mother?'

'You think she's dead, don't you?' I snap.

'No. Not at all. It is important they take time with someone as special as her. But while we wait, I think we both could use a way to soak up the time, and if I have any more sugar and coffee I might need a doctor of my own.'

I force my lips to curl into a smile of acknowledgement.

'I can't think of a favourite memory. She was just a really good mum. She always made my costumes for school plays and arrived for the plays early so she could sit at the front. I remember one teacher asking her how she could never get me to school on time but could always arrive early to my shows. She was cool about everything when I was a teenager . . . she's not just my mum, she's my best friend.'

My phone begins to buzz from an unknown number.

It must be the surgeon.

They said they'd call me when it was all done to tell me how it went and where to find her. I think they wanted to do it personally because they could see how worried I was.

In the second it takes to slide my thumb over my phone to answer it and bring it up to beside my ear, a whole lifetime could pass.

It doesn't matter how quickly my hands move, everything slows down, because right now, in my head, she's both dead *and* alive. Anything could be true.

All I know is, this call will decide the direction of my whole life.

Chapter 52

Mia 2025

'What did they say?' Dimitri has gathered everything into a plastic bag and pushed his chair back, ready to stand.

'It went as well as it could.' My throat is so dry my voice comes out as though I haven't spoken for a week.

'You look pale, is everything—'

'She hasn't come round yet. From the anaesthetic. She's still unconscious. Her blood pressure dropped, from a bad reaction, they think . . . they don't know.'

I stare down at the picture on my phone's lock screen of all of us together from our last night in Kos. We asked one of the waiters to take our picture. It's not the best photo in the world. My eyes are puffy from crying and Mum's cheeks look flushed, but we're holding up drinks and saying *yamas*, to good health.

The screen fades to black.

'What does this mean?'

'They don't know. We can come up and see her.'

Dimitri covers his mouth and mutters in Greek behind it before flicking his eyes back to me. 'Where is she?'

I scramble through my memory of the conversation with the doctor. 'They didn't say . . . or I've forgotten.'

'Look.' Dimitri points towards a familiar face marching towards the curling line in the café. 'Dr Bouras!' Dimitri stands and calls out to her. He chassés between tables and chairs to catch her, leaving me confused and stumbling over my thoughts.

He begins talking to her in Greek, leaving me even more confused, but I can read body language well enough. Studying performing arts means studying acting, and acting, in essence, is the study of reactions. She looks genuinely sorry. As soon as I'm close enough, she flips into English.

'It is very rare for someone not to come around from the anaesthetic right away. Hopefully, she will be awake soon. The surgery went well, we hope she will recover, but we won't know about nerve damage until the swelling has gone down.'

'*If* she wakes up,' I add, blankly.

Dr Bouras's dark eyes briefly lower and she nods. 'She's in the best possible place for recovery.'

'Do you know where she is?' Dimitri cuts in.

'She was taken to F7. Go and see her. Hearing you might help to bring her round quicker.'

'Thank you, Dr Bouras.' Dimitri places a hand on her arm. '*Efcharistó poli.*'

She nods and we leave her to stand in line for her late lunch. She looks drained, but still not as bad as I feel.

Dimitri and I march through the endless corridors with the rows of signs.

'F7.' I point at one of the signs and then we're off into the maze, hoping we can find answers and bring Mum back to us.

As we turn into the corridor housing Mum's ward, Dimitri grabs my arms. 'Wait, Mia Zoí.' His eyes have been dragging along the floor, but they pull up to meet mine. 'Your mother wanted me here to help you. But I also want to be here for you. When a baby is born, you don't have to know who they will become to know you will love them. They are yours and you would do anything for them, die for them, kill for them. You are my child, and no matter the problem, I am here for you, and I love you with no conditions.'

I sniff back the tears that threaten to take over again.

Words fail me, all I manage to do is nod.

He grips my shoulders and tilts forward to kiss me on the forehead in the same way Mum always does.

'Come on,' he says. 'Let's find her and bring her back to us.'

A nurse in powder-blue scrubs is on the phone, doing her best to keep calm even though she's obviously irritated with whoever is on the other end of the call. We do our best to not hover and pressure her further, even though we're desperate to ask where we should go.

She slams the phone down, takes a measured breath and smiles up at us from the desk.

'How can I help?'

'We're here to see Sara Barkley, she's just had surgery. On her spine. She's still unconscious,' I blurt.

'There's a doctor in with her now. Go to the end of the hall and her room's on the right. She's under surveillance but they're hopeful she'll come round soon.'

'Thank you,' we both chime before swiftly walking the last stretch.

There're rooms with windows and curtains containing people who don't feel like themselves, who would do anything not to be here. Some will never leave this place, some will heal and continue on their journey. Not everyone knows which way the scales will tip.

I'm not prepared for what I see when I turn right at the end of the hall. If I thought Mum looked fragile earlier, now she looks like a shade of her previous self.

Wires spread from her like she's a fly caught in a web, there's a bruise on her cheek like someone's punched her and she's completely lifeless.

My mum, the one who is always larger than life, is still and empty. It looks more like my mum shed her skin and that's what she's left behind, and now someone's trying to convince me this is her. But it can't be her, because she's all soul and this is all shell.

I drop my bags next to the door, barely acknowledging the doctor.

'Mum.' I walk straight to her and take her hand in mine.

Her fingers wrap around mine with the flicker of a squeeze.

'She squeezed my hand,' I announce to the doctor, my eyes painfully wide.

'I take it you're her daughter?' he says.

'Yeah, Mia. This is my father, Dimitri.'

'Hello, Doctor. How is she?' Dimitri enquires politely.

'Well, it's good that she is reacting to touch. There's a scale, the Glasgow Coma Scale, to measure the levels of consciousness. Reacting to touch is very positive.'

'Coma?' Up until this moment I hadn't thought of this as a coma. This was just a delay because my mum is the most awkward person in the world.

The doctor nods. 'Her blood pressure dropped during the surgery, but the anaesthetist caught the hypotension early. If he hadn't, there could've been extensive damage to her organs. As it is, we think that's the reason for the delay in rousing her. Outside of this, the surgery seems to have gone as well as it could. The tumour needs to be sent off for analysis, but we don't think it's cancerous. We are still of the consensus that this is a benign vertebral tumour. Obviously, the sample we've sent off will confirm this. For now, keep talking to her, sitting with her. Being near her could help to bring her round quicker.'

'And if she doesn't come round?' I lock eyes with the doctor, a young man with hair as light as his skin and a smattering of freckles over his nose.

'Let's get through today before we ask those sorts of questions. The surgery took longer than expected as the tumour had wrapped itself up nicely, it was a lot of trauma . . . Look, if there's any change, press this button to call for help.' He indicates the button attached to one of the many wires. 'I'll be back in about ten minutes or so to check on her again.'

'Thank you, Doctor.' Dimitri steps out of the door to let the man pass before moving around the bed to carefully take Mum's other hand.

'I don't think my mum has ever been really ill before. I don't remember her being ill. The odd cold, yeah, not *really* ill.'

'She is strong. She just needs time to rest. Time to heal. What has been the hardest time together? Something you have had to suffer through?'

People's footsteps clomp about the corridor and someone in the distance is crying out for a nurse in a monotonous drone among the constant beep of machines.

I do my best to think of the worst possible thing to happen to us as I look across at the man who should've been there, who should know the answers as well as I know them.

'I guess, watching her try to find happiness was the hardest thing. When I was younger, I never saw her date, but as I got older, I'd watch her get to know good men and I could never understand why it didn't work out. There was one man, once, and I really thought he might be *it*, but she broke it off. It was like she couldn't be happy with anyone. It always seemed so sad to me, and I wondered if I'd be the same. Never able to find love . . . maybe even unlovable. I was proud that she was OK on her own, like she didn't *need* anyone else, but something didn't sit right. Some people are happier alone, but it didn't fit with her personality. At least now it makes sense.'

'It does, and yet,' Dimitri shrugs, 'none of it makes sense to me. Before Sara, I was not looking for someone, I was . . . having fun, but then it all changed. She changed me.'

Dimitri releases Mum's hand, drags the chair on his side of the bed closer to her, then, careful not to move any of the tubes or wires, weaves his hand along the sheets to take her fingers in his again.

'Sara, we are here for you now. Mia Zoí is with you now, and me, Dimitri. They tell us you are strong and the surgery went very well. You will be out of here in a week and I will make you both a big Greek dinner.'

It's hard not to smile as Dimitri's face becomes animated talking to Mum as though she's really listening.

'Maybe a meze. Yes, I think it will be a meze, and I know what you will say, your kitchen is *no good for a meze, it's too small.*' He puts on a slightly higher voice for my mum's role in the conversation.

I carefully place myself down on the edge of the bed and watch my mum's still features as he continues.

'We will have fish, meat and vegetables—'

'I'll stick with the veggies, thanks.'

'You eat fish, *nai*?'

'Sometimes,' I concede.

'We will have *tirokraso*, the cheese in wine,' he confirms for me with a nod in my direction. 'It is a local cheese for me, but I will find a way to get it here. I will get octopus for *chtapodokeftedes*, you will love all the herbs and the spices for this one.'

I'm not sure I'd love eating the very intelligent creature, but I don't want to stop his flow, because he's doing what I can't, he's talking. If I open my mouth, it might flip a switch in my head that releases tears instead of words. The idea of talking to her and there not being a silly response hurts too much.

He continues telling her about the things he'll make and the ways he'll care for us both when she wakes up.

'You would be very proud of our Mia Zoí, Sara. She has been very strong, holding her head up and letting me buy her sugar to make this old man feel useful.'

'I haven't done anything,' I croak. 'You've looked after me all day like I'm still a child. I don't know what I'd have done without you here. You even ran across the café and stopped the doctor before I managed to stand up . . . you've been amazing.'

'Good.' A voice coming from the bed startles me enough to make me flinch.

'Mum?' She's in the same pose as before.

Did I imagine her voice?

'Did you hear that?' I give Dimitri a sharp look.

Dimitri nods, his eyes bulging as he looks from me and back towards Mum.

'It's because he loves you.' She doesn't sound like my mum. Her voice is gravelly and monotone. 'I had a really strange dream.' Her eyes squeeze even more tightly together.

Neither Dimitri nor I move to hit the buzzer to alert anyone about Mum's new vocalisations. We're both transfixed by her mouth.

'Everyone had their expiry date tattooed on their bums. Some people wanted to look at them and some people didn't.' Her eyes stay shut but one eyebrow flicks up. 'I wanted to look at mine but you two wouldn't let me. You both kept saying *we all have an expiry date and it won't change if you know it, so why look? Why count down?* Then a big rat came in and stole our cheese.'

'Push the button for the nurse,' I demand, as Dimitri's nearest to it.

He quickly presses it and before long we hear the sound of worn Crocs hitting along the floor in our direction.

'Everything OK?' A nurse with her hair in plaits pops her head round the door.

'She was talking but she hasn't, she hasn't opened her eyes.' I speak so quickly I trip over my own words.

'Sara?' the nurse says more firmly as she comes in the room. 'Can you hear me?'

'Maybe.' Mum frowns over closed eyes.

A laugh falls out of my chest and tears tumble and sting their way across my cheeks. But these are different – they may still burn, but these are tears of sheer relief at hearing her broken voice and it not being something only audible inside my head.

'Can you open your eyes?' The nurse moves around, checking wires and drips.

'Probably.'

'Could you, please?'

'I really don't want to.' Mum squeezes her eyes tightly closed and that's enough.

That's enough for me.

She's going to be OK. Everything's going to be OK.

Epilogue

Mia 2026

'. . . *Happy birthday dear Dad, happy birthday to you.* Make a wish!' I urge as Dad blows out the candles.

'But I don't need to.' He gives me *that* look. The look of a man deeply content with his lot.

I already know what he's going to say next, so I go to say it for him.

'Because you already have everything you want,' Mum and I chime in unison.

He looks from me standing in front of him to her sitting by his side at the same old kitchen table.

'Exactly. Who is luckier than me?'

Behind Mum and Dad, Leonidas puts his hand up like Dad is wrong and the answer is him. He shoots me a look laced with a giggle to go right alongside it.

Dimitri rocks back on the kitchen chair, with a grin just for Mum.

A crunching sound cuts through the air and Leonidas's face crumples in the same instant. His arms reach out and he catches Dad moments before he crashes to the floor.

My heart pounds and we all begin talking at once, *What just happened? Are you OK? What was that?*

It's quickly deduced that one of the old kitchen chairs has given up the ghost. The leg snapped and toppled underneath itself.

'See,' Dimitri begins, now holding the chair up like it's a painting for us to coo at. 'I say we can get all new tables and chairs and then you get all sentimental and say we should keep them. One year with you and I could've been killed,' he tuts, but there's still a laugh caught on the corner of his mouth. It's never really faded, not since Mum opened her eyes after the surgery, grabbed his face and kissed him.

There have been some ups and downs from then to now, but Dimitri's light always seems to shine.

'I think you should be wishing on your candles to keep your luck,' Leonidas taunts as he brings over four plates from the counter. 'First it rains, now you're falling from chairs. Maybe you *should* make a wish.'

'It's too late now,' Dad huffs as he discards the broken wood to a corner of the room not far from the oven.

'We'll have to get some new kitchen furniture to match everything else now.' Mum rolls her eyes like she never told him to keep it in the first place. 'I did tell you to get something new . . .' She tucks in her smile and winces, knowing she was the one who decided it was *nice* to keep something that *reminds them of their very first meal together*.

Dad shakes his head, picks up the chair again and waves it in her direction with a jovial growl.

'Oh, that reminds me . . .' Mum slaps her hands down on the table and proceeds to stand with more care than would've been imaginable just over a year ago.

Even now, her dainty way of getting up and down catches me off guard. She used to be the one to bound about and jump on furniture with great abandon.

'. . . There's one more gift.'

As Mum takes Dad's hand in hers and gently moves out of the room, I'm overwhelmed with gratitude towards the man who up until this time last year didn't even know I existed. I'm grateful for him being there for me and Mum after the operation and helping me to nurse her back to health. He spent every waking hour with her as his primary focus, all while checking in on me too.

Some people may be sceptical, but there isn't a doubt in my mind that she is as good as she is because of him. The doctors said there was some nerve damage that could cause pain or numbness going forward, and she might even feel more comfortable in a wheelchair at times. It was Dimitri who told her she was going to be OK, Dimitri who said he would help her . . . and he did. That's when I casually started calling him Dad.

He spends time every single day trying to heal her with energy from his hands and from the volcanic energy of Nisyros. I have no idea whether it's the energy that's achieving the goal or her belief in him, but she's almost never in pain now and only occasionally numb along part of one leg. She rarely has bad days, and on those days she's just careful with how long she sits down and how she stands up.

She swears it's Dimitri, that he has healed her, and I agree.

He's even been helping me to learn how to use my hands and energy to heal others. So far I mostly practise on Mum, but she says she can feel a heat from me even when I'm not touching her, which is a really strong start, according to Dad.

'Come on, you lot. We haven't got all week,' Mum jokingly chides us from the kitchen door. 'Not with you two running off back to the recording studio tomorrow.'

Leonidas's hand wraps around my left hip as we follow on behind my parents. We've been recording an album together. Twelve songs we've written. One for each month we've been together.

The first few months of *us* were hard. I didn't even get to see Leonidas for three months after Mum's operation. He came to visit me in England when he didn't have any of Dimitri's private tours to take. I knew then and there that I was all in. I think I knew before that, but if there had been any doubt, it vanished when I saw his face in the airport terminal.

I saw him before he saw me.

He was desperately scanning faces and signs with people's names scrawled on. I called out to him, and he nearly threw down his bag just to get to me that little bit quicker . . . like we had been away from each other as long as my parents had. I felt the same way about him. We'd only seen each other for a matter of days, but after three months of calls and talking about everything the world has to offer, I was completely hooked. It turns out, so was he.

'Do you know what the present is?' Leonidas whispers in my ear as I step forward to walk ahead of him up the stairs.

'Yeah, it means *right now*. You know: past, present, future . . .' I glance over my shoulder and pull a silly face at him.

'With sarcasm like that, I think you have been spending too much time with Sara.' Leonidas taps my bottom as I do my best to push thoughts of his hands out of my brain.

I really don't know what this gift will be. I knew about the photo of us all in a beautiful frame and the new mobile phone, which Mum found funny for some reason I don't understand, something about the idea of Dimitri caring about phones nowadays . . . but I thought that was it.

Mum takes us all the way out to the balcony. There's a pause in the rain, and the sun is streaming in between the clouds, at least for now, but water's still dripping off the lavender and the thyme at a steady rate. The forecast said it was set to continue for the rest of the day, and tomorrow.

Dad follows on behind Mum as she goes towards a new piece of furniture they chose together. It's a wooden outdoor ottoman with storage. It sort of reminds me of pirate treasure, even though it's nothing like it. She lifts the hinged lid and pulls out an A4 envelope.

'Read this,' she demands.

Dad goes about opening it up. There's a piece of paper that I can read over his shoulder. It says: THIS WAS A DISTRACTION.

Leonidas's elbow sticks in my ribs with four sharp jabs.

'What was that for?' I mutter under my breath, but then I see exactly what it was for: my mum, down on one knee.

Dad notices at the same time as me, with a strangled gasp.

Leonidas squeezes me in close to his chest and we watch on like we're at the cinema. I feel strangely detached, waiting to see what happens next.

'I needed a moment to get down here. Hence the card,' Mum says as she sniffs back tears. 'Dimitri, I have asked you to forgive me, and you've gone so much further than humanly possible. I know it might sound ridiculous, but I'm grateful to that stupid tumour. It forced my hand, and it made me come back here. I'd take a lifetime of pain just to be here with you for one minute more. If having that tumour meant we could be together, then it was worth it. I'm so sorry it took that to get me here.' She hesitates, steadying her breath. 'Now, as well as your forgiveness, I need to ask you something else.'

She exhales a trembling breath as mine traps in my chest with a mix of excitement and nerves. 'In hospital, staring at the walls, I realised that time is a currency. Sometimes we spend it on stupid things without even noticing, and we forget how important it is. None of us knows what insane thing is going to happen next, but what I do know is, I want to spend the rest of my currency on you . . .' Mum raises a hand. Her fingers unfurl to reveal a ring.

Rain begins its decent on the scene as Dad puts the paper down on a wet table to his left and drops to his knees in front of Mum like a man half his age.

'Sara, I know what you want to ask.' He curls the ring she's clutching back into the folds of her hand. 'But can I show you something before you do?'

Mum nods. 'As long as it doesn't take more than a few minutes, or we might have to live down here forever.'

I can't see Dad's face, but he slides his hand into the back pocket of his jeans, pulls out a velvet pouch and passes it to her.

'You know, many years ago I bought a ring for you, and I wanted to say these words of the future, but I was afraid. As I look back, I don't know what I was afraid of, because the worst thing was what happened. I don't want to live in fear of losing you. I already know that pain, and I never want it again. Sara—'

'Will you marry me?' they say together. 'Yes,' they chorus.

Dimitri pulls Mum into him, and they curl into a ball of laughter and tears as the rain begins to pour over us all.

'I can't believe my parents are getting married.' I look up at Leonidas, with tears and rain blurring my vision.

'Congratulations, Mia *mou*.' Leonidas turns to the two people pretzeled on the ground. 'Congratulations!'

'Yeah . . .' I snatch a breath. 'Congratulations.' I cover my mouth with my hand and begin to sob behind it.

It's not because I'm sad, but because I never thought this day was possible. It's not how I dreamt it would be in the eyes of a child. It's better than anything my imagination could've given me. I'm almost afraid of the future, because surely nothing could be more perfect than right now.

Mum and Dimitri help each other to their feet, their clothes sticking to themselves and each other from the downpour.

Turning to me, Mum says, 'Don't worry, I won't make you wear a bridesmaid dress that's *too* ugly.'

Laughter bubbles up as she wraps her arms around my neck.

'Love you, Sweetpea. I'm sorry this didn't happen the way you wanted when you were ten.'

'Love you too, and I'm just so happy we're here at all.'

There will always be a part of me that wishes Mum had made a different decision all those years ago, but I love what we all have now: her and Dimitri, me and Leonidas. I wouldn't change it, because who knows how it might end if I did?

ACKNOWLEDGEMENTS

It's impossible to write an acknowledgements page without first thanking those who push you to be a better writer and create a better book. In this case, it's my wonderful editors Victoria and Lindsey! I'm always truly grateful for your insight and help.

Thank you to my copy editor, Jenni, and all proofreaders involved in this book. It wouldn't be the same without your incredible technical capabilities.

I'd like to thank all the lovely people of Kos and Nisyros who stopped and chatted to me and my husband while I was there researching *Reminders of Greece*. I'd also like to say a big thank you to the Facebook group 'Ex Holiday Reps' for sharing their experiences with me and helping to make some of the 1998 details more authentic.

Thank you to Paige at Millmead Business for your ongoing help with all my admin and business stuff. Knowing you're on top of things really helps to give me space to write. Also, for supporting me with our wonderful book club and book boxes, Gaia's Library!

Finally, I would like to thank my family for your ongoing support and putting up with me when I wake up from my writing daze with fuzzy eyes and a confused brain. Your love keeps me going!

If you enjoyed Mia and Sara's story in *Reminders of Greece*, you'll love *Greek Secret*. When Ruby arrives in Corfu, she's greeted by a sparkling sea, hot sand and a new future. She's certainly not going to be distracted by Yianni, her handsome new colleague. Because getting close to someone again means facing up to her past – and the reason she was so desperate to get away from home in the first place. Available now, or read on for an exclusive extract.

Prologue

I feel like a used-up butterfly, with tatty edges.

If I had wings, they would be battered beyond repair, with frayed tips leaving dust on everything they touched, but at least I'd be able to fly away.

As it is, I don't have wings, I have family problems.

I guess I really thought, for a moment there, that I did have wings. I really believed I could fly and that I could have it all.

What goes up must come down. After today, I feel like I've crashed down and hit my head on concrete. My eyes burn and the skin underneath them feels raw.

My heart feels scorched with the pain only a child can feel, even though I'm fully grown. It's as though I've lost my footing on a ledge. I was momentarily suspended before suddenly dropping, falling, making my stomach lurch and churn.

Nothing makes sense now.

My grounding has gone, and my belief system has run away. I wonder if this is how other people feel when they find out their parents aren't together anymore. Or is it reserved for those of us who truly believed their parents were perfect, right up until the point we were told they're not?

Maybe some people feel relief, maybe even joy. There's part of me that's felt paralysed with shock since this morning.

My key slides in our door and all I want is to curl up next to Jonah and for him to tell me he loves me, and that my parents love me, and that I'm not losing anyone. His hand on my knee or his arm around my shoulders. That will be enough to keep the tears from starting up again.

What I really need is for him to tell me that they'll both be at our wedding and that they won't fight or cause a scene.

If Dad wants to bring this woman he's off with, I have no idea what I'll do. I can't even handle the idea of him being with someone other than Mum, let alone him bringing someone else to our wedding.

Would she be in all the photos? What does she even look like?

I don't want her there, whoever she is, and if he can't handle that, then I don't want him at the wedding either.

The house is dark as I slip in through the barely open door. A muddle of shapes and shadows. I quickly close it behind me, the way I always do.

'I'm home,' I call into the abyss.

It's never normally this dark. Normally there's a lamp, the TV, something.

I slide my hand over the smooth surface of the wall, searching for the light switch.

The only message I've had from Jonah today was a quick *I love you, be safe xx* and nothing more. I didn't want to tell him about my dreadful day via text. A day that should've been spent looking at dresses, instead spent finding out that one of my parents is out of the country with someone else and the other wants to leave England for good.

I stand in the dark for a moment to catch my breath. Thoughts drag their heels around my mind. How can any of this be real?

I hit the switch, making the bulb burst into life with a click, leaving me squinting.

A gasp fills the hall. My gasp.

My shock.

Everything's been turned over.

I dash about calling for Jonah, with no answer. I trip over a broken vase that's shattered over the floor.

It doesn't slow me down. When he isn't in the living room, I skid along and up the stairs to our bedroom. Fear explodes in my chest like TNT.

Everything of value is gone. The TV, my laptop . . . Jonah.

The bed looks much the same as when I left. The same crumpled mess, but he isn't there, filling it. His messy hair isn't peeping above the sheets.

But it's not empty.

An envelope rests there on my pillow, with *Lorena* written on the front.

Chapter One

'We can't stay here. No way.' Serena spins to gawp at us. Her mouth wide and her eyes bulging, exaggerated by the thick layers of mascara.

'Don't be a princess, Serena.' Mum moves around the space as though it's full of furniture instead of echoing with every step.

I want to agree with Mum. I want to tell my sister she's exaggerating, and that she really is being a princess, as usual . . . but I can't. Not that I'll side with Serena either, Mum doesn't need that right now, but I don't think she's being a princess. Not this time.

This house isn't what I expected when Mum invited us to live in Corfu, where she grew up. Even when she said we could fix up an old beach house her parents left her in their will years ago, this isn't how I thought it would be.

In my imagination, we would be jetting off to something from a postcard. Those ones where all the buildings are crisp white with bright-blue doors, and pretty pink flowers line them, or olive trees sprout up here and there. That's what the beach house would look like, but maybe a little overgrown, waiting for us to turn up and show it some affection. That maybe some shutters would need screwing in a little tighter and weeds would need to be pulled up and then we would be living in luxury by the sea.

It was meant to be sunsets and fresh fish for dinner, lying back and healing in the sun.

This is nothing like how I thought it would be. The beach house is half finished and falling apart from being left for so long. The door into the kitchen is sagging and the floor is so filthy it looks as though half the beach has been dragged in.

It has a roof. A structure. Walls. That's an advantage over the places that have the rebar sticking out at all angles. That's something to be positive about, I suppose.

But then, if it was all perfect here, surely Mum would have brought us to Corfu years ago. With her parents gone, she always made out like there was nothing here for us. Until now, that is. Now she needs change.

'Seriously, Mum, you said we would have this place liveable in no time. If this is where you were living when you were last here, no wonder you never came back . . .' Serena's voice trails off as she slowly spins in the centre of the expanse.

'This is not where I lived.'

'Where then?' Serena stops spinning to address my mum again, her arms crossing over her chest. 'I still can't get over you inheriting a place by the beach and never mentioning it before.'

'It didn't matter before—' 'And now it does?' I cut in.

'Now is the right time. We needed a place to stay, and here it is.'

It's tempting to point out that we could've stayed at home in England, but I can understand why she's decided to run away instead, rather than face Dad. Mum continues, 'It'll be fine. We will find people to help. I know it. Tomorrow, I will take you to meet some people.' Mum takes a few steps and runs her finger through a thick layer of grime on a windowsill, then adds under her breath, 'I'm sure they will help us.

Mum lets out a deep breath and mumbles as she rubs away the dirt between her fingers.

Mum and Serena have discarded their bags and suitcases, their eyes flicking from one empty corner to the next, leaving me gripping the handle of my cases by the door. I'm not sure I'm able to move yet. Even though there's nothing here, it's all too much to take in.

The entrance must also be the living room, as there's a chimney breast to the left of the room and it's a reasonably good size too.

No one's even bothered to shut the front door. Outside, our front garden is made up of wiry grasses that look like lightning strikes where they've been scorched by the sun. The grass looks how I feel. Dried up in its prime.

It's not just my soul that feels that way; my lips feel dry from the plane. My skin feels tight, like it's trying to shrink and squish me down. It felt that way before the plane. It's felt that way for days.

I need to move again, standing still is the worst. It leaves me feeling open to my own thoughts.

'Where shall I put my cases? Upstairs?' I tip my head towards the wooden steps trailing up the right-hand wall.

'Yes, Lorena mou. The bedrooms are upstairs, let's hope it's better up there.' Mum shoots me a smile, but it doesn't carry up to her eyes.

The wheels of my cases rattle along the worn wooden floor and the grit of sand and dirt. I struggle for a moment, trying to take both cases up the stairs simultaneously as my mum and sister move into the next room, away from the expanse of the open entrance.

Everything I own now fits into four large suitcases.

Two are here with me, and two I left in England, stuffed with childhood things and some photos that I don't want to look at.

That's all I could bear to hold on to from my old life. The life that took years to build and moments to pull apart.

With Jonah in the wind, everything we had purchased together, or anything that remotely reminded me of him, or anything he had even touched, I didn't want to see again. So I did a car boot sale to cleanse myself of our life together.

Not that he left anything of value when he disappeared.

I managed to scrape back two hundred pounds of the thousands he took from our joint account. It wasn't even enough to cover the taxi to the airport or the flight out here.

I leave one case behind and heave the other one beside me, grinding and banging on each step as I go. As soon as I get to the landing, my heart plummets all over again.

Up here is no better than downstairs. Nothing's been finished. The landing's filled with unpainted doors and plasterboard walls and the floor is more sand than wood.

I swing open the first door. Behind it there's a room with a loo and a sink. That'll be fun to tell Mum and Serena, there's not even a shower or a bath yet.

A toolbox with tools scattered about decorates the floor. It reminds me of Pompeii, where everyone stopped what they were doing and ran away from the clouds of ash. Someone was working here, then everything stopped. It all ended.

My grandfather, I guess. It must be his old toolbox that was left here. It must have been him hard at work, only to leave and pass away before he got to finish what he was doing. All Mum told me was that he died peacefully.

It feels odd to step into the world of someone I've never met and see a dusty snapshot of their past. It's like seeing a ghost but without feeling afraid, only a little resentful that they won't talk back.

Abandoning my own case, I twist the tap. The piping moans but, to my relief, water coughs out.

I turn it back off with a squeak before briefly touching the tools, feeling the weight of a spanner in my hand.

My grandfather held this in his hand. It's the closest I've ever been to him.

I wish I could've met him. At least it's nice to be in the place where he spent his life. I've always assumed it was too painful for Mum to come to Corfu with no one left here for her, no parents to greet her on arrival. It's the one thing I could understand. But now, with Dad off with someone else, I can understand wanting to come home to start all over again.

I place the spanner back in the toolbox, along with the other items that have been accumulating dust for the past few decades. I don't want them to upset Mum further when she's doing so well to hold her head up.

In my whole life she's barely ever spoken of her parents. I've never tried too hard to push the matter and I've only ever seen one photograph of them. One where they're both laughing, arms wrapped around each other. Mum told me it was from Easter when she was a young girl.

Leaving the room slightly neater than it was when I found it, I investigate the first of the three bedrooms, the one next to the bathroom. There's no bed, but it's cleaner than the hall and it looks more finished too, with all the walls already plastered.

It's stuffy though, with the shutters open but the window shut. I lean in to peer out towards the road and over to a sweeping villa that looks ready for a romantic getaway. It's all white, with pink flowers. Just the sort of place I was hoping Jonah and me would go to on our honeymoon.

I push the thought of what was meant to be to the back of my mind and close the door to the room behind me.

The air in there is so hot it feels like it's burning my nostrils with every inhale, making my lungs want to collapse. To step back on to the landing is a relief by comparison.

The room opposite is bigger and has space for an en suite but not even a sink inside yet. The shutters are closed, making it cooler than the first room. I slip out and make my way to the last room, back towards the staircase.

I walk in, and I see it, what I've longed to see.

There in the third room, I feel like Goldilocks: this is my *just right*.

It's not as big as the second bedroom, or as finished as the first, but none of this is what matters or what catches the breath in my chest.

A view out across the rolling white-gold sand and the glittering azure. It's the first thing to really lift me in days.

A few weeks ago I was filled to the brim with excitement, saying goodbye to all my lovely colleagues to start my own company, only to have it all snatched away by the one person I trusted the most.

Everything has been grey from that moment to this.

Somehow, this view manages to remind me the world is a big open expanse and I'm only a small part of it. I'm just a grain of sand rubbing shoulders with everyone else.

I have to have this view.

'Shotgun,' I holler over my shoulder.

There's no going back now. I can't let the past week be what defines the rest of my life. Jilted and robbed before even making it to the altar.

No.

I have to find a way back to something of my own, and it starts here, with this room.

ABOUT THE AUTHOR

Photo © 2023 by Samuel Thomas

Francesca Catlow writes bestselling fiction filled with passionate love stories that feature flawed, and sometimes broken, characters as they face a crossroads in their life. She often explores heartbreaking themes while also whisking readers off to beautiful locations.

Francesca loves to travel. Born and raised in the heart of Suffolk, England, she has travelled extensively in Europe with her French husband and, more recently, their two children. In 2024 she relocated to France where she spends her days dreaming up stories and her evenings sitting in her garden relaxing with her family.

In 2023 Francesca was a finalist for the prestigious Kindle Storyteller Award, and was nominated for an Innovation Award for her work with libraries in Suffolk.

Francesca loves to hear from her readers – if you would like to contact her, you can do so on her social pages, or subscribe to her newsletter.

To stay up to date, and for free content, please visit https://francescacatlow.co.uk/subscribe

Facebook: @francescacatlowofficial

Instagram: @francescacatlowofficial

X: @francescacatlow

TikTok: @francescacatlow

For trigger warnings visit: francescacatlow.co.uk/trigger-warnings/

Follow the Author on Amazon

If you enjoyed this book, follow Francesca Catlow on Amazon to be notified when the author releases a new book!
To do this, please follow these instructions:

Desktop:

1) Search for the author's name on Amazon or in the Amazon App.
2) Click on the author's name to arrive on their Amazon page.
3) Click the 'Follow' button.

Mobile and Tablet:

1) Search for the author's name on Amazon or in the Amazon App.
2) Click on one of the author's books.
3) Click on the author's name to arrive on their Amazon page.
4) Click the 'Follow' button.

Kindle eReader and Kindle App:

If you enjoyed this book on a Kindle eReader or in the Kindle App, you will find the author's 'Follow' button after the last page.